The Cure

The Cure

CARLO GÉBLER

HAMISH HAMILTON · LONDON

HAMISH HAMILTON LTD

Published by the Penguin Group
Penguin Books Ltd, 27 Wrights Lane, London w8 5TZ, England
Penguin Books USA Inc., 375 Hudson Street, New York, New York 10014, USA
Penguin Books Australia Ltd, Ringwood, Victoria, Australia
Penguin Books Canada Ltd, 10 Alcorn Avenue, Toronto, Ontario, Canada M4V 3B2
Penguin Books (NZ) Ltd, 182–190 Wairau Road, Auckland 10, New Zealand

Penguin Books Ltd, Registered Offices: Harmondsworth, Middlesex, England

First published 1994
1 3 5 7 9 10 8 6 4 2

Typeset by Datix International Limited, Bungay, Suffolk
Printed in England by Clays Ltd, St Ives plc
Filmset in 11/13.5 pt Monophoto Baskerville

A CIP catalogue record for this book is available from the British Library
ISBN 0–241–13206–1

For Tyga

Author's Note

My attention was first drawn to the story of Bridget Cleary by Hubert Butler's justly celebrated essay *The Eggman and the Fairies*.

Of course that work is an interpretation of events by a historian, while *The Cure* is an imaginary account by a novelist. Our sources are the same real events, but our conclusions are very different. None the less, I am not only grateful for the insights which Hubert Butler offers, but I am happy to admit that without his essay there would probably be no novel.

I would also like to thank Colette Blair, Dr Bob Curran, the proprietors of the *Nationalist*, Clonmel, the staff of the County Library, Thurles, Co. Tipperary, and I gratefully acknowledge the financial support of The Arts Council/An Chomhairle Ealaíon, the Arts Council of Northern Ireland, and the Tyrone Guthrie Centre at Annaghmakerrig.

All mistakes are my own.

Fairy – mythical small being with magical powers

Rath – prehistoric hill-fort (Ireland)

The Concise Oxford Dictionary, 1986

PROLOGUE

As garlic lingers on the breath, so all the books I have read show in what I write.

It seems to me that I have no prose style, everything which I have is borrowed from others.

If my father is in heaven and looking down on me sitting here at my table in Belfast, he would doubtless say this is typical of the special pleading which he believed I made my life's work.

'Oh, dearie me! So your head is so full, you've got no literary voice of your own,' is what he might say.

'And it's all too bloody true,' he might continue, squeezing every last drop of hurt from each word. 'Give up this novel, Jim boy, and save a tree.'

'But father,' I want to shout back, 'you never finished off, did you? You never completed what you started, and now your son is trying to make that right.'

My father always wanted to be a writer.

'We journalists simply cover stories,' he used to say, 'but writers make 'em up and they have a lot more fun than us hacks.'

There was a problem, however. As my father knew only too well – and he did know himself – he never was going to be able to make something up. Frankly, he had no original talent.

He was, therefore, always on the lookout. To him, a story was like a rare butterfly and he was the lepidopterist with the net. It was out there; all he had to do was catch it.

3

The fact that he was intending to use another person's raw material struck me and strikes me still as perverse for a socialist (which he was), but my father believed otherwise.

A story was not a natural resource like copper or rubber, he said, which only belonged to the proletariat.

A story, like the air, belonged to anyone and everyone. If you caught it, that was your good fortune.

On hearing the news of my father's death, my wife Marianne came straight round to the library where I work, bringing with her a bunch of red and white carnations. Here, in Belfast, they symbolize tears but she brought them for an altogether different reason. After he retired from London to Dublin, my father used to grow carnations and enter them in local horticultural competitions. He won several cups and they were the only living thing which he and I agreed that we both liked.

'I warn you,' said Marianne, as we turned to talking of the funeral, 'my skirt will be short. I'll drive your father's cronies mad.'

In the event she wore a modest black dress and a hat with a veil, and we were the only mourners. The ceremony in the crematorium chapel started with 'The Lord is my Shepherd', played on a warbling organ, continued with a short address from a minister who had never met my father, and ended with the noisy conveyor belt trundling the coffin through a grey curtain to the secret world of the crematorium ovens behind.

I was not crying although I felt I ought to be: this was, after all, the end after forty years' coexistence. I looked down at the floor. It was tiled with orange squares, blue triangles and green oblongs. I was reminded of the glass pieces in a kaleidoscope and I knew, as I gazed at them, that whenever I thought of this day in time to come, I was always going to remember them first. The next moment someone opened the

4

side door of the chapel and we were invited to step outside. Another funeral party was expected.

We collected the ashes and then came the grisly business, over the following weeks, of dealing with my father's assets. Item: one large, rambling house in ever so desirable Howth; item: one kitchen, crammed with back-copies of the *Sunday Times*, the *Observer* and the *Irish Times*, dating from the nineteen-seventies to the nineteen-nineties; item: one conservatory, piled knee-high with seed packets, paper bags and bundles of string; item: one master bedroom stuffed with all my father's tax returns, starting in the mid-nineteen-thirties when he was a young reporter in Kilkenny: item: one music room stacked with day books in which he detailed his bowel movements since 1967 when the *New Scientist* first alerted him to the danger of cancer of the colon; item: one garage packed to capacity with the said *New Scientists*; item: one library, its bookcases laden with diaries in which he catalogued his hatred for his wife and simple-minded son; and finally, item: one study containing vast and hideous German desk, its drawers crammed with papers except for the one on the bottom left, where I found the Jacob's biscuit tin.

I have the contents with me now in Belfast but let us stay awhile in my father's crowded and chaotic study in Dublin . . .

There was a casement window to my left; the yellow blind was down and the tattered red velvet curtains were drawn to deter burglars.

Somewhere in the house, which she had taken to calling The Lair of Howard Hughes, Marianne was filling a black plastic bag with my father's rubbish, ready to carry it down the steps and heave it into the skip parked in the drive.

But I was not with Marianne, sorting the accumulated clutter and throwing it out. I was staring down into the drawer which I had just pulled open, at the Jacob's tin, and at

5

the label on which my father had written in his unmistakable, pointed handwriting, 'Easter, 1966', and as I sat looking down, the memories started to flow . . .

In Easter, 1966, I was twelve and Father was fifty-two and we were living in the north London suburb of Wembley.

It was the time of my school spring holiday but I was hating being at home. My father worked all night on the newspaper (this was his choice), came home at six, went to bed and slept for the rest of the day. I was forbidden to leave the house or to make any noise in case I woke him (which ruled out both going to the houses of friends and bringing them home). So I spent my time by myself, sitting in a deckchair in the garden greenhouse, warmed by the pale April sun, reading Enid Blyton novels borrowed from the library.

Then, one morning, when I came into the kitchen for breakfast, instead of finding the usual message on the table, stating when he was to be woken and what kind of tea I was to bring him (Earl Grey, Lap Sang Souchong or Irish Breakfast), I was greatly surprised to find himself sitting there. He was eating prunes and spitting the stones into the ash pail on the floor beside him. With each projection a small cloud of dust rose upwards.

'We both need a holiday,' he said. 'So I've decided we're going to see Mavis.'

Mavis was his Model-T Ford and she was stored in a barn on the Irish farm of my mother's people.

'Pack your bags,' he continued, and within two hours, Father and I were cruising past the Hoover building on the A40 in his Austin Cambridge estate; destination, Fishguard, Wales.

Because the Model-T Ford was on the farm of my vanished mother's parents, I had a vague idea (which naturally I kept to myself) that the real motive for the journey was to do with her. Maybe she was going to be waiting on the farm for me?

6

Later that day, father and I boarded the ferry and stood stiffly on deck as MV *Pride of Erin* started to shudder away from the dock. In the dark, dirty Welsh waters slopping around the bows, my father pointed out an enormous, blood-red and mucus coloured hemispherical object with long trailing tentacles. This was a Portuguese man-of-war, my father told me, and should any unfortunate swimmer ever tangle with the tentacles, death immediately followed.

I, who was a keen believer in omens, received this information with a sinking heart. No, I realized, my mother was not going to be waiting at the end of this journey. Later, I remember, curled up in my bunk, I cried before I fell asleep. Of course I did so quietly, for Father snoring in the bunk below was a light sleeper. If I had woken him he would have demanded to know why I was crying. I would have refused to tell him for a while but in the end he would have wormed the truth out of me. Then he would have denounced me as a mother's boy. My face would have reddened, I would have begun to stammer as I defended myself, and by the end of our little session, I would have been as angry with myself as with him.

The next day found us driving across Ireland, then in the throes of celebrating the fiftieth anniversary of the Easter Rising. We stopped in a town somewhere in the Irish midlands. Triumphal arches hung with green, white and orange bunting and pictures of Countess Markiewicz, Patrick Pearse, James Connolly and other leaders of the rebellion, were strung between the elm trees which lined the mall.

A lorry with a flat bed was parked at one end and we joined the crowd which had gathered to watch 'The Pageant of Ireland', a history acted by local children. One scene involved a nineteenth-century eviction. Two youths in old Royal Irish Constabulary uniforms, which were several sizes too big for them, armed with wooden rifles and speaking in appalling mock-cockney accents, drove a group of children in shawls from their cardboard 'Oirish' cottage, and then knocked it to the ground with their rifle butts. Meanwhile, the audience hissed with outrage.

The performance ended, we strolled away under the bare trees.

The two youths who had played the policemen were sitting on a bench, hatless, their guns beside them. They were eating ice-creams held between wafers and their licking tongues were stained pink and white.

'Did you hear the English accents?' Father asked.

I nodded.

'Ridiculous. The RIC were all Irish, and a country which doesn't know its history is bloody doomed,' he added.

Climbing into his Austin Cambridge a few minutes later, I heard my father saying, 'I feel a change of plan coming over me. Sorry, Mavis.'

Settling on to the blue leather seat in the back I thought, yes, I had been right to abandon hope on the ferry when Father had pointed out the huge jellyfish. Mother was not to be found, not on this journey at least, because now we were not going to her people's farm.

We drove back through the square as we left the town. The youths, their ice-creams now finished, were drilling with their wooden guns.

'We're going to meet a real RIC man,' said my father, 'which is more than the people who did that thing have ever done.'

He gestured at the lorry as it flashed past the car window. On the flat bed, two priests were rebuilding the demolished cardboard Irish cottage for the next performance.

'You know the trouble with history in this bloody country,' he continued, 'it's never about putting yourself into someone else's shoes. Oh no, history here is all about proving the other lot were always wrong and for that reason you, us, the Irish, whoever, were always bound to win in the end. It's a bloody

8

travesty, wouldn't you agree?' But in the back I stayed silent, knowing better than to speak.

Sometime later that afternoon, we reached a farmhouse. It was an old, crooked, two-storey building with a boot scraper at the door and a coloured fanlight overhead. The occupier was called Mr Egan and he spoke in the thin, high-pitched, wavering, feminine voice of the very, very old.

I remember standing in the living-room. It was cold and smelt of apples, and there was a marble mantelpiece with framed photographs lined along it. The largest was a black and white one; it showed a youthful Mr Egan in uniform with several other men, also in uniform, in front of a large building with pillars. There was a Union flag fluttering from a flagpole. As I stared at the photograph, Mr Egan came up behind.

'That was taken in front of the depot in Phoenix Park on my nineteenth birthday,' he whispered. 'That was the June day, 1890, the third it was, when I became a policeman in the Royal Irish Constabulary.'

I looked up at the old man who was bending towards me and smiling. His mouth was open and I saw there were two neat grooves in the bottom teeth into which, I guessed, the top teeth fitted exactly.

'How old are you now?' I asked. A certain directness was one of the few advantages there were to being a child.

'Ninety-five,' replied Mr Egan, and laughed.

This moment, like the tiles in the crematorium, was the memory from that time which stood out in greater relief than any other, and it flooded back to me as I lifted the Jacob's tin carefully from the drawer. In my childhood it was shiny but now it was a dull grey. I pulled the lid off and up came a musty, papery smell. Inside, there was a parcel of waxy brown paper tied with coarse string, its knots sealed with darkened sealing wax.

I got the package out, cut the hairy twine, and peeled back

the paper. The contents of the package consisted entirely of identical notebooks with black oil-skin covers.

I took one from the top of the pile. It was held closed with a loop about the thickness of a shoelace that was attached to the front cover.

The fastener, as I undid it, felt powdery and brittle. Of course that was only to be expected, I thought. It was, after all, over a hundred years old.

I flicked through the pages. They were closely covered with handwriting (as were all the notebooks except occasionally where there were newspaper clippings stuck in). The writer had used indelible black ink and his copperplate style was the one which was taught to every Victorian child who passed through Ireland's National school system.

The handwriting was that of Mr Egan and in 1895, the year he filled these thirty-odd notebooks, he was twenty-four years old. He had been a full-time member of the Royal Irish Constabulary for five years and he was based in the small village of Drangan, in County Tipperary. It was quiet but not entirely remote and Acting-Sergeant Egan (as he then was) rather liked the life he lived there.

Then something huge happened in this little backwater: there was a vile crime; journalists came from all over the world. Egan attended all the hearings, collected the newspaper reports, spoke to everyone. His intention was to write a book.

But he never did. He sired six daughters instead and rose to the rank of district-inspector. He was a popular policeman and when, following the Treaty, the Royal Irish Constabulary was disbanded and the Garda Síochána set up in its place, District-Inspector Egan transferred to the new force.

Then his wife Mary died and Mr Egan, perhaps bored, certainly lonely, returned to the subject which had so engrossed him sixty years earlier. He wanted now to do something with his story.

At this time, a grandson called Gerard was the advertising manager on the *Hendon Gazette* where my father worked. Gerard told my father about Mr Egan, and while we were on our way to the mothballed Model-T Ford, my father, his memory jogged by the eviction in the awful pageant we had seen, suddenly thought to himself, 'To hell with the car, I've got to get the story from Mr Egan.' And that was how we came to pay our first call.

The next day we went back and sat in the kitchen. There was an Aga against one wall with a rack above where Mr Egan's old-fashioned underwear lay warming in the heat.

Mr Egan sat with his back to the kitchen window. There was honeysuckle growing up the wall outside and, further away, a small orchard of stunted crab-apple trees with green bark like corroded bronze.

My father sat at the opposite end of the table from Mr Egan. The table top was formica, pillar-box red, except where it was worn around the edges and it was ivory.

My place was by the Aga. I was an asthmatic child and my father believed I needed to be near warmth whenever possible. There was a silver rail for hanging towels and I was able to lean an elbow on this and place my head in the palm of one hand.

Mr Egan was directly in front of me. He was smoking a cigar and the light from the window behind was shafting through the smoke as it coiled and tumbled through the air.

Mr Egan began his narrative using the first notebook (he also had some carefully preserved old newspaper cuttings, but those only came into the picture later) while my father, at the other end of the table, sat listening attentively. As day followed day he sat without speaking except when he interrupted to ask questions and then carefully noted down Mr Egan's answers in one of his spiral-bound reporter's notebooks. (He used several; I found them all in another drawer in his desk.)

I was mesmerized hearing the story for the first time, and so was my father. Here it was, his passport out of journalism and into respectable authorship; he continued to say this through my adolescence. But it never happened. He never wrote the material up and fashioned it into shape.

All that he was able to do, as I discovered while Marianne emptied the house, was to comb through Egan's notebooks editing and subbing the text, and then cross-reference it both to Mr Egan's answers, which he had transcribed word for word in his reporter's notebooks, and to the trial transcripts in the old newspapers.

These tasks complete, my father left his raw materials in his desk until I rescued them and wrote them up in my own style and with my own additions and subtractions, more than thirty years later.

PART I

CHAPTER ONE

This was how Mr Egan's account began.

The year was 1875; the time was summer; the place was a farm near Drangan in County Tipperary. It was about three o'clock in the afternoon and it was raining.

Bridget Boland, five years old, was standing in the middle of the kitchen floor of the cottage where she lived with her mother and father.

Bridget Boland was wearing black leather boots that were two sizes too big for her. In order to stop her feet swimming around in them, her mother had stuffed newspaper into the toes. Bridget was also wearing a Victorian child's dress. It was blue. There were big black buttons up the front. She liked to twist and turn the buttons but never in her mother's sight, for her mother always slapped her hand if she caught Bridget doing this, and scolded her saying, 'Children must not fiddle.'

Set into the thick wall in front of Bridget was a small window with no glass. Beyond this – and this was what Bridget was looking out at – there hung what appeared to be a sheet of grey water. In fact this was rain running off the thatch roof overhead and plummeting to the ground.

Bridget now shifted her gaze to the chestnut tree at the end of the lane. The green leaves were glistening and shining with wet to her childish way of seeing things, and her father's three cows, with their big, wide, white eyes, were sheltering in the shadowy area beneath.

Bridget went and sat by the fire. Then, after a few minutes, she thought she heard something. A shout? An oath? – she wasn't sure. She got up and ran back to the window.

At first she saw only the dripping stone walls of their farmyard, the chestnut tree and the dark sky.

But then she noticed that the gate from the road was open. Suddenly, she became aware from the nervous movement of their cows that something else was crouching in the dark, green place beneath the chestnut. Then her heart started to knock against her ribs, for she saw what was crouching near the cows. It had a hard shell for a back and protruding spikes that stuck several feet into the air.

Next thing, the monster bolted forward and started to hurtle towards their cottage. It was like a fiendish tortoise except that it was upright, running on two legs. All that she could think was that when the monster got inside the cottage, it was going to devour first herself, next her mother, who was out in the shed at the back splitting sticks, and finally her father when he returned home.

The monster passed the window, heading for their door, and it was now, at this moment of ultimate dread, that Bridget suddenly saw what she had not seen before. The monster was in fact nothing more than her father Pat, who was carrying an old-fashioned bentwood seat upside down over his head. The spikes were the chairlegs sticking up in the air, and the shell was the chairback hanging down over his shoulders. It was his umbrella from the rain.

The half-door of the cottage burst open and her father ran in.

'Some shower,' he muttered.

He knew immediately that something was wrong. He could tell from the child's face, the downcast eyes, the paleness of the cheeks.

From out of the dresser he fetched a piece of old flour sack and tore it in two.

'Come on you,' he said.

When she took the square Bridget felt the special thinness of flour sack after washing and re-washing, use and re-use.

She held it up to the window and saw pinpricks of light shining through between the meagre threads.

She began to dry the chair. The cloth went immediately dark as it soaked up the water. She noticed the faint flour smell. It never washed away, it seemed. Some things never did.

'Just the big drops,' her father urged, 'and mind the joints.'

The knot in her stomach was undoing.

'This is going to be the chair where you tell your stories,' she ventured.

'Yes,' he agreed.

Bridget's mother, Rosemary, was quiet, mild and pious, had few friends and no interest in other people's business. Bridget's father Pat, by contrast, was much better known. Besides keeping a few cows, he was a labourer and he built stone walls, mended fences, hung doors, drove cattle, made hay, and generally turned his hand to whatever he was offered. He supported his family well and he had no vices, it was acknowledged, except that sometimes he drank too much.

Bridget's childhood was normal, that is to say unexceptionable. At seven she made her first Holy Communion. At thirteen she began to menstruate. At fourteen she left her National school. She was literate, numerate, and Mrs Leary, her teacher, wrote an excellent report for her to take away with her. Bridget was apprenticed to work in a haberdasher's. At the age of eighteen she met Michael Cleary. They courted and married.

Michael was a cooper. He made barrels in Clonmel. His trade gave him a steady income, on the strength of which the couple secured the offer of a labourer's cottage soon to be built in Ballyvadlea, twelve miles from Clonmel town and not far from where Bridget had grown up. Bridget's mother was now dead and the newly-weds agreed to take Bridget's father into the house to live along with them.

A cutting from the *Nationalist*, Monday 11 June 1888:

Saturday last saw the inauguration at Ballyvadlea of a new dwelling which is being built under the direction of the Cashel Guardians. Mrs Cornelius O'Ryan, wife of the Chairman of the Board, Mr Cornelius O'Ryan, JP LL B, generously undertook to perform the laying of the foundation stone. It is anticipated that it will be some three months before the house is ready.

Other members of the board, notably Mr Gerald Finnegan, Henry Hackett, Esq., Major Wesley Armitage, Mr John Maguire, Mr Fred. O'Casey, and their wives, were also in attendance.

The site of the house, which stands a mile from the Drangan to Cloneen road and which commands splendid views across rolling landscape to our most notable and picturesque local feature, Slievenamon, was a common theme during the speeches afterwards at a small private dinner in the Royal Hotel. Praise was also given to the Board and its splendid efforts in the housing arena, with several speakers noting, and with justifiable pride we feel at this newspaper, that the Ballyvadlea enterprise now brings to one hundred and fifty, the number of dwellings which the Guardians have erected.

One morning about a year after her marriage to Michael and their settling at Ballyvadlea, Bridget woke very early in bed beside her husband. Sunlight streaming through the half-opened shutter formed a golden rectangle on the wall behind her head.

Lying there, drowsy and faintly mesmerized by Michael's breathing, she noticed her lips felt puffy. Then, feeling along them with her tongue, she found a cold sore in the corner, an infallible sign that her period was coming.

After Michael left for work, she put on her boots and stockings, bid her father goodbye and went out.

The house of Michael and Bridget was a slated, three-roomed dwelling, with a path from the front door and a gate on to a narrow lane. To the left lay the way to the villages of Cloneen and Drangan but Bridget turned the other way.

The day was warm. In the hedgerows ragged-robin and

meadowsweet, cuckoo-flower and tufted forget-me-not grew in rich profusion, interspersed with long dense stretches of bramble. The hard green fruits which would become the autumn blackberries were already beginning to show, and vaguely reminded her of a baby's clenched fist.

At last the monkey-puzzle tree which grew at the front of Joanna Burke's came into view. Bridget turned down the track.

Her cousin Joanna's home was slightly larger than hers. It was a two-storey dwelling with two bedrooms upstairs, a kitchen and a parlour downstairs. In the window above the front door stood a statue of the Child of Prague. His round body was enclosed in a white robe and hanging from his shoulders was a sumptuous white cloak, the edges fringed in red. In his right hand he held an orb adorned with the cross and on his head sat a crown. His eyes were violet and followed, it seemed, her every step as she approached.

The statue had been Bridget's gift to Joanna after her cousin married Thomas. It was immediately put in the window with a silver sixpence under its base, and its effect was instantaneous. No calves died; it was a bumper summer for hay; and in answer to her prayers, Joanna became pregnant with Katie.

Bridget circled the house and found her cousin sitting on the back step drinking tea, Katie, now two years old, sleeping beside her in a basket.

Bridget sighed as she sat.

'Oh, don't tell me. I can guess,' said Joanna.

'We've been married for a year now,' Bridget said quietly.

'We'll go and see Mrs Whelan,' said Joanna.

Before she married, Mrs Whelan was in service on a large farm in County Kildare. One morning the cowherd came into the dairy where she was washing the churns. He was breathless and greatly excited.

She followed him to a field where she saw what she later

described as a glowing pile of foam. It was resting on the ground and great heat was coming from it. All the cows gathered around were contentedly chewing, and an all-black Guernsey was actually licking the cloud.

Mrs Whelan drove the cows to the byre. When she milked the Guernsey it produced milk that was exceptionally yellowy and thick and Mrs Whelan filled a cup for herself to drink.

It was warm and sweet to taste but she had no sooner finished than she fell down in a faint. The cowherd found her. She was murmuring and smiling. Later, Mrs Whelan reported that while she was on the byre floor, she was dreaming of an old fairy woman who was telling her the secrets of life.

A week later, Mrs Whelan quit the farm and began her new life, as a helper to the infertile. In time she married a horse trader and produced two sons who later emigrated to America, where one drowned in the Missouri river and the other prospered working in a factory which produced pianos in St Louis. Aged fifty, Mr Whelan was kicked in the head by a horse and subsequently died of his injuries in Clonmel hospital, where he had been taken suffering from concussion.

Mrs Whelan lived alone in a cottage off a back road in the desolate hills to the north, and the following week the two cousins found themselves knocking on her door. Joanna carried Katie in her arms.

After a moment or two, the door scraped back. Mrs Whelan was a stout old woman with short crinkly grey hair and a mannish voice.

'Come in, girls,' she said boisterously as she pulled the door wide.

Bridget and Joanna stepped quietly in and Mrs Whelan closed the door behind. They found themselves in a small, dark, smoky room with numerous corn figures hanging from the low ceiling which brushed against their heads.

They settled by the fire and a cat jumped on to Bridget's

lap, its claws reaching through her skirt and stockings to her skin.

'Christopher, that's Christopher,' said Mrs Whelan.

The old woman's face was tanned and deeply creased. She wore big gold ear-rings and she had lovely white teeth.

'This is my cousin Bridget Cleary,' explained Joanna. 'As you were of great service to my mother's sister, I wondered if you could help her?'

After asking several questions, Mrs Whelan laid three lines of salt out on the table. She enclosed the first row with her arms and, touching her head against the thread of salt, she began to recite the Lord's Prayer.

'Our Father, who art in heaven, hallow'd be Thy name . . .'

Lifting her head after the third repetition there was a band of salt stuck to her face. Moving slowly, as if through water, Mrs Whelan repeated the process with the middle row and again with the last.

'Come,' she said, and still with the grains of salt stuck to her, she led Bridget outside and turned her face towards the sky.

'By the power of the Father and the Son and the Holy Spirit,' she began, 'let the disease disappear and the spell of the evil spirits be broken. I adjure and command you to leave Bridget Cleary. In the name of Christ, I adjure. In the name of the Spirit of God, I command and compel you to go back and leave this woman free. Amen. Amen.'

There was a low wall in front of Bridget and a bog beyond filled with purple heather and white wispy bog cotton. She saw a black line some distance away where a trench had been made and turf cut, and beyond, a clump of dark green gorse. Otherwise the landscape was empty and featureless.

'Come with me.'

Holding her by the hand, Mrs Whelan led Bridget through a narrow gateway in the wall and away across the bog along a winding path of beaten brown earth until, at last, still hand in hand, they came to the outcrop of gorse Bridget had noticed earlier.

There were several bushes growing here which together formed, what looked like to Bridget at first sight anyway, an impenetrable clump. However, hidden at the side was a small pathway along which Mrs Whelan led the way, bringing her finally into the middle of the bushes. Here she found a small grassy area with an enormous boulder sitting in the middle. The stone was freckled with white lichen.

Mrs Whelan released Bridget's hand, knelt on the ground beside her, unlaced her boots and gently pulled them off. The coarse bog grass felt springy to Bridget beneath her stockinged feet.

'Take off your clothes,' Mrs Whelan said kindly.

Bridget was surprised and alarmed. Joanna had not mentioned this as they had made their way to Mrs Whelan's door. Joanna had only told her about the salt and the prayers.

'Don't worry,' said Mrs Whelan gently, unbuttoning Bridget's jacket and blouse, 'this is part of the cure.'

Well, her underclothes, Bridget thought as she stepped out of her skirt, Mrs Whelan would surely leave her standing in those. But no, for a moment later she felt old Mrs Whelan's surprisingly nimble fingers undoing the stays at the front of her bodice. As her breasts were exposed, she automatically covered them with her arms and a second later she felt her bloomers and her stockings being tugged down.

'Shift your feet,' said Mrs Whelan. Bridget did not want to cooperate; none the less she found herself lifting one foot and then the other and she was finally naked.

Bridget looked up involuntarily. The pale blue sky above was ribbed with cloud and the wind blowing across the heather brought goose-bumps to her arms and down her back. She heard Mrs Whelan moving and turning, she saw the old woman with all her clothes over one arm and her boots in her hand, disappearing away down the path between the gorse bushes.

'Where are you going?' she called out in faint alarm.

'I'll be back,' said Mrs Whelan and disappeared.

Bridget quickly scanned the countryside over the spiky top of the gorse. There was not a soul in sight, she was relieved to see, and nothing moved in Slieveardagh except the grey smoke floating up from Mrs Whelan's chimney.

Mrs Whelan returned saying, 'You must not dress yourself until I say.' Then she took Bridget's hand again and led her over to the boulder. It was about four feet high and a couple of feet wide, with a flattish top which dipped in the middle and rose to a crest, somewhat like a saddle.

Mrs Whelan patted the stone.

'Sit up,' she instructed Bridget cheerfully.

Bridget made as if to sit with her back to the pommel but Mrs Whelan stopped her, turned her round and made her sit the other way so that it was between her legs, just as if it really were a saddle she was sitting on.

'Close your eyes.'

Bridget closed her eyes.

Mrs Whelan began to recite and Bridget listened. The old woman's voice was high-pitched and what she said made no sense. Yet Bridget did not doubt that there must be sense in it, only it was one she could not understand.

She felt Mrs Whelan's hand come on to her head, pressing down her hair on to her skull. Still chanting, Mrs Whelan now began to circle round her slowly, with Bridget as the spindle.

Bridget now felt herself quickly growing colder and colder; the heat of her body was vanishing at a bewildering speed. It was not going to be long, she realized, before her teeth would be chattering and she would be shivering. Would that affect the cure? she wondered.

She opened her eyes and glanced sideways at Mrs Whelan,

hoping to catch her eye and communicate that she was freezing, but the old woman had her eyelids shut, and with her hand still resting on Bridget's head, she continued circling her.

Bridget closed her eyes again to wait for the waves of cold to begin. But when at last the moment arrived, when she expected they were going to start, she felt instead a kernel of warmth inside herself.

It started behind her groin right in the middle of her being and gradually radiated outwards until not only was she warm but also the rock beneath her as well. She was warm, as warm she thought as when, after splashing about in the river as a child, she basked in the summer s sun.

Mrs Whelan's hand came away from the top of her head and Bridget opened her eyes. She heard the squawking of ducks and looking up, she saw a mallard drake with two females beating across the sky. There was a thick bar of cloud behind them, and together birds and cloud made the sign of the cross.

As the ducks vanished and the wind moaned, Bridget felt a powerful sense of calm stealing over her.

'Do you feel well?' asked Mrs Whelan, speaking now in her normal talking voice.

'Oh, yes,' Bridget agreed cheerfully.

'All that matters,' continued Mrs Whelan, 'is that you believe, and that you love, and that you are good, and God's will shall follow, whatever His will shall be. But remember, I make no promises. Whatever is His will, that is what will prevail no matter what you wish to the contrary. Do you understand?'

'Yes,' said Bridget, and the next instant the warmth in her body vanished, she felt the coldness of the stone again, and goose-pimples reappeared along her arms and down her sides.

Mrs Whelan disappeared between the bushes and came back a moment later holding her clothes. Bridget dressed quickly and followed Mrs Whelan back down and into the cottage. The old woman instructed her to sit as before on the bench beside Joanna.

'Now,' said Mrs Whelan. She took down a half-finished shape made of corn straw and began to tie and twist and plait the yellow straws, while the visitors watched and the room was silent, except when the turf sods settled with a sighing noise.

After a few minutes there was a finished object. It was a female figure in a long skirt.

'Take this. Let no man see it. Let no man know you have it. Place it under your mattress but above the bedstead on your side of the bed.'

Mrs Whelan closed her eyes, kissed the effigy and handed it over to Bridget.

When she got back home later, Bridget found her husband Michael and her father Pat sitting outside the house on the kitchen chairs. They were basking in the evening sun slanting from the west.

As their eyes were closed, she was able to stuff the corn figure under her short jacket, and saying 'Hello', she sped past the men.

Inside the house she went straight to the bedroom where she and Michael slept. She lifted back the mattress from the Vono bedstead on which it rested, carefully placed the doll on the metal mesh underneath on the side where she slept, then lowered the mattress down again.

The doll was going to be crushed, but she presumed this was not going to interfere with its effect. Or why else would Mrs Whelan have given her the instructions she had given her? Bridget got down on to her knees and, peering under the bed, she saw there were already pieces of straw on the floor, glistening like new snow.

She combed her hair, took out her gold hoops and put in

25

her best ear-rings. These were bunches of grapes made from red coloured glass that dangled from gold circles.

It was a wise precaution because as soon as she reappeared at the front, Michael asked, 'What were you doing in the house?'

'Changing my ear-rings,' she said.

'What was wrong with what you were wearing?'

'I wanted to change them.'

Michael went inside, returning with a chair for her.

'Thank you,' she said and sat down.

The leaves of the hedge on the other side of the lane were translucent in the sloping sunlight, while the landscape beyond was an arrangement of light green squares running to the foot of Slievenamon, at which point the green gave way to olive-brown, for the slopes were in shade this summer's evening.

She let her gaze rise. The outline of Slievenamon stood out this evening with particular clarity against the sky which was pale blue and without even a trace of the mackerel cloud which Bridget had seen earlier outside Mrs Whelan's.

Slievenamon, she had often imagined, had once had a rough outline to it, but over the centuries, through the action of wind and rain, it had become the soft and rounded hump that she knew. She sometimes thought it was like a breast, although when this thought came into her mind as it did now, she was quick to banish it.

From the upper reaches of Slievenamon, she let her eyes slowly sink back to the foothills again, and she watched them now as they turned from dark olive through purple to the shade of violet which had mesmerized her, as had no other colour, when she was eight, ten, twelve years old and a child in the local National school. Mrs Leary was her teacher then, or Bleary as she was known to the wits of the schoolyard, and one day Bridget remembered now, as she sat gazing into the distance yet with her mind's eye turned towards memories of the past, Mrs Leary chalked on the blackboard, 'Slievenamon', and then beneath she wrote, 'The Colloquy of the Ancients'.

What was a colloquy? Bridget had wanted to ask her teacher but she did not dare in case it was just a simple word and Mrs Leary mocked her . . .

Her father, Pat, stirred in his chair beside her and lit his pipe. Bridget blinked. She heard the stem knocking against his teeth and his saliva bubbling in the bowl. Yet, she went on staring at the purple slopes as she might gaze at water, until everything immediately around her began to fade slowly and into the centre of her attention now moved the big square draughty schoolroom, the rows of crooked oak desks carved with initials and stained with ink, and the lectern at the front behind which, on a high stool, sat the teacher.

Mrs Leary was thin and intense. She always dressed in a long black swishing skirt and a white blouse and she always carried a three-foot ruler. When she was talking she would hold the ruler in both hands and flex it upwards and downwards, or point with it at the board. Very occasionally she hit with it.

Mrs Leary had a gap between her two front teeth and when she spoke she lisped her sibilants, which made her voice strangely endearing and utterly unforgettable. Bridget heard Mrs Leary now in her mind as she began, 'Today, boys and girls, I am going to relate a story from "The Colloquy of the Ancients", a story which was told to St Patrick.'

Mrs Leary paused and rubbed her front teeth with her tongue, cleaning them, it seemed, in readiness to speak; and from where she sat in the front row, Bridget glimpsed the darting red wet muscle in her teacher's mouth, bright red, frightening and fascinating.

'Once upon a time,' Mrs Leary started, 'the Chieftain Fionn and five of his men raised a fawn in Donegal in the north-west of Ireland and followed her here to the south-east where they then lost her.'

27

Forty pale upturned faces stared at their teacher, blinking, swallowing, rapt.

'It began to snow and one of the huntsmen, in the course of searching for shelter, found a door in the side of our mountain here, Slievenamon, but it was not any door, it was an entrance, boys and girls, to a fairy palace.'

Mrs Leary was speaking in the hypnotic monotone which she always adopted for stories and her face hovering above Bridget was white and her eyes were bright.

'Once they were through the door, the hunting party found themselves in a huge hall,' she continued, 'and in that hall there were a thousand mirrors, many warriors and many, many beautiful and comely women, some singing, some playing musical instruments, some working at their tapestries.'

Mrs Leary's tongue again, behind her teeth.

'The parties feasted together, consuming one sumptuous dish after another and drinking wine. When they were finished one of the huntsmen asked, "Who are you?" to which the leader of the hosts replied: "We are the sons of Midir, and are banished to this obscure place by the king of the Túatha Dé Danann."

'The speaker went on to explain that, as it happened, this king was coming the very next day with his men to give them battle. As for the fawn, he confessed, it was in fact a woman who had been sent to lure Fionn and his party there.

'The following day the battle began at sunrise and it went on without ceasing until sunset. Naturally, Fionn and his men fought beside their hosts and, in the end, because of the valiant efforts of Fionn and his men, the defenders triumphed. Thus the sons of Midir were able to remain in their palace, where they possibly survive to this very day, quietly living their fairy lives.'

Mrs Leary instructed the older boys and girls to copy the story into their exercise books; the younger ones used slates. Bridget was twelve and wrote with a dip pen. Her nib squeaked, the ink in the porcelain pot in her desk had a bitter smell like carbolic soap, and her eyes were smarting because the turf-burning stove was leaking smoke from the chimney.

As she wrote slowly in her rounded, looping copperplate, Bridget sensed Mrs Leary in her button boots, clumping along the pine floorboards, up one row of desks, down the next, until she passed at last by Bridget's own desk. As she did, Bridget smelt her teacher's special smell, which was like cow parsley. After Mrs Leary was gone, Bridget stole a quick glance at the disappearing shape, cinched with a belt round the middle. She felt infinitely relieved that Mrs Leary had not stopped to check her work over her shoulder.

Mrs Leary only beat the boys; the girls she scolded. So it was not the three-foot ruler which frightened Bridget; it was Mrs Leary's tongue. Of the two, Bridget believed, as did all the other girls, a verbal lashing was the worse.

A beating, although it was extremely painful while it lasted, was of short duration and invariably, unless he cried, the recipient of Mrs Leary's strokes was always a hero afterwards amongst his peers, if only for a day or two.

Words, on the other hand, had a way of lingering on for weeks, either in the memory or, more usually, in the chants of other children. Mrs Leary had a memorable turn of phrase. Once, she had described Bridget to the class as 'soft and runny, like an uncooked egg', and even if Bridget had been able to put out of her mind what had deeply hurt her, the other children would never have let her forget. For weeks afterwards, 'Eggy-Weggy' was called after her, as she made her way home . . .

A blackbird trilled in one of the trees behind the house.

'Penny for your thoughts,' she heard Michael saying beside her, and like a dream vanishing on waking, her school memories disappeared.

'Oh, nothing.'

'That sounds suspicious.'

'No, it was nothing. I was thinking about school and something Mrs Leary taught us.'

'Oh, that old witch,' said Michael. Michael disliked Mrs Leary. He had done so ever since his wedding, for at the party afterwards she had taken him aside and said, 'Are you going to look after your wife?'

Mrs Leary had been retired many years by this stage. Her hair was grey and her face was creased. She had been crying at the marriage service in the church and, because of the wrinkles in her skin, her tears had not run down her face but remained trapped around her eyes where they formed a pool.

'Of course, I'll treasure her,' Michael had replied. Although he was furious the old woman should ask such a question, he had none the less managed to make his answer seem light and throwaway, at least he thought so.

'We'll be watching you,' Mrs Leary had continued, 'she's a very fine woman is Bridget . . .'

Michael stretched himself and then, turning his hands inside out and clicking the knuckles of his joints, he asked, 'What did Mrs Leary ever teach that was so unforgettable?'

'I can still remember what she taught us about Fionn and Slievenamon as if it were yesterday,' replied Bridget.

'She wasn't a teacher, she was a terrorizer. You said so often yourself,' said Michael categorically.

'Yes, I suppose I did,' agreed Bridget. 'But I can still remember some of what she said so well, because of the way she said it.'

Michael stood with a snort and announced, 'I'm going to make tea.'

Then, picking up his chair, he went through the gate and down the path and in through the front door.

Shadows were lengthening across the fields and it was growing cold but Bridget, her father still smoking beside her, remained as she was, letting her gaze drift across the landscape. She felt calm and happy and it was comforting to know she was never going to fear Mrs Leary sweeping past, or 'Eggy-Weggy' booming after her as she made her way home along the lanes. She remembered Mrs Whelan's and she was filled with an inner certainty that the cure was going to work.

But despite her optimism Bridget did not conceive the next month, or the next month or the month that followed.

To begin with, as it gradually became clearer and clearer to her that she was not going to get pregnant, she was bitterly disappointed that Mrs Whelan's corn doll was not a success. But then, as she reflected on her visit, she remembered the old woman's last remarks to her when she had been sitting on the stone and staring across the bog. 'All that matters,' Mrs Whelan had said, 'is that you believe, that you love, and that you are good, and God's will shall follow, whatever His will shall be.'

It was not His will, she decided, that she and Michael should have children. So gradually, over the months and years, she resigned herself to being a married woman with no children and concentrated on Michael and the marriage instead. Fairy magic, she decided, which worked so well for others, was probably not for her; only God could help her and there was nothing she herself could do.

The story of Michael during the years of the marriage was quite different. In the beginning he was not keen for himself and Bridget to have children at all. As he put it, he did not want bawling brats around the place; he wanted peace and quiet. He also felt they already had a child, in the form of Pat, living with them. If Bridget moped – as she did when her period came in the early days – Michael would sometimes say, 'Thank God, the red flag's out. That's another month we get to ourselves.'

However, as relations and friends of their own age began having children, and then more children, Michael decided they should too. Michael only appeared to be indifferent to what other people did. In fact, he was thoroughly conventional and if he did not have what everyone else had, in this case a growing family, he became very unhappy.

Michael started to dread Bridget's periods, and as one month followed another without her conceiving, he became more and more despondent. Why was she not able to get pregnant? What, he asked, was wrong?

In the fourth year of their marriage, he took Bridget to see Mrs Whelan. Bridget naturally did not let on that she had visited once before and the old woman herself, when she opened her door and saw Michael and Bridget standing in front of her, had the good sense to keep her mouth shut.

While Michael stayed outside, Mrs Whelan repeated the prayers over the lines of salt and then took Bridget up to the stone in the middle of the gorse bushes. This time, however, no feeling came as she sat on the rock and she remained cold and covered in goose-pimples. Naturally, Bridget said nothing.

When they returned to the cottage, Mrs Whelan made another strange figure and repeated, word for word, her previous instructions. The visit of four years before was never alluded to, which Bridget thought was strange.

Bridget and Michael walked off in silence and when they reached home, Bridget excused herself and went into their bedroom, locking the door after herself.

She lifted the mattress. All that remained of the first doll were a few wisps caught in the wire mesh, and a puddle of smallish shreds on the floor beneath. Bridget put her new doll in place and dropped the mattress.

The second visit to Mrs Whelan was no more effective than the first and, before long, Michael became desperate. Sometimes he blamed himself, sometimes Bridget. Her solution to his moodiness was to make love more passionately and more often.

However, the house was small and there was a lack of

privacy. For this reason, Michael and Bridget always preferred to make love when Bridget's father, Pat Boland, was out.

Two or three evenings a week, Pat was in the habit of walking down the lane and calling on his sister, Mary Kennedy as she was called, who was also Bridget's aunt. Mary Kennedy lived in a small cottage at the point where their lane met the main road; and while Pat was away visiting Mary, Michael and Bridget felt free as they never did when he was at home.

But one winter's evening, while Pat was down visiting his sister, some young men called into Mary Kennedy's cottage.

The young men found the company of the old people uninteresting. Bridget and Michael were a better prospect.

'Where's Michael?' one of them asked. 'Up at the house, is he?' to which Pat replied without thinking, 'Yes.' Later he was annoyed with himself for having done so. He was also slightly anxious that Michael might be cross with him. Pat was always a little frightened of his son-in-law.

The young men left Mary Kennedy's and walked the mile up the dark lane to Cleary's.

Approaching the gloomy house, however, the visitors were disappointed to discover there was no light burning in the window. But drawing closer and hearing cries of pleasure and encouragement coming from inside, they understood why the light was quenched. Then, quickly grasping the comic potential of the situation, they decided that they would stay as they were, hidden in the darkness, and listen to the proceedings within.

From then on, if Pat was discovered to be visiting with Bridget's old Aunt Mary, young men would gather around the Clearys' house to listen or amuse themselves by offering a running commentary on the progress of the lovemaking which they could hear going on in the house.

This continued until, one autumn evening, Acting-Sergeant Egan of the Royal Irish Constabulary was cycling down the lane on his way see a farmer about a bull licence. As he came up to Cleary's, he was very surprised to find three young men standing in the darkness, though not nearly as surprised as they were when he appeared.

'What are you doing?' the acting-sergeant demanded.

'We're on our way to Mary Kennedy's,' one of them replied. He spoke with a definiteness which was suspicious to the acting-sergeant.

'Where have you come from?' the policeman asked.

At that moment there was a cry of joy from inside the house and none of the young men could come up with an answer to the acting-sergeant's question.

'Go away,' ordered the policeman, and the young men shuffled off.

Acting-Sergeant Egan went on his way, saw the farmer and only then, on his way back, dismounted and knocked on the Clearys' door. It was Michael who answered.

'There were some young men hanging around your house earlier, Michael Cleary,' he said. 'This was about an hour ago.'

Acting-Sergeant Egan waited for this to sink in and then he added politely, 'An hour ago you were sleeping I suppose, because there were no lights on in your house at that time.'

'Yes,' agreed Michael.

Bridget appeared behind her husband. She was pinning her hair in a bun on top of her head.

'Mrs Cleary,' Acting-Sergeant Egan greeted her.

'What is it?' asked Bridget.

'Some young men were loitering in the lane earlier. I sent them on their way. They shan't be back.'

Acting-Sergeant Egan left. 'How dare they come and spy,' Michael shouted, while Bridget sat silently dragging her teeth over her lower lip. This was what she always did when her husband was angry and she felt anxious.

'Do you think this was the first time?' she asked.

'I wouldn't think so,' said Michael furiously, and after making enquiries in the district he found he had guessed correctly.

With a view to retaliation, Michael purchased a pickaxe handle. He hid it, wrapped in sacking, at the back of the turf pile in the shed.

Inevitably, Bridget found it and demanded to know what it was for.

'My own handle is split,' he mumbled. He was not an accomplished liar.

'Well, why was it hidden under the turf?'

'Was it? To keep it dry,' he continued lamely.

When she had drawn out the truth, which did not take her long for she had already guessed the true purpose for which Michael had bought the handle, Bridget began:

'One beating you might get away with. But by the second or the third, Acting-Sergeant Egan will have worked out it's you, and then he'll come here and arrest you, that is if that gang of hooligans haven't come and thrashed you half to death first.'

Michael saw his wife's argument was compelling. In the search for revenge he was either going to end up feuding or in prison, or both.

Then he recalled that outside Fethard there was a woman called Irene Callaghan. Some said her father was a fairy; others said that her father was a tinker and that her mother conceived after the couple made love on a fairy stone in the middle of a rath. However, the most popular explanation for Irene's power was that her father was an English soldier, itself not a cause for harm except that one day when she was pregnant, Irene's mother denied the fact she was having a baby in the hearing of a neighbour who had the power of giving the evil eye, so ensuring, perversely, that this talent was passed on to the infant in the womb.

So one evening, Michael bicycled over to her house after

work. Irene Callaghan lived in a small but neatly whitewashed cottage in the middle of a copse on an old demesne. The windows and the doors were painted bright red by order of the landlord and there were two lovely flower beds.

Michael knocked, the door opened and he saw, standing in front of him in the fading light, an oldish woman with very dark, sad brown eyes. She brought him into her kitchen and he sat on a green horsehair sofa piled with cushions and told her his story. Then he drank peppermint tea while she smoked an old brown clay pipe.

Finally she said, 'I will do,' and in that way Michael gathered she had agreed to help him.

'You go now. Leave this to me. You must never discuss this with anyone.'

A fortnight later, in a blacksmith's forge, a rogue spark entered the eye of one of the voyeurs. The aptness of the punishment was pleasing to Michael, his sense of grievance was now assuaged (so much so he now lost all interest in the other miscreants) and the news vindicated one of his deepest beliefs, and that confirmation was a great comfort to him. There was another power in the world, if one only knew when and how to invoke it.

CHAPTER TWO

When Michael Cleary was a child, his father and mother often told him that if he misbehaved, the fairies would steal him in the middle of the night, take him to Kearney's ringfort which was near his childhood home, and drag him down to their kingdom underneath the fort, from where he would never be able to return. His mother and father never said exactly what happened to the captives underground or what would happen to him, and of course their vagueness only made the idea more ominous.

Michael was a solemn only child, well behaved and biddable. His only shortcoming was that when – to his mind – his sense of natural justice was violated, he was gripped by a terrible temper. His rages when he was in this state were so overwhelming that as he screamed and shouted he made no sense whatsoever.

Michael's mother was Agatha. She was a heavy woman with a round head balanced on a round body. Her cheeks were permanently flushed; however, although she gave the appearance of always being hot to the touch in fact she was always cold, her hands especially. Agatha's eyes were grey and she was an accomplished maker of jams and jellies.

For Agatha, making jam and jellies was far beyond a duty and far greater than a pleasure. Seeing the dark full jars in her press was a greater comfort to her than anything else in life, with the exception of her faith.

Agatha collected jam jars and so did her friends, and because she was so very good at jam and jelly making, they gave her sugar and fruit and in return she made them all they needed.

It was an afternoon in the summer, the time of strawberry jelly. Michael was seven years old. After boiling and reducing, Agatha ladled the jelly into a sock of muslin to strain. The muslin was suspended from an ash-plant stretched between two straight-backed kitchen chairs.

Michael was chasing around in the kitchen with some neighbour's children. Timmy, the dog, was running about as well. Somebody jogged the ash-plant. The muslin bag fell. There was a pan underneath but unfortunately the bag missed and hit the edge. It split and pounds and pounds of jelly poured out on to the earth floor where it formed a steaming puddle.

Smelling the jelly, the dog ran straight over but the mixture was so hot Timmy had to spit out the first gobbet he stole. A moment later a two-year-old tripped and fell head-first into the pool. Someone stood him up. The hot jelly was stuck to his palms and his face. His mouth opened and out came a cry. Agatha tried to wipe the jelly off him with a rag. The child, who was in considerable pain, panicked and ran screaming towards the corner. Agatha grabbed him and, trapping him between her knees, she managed to rub the jelly away.

'Just look at that,' she shouted when she had finished.

Suspended in the jelly were bits of dirt and twig and several hen feathers. These came from the hens who were pecking away under the kitchen table.

'Just look where your tearing around has got us,' Agatha continued, while the little knot of children stood quite still and stared up at her, none daring to speak.

It was not Michael's fault yet Agatha blamed him now. She took the ash-plant, dragged him outside, and hit him on the back of the neck with the nobbled end.

'I didn't do it, it wasn't me,' Michael shouted back at her.

It was bad enough, she thought, to do what he had done but now on top of that to lie, it was beyond the pale. Yes,

Michael was the culprit all right, she thought, there was no doubt about that now.

'Don't lie, don't lie, don't lie,' she shouted, whacking him on the back and the neck as she did.

Michael fell to the ground and rolled himself into a tight ball.

'Stand up, you.' She stabbed at him ferociously with the point of the ash-plant but Michael curled up even more tightly.

'I didn't knock down the bag of jelly,' he shouted.

There was something about the way his lips quivered and the way his eyes were filled with tears which made her even angrier. Still holding out, still denying, she thought, and she hit him across the legs.

After lashing Michael several more times, Agatha began to tire and feel faint. She felt breathless from all the exertion.

'To bed. Now!' she shouted at Michael, curled at her feet.

Michael got up and hobbled into the kitchen, Agatha following behind. The anxious faces of the other children were staring at him. He could tell from their eyes just how grateful each of them was that he or she had not been selected for punishment.

He climbed painfully up the ladder to the space under the roof and lay down on his mattress there where he slept. In the kitchen below he heard his mother reprimanding the other children.

'This is what happens when you all tear around in here,' she shouted. 'Look at the trouble you've all caused. Look at my jelly! Ruined. Now, go away! All of you.'

Michael listened as his friends slunk out through their back door and made off across the yard. No one spoke. They were too terrified, he imagined. The house went quiet and then he heard a strange scraping. He peered down through the hatch-way and saw Agatha scooping up the jelly with a spoon and dumping the mess into a filthy cardboard box. When Agatha finished she threw the box into the fire.

Michael lay down on his mattress and listened to the hissing of the jelly burning, smelt the burnt-sugar smell wafting through the rafters, then heard Timmy the dog as Agatha caught him by the scruff of the neck. He could tell she had done this because of the combination of Timmy's yelping with the scratching made by his back paws on the ground.

'Come on now, you! Don't think you're getting off lightly,' came her words from the back door.

Michael got painfully to his knees and squinted out of the tiny window set in the gable wall.

In the yard below, he saw Agatha dragging a whining and protesting Timmy to the turf shed. She pulled him inside where she tied him up, Michael presumed, then came out again, shutting the door after herself.

'That was twenty-eight pounds of jelly ruined,' she shouted through the wood at Timmy, and stomped back across the yard.

Michael lay down. In the shed, Timmy started to bark. It was a bark Michael recognized. It was going to last and last, for hours perhaps. It was a cry of pain and hurt which he perfectly understood.

Then he remembered the fairies with which he had been threatened so often. If they could take him away, he thought, then why not his mother?

He raised his face again to the tiny window. He saw the tin roof of their byre, rusting around the edges where the green paint was worn off, and the dark, mashed-up earth which their two cows churned up on their way backwards and forwards to milking. Then, raising his eyes, he looked across at Kearney's rath, a perfect circle of trees on the top of a hill. Kearney's Hill, as it was sometimes called, stood on a neighbour's land.

'Please,' he whispered, 'if you are listening in the trees, will you please come and take her away from me, please.'

When he woke the following morning, Michael was still bruised and stiff from the beating. He lay under the blankets for a few moments. He ached even in the little spaces between the vertebrae down his back.

He sat up slowly. That was when he noticed there was something wrong. The house was abnormally quiet, like a sick house.

No sound of his mother below, making the fire ready or boiling the kettle for the tea.

He climbed down the ladder. There was nobody about in the kitchen but from the teacup and the glass on the table he could tell that there had been. The glass was empty and when he lifted it up, he could smell whiskey.

'Mother! Father!' he called.

No reply. The old alarm clock on the mantelpiece was ticking loudly.

His mother was vanished. His father as well.

Michael peeled an onion and broke off a piece of bread from the loaf on the side of the dresser. He fled to the byre and sat deep in one of the stalls with old yellow straw piled around him. The smell of the cows was a comfort. He took a bite of the onion and a mouthful of bread. The onion was sharp, the bread dry. Tears rose into his eyes. He blinked them back. In his stomach there was a fluttery feeling. He wanted to cry but not from the onion; these were real tears but, he told himself sternly, he was not going to let that happen.

'Michael,' he heard his father calling.

He clambered from the stall and crept out through the byre door.

His father, James, appeared round the side of their house. He was carrying Timmy's bowl.

41

His father's hair was very black and his head was very square. There was a mole just below his left eye. When he was talking, James would sometimes squeeze the mole between finger and thumb, and by turning and pulling it, he would expose the red part under his eye.

'Were you in the byre?' his father asked even though it was obvious this was where Michael had been.

Yet Michael nodded. 'Yes,' he said. He always answered his father.

'Did you eat?'

'Yes.'

'Good.'

His father disappeared through their back door and Michael followed him into the kitchen. The half-panelled walls were painted mustard yellow but along the skirting great chips had been kicked away and the bare wood which showed through was a brownish black, the same as rotten teeth, Michael's mother sometimes said. The St Brigid's Cross over the door was dusty in its crevices. The empty cup and glass were still on the table.

'Let's get this fire going.' His father knelt, took the tongs and scraped away the old white ash until he came to the turf embers in the middle, glowing red and hot. Michael looked up at the mantelpiece, at the white-faced clock with no glass – consequently the numbers were almost rubbed away – and the tea caddy beside it, with the picture on the side of two Chinamen with long pigtails.

Michael, still standing by the table, now stared at the back of his father's jacket. There was a seam in the middle joined by big stitches; it was something like a vein.

Where was his mother? Michael wondered to himself.

She was gone, replied his inner voice.

So why didn't his father mention her? Or say where she was?

He thought for a moment or two and then he told himself

that obviously she had been taken away or gone off with the fairies. That had to be the answer. Otherwise, his father would tell him, wouldn't he, where she was.

Your wish has come true, he thought.

He heard the words inside his head. It was as if he were speaking them.

His wish had come true.

His legs started trembling. He sat, put his head down on the table and looked along the bumpy, wooden surface to the cup at the other end.

With the sunlight streaming through the open door behind, the porcelain suddenly seemed whiter than it really was and thinner.

Michael reached forward to touch the cup, misjudged and knocked it over. There were some tea dregs in the bottom and they spread out across the table in a brown puddle.

'What are you up to?' his father asked.

Michael stood the cup back in the saucer as his father turned to see what was happening.

'Not messing, are you?' his father demanded. He was often cross like this.

'No,' Michael said.

His father turned back to the fire.

He had asked and his wish had been granted, Michael thought.

He went out, sat down by the cattle trough and stared into the dark, still water. This was where he always went to think or when he felt sad.

Timmy, still locked up in the turf shed, was whining and barking, and these sounds as they echoed off the stone walls and tin roof seemed unusually plaintive. The rooks were cawing in the trees. This was another sad noise, he thought.

As he sat there, Michael gradually realized what he had done. He had asked and his mother had been taken. She was gone and she was never coming back.

He grew appalled, and the more the truth sunk in, the greater his anxiety became. He had lost his mother, he thought, and he was never going to see her again.

Michael began to cry and at one point he caught sight of his reflection on the water as he dragged the cuff of his jacket across his pale face . . .

After a while his father came out of the cottage and Michael heard him stamping towards him in his boots. Michael blinked furiously, his usual resort when tears had to be hidden. If his father started on the questions, he thought, he would be caught, and if caught, it was going to be more than just a beating he was going to get this time. His father would probably kill him.

And Michael did not want that to happen, because now he knew exactly what he had to do in order to get his mother back.

'I'm going to bring in the cows,' his father muttered, passing behind him. 'Come on.'

Michael followed his father along the lane to the first gate. The animals were in the small field beyond, the one they called the Quarter. Michael followed his father in.

Dotted about the field were several clumps of gorse, dark green and dusted with yellow blooms, as well as some very large slabs of rock which were half-buried in the ground. When the sun shone the rocks heated up and Michael liked to lie on them and feel the warmth soaking out of them into his body. Sometimes, the cattle would lick at the rocks with their furry tongues, making a strange rasping noise.

'Auk, auk, auk,' James began. His father always made these guttural calls when he fetched the cows. The older cow appeared first. She was black and white, her udders swaying beneath her belly. The second one followed. She was scrawnier and her pelvis stuck up through her pelt.

They drove the cows to the byre and chained them to the

44

wall. His father sat, gripped the bucket between his knees and began to pull at the teats. The milk squirted and tumbled and frothed in the bucket. Michael stealthily backed through the door, turned and ran into the house.

The kitchen dresser stood against the partition wall. It was dark blue except for the creaking doors, which were cream. He opened the bottom doors and smelt the linseed oil and flour and jam smells of the dresser.

He reached his tin box down from the shelf and took off the lid. His spinning top, his eight lead soldiers and his three halfpennies were lying inside, along with some bits of wood and some painted stones.

He did not want to take the box, he decided, because then his father might realize that he was up to something. None the less, he needed something to carry his treasures in.

He looked around the room. His glance took in the salt box above the hearth, the turf piled by the fire, the table with the drawer hanging open and the cup which he had knocked over earlier with the glass beside it.

He turned back to the cupboard and that was when he saw the muslin bag which had been the start of it. His mother had rinsed it out and dried it in front of the fire. Now, here it was, neatly folded and lying on the shelf.

He opened it out. The tear was down the side but it would do. He put his treasures in and twisted the slack of the muslin sock into a plait which he loosely knotted.

He put the lid back on his tin box in which he had left the painted stones and pieces of wood, replaced it, closed the dresser doors and ran out of the house. He ran down the lane and climbed into the Quarter field. The hurt was aching inside him, yet the movement and the knowledge that he was taking action made him feel better. Much, much better.

Breathless, Michael arrived some minutes later on the cusp of Kearney's Hill.

Through the trees he saw that it was dark inside the rath which stretched in front of him. He felt his stomach falling, the same feeling as when he swung on the rope over their stream, and looking down he saw the bank falling away and the wet rocks below. However, that was a nice sensation and this was not.

'Go on,' he said out loud to himself. 'Go in!' It was the same tone in which his father would speak to a donkey.

Michael gripped his precious bundle with both his arms and went through the gap in the bank which formed the circle from which the trees which comprised the rath were growing.

In the fields through which he had run on the way to Kearney's ring-fort, there had been a grassy smell typical of a summer's day which was mild and warm; but once he was inside the circle of trees, the nice smell was gone and the new smell was of wet and stone and moss.

There were leaves on the ground. They were old and brown and stuck together like pieces of wet paper which had dried hard. As Michael walked they rustled underfoot.

In the middle of the rath there was an enormous boulder as high as his chest, where sheep sheltered and scratched themselves. Clumps of their browny-white wool were lying around everywhere. There were even strands of wool stuck to the bark of some of the trees.

Michael halted in front of the rock. It was broad at the top but narrowed down to a point which was buried in the earth. Because it resembled a triangle resting on one of its points, the rock looked as if it ought to topple over. But when, once, he had asked his mother why it did not, she had told him it was a special rock because it was inside a fairy fort. That was the reason why it never fell over.

Michael knelt and opened the muslin sack. He took out his spinning top and put it under the overhang in the dark dry place at the back, sticking the point into the earth to make the top stand up. The spinning top was made from tin. It was white with blue lines on it, but when it was spinning it was all blue. He closed an eye and squinted, checking the top was standing up straight, then he got to his feet and arranged his lead soldiers in a line on top of the rock. He laid his three coins in a half-circle in front of them.

'Please, please,' he shouted, 'can I have my mother back and you can have my soldiers and my money and my spinning top.'

He went home uncertain but contented. He had made his offering and it would only be a matter of time before his mother was back. He sat for a while in the kitchen, staring at the open door, expecting his mother to walk through at any moment. However, by the early afternoon when she still hadn't shown up, he started to grow despondent again. Perhaps she was never coming home, he thought.

The anxiety trickled back. He kept running to the door.

His father came in for tea and told him to sit still.

Michael took himself off to the water trough again.

When his mother came back, he thought, she would have to come up the lane.

He squinted down to the point where their lane curved and disappeared behind a clump of alder trees.

He saw something moving.

She was coming, he thought. His heart began to thump.

But it was nothing, he realized a moment later. Just the wind blowing the trees. At the back of the throat he felt raw, the same as when he cried only now he wasn't crying.

He hung about the water trough until it was dark, by which time his stomach was tight again. He heard his father calling, 'Michael,' and turned towards the cottage.

For supper, his father gave him a dish of porridge, a knob of yellow butter melted in the middle. Michael ate slowly and then went up to bed without his father telling him to go. Under the covers he cried at first. Later, he fell asleep.

When he woke up the next morning, he knew at once that something was wrong, only he could not remember what. He lay there for a moment until he remembered, and then he felt sick in his stomach again.

He dressed and went down. His father was milking in the byre. He ran across the fields towards Kearney's ring. There was a thin mist lying on the ground. As he ran it seemed to open in front of him, then after he had passed, it seemed to close over his tracks again.

At the entrance to the rath, with the tree trunks rising on either side, he stopped for a moment, then he ran on. Inside, he stopped again. He blinked. His feelings somersaulted.

Where he expected to see his line of lead soldiers in their red coats, there was just an empty expanse of rock.

He blinked again. They were gone.

He ran over to the rock and threw himself on to his knees. He peered into the dark overhang and right to the back.

Yes, the top, it was gone too. Quite gone.

He put his little finger into the hole which he had made when he had jammed the point of the spinning top into the earth the day before.

He stood up and ran his hand over the top of the rock. The stone was smooth and cold.

The sad call of a cuckoo sounded. The canopy of leaves overhead was dark with tiny points here and there where the sunlight showed through.

'Please, can she come home today?' he called.

He got on to his knees again and stared into the dark space at the back of the overhanging rock. For the first time it struck him it was nearly a little cave.

'Please, can she come home today?' Michael shouted once more.

For the rest of that day he stayed by the water trough, every now and again running down to the corner where the alders grew, to get a look along the next stretch of the lane.

48

The movement of the trees had betrayed him too many times the day before. By evening, however, there was still no sign of her.

He went into the kitchen and ate with his father, potatoes and rashers.

'Why so silent?' his father asked, tugging at the mole on his face and showing the red moist part under his eye.

Michael shook his head, saying nothing.

His father sent him to bed when it was still light. On any other evening, Michael would have objected, but not tonight. He wanted to be in bed. He wanted to be asleep.

He slipped beneath the blankets. The ache had moved from his stomach to the back of his throat. A few salty tears ran down his cheek.

Waking the next morning there was no gap between feeling unhappy and then remembering why. Opening his eyes, it came to him instantly. His mother was gone and he was to blame.

But what about the soldiers, the spinning top and the money? he asked himself.

He went back to Kearney's rath, knelt in front of the rock and once again begged the fairies to let his mother come home. Then he retraced his steps to the cottage feeling disconsolate. He had to keep reminding himself that his toys and his money were gone.

In the afternoon, while he was in the kitchen, he heard the rumble of iron wheels coming from the lane.

He had been waiting for something to happen for three days and he was exhausted by it. He was wrung out.

He listened. The rumble of the turning wheels drew closer.

He got up from the chair and went to the door.

It was their neighbour, Mr Henry, driving his blue cart up their lane. Mr Henry was standing up on the front of the cart. He was wearing a bowler hat and a red handkerchief was tied around his neck.

49

Not daring to allow himself to think what he hoped, Michael clambered on to the window-sill in order to get a more top-down view.

The sides of the cart were high, as Mr Henry used it mainly for moving turf or sticks. But it was not filled with fuel today, Michael saw.

No, instead of sticks and turf there was a someone in the back. It was a woman, with a scarf over her head.

Michael jumped down and started running down the lane. He stumbled but he did not fall.

Mr Henry lifted a finger, acknowledging the approaching boy.

'Michael,' he called.

Michael ran past and swung round.

'Mother,' he shouted, and the face under the scarf looked up at him. It would have been shocking if Michael had not been so happy. Agatha's characteristic flushed expression was vanished. She was pale, white, and her eyes were dim and lifeless. She smiled weakly at him.

'Mother,' cried Michael.

He leapt up on to the back of the cart. Agatha's arm went round him and Michael's head went on to her lap.

'Mother.'

Inside the cottage she shuffled straight away over to the chair by the fire and lowered herself carefully down on to the seat.

'I was unwell. I am tired,' she said slowly, and shivered.

James came in and told Michael to sit quietly. His father made tea and Michael sat on an orange box at his mother's feet. She drank thirstily, greedily, then when she was finished she gave Michael the cup and stood up painfully.

'I'm to bed,' she said, and added, as if apologizing, 'I must.'

Michael had not asked the question which he had been longing to ask since he jumped up on to the cart beside her. Now was his chance, perhaps the last he was going to have.

'Where have you been?' he said.

'Where have I been, darling?'

She was swaying on her feet.

'Up in Kearney's,' his father interjected.

'Yes, and don't ask me any more,' she continued. 'I'm tired.'

'With the fairies,' his father added.

James took his wife's arm and steered her into the bedroom off the kitchen, shutting the door behind.

Michael heard the voices of his parents drifting through. Mother sounded frail and broken; Father was cajoling and mock jolly.

He ran outside. The day was blustery and the blue sky was littered with great white summer clouds. He slipped through the gate into the garden where they grew their vegetables.

There was a hedge around the plot and in the hedge there was a hole where the dog, Timmy, hid from the rain and sheltered from the wind. Over the years, the hole had rounded to Timmy's shape, and on the sharp branch ends wisps of his fur had caught and stuck, until at last the place had become a little fur-lined cave. If it was not to the water trough then it was to here that Michael crept when he was troubled.

He backed into the hole and rolled up like an animal. The meaty dog smell of Timmy was all around him.

Michael listened to the sound of his breathing. His body was shaking. He waited while it gradually stilled. He was exhausted.

He began to think. He had had the closest, the narrowest of escapes. The worst thing that could happen almost had happened. He had nearly lost his mother. But then, somehow, at the last moment the calamity had been averted and she had come back home.

But what about the part he had played? If he had never made his wish, nothing would have happened, he thought, and all would have been well.

After this thought, he felt a great wave of fearfulness. Then he remembered the summer before, climbing up the beech tree at the back of their house. He had gone up happily, gaily even. However, when he reached the summit and looked past the branches and the leaves at the ground far below, panic had overcome him and his legs had begun to shake. In the end, his father had to fetch the ladder and bring him down on his shoulders.

He was experiencing that feeling of terror again, only now it was ten times worse. It was not that he had nearly lost his mother – which was bad enough – it was that *he* had asked to lose her and it had nearly happened.

But no one had heard him at the window and so far he had escaped detection for having begged the fairies to take his mother away. He felt a sense of gratitude and relief that he would not have been able to put into words.

But what Michael did not know was what had actually happened.

In the middle of the night following the day Agatha had thrashed him and long after he had fallen asleep, his mother suddenly began to salivate and to run a high fever.

Her husband in the bed beside her woke up.

'I'm ill,' she said. 'God help me, James, for what I have done.'

They were lying on a sheet made of two old flour sacks sewn together. James put his hand towards his wife. He felt the sheet where she was lying was wet with sweat. He touched her forehead. Again, it was hot and wet.

He got out of bed and lit the candle.

'I'll fetch you some water.'

He put on some clothes and went out to the kitchen.

He filled a tin cup from the enamel bucket by the dresser and came back to the bedroom.

By the wavering candlelight he saw Agatha's eyes rolling wildly.

'God help me,' she said. 'God forgive me.'

She rolled her head from side to side on the bolster. Little bubbles of saliva appeared around her mouth.

'Can you hear me?' he asked, but he doubted if she could.

He lifted her head up and pressed the tin rim against her lips.

'Drink,' he said.

The water ran over her mouth and down her chin.

James lit the storm lantern and hurried down to the house of their nearest neighbours, the Henrys, and banged on the door until Mr Henry woke up and came to the door.

'My wife is sick,' explained James.

Mr Henry wore a long, striped nightshirt. Mr Henry was groggy and unshaven.

Mr Henry dressed and together the two men went into the field behind the cottage. James held the storm lantern, the heat from the flame rising around his wrist. He spotted the dark shape of the donkey standing near a clump of nettles.

Together, James and Mr Henry got a rope round the animal's neck. Then they dragged it to the yard and they hitched it to the blue cart.

Returning to Cleary's cottage, James and Mr Henry hurried inside. They found Mrs Cleary lying in bed, shaking and juddering. As she did not reply when her husband asked, 'Are you all right? Can you hear me?' James assumed his wife had fainted.

'Come on,' he said.

Mr Henry took her feet and James took Agatha under her arms.

They carried the sagging, bowed body of Agatha across the kitchen and out to the cart which was standing at the front door.

'Easy, easy,' mumbled James and they swung her up and on to the blanket which Mr Henry had thoughtfully laid out in advance. Having stretched her out, Mr Henry then folded the blanket slack over her.

What about the boy? James now wondered. He turned back towards the house but then stopped.

If the arrival of the cart and the carrying out of Agatha had not woken him, Michael would now certainly sleep in until morning, he calculated, by which time either he would be back or he would have sent Mr Henry home with a message. Yes, it was best to let him sleep. Michael had had a lot to contend with that day.

James closed his door and got up on to the cart. Mr Henry snapped the reins and they set off for the hospital twelve miles away.

It was a cloudy summer's night. All James was able to make out were the stones in the ground like dark lumps in a river.

At the hospital, two orderlies carried Agatha into a cubicle on a stretcher. They put her on to a padded bench covered with a sheet. It was a clean sheet but there was a hole in it. The name of the hospital was stitched on the edge in big red letters.

The doctor unbuttoned Agatha's nightdress at the neck and put his stethoscope to the pale triangle of skin which was exposed. As he listened to her breathing, the doctor raised his eyes to the ceiling.

The doctor looked drunk, thought Michael's father.

Then he thought, no, on second thoughts, he didn't.

A nurse with a scrubbed face brought a bottle of salts. The cork came off and it was lifted to his wife's nose. The acrid odour of smelling salts filled the room. Agatha opened her eyes. Michael's father felt a strange stirring in the middle of his body.

He had been in the grip of an unacknowledged terror from the moment he had felt the sodden sheet on their bed. It was a terror of Agatha dying, a terror of losing her. But now, as he saw Agatha's eyelids opening, he realized there was no longer any cause to be terrified, for she was not dying. She was going to live, and knowing that, he was now free at last to acknowledge the terror which had gripped him earlier.

They moved Agatha to a ward. The patients in the beds all appeared to be breathing in unison. James stood and watched as Agatha was tucked in. He wanted to speak to her but he felt intimidated by the doctor's white coat and the starched frocks of the nurses. The doctor led him out into the corridor.

There was a gas lamp on the wall burning very white. They stood underneath. For the first time Michael's father was able to take in the doctor's features. He was a large man with a large head. He was balding but what hair remained was jet black like his own.

From the domed head James's gaze slid down across the forehead and came to rest on the man's cheekbones. These appeared to be sticking out from under his skin. James was reminded of the little horns on a heifer pushing up through the animal's pelt. Suddenly, his own hands felt too big to him and James rammed them into his pockets.

'We will keep your wife,' said the doctor.

He was English. Michael's father wondered why he had not noticed that before.

It was probably that he had been too much in his own world to notice, he thought, and he nodded and said 'Yes,' in the humble, unquestioning manner that doctors and other officials always brought out in him.

'As soon as we're certain there is nothing wrong, we can let her go home,' continued the doctor. 'That would be in a day or two, I would think.'

Sister was hovering. The interview was over.

The doctor pointed him towards the entrance and James walked away along the corridor painted a sickly green. Government buildings, he thought, were always this awful colour.

In the front hallway of the hospital, James found Mr Henry

sitting bolt upright on a bench, his hat hanging off his left knee. An enormous oil painting was hanging on the wall behind which showed a man – one of the founding fathers of the hospital – in a black top hat and a grey waistcoat, a gold fob chain stretched across his stomach.

Outside, James and Mr Henry climbed into the cart and set off for home. It was still dark and, listening to the rumble of the wheels below, James, for no reason which he was able to grasp, was suddenly reminded of the mill where he went with his father as a child. It was dusty, smelling of flour, and filled with the grumbling roar of the millstones as they turned.

Drifting out of this reverie of his childish self, his own tiny hand lying inside his father's huge and calloused one, he heard Mr Henry coughing at his side.

James gazed at Mr Henry's face, and noticed the pointedness of his chin was somehow made the more acute by the fact of his not being shaved. Even in darkness he could make out the bristles. His neighbour wanted to ask what was wrong with Agatha. James could tell he was desperate to ask from the way he kept coughing and shuffling on his seat. However, he realized, Mr Henry had not brought the subject up and nor would he.

Why? James wondered.

He decided it was either because Mr Henry lacked the necessary courage, or because he thought it would be indelicate in case she was dying. James turned the matter over in his mind for several minutes but in the end he was not able to decide which it was.

Eventually, James took pity on Mr Henry and he said, 'My wife will be coming home tomorrow, or the next day. Maybe you will bring her home for me?'

'Please be to God,' said Mr Henry. And he added quickly, 'Of course I will bring her back. Why wouldn't I?'

'There's nothing wrong with her, or the doctor doesn't think there is,' continued James.

56

Mr Henry nodded sagely. The wheels rumbled beneath them and the hedgerows on either side unrolled as they trotted past. Suddenly, James was aware of a curdled feeling in his stomach. For a moment he thought he was going to be sick and in order to dispel the nausea he opened and closed his eyes frantically several times, which was his practice when he feared he was going to be sick from whiskey.

'Look around,' he heard his inner voice urging, 'and don't be sick.'

Light began to show behind the distant hills, a very faint shading. A bird trilled. He did not recognize what it was.

He had left his wife and she was apparently on the mend but what, he asked himself, if she took a turn again for the worse?

The idea of losing her came again and the idea was unbearable. He was overwhelmed by a sudden sense of the blood inside his body. It was surging and pulsing as it shoved its way through his veins. However, at any moment they might split apart and out it would pour. He started to shake.

'Please,' James pronounced under his breath, 'please let it be all right with Agatha.'

Mr Henry, hearing the whispered words, glanced over quickly then looked ahead again at the road.

At last they reached the cottage. James got down from the cart and nodded goodbye to Mr Henry.

Dawn was still some way off. James made his way along the path and opened the door. He could hear the wheels of the cart crunching behind him as Mr Henry rolled away down the lane.

Having told himself so often on the journey home there was no need to worry about his wife, he had come to half-believe it; however, coming into the kitchen, James's conviction crumbled. The chair by the fire where she sat, the tongs with which she turned the turf sods, the honeycomb on the window ledge which she had brought home wrapped in brown paper and was not yet opened, all conjured her up before his mind's eye.

He poured a glass of whiskey and took a sip. It made him feel nauseous again.

He tried to pour the drink from the glass back into the bottle but his hands were shaking and the liquor flowed down the side, wetting and staining the paper label.

He felt extraordinarily annoyed not to be able to put the drink back into the bottle again. He flung the slops into the fire and the embers hissed.

Then he remembered his son.

He climbed slowly up the creaking, homemade ladder and put his head into the loft.

He was not able to see anything so he listened. He heard Michael breathing. It was the slow, gentle breathing of a sleeping child.

That was good, he thought.

His eyes were now adjusted and he could make out Michael's shape under the blanket on the pallet.

The child seemed to him suddenly so very frail. He was like a stick, he thought, and like a stick Michael could be snapped in two, just like that.

He was filled with love and concern for his only child, and it was then the idea came to him. He decided he wasn't going to tell Michael about what had happened to Agatha at all. Children were easily upset, especially when their mothers were taken sick, he thought, and if he mentioned to Michael that Agatha was in hospital, it was only going to make the boy unhappy.

The best way to proceed was just to leave Agatha's absence uncommented upon, he thought, and after Agatha came home in a day or two, as the doctor had said she would, the whole matter of Agatha's disappearance would soon be quickly forgotten. Having made the decision, James felt much better.

58

He descended the creaking ladder and regretted now that he had thrown away the undrunk whiskey.

He poured himself another glass and sat down in front of the fire.

As the light outside began to show through the window, he fell asleep.

James awoke in the chair with stiff legs and a cold neck. It was early. He climbed up to the attic. Michael was still sleeping, as he saw it, the untroubled sleep of a child.

He boiled up some water on the little primus which doubled as a lamp and drank his tea heavily sugared.

Timmy was barking. He prepared a dish of bread and milk and went out to the shed. As he pushed open the door Timmy rushed towards him, his body twisting with joy on the end of the rope which attached him to the wall. He reminded James of a fish on a line.

He put down the bowl and watched Timmy's tongue dart forward, curl around a piece of bread and lift it into his mouth. The appetite, the energy, the enthusiasm of a hungry dog was always a marvel to him.

Within a few seconds the bowl was empty but Timmy went on licking, and the bowl rocked and clattered on the floor from the force of his tongue.

'Come on, you,' he said finally.

Timmy looked up, one eye blue and one eye brown. James bent down and took the bowl carefully by the edges. He did not like to have a dog's saliva on his fingers. He found the meaty smell of their spit disgusting.

'Go and lie down,' he ordered Timmy.

Timmy dropped his head and made his way back to the side of the turf pile and lay down. James wondered if he should let Timmy out. He looked about to see if the dog had fouled the floor but there were no stools that he could see anywhere. And the dog seemed willing to stay, he thought, as if Timmy sensed he had not yet served his time for trying to eat the jelly off the floor. James decided he would leave him be.

James turned and left, closing the door after himself. He walked across the yard towards the cottage. The door of the byre was open, he noticed, and then he thought he heard someone inside.

'Michael,' he called, and the child crept out with a strange, woeful expression on his face.

And seeing the expression, the tenderness he had felt for the boy the night before vanished, and James felt himself growing irritated. Damned child, he thought.

What the hell did Michael imagine that his father had been going through? he wondered angrily, having to trek over to the hospital in the middle of the night, and then having to leave Agatha there. And God only knew what was going to happen or when she was coming home. If anyone had the right to a long face, James thought, it was him, not his son.

Then he paused and reminded himself, of course the boy didn't know what had happened to his mother and why she wasn't there, and he was worried as any child would be. Still, the boy did seem strangely unable to think about anything but himself.

James went through the door into the kitchen, Michael following. The clock was ticking on the mantelpiece. James knelt down and began attending to the fire. He could feel that his son, who was standing near the table, was staring at him.

Michael obviously wanted to ask about Agatha, he thought, but he wasn't going to tell him, was he? No, the matter was settled and silence was the best course of action. He had no doubt about that.

However, to his great surprise, the child said nothing, ran out and spent his time hovering around the trough with the same mournful expression which he had been wearing when he had come out of the byre.

And when James went out later that morning to get the cows, the boy's expression was unchanged.

James felt his irritation not only returning but growing. His son did nothing but brood and hang about. As usual, he thought, Michael was only thinking about himself.

Well, I'll shake you up, young fellow, James said to himself.

'I'm going to bring in the cows,' he muttered, passing behind Michael. 'Come on.'

Michael slunk down the lane after him to the Quarter field.

What did Michael think he was up to? wondered James, as he lifted up and opened back the five-barred gate. They had made this together from rope and long lengths of ash cut from the hedges.

And what did Michael think his father was feeling, James wondered, getting on with the day and no Agatha at home?

James was annoyed now that the boy had not spoken. It seemed so careless, so selfish, so unholy. Why didn't he ask questions? He'd always said it. There was something unnatural about his son. Something hard. He didn't like to have to admit this but the child was a stranger, an outsider. He was, and James hardly dared frame the thought, he was not human in some sense.

James walked towards the gorse bush in the corner, calling out to the cows as he went. The animals appeared from behind.

Well, Michael would be a damned sight more long-faced, he thought, and a damned sight more sorry for himself if he knew where Agatha was at that moment. The child, the child, the infuriating child, he would try the patience of a saint.

They got the cows to the shed and chained them up. James sat on the stool, got the bucket between his legs and began squeezing the teats of the big cow whom they called Apple Blossom.

Michael was behind him and James could feel, as he had at

the fire that morning, his son's eyes drilling into his back. Then suddenly he was aware that Michael was gone.

He got up from the stool and went to the door.

No sign of Michael.

He saw the back door of the cottage was slightly ajar. He crept over, taking care not to let his heavy boots scrape on the stones, and peered around the lintel.

In the kitchen he saw Michael putting his lead soldiers, his spinning top and his coppers into a muslin sack. Then Michael closed the doors of the dresser carefully. It was, James recognized, clearly the act of someone up to some wrong and trying to cover their tracks.

Michael got up and ran out of the front door.

James waited a moment or two, crossed the kitchen to the other side of the cottage, and looked out through the front door.

He saw Michael running down the lane. James set off after him at a gentle trot.

Halfway down the lane, he saw Michael climb over the gate and leap into the Quarter field. James hung about for a few moments and then went down to the gate himself.

Michael was halfway across the field. He seemed to be headed for the fairy rath on Kearney's Hill.

James crouched and watched for some minutes as the figure of his son grew smaller and smaller as he toiled up the hill. When he reached the top, James saw Michael stopping for a moment and then disappearing into the ring between two enormous trees.

James went back to the byre and finished milking. He didn't like what he had seen. He wanted to go and see for himself if Michael had done anything in Kearney's ring. However, as the boy hung about the lane all day, James recognized that he was going to have to wait until later if he did not want Michael to know what he had done.

In the evening, James gave his son a dish of porridge.

Michael ate slowly, as if he had no appetite, and when he was finished he voluntarily took himself off to bed to James's great relief.

It was still early, still light outside. James milked again then sat for a while by the fire. Then he checked that Michael was asleep, took the storm lantern, and in the gathering dusk walked over to Kearney's Hill.

Reaching the edge and standing between the same two trees he had watched Michael passing through earlier, he felt nervous. What he saw stretching ahead of him was almost as dark as if it had been a cave with a roof. The branches of the trees sighed eerily overhead.

He listened carefully for other sounds but was unable to detect any. He stepped forward. Beech nuts and leaves and twigs sounded underfoot. He had been up here in the day hunting rabbits and that was one thing. But now it was evening, nearly night, and that was something else. One had to be careful in a place like this. Other powers ruled here at night and as he stood between the two tree trunks, a gloomy mauve as they rose upwards beside him, he could feel their presence.

It was a remarkable and brave man indeed who entered this place after dark, he thought, and he remembered that Quinn had done just that, and how the following morning, shaken and ashen-faced, Quinn had come to their cottage for his breakfast.

James had been a boy then, Michael's age, but he had never forgotten Quinn sitting by their fire, rocking and spitting and using both his hands to hold the mug of tea which he had been given. Even though he was only a boy, James was able to recognize the symptoms of terror when he saw them.

And in the evening, lying in the same bed where Michael now slept, James had listened to his parents and Quinn as they talked in low voices by the fire. In this way, he learned that Quinn had passed the night on the stone in the middle of the ring in order to acquire the power of the fairies. And later, James had heard it said around the district that Quinn had indeed been successful, and later again, he had noticed how Quinn was consulted by the local people as to who was harming either them or their cattle.

So what was Michael doing in here? he wondered. James didn't like this. His son in Kearney's rath, it gave him a bad feeling. It made him anxious. It made him fearful. They had enough trouble with Agatha away, without meddling with the fairies.

But there was only one way to deal with this matter. That was just to go in and see, and then leave. It was not yet completely pitch dark, and so the powers would not yet be out. Or so he hoped, anyhow. Besides which, if they were and they challenged him, he had an answer. His son Michael had been up there that very afternoon with his toys. What had the boy been up to? He was Michael's father, and he was just coming to find out. That was all. Nothing more.

'I'm the boy's father.' He rehearsed the sentence in case he was challenged. 'I've just come to see if he's been up to any mischief.'

James stepped forward quickly, his heart beating and swallowing hard. He went straight towards the stone in the middle. It seemed the obvious place to head for.

As he approached he saw the blur of something on top of the stone. For a horrible moment he thought they were the figures whom he dreaded above all others and then he saw he was mistaken. They were Michael's lead soldiers laid out in a line. There were eight in all: two in kilts and forage caps; four of them in redcoats and pointy hats; an officer on a horse wielding his cutlass; and a sergeant with stripes on his shoulder and a baton folded under his arm.

When he got up to the stone he saw the coppers were laid out as well as the soldiers.

James's mind started racing.

Why had Michael left them here? he wondered. No, he did not like this. This wasn't right. It was . . .

He did not finish the thought because suddenly it seemed to him as if the soldiers had started to move. They were fairies. He turned and headed back towards the gap in the old earth rampart, between two tall trees. He longed to break into a run. However, he told himself that at all costs that was the one thing he must not do. The powers smelt fear; it attracted them. The slightest sign and thousands of them would swarm out from their palace under the rock and pull him to the ground. They would take him prisoner, bind him with ropes and carry him away.

He passed under the trees and into the field beyond. Gnats crowded around him to form a haze of dancing black points.

He looked across the darkening landscape of hedges and trees. He could see their cottage in the distance with the lamp showing in the tiny window. Their walls were whitewashed and the front door was red. It was safe down there. He wanted to be inside and the door closed and locked.

He walked home rapidly, closed and locked the door after himself just as he had imagined he would, and sat down by the fire.

He tried to puzzle matters out. His son had left his soldiers – and now he was calm James was almost certain that was what he had seen – as well his coppers on the rock in the middle. And no doubt the top, although he had not seen it, was somewhere around. It had to be. But what had Michael been up to earlier? Quinn passed a night on the rock and emerged from the ordeal with the fairy power to determine who was harming man or beast. What had lead soldiers to do with that? Or coppers? Or a top?

James slept uneasily and woke early. When he had gone to bed the night before he did not know what to think; however, now he did.

It was always better to sleep on things, he thought.

He dressed quickly and made his way back to Kearney's rath. The grass was wet with dew and he felt his trouser bottoms growing damp around his ankles as he walked.

He reached the cusp of the hill, the trunks of the trees on the bank above like the gateposts of an ancient city.

Yes, he thought, to sleep on a matter was always good. Problems were sorted out in dreams, painlessly, effortlessly, whereas in the light of day problems were made worse by thinking.

His son had left some toys for them. Fair enough. With good luck, that's how they would be seen – as the toys of a child who had no sense about what he was doing.

Michael was just an ordinary boy, and like any ordinary child, he just wanted his mother back.

And if the toys had been seen in the night and judged as he hoped they would be, as the leavings of a child who didn't know better, then he was going to take them away with him and hide them at home.

But if they'd been taken, then, oh God, they were probably in for it. Quite frankly, the leavings were an insult.

He breathed heavily. The rooks were cawing above.

'Well,' he said out loud to himself, 'there's nothing else for it. I'll just have to go and see.'

He stepped through the gap and headed towards the stone in the middle. His heart was thumping.

For a moment he did not dare to hope and then he saw what he had desperately wanted to see.

Yes, there they were, as he had left them the night before.

But the top, what about that? he wondered.

He dropped on to his knees and peered into the dark space underneath where the rock jutted out.

His heart soared again.

There was the tin top. It was jammed by its point into the ground and leaning over at an angle.

He reached forward and took the top and put it into his pocket.

James stood up. He untied the handkerchief around his neck and spread it out on the rock. He put the lead soldiers and the coppers in the middle, tied the corners and put the bundle into his other jacket pocket.

He turned and started to walk towards the edge of the rath. His heart was beating. Any moment he expected small figures to rise up out of the ground and challenge him. That would be like the fairies, he thought, to stop him at the very last second.

However, a moment later he passed under the great beech trees sighing overhead and he emerged into the field. He looked down the sloping hillside towards his own house.

He began to walk forward. At the gate at the bottom he stopped. He was trembling and shaking. He climbed slowly over and went on.

At the Quarter field, though it was earlier than usual, he rounded up the two cows and drove them up the lane and into the byre. He chained the animals to the wall, then got up on his stool and reached up over the lintel above the door.

His fingers found the loose stone and he carefully pulled it forward. A small cloud of mortar dust came away, trickling on to his shoulder.

James put the soldiers and the spinning top into the hole and replaced the stone. The coppers went in his pocket.

He got down dusting his shoulder, then carried the stool over to Apple Blossom who stood waiting patiently, her heavy udders drooping towards the ground.

After milking he threw a cupful of milk on to the ground outside the byre. He did this in order to propitiate any powers who might come around the house. He remained troubled by the offering which Michael had left. He still feared it might be judged insulting.

And come evening, his feelings were unchanged. He gave

Michael potatoes and rashers and sent him to bed, and after milking the cows he again threw milk on to the churned-up ground outside the byre. This time, it was two cups' worth.

Then he went down to Mr Henry's where he learned that a message had been sent from the hospital to Corrigan's shop and passed on to Mrs Henry. Agatha was to come home. Could she be collected the next day?

Although he knew he ought to go, James detested the hospital and its smell, in the same way that he hated the saliva of a dog. So he coughed and said nothing and Mr Henry said he would go.

'Thank you,' said James. 'I can't go in the day,' and he added the usual feeble excuses about cattle and milking and chores.

'What are neighbours for?' said Mrs Henry pleasantly.

'Could you give Agatha a message, please?' said James.

'Yes.' Mr Henry looked at him with his most obliging expression.

'She's not to say to the boy where she's been. Tell her that. I don't want him being worried.'

'Indeed,' Mr Henry agreed, 'I will tell her.'

James was splitting sticks when Mr Henry came up the lane. He waited until his wife was in the cottage and then he went in by the front door.

Agatha was in the chair and Michael was on a box at her feet. The boy did not see him, his back being to the door. Agatha looked up and James, catching her eye, put his fingers to his lips.

His wife looked back at him, perplexed.

'Don't say where you've been,' he mouthed without sounding the words.

James made Agatha tea and when she finished, inevitably, Michael asked the question; 'Where have you been?'

James caught Agatha's eye.

68

'Where have I been, darling?' she said.

She was swaying on her feet. She wanted to speak but had no words to say.

'Up in Kearney's,' said James suddenly.

'Yes, and don't ask me any more,' she agreed, 'I'm tired.'

'With the fairies,' continued James, and taking his wife by the arm, he steered Agatha into the tiny bedroom off the kitchen, shutting the door after them.

Left alone, Michael wandered outside and went and curled up in Timmy's hole in the hedge.

Surrounded by scraps of the dog's fur and Timmy's meaty smell, Michael began to grow calm. Then from deep down the thought rose up into his mind, like a bubble rising to the surface: whatever happened in the next days and weeks and months, he was never going to admit to his crime, that he was the one who had asked that his mother be taken.

Michael kept his secret through childhood and adolescence – he only ever nodded and smiled when the subject of Agatha's three-day sojourn with the fairies was mentioned, as it often was in the family – and well into his marriage. Then, one night, when he was lying in bed with Bridget, she whispered, 'What was the worst thing you've ever done?' and he did what he had often longed to do: he told her simply and straightforwardly of the terrible crime he had almost initiated in a moment of childish rage.

Bridget listened silently as Michael related the story, twisting strands of his hair between her fingers, and he found the telling was far easier than he had ever dared to imagine it would be during the preceding years.

'You weren't to know, you were only a boy,' she whispered, when he finished, and then she added; 'Did you ever tell anyone else about that?'

'No.'

But then a few weeks later, emboldened by having given an

account to Bridget, he did repeat the story, this time to John Dunne, an elderly bachelor and a neighbour whom Michael was somewhat in awe of.

'I told John Dunne the story about my mother,' he boasted to Bridget when he came home that same evening, and Bridget sensed how important it had been to confess to someone who was not family, and moreover, just as she had, how important it had been that John Dunne had absolved her husband at the end of the tale by saying, 'You couldn't be expected to know better. You were only a child.'

A few weeks after this, John Dunne fell ill.

'I think the poor fellow needs looking after or he'll be at death's door,' said Michael, when he came back from making his first sick call, and Bridget agreed to go down to Michael's special friend's house on the main road every day, even though, as she said, he smelt of boot polish.

For the first week John Dunne was feverish and appeared not to know who was coming into his house and looking after him. Then his fever dropped, and by the end of the second week his temperature was normal, although he was still very weak.

One morning, this was at the start of the third week, John Dunne was lying in bed and Bridget was carefully soaping his face in order to shave him.

His eyes were closed but suddenly he opened them, looked straight up at her and said, 'Would you like to wash me all over?'

'Certainly not,' she said. 'You get yourself up some water from the spring when you're well, and you have yourself a bath, and until then you'll do rightly.'

John Dunne closed his eyes and she went back to soaping his face.

The following day, as usual, Bridget brought him down his lunch on a tray. When he finished eating, John Dunne asked if she would read to him and she agreed. The book was Robert Louis Stevenson's *Kidnapped*.

Bridget took her place by the fire under the paraffin lamp on the mantelpiece, while John Dunne settled himself back in the bed on the other side of the room, his head propped up by the bolster.

Bridget opened the book at the page which was marked with a squashed cigarette box and cleared her throat.

'Chapter Eight,' she began, 'The Round-House.

'One night, about twelve o'clock, a man of Mr Riach's watch (which was on deck) came down for his jacket; and instantly there began to go a whisper about the forecastle that "Shuan had done for him at last." There was no need of a name; we all knew who was meant; but we had scarce time to get the idea rightly in our heads, far less to speak of it, when the scuttle was again flung open, and Captain Hoseason came down the ladder. He looked sharply round the bunks in the tossing light of the lantern; and then, walking up to me, he addressed me, to my surprise, in tones of kindness.'

Usually, Bridget read well and strongly, and she admired the way Stevenson led the reader by the hand from situation to situation without faltering; however, this afternoon, because of the comment Dunne had made when she had been preparing to shave him, she felt uncomfortable, her appetite for the story was depressed, and she was unable to stop herself glancing up from the page to check on him every few lines.

Of course all there was to see each time she did this was John Dunne in his striped nightshirt, his eyes closed, and his hands resting on his chest.

And after the thirtieth or fortieth sighting of Dunne in this habitual listening pose, Bridget remonstrated with herself. The day before, he had been uncouth, she thought, but now he was back to his normal self.

Bridget continued reading but no longer letting herself glance up from the page. Within a few moments she felt herself growing calmer. Her sense of the narrative quickly returned, and very soon she was completely engrossed by Stevenson's description of David Balfour and the awful death of the cabin boy Ransome aboard the brig *Covenant* of Dysart, bound for the Carolinas in the New World with a cargo of slaves.

Bridget went on reading happily and animatedly for some minutes until, reaching the point where Captain Hoseason comes to remonstrate with the cabin boy's murderer, she glanced up with the vague intention of seeing how the story was affecting her listener. What she then saw froze her heart.

John Dunne was stretched out in his bed, more or less as he had been when she had last looked across at him; except that now his head was turned towards her, his eyes were open – and it seemed to her they were almost glowing – and his hands were between his legs underneath the bedclothes. He was holding himself.

Her heart started to race. She said nothing. Her eyes flicked downwards. She felt her palms had gone hot in an instant. She read on:

'Mr Shuan was on his feet in a trice: he still looked dazed, but he meant murder, ay, and would have done it, for the second time that night, had not the captain stepped in between him and his victim.

'"Sit down!" roars the captain. "Ye sot and swine, do ye know what ye've done? Ye've murdered the boy!"

'Mr Shuan seemed to understand; for he sat down again, and put up his hand to his brow.

'"Well," he said, "he brought me a dirty pannikin!"

'At that word, the captain and I and Mr Riach all looked at each other for a second with a kind of frightened look; and then Hoseason walked up to his chief officer, took him by the shoulder, led him across to his bunk, and bade him lie down and go to sleep, as you might speak to a bad child. The murderer cried a little, but he took off his sea-boots and obeyed.'

The ability of her lips to make the sound of one word after another was nothing short of miraculous but she was no longer with David Balfour in the brig's round-house, marooned amidst murderers. She was in John Dunne's kitchen, every muscle tensed, her ears straining to hear the slightest noise from the other side of the room, quite terrified and yet, as she also knew, quite unable to move. But then, mercifully, she reached the last paragraph:

'The shadow of poor Ransome, to be sure, lay on all four of us, and on me and Mr Shuan, in particular, most heavily. And then I had another trouble of my own. Here I was, doing dirty work for three men that I looked down upon, and one of whom, at least, should have hung upon a gallows; that was for the present; and as for the future, I could only see myself slaving alongside of Negroes in the tobacco fields. Mr Riach, perhaps from caution, would never suffer me to say another word about my story; the captain, whom I tried to approach, rebuffed me like a dog and would not hear a word; and as the days came and went, my heart sank lower and lower, till I was even glad of the work which kept me from thinking.'

Thank God, she thought as she pronounced the last word. At that she heard a low moan, the source of which she easily guessed. She closed the book smartly, stood up and returned it to the mantelpiece where it lived. Then, without allowing John Dunne to catch her eye, she announced she would be back with his supper in the evening, picked up the tray and marched straight out.

When she came back at six, Bridget brought Joanna with her and from then on her cousin was never not with her.

A couple of days later Michael noticed this.

'Did anything happen?' he asked. 'Are you frightened to go down to Dunne's place alone?'

Bridget said nothing. Old Boot Polish, as she and Joanna

now referred to Dunne, might be contemptible; however, telling Michael was only going to lead to an almighty row which, they had agreed, would be very ugly. The matter, they had decided, was best forgotten.

'Not at all,' said Bridget blithely to Michael, for when she had to she was able to lie effortlessly. 'It's just Joanna and I haven't seen one another much recently. So she comes with me and we talk as we go down and as we come back.'

Michael shrugged. He was glad to know nothing had happened.

A week later John Dunne was back on his feet and completely recovered. On the last day Bridget and Joanna came to feed him, he presented Bridget with a pair of ear-rings which he had had someone buy for him in Clonmel.

'Thank you for looking after me,' he said, gazing directly, and as Bridget fancied, somewhat longingly into her eyes.

Bridget and Joanna fled as soon as they decently could, dragging Katie after them.

'I saw those eyes, I saw those eyes,' said Joanna, as they turned up the Ballyvadlea lane and began to hurry towards Bridget's home. 'Did you see them?'

'Did I, did I?' exclaimed Bridget in reply. 'Those were the eyes when he was you-know-what.'

When they were gone a good way up the lane, Bridget stopped and opened the box to get a good look at the present. They were pendant ear-rings, glass, with the profile of a woman's face engraved on the sides.

'Quite nice,' said Joanna.

'Yes,' Bridget agreed, but that evening when she went to their well, she tossed them at the deep, dark water and heard the splash they made with infinite satisfaction.

Her benefactor, unfortunately, was not so easily got rid of. Some months later, he was among several callers who were up at the house one evening. Bridget went out to get turf from the shed, and walking back by the gable, for their house had

74

no back door only a front one, who did she find waiting there but John Dunne.

'You never wear my gift,' he said, his boot-polish smell enveloping her in the darkness. She touched the hoops in her ears.

'Oh, but I do, or did. They're lost.'

'How can you lose a pair?'

'Very easily. You take them out, as I did, and you put them down somewhere and then you forget where you've put them, and then when you remember and go back, they're gone; taken by the fairies, who knows? Why do you think we women need so much adornment? We're always losing things, you see. Now as you're out, you'll have to help me.'

She thrust the basket into his arms, slipped round the corner to the front of the house and into the safety of the room.

CHAPTER THREE

Bridget woke. She had been dreaming. She lay still with her eyes closed. She had been running. No, not her. It was a young tinker girl, and she was being chased by older tinker women.

They were heavy, bulky females, with brown, weathered faces and heavy gold ear-rings which flapped up and down as they ran after the girl across a field. The girl had done some wrong. They were going to catch her and teach her a lesson.

One of the older women was lagging behind. She carried a bucket filled with curdled milk. When the girl was caught and stripped, the women were going to kneel her on the ground and make her drink . . .

In her mind's eye the dream continued. The girl got to the edge of the field but could go no further. The hedge was impenetrable. There was a moment of prolonged terror with the inevitable looming and yet no action being taken to avoid it. Bridget particularly hated these moments in dreams.

Then, inevitably, the old women appeared and caught hold of the girl. They began to pull at her. The girl struggled. They pulled her clothes off item by item and threw them across the hedge one after the other. The girl's skin was very white and the hair between her legs was very black.

Bridget shuddered and turned the wedding ring on her finger. Dreams like this were not welcome. She shifted in the bed towards Michael beside her. She put her face against his and felt the bristles on his chin. He smelt of soap and blanket and he was warm.

She turned and looked at the clock on the chest beside the

76

bed. The clock was painted green and where it was chipped it was black, and it had a comforting tick. It was time to get up. It was Thursday and Thursday was Mr Hagan's day and there were many things which she had to do before their appointment.

She climbed down from bed and went out to the kitchen.

It was the biggest room, the principal room in the house; it was about fourteen feet square, with pitch pine boards on the walls and a flagged floor. At the front there was a door which opened on to the path which led to the lane, and at the back there were a set of steep stairs which led to the loft where she sometimes slept with Michael in the summer. On the gable wall was the hearth and in its basket grate she saw the red embers of the previous night's fire were still glowing. The doors to the two downstairs rooms, from one of which she had herself just emerged, were opposite the fireplace, and between the doors stood the dresser, shelves at the top with her plates and glasses arranged on them, the press below where she kept food and groceries.

Bridget padded across the room to the fireplace. It was nearly dawn and she could see the outline of the front door, the stairs and the dresser. She had filled the big black pot with water the night before and hung it on the crane to warm on the fire overnight. Now she swung the crane towards her, and as she removed the lid from the pot a wreath of steam rose up into her face. She tested the water with a finger. Warm, not boiling.

With the pint pot she ladled hot water into the enamel bowl with the pink rim, then carefully carried it with two hands to the table which was in the middle of the floor, halfway between the hearth and dresser and opposite the front door. She unpinned her hair, combed it and pinned it again. Then she took a flannel from the rack hanging over the fire, dipped it in the water and began to clean her face. This was the way Michael liked her to wash, indeed insisted. It started after they married, when he found her one morning, naked, standing in the bowl in the kitchen. She was washing herself from the feet upwards. He had been horrified.

'That's wrong,' he had said, 'it's always the face to begin with and then you do the other parts,' and since then she had always done it this way.

After washing her ears and her neck, Bridget listened for sounds of her father. He slept in the other small room leading off the kitchen. He was awake for she heard him moving around, but by custom he would not come out until she called him.

She took off her nightdress and threw it across the chair and washed under her arms and her breasts. The water was soapy by the time she lifted the bowl down to the flagged floor and stepped into it. She washed her legs and finally her feet and then she noticed she was shivering. It was always that way; water was warm to begin with but it quickly went cold, not like when she filled the tin tub and she was able to steep herself for half an hour. That was lovely but it only happened once a month when she washed her hair.

She lifted the towel to her face. It smelt of flour. As she dried herself under her arms and on her front, she noticed that she felt sore. She felt the soft spots on either side of the bony centre of her throat. They were lumpy and tender to the touch.

She stopped for a moment and noticed, which she hadn't before, that it was painful to swallow, and her head was heavy and muzzy. But today was not the day to be taking to her bed, she told herself.

She went back to towelling herself and did it vigorously, as if the action could banish any sickness.

She was dry. She pulled her nightdress on and went back into the bedroom to dress and wake her husband.

Some hours later, after Michael had left for work and she had given her father his breakfast, Bridget opened the front door and stepped out. It was ten o'clock. A basket of eggs swung from the crook of her arm. She closed the door.

Bridget went down the path, through the little gate and left down the lane. After a few steps she stopped by the bank on the far side and peered under the hedge at the small, vivid green shoots of the snowdrops which were shoving their way up through the earth. Spring was not now that far off, she told herself, even if it was still only the second week in January.

Bridget continued. Her legs were tired and odd pains were shooting up and down her back. She sneezed twice.

After about a hundred yards the lane bent savagely round to the right, almost forming a right-angle, and situated on the point was a gateway which opened on to a yard surrounded by sheds, outbuildings and a low, grey, single-storey farmhouse. The story, as Bridget had it, was that some years previously the owner had put out the old tenants after they defaulted on their rent and installed the elderly couple who lived there now, William and Minnie Simpson, as the emergency caretakers.

When Minnie and William moved in, there were mutterings around the district. Those of nationalistic opinion argued it was wrong for the old couple to have agreed to manage the property. They were profiting from another's downfall. The only proper course was a boycott.

However, the remarks stopped once William let it be known in the district that he was the proud possessor of a Colt 'Double-Action' army model revolver – it was a gift from his brother in America – and that, furthermore, he would not hesitate to defend himself and Minnie.

Yet the Simpsons remained fearful of attack by some hothead, and at night the old couple always closed the gates and locked and bolted their front door.

This morning, however, the heavy black gates were thrown

open as usual, and Bridget saw Minnie on the far side of the yard. She was pouring meal into a crude wooden trough of two planks nailed together in a 'V'. Around Minnie's feet swirled the hens, a clucking mass of brown and white and black.

'Come on, come on there,' Minnie shouted, turning and walking away through the squawking birds. Several feathers wafted in the breeze around the yard.

'Hello, Bridget,' Minnie now called out, acknowledging the younger woman. 'They're waiting for you.'

She pointed at the bag hanging on one of the spears of the gate. Bridget lifted it down and looked inside. Minnie's eggs lay in the bottom. They were white and brown and had the scrubbed look which came from a thorough cleaning with bicarbonate of soda.

Bridget began transferring Minnie's eggs to her basket two at a time. She noted that Minnie had nineteen eggs for sale, against her twenty-three.

'How are you?' enquired Minnie when she reached the gate. Bridget had emptied Minnie's bag. Her neighbour's face was small with a tiny mouth and surprisingly neat white teeth.

In her youth, Bridget imagined Minnie had been pretty, like the actresses and singers in the hand-coloured portraits which were sold at fairs. But Mrs Simpson was no longer young; her hair was grey and her cheeks were red from broken veins.

'I'm well,' Bridget said. She coughed and shook her head. 'No, I'm not actually.' Bridget moved her hands in an equivocal manner. 'I'm not feeling well.'

'You should go home, go to bed.'

For a moment Bridget wondered if Minnie was offering to walk down to meet Mr Hagan in her place, but no offer followed, of course. Mrs Simpson only ever said the right thing, she never did it.

80

'I'll be up later with the money,' said Bridget curtly and walked off.

'And don't worry about me, I'll be all right,' she then called back over her shoulder, but turning she saw Mrs Simpson was already halfway across the yard, and of course she had not heard her.

Silly old woman, thought Bridget.

A few yards further on there was another bank which was crowded with snowdrop shoots, on one of which there showed a single, trembling white bloom.

Was the spot more sheltered, she wondered as she bent down, than the bank outside her house? She touched the petal of the single snowdrop. It was cold and fleshy.

Then her mind moved back to what had just happened at Minnie's gate.

What was disappointing, she thought, was the way a few people in the district believed Mrs Simpson was caring. Even she herself had believed it when she had first got to know her.

But now she saw the older woman more clearly and she saw that she was not caring. However, Minnie was her neighbour and Bridget made certain that relations between them were cordial.

She straightened up and sniffed at the finger which had touched the bloom. In just a few weeks she would be able to pick a flower and thread it through her buttonhole on Thursday mornings.

She walked. Yes, thought Bridget, she must never forget there was something fundamentally untrustworthy about Minnie Simpson and she wasn't to be relied on.

From the Simpsons' farm, the lane wound on for about a mile through fields, hedgerows and copses, until it hit the main road which connected the hamlet of Cloneen to the south with the village of Drangan to the north. The house of Bridget's aunt, Mary Kennedy, the house which her father would often visit in the evening, stood here on the corner. It was a small whitewashed cottage with ragged, brown thatch, a blue painted gate and red fuchsia growing by the door in summer.

As she approached, Bridget saw Mary was standing at her front door, as she was faithfully every Thursday morning. She was waiting for her niece.

Her aunt waved at her and came forward to the gate.

'Thursday again,' called Mary.

Her aunt's hair was crinkled and still retained its colour. She wore it pinned to the back of her head with a silver comb. Mary was heavily built. Her forearms, which she now folded, were especially thick. There was a tooth missing at the front of her mouth, and she whistled strangely as she spoke.

'Thursday again,' agreed Bridget.

'I don't know,' said the old woman. 'It's Thursday one day, and then suddenly it's Thursday again, and I don't know what's happened to the days in between. What have I done with all that time?'

This was a habitual observation of Mary's. Her four sons, William, James, Patrick and Mikey, were fully grown and often they were away from home, with the consequence that not only was her aunt growing more lonely, but – as she frequently complained – she was losing track of time.

'You washed a blanket,' said Bridget cheerfully.

There was one thrown over the hedge to dry.

'My Liza didn't come home last night,' said Mary abruptly.

This was her tortoiseshell cat.

'But that Peter,' Mary continued irritably, referring to Peter the brown tom, 'he was home as usual this morning for his breakfast, and he wolfed it down. Just like any man, it's home to eat and then he's off immediately he's got his feed.'

People were a strange mixture, thought Bridget. As Mary was at pains to emphasize, she was longing for her sons to marry. She did not want to look after them any more. Yet at the same time, her aunt was also dreading the day her sons married, as she often admitted, for then she would be quite alone except for her animals.

Bridget and Michael were also dreading the day. They often said to one another, only partly in jest, that once the Kennedy boys were married, Mary would be up at their home incessantly. She would drive them mad.

'I'll look out for Liza on the road,' said Bridget helpfully, 'and I'll ask Mr Hagan. He might have seen her on his travels.'

'Thanks.'

Bridget walked away but Mary remained where she was, and she would stay there, as Bridget knew, for some minutes, just on the off-chance that she might have to go back for some reason to ask her aunt something.

Usually this knowledge touched Bridget. However, this morning, because she was not feeling well, Mary's loneliness quickly passed out of her mind.

The spot where Bridget waited for Mr Hagan, the eggman, was down the main road about fifty yards, beneath an ash tree. Turning the corner from the lane Bridget's eyes darted ahead, for she was hoping to see Mr Hagan's trap and his brown horse waiting there for her. However, all there was to see was the ash, its pale white bark smudged with green mould, its canopy of fine branches reaching up towards the sky like outstretched hands.

Bridget felt cold and shivered. She stopped and put down the basket of eggs and stared along the road. It led away past the ash tree and on to the village of Drangan, two miles to the north. It was empty. Nothing moved. She did up the top button of her jacket and picked up her basket again. Where was Mr Hagan?

Bridget took her place beneath the tree and now looked

back the way she had come. On her right was the entrance to their lane, while on the other side of the road, about fifty yards away, was the small cottage where the greatly disliked John Dunne lived. Behind this rose a low hill crowned with a ring of trees. This was Kilnagranagh rath, about which she had heard almost as many stories as Slievenamon. Yet she had only ever been up to the summit once, the summer before as it happened, on a Sunday when she and Michael had been out walking and picking flowers.

At first, when they got to the top of the hill, they were uncertain about going inside the rath. So they walked around the outside. There was a low earth bank about as high as her waist. The bank formed a circle about fifty yards across and there were two entrances cut through it.

Out of the bank grew the trees which could be seen from the road below. They were all either oaks or beeches with moss-covered trunks.

'It's like Kearney's ring,' said Michael, predictably she thought, as this was a place about which he often spoke, now he knew his secret was safe with her.

After making two or three circuits Bridget said, 'Let's go in,' for she no longer felt nervous, and Michael agreed.

They went to the nearest gap and walked through. Inside the circle of trees and under the huge branches which arched above, the sunlight was subdued and green. It was as if it were coming through stained glass and it reminded Bridget of Drangan church.

Yet looking up, she saw that the leaves on the branches overhead, far from being like glass, were in fact silvery and shimmering, and she could not see through them for the sun coming from behind.

She lowered her gaze and saw now that the trunks of the trees were like columns, vast and monumental, framing views of the countryside as it stretched towards the distant horizon.

She started to walk in a circle. The floor underfoot was a

mixture of beech nuts, twig and leaf-mould. It was damp and woody and springy to walk on.

There was a summer breeze blowing and the boughs of the trees were moving, but inside the circle the wind was a hiss, almost inaudible, while the braying of John Dunne's donkey seemed miles away, rather than what it was, which was just a few hundred yards . . .

She stamped her feet and looked along the road. There was still no sign of Mr Hagan. She felt feverish. She looked for somewhere to sit but the ground was wet. The hotness passed on and she felt cooler again. The memory of Kilnagranagh returned but instead of lingering her mind moved to an article. She had read it in their local paper, the *Nationalist*. It was written by a Protestant minister from somewhere in Tyrone.

Thousands of years ago, he had begun, the raths were literally ring-forts – earth ramparts with a gate – and they were on hilltops all over Ireland. The earthworks were thrown up by men and then trees and thorn bushes were encouraged to grow on them. This was to better protect the families who huddled inside with their cattle at night or in times of war.

Then came the movement of people in Ireland to lower-lying lands and the arrival of Christianity. But the raths remained and now, instead of being the sanctuary of ordinary people, wrote the minister, they became instead the refuge of immortals, the fairies.

According to some legends, the fairies were those in the heavenly host who were indecisive during the great struggle between God and Lucifer, not knowing with whom to side. After Satan's defeat, there was no longer a place for them in heaven, yet they did not merit the punishment of hell, so God banished them to earth, where they took up residence in the abandoned hill-forts.

However, according to other accounts, they were pagan gods and warrior chieftains from pre-Christian Ireland, who went underground when St Patrick arrived, where they had remained living ever since.

But whatever their origin, there was universal agreement in Ireland on their character and qualities. They were small, elfin-looking, with very neat hands and feet, and with an attitude towards those with whom they shared the country that could best be described as tolerant, and was sometimes cruel and unkind.

They happily stole milk, honey and other foods. They also stole babies, children, even grown men and women, in place of whom they would leave foundlings, which though they looked almost identical to the stolen person, always had a foul temper and an appalling manner. But woe betide anyone who blocked one of the numerous fairy paths along which they moved through the countryside, day and night, or worse, cut down the trees or interfered with the ramparts of a fairy fort . . .

Bridget's thoughts drifted back to Kilnagranagh. The afternoon when she and Michael were up there, there had been flowers growing in profusion from the low earth bank. Red poppies, blue bugles and yellow marsh marigolds. She was about to pick a poppy when Michael said not to, and after reflecting a moment or two, she had agreed.

There were just some things one did not do. And to interfere with a fairy ring in any way was one of them.

'Hello, Bridget.'

It was Mr Hagan perhaps, she thought, but a moment later she saw it was John Dunne. He had come through his gate and was walking towards her. Like Mary, he was another regular feature of her Thursday runs.

She had never forgotten the glow in his eyes as she had read from *Kidnapped*, and he knew that she remembered. They shared a secret, of which the consequence was that not only did she loathe him, but he loathed her.

John Dunne drew level.

'Hello,' he said.

'Hello.' The basket hung from her folded arms covering her front.

'Not a bad morning.'

'No.'

'How's Michael?'

'He's fine.'

The conversation trickled on, with each questioning the other on mutual friends and the other replying with frigid precision.

Please let this be over, she wished after several minutes of tedium, and suddenly the clip-clop of an approaching horse interrupted them.

She turned and looked towards Drangan. It was Mr Hagan bowling towards them.

'I won't detain you from your business,' John Dunne whispered behind her, and he slid away down the road back towards his cottage.

'Goodbye,' she called, but he did not turn, just raised an arm in acknowledgement. She had seen the local Clonmel MP do exactly this when he was cheered once in the streets.

Mr Hagan drew up and smiled down at her as he tugged on the reins. The horse's head dropped towards its chest and the cart came to a halt with a clatter.

'Good morning,' called Hagan cheerily.

'Good morning,' she replied.

Mr Hagan was not alone. The German music teacher from Clonmel was sitting up beside Mr Hagan. Mr Hermann was wearing a black coat, a black scarf around his neck, and a black bowler hat on his head.

'Good morning, Mrs Cleary,' he said. Mr Hermann's accent was foreign-sounding but melodious.

Bridget smiled.

'And how are we today? Are we well?' Hermann continued.

'If Mr Hagan is in a generous mood today, then yes, I'm very well,' said Bridget laughing.

'There's more to life than money,' said Mr Hermann.

'Indeed!' Mr Hagan agreed, raising his eyes at the sky.

Mr Hermann always said the obvious.

Mr Hagan climbed down from the seat. He took Bridget's basket, walked round to the back of the cart and opened the door to reveal the racks of empty trays waiting to be filled with the eggs.

'How is Mildred, Mr Hermann?' Bridget asked politely. Mildred was his sweetheart.

'Well. We are well. At the moment we are killing Schubert.'

Mildred was a soprano. Mr Hermann accompanied her on the piano.

'You'll be able to play all day when you're married.'

Mr Hermann began to sing in German.

Mr Hermann was an ugly man. His hair was thinning, his nose was bulbous, and his eyes behind the glasses perched on his nose were slightly crossed. Yet listening to his low, gravelly voice, Bridget felt herself growing drowsy as the words flowed around her.

When she had once asked Mr Hermann about himself he had told her that he was born in Bohemia in 1870. When he was fourteen he enlisted in the Austro-Hungarian army and was assigned to a regimental band. When he left four years later, he was an accomplished musician who spoke German, Italian and Hungarian, as well as a smattering of English and French.

Mr Hermann became a touring musician, playing in orchestras all round Europe, eventually settling in Ireland where he became the teacher of music in a number of convents in County Tipperary and engaged to Mildred.

Mr Hagan appeared at Bridget's side and Mr Hermann stopped singing. Mr Hagan wore a leather money-pouch belt around his waist. He took out a fistful of change and counted some coppers into Bridget's outstretched hand.

'A pleasure to do business, Mrs Cleary.'

Mr Hagan bent down to lift Bridget's basket from the ground and hand it back to her. At that moment there was a huge gust of wind. Leaves and twigs from the ditches were lifted up into the air, and the basket started to roll away down the road at a fantastic speed.

Bridget ran half a dozen steps and stopped. Her chest and her neck hurt, and pieces of grit from the road were stinging her eyes. She heard the moaning of the wind as it whistled through the hedgerows. She even thought she could hear the boughs of the oak and beech trees on Kilnagranagh sighing. Then the jingling noise of the coins in Mr Hagan's money pouch came up from behind, passed her and disappeared as Mr Hagan, she presumed for she couldn't see anything, made off down the road.

She blinked and opened her eyes in time to see Mr Hagan draw level with her basket. However, just as he was about to grasp the handle, the wind gusted and the basket took off again. It moved away along the road like an ungainly brown animal, while leaves and twigs frantically whizzed through the air around it, and Mr Hagan lolloped behind. His pace was slow, his gait flat-footed, and Bridget distinctly heard Mr Hermann guffawing in the cart.

'Run,' Mr Hermann shouted after his friend.

At last, the tradesman drew level again with his quarry, and this time he got his foot on the lip of the basket and trapped it on the road.

'I have you,' he exclaimed.

He bent forward, his pouch upending.

'Mr Hagan,' Bridget shouted her warning; however, it was too late, and all his money poured out in one swift, unstoppable stream.

'I'm so sorry,' Bridget apologized breathlessly, as she drew level with him. Her head was splitting from the effort of running and the light was hurting her eyes. 'I've made you spill your money.'

'None of it's gone far.'

She saw his pennies, halfpennies and farthings were spread across the road. There was even a sixpence at the verge, standing upright, trapped between blades of grass.

Hermann came over and together the three scooped up the change, then searched for missing coins along the edges. As she poked through the undergrowth with a stick she had found, Bridget felt feverish and ill again, the way she had felt that morning when she was washing, only worse.

At last, they called off the search. They went back to the cart where Mr Hagan arranged his coppers into shilling columns on the front seat.

'All but a penny accounted for,' he said at last.

Bridget's hand went towards her pocket. 'Here,' said Bridget.

'I wouldn't hear of it,' said Mr Hagan.

Because she felt ill, she had intended to ask Mr Hagan if he wouldn't mind running her home, but after all this business with her basket and the money, she didn't feel that she rightly could.

Mr Hagan swept the coins into his pouch and fastened the clasp. Mr Hermann handed Bridget her basket.

'Thank you,' she said. She set off down the lane.

The men climbed up into the seat.

'See you next Thursday,' Mr Hagan called. He shook the reins and the cart rolled forward towards Cloneen, where Mr Hermann was due to give a piano lesson punctually at eleven o'clock.

'Lovely woman,' said Mr Hagan.

Bridget passed by her aunt's cottage, grateful that Mary was inside, and went on. Pains were shooting up and down her back again, and there were small beads of sweat above her lip. She wiped them away and touched her forehead. She was hot. Overhead the sky went dark. It was going to rain. She quickened her step but after fifty yards she was hot and tired.

She sneezed and sneezed again. She heard the whispering sigh of the rain as it started to fall on the grass and hedgerows. The land might almost be human, she thought, making that noise. The rain droplets were heavy and thick. Within seconds, loose strands of her hair were plastered to her hot forehead, and the rain had soaked through her jacket and her blouse to her skin.

As she moved on, alternating between a fast walk and a slow trot, she wished now she had asked Mr Hagan to bring her home. He would not have minded, would he? she thought. If only the basket hadn't bowled off and then his money spilt everywhere.

Her head was hurting, deep in the middle. In her mind's eye she saw her room, her bed, the cool bolster and her cheek resting on it. She wanted to be home.

When she had first noticed that morning that she did not feel well, she assumed the worst she was in for was a short fever or a mild chill. She hadn't an earthly idea that in a few short hours her brain was going to be hurting so badly, or that every step she took was going to register as a pain inside her skull. She had never felt as bad as this before, ever.

By the time she reached the door of the house, Bridget was soaked through, cold with wet and at the same time feverish. She turned the handle of the door and hurried in.

'Thank goodness to be home.'

Her father, Pat, was behind the kitchen table, stropping his cut-throat razor on a leather strap. Her father was in his vest and his scrawny forearms juddered as he stroked the blade up and down.

'You're wet,' exclaimed Pat.

Bridget closed the door.

Her father's face hovered before her in the steam. His hair was sticking out from his scalp in barbs, like a cock's coxcomb.

'I'm to bed,' said Bridget. 'I'm not well.'

Her father reached his teeth out of a cup and popped them between his lips. With his false teeth in, his cheeks filled out and his chin appeared to shrink miraculously.

Bridget sneezed.

'Lord help me,' she said.

She put the coppers on the table in two columns.

'If Mrs Simpson calls, there's hers,' said Bridget, indicating the pile.

Bridget rushed into the bedroom and started to pull off her clothes. All she wanted to do was to get into bed, to close her eyes and be still. It was the only way to stop the pain inside her head.

'Father,' she called feebly.

Her nightdress was on and she was pulling back the bedclothes.

'Daddy . . .'

She was in bed when Pat came in, her eyelids closing.

'Take my clothes and hang them to dry.'

Bridget had kicked her bloomers under the bed but left the rest of her clothes on the floor. Her father gathered everything up in his arms.

'Daddy,' she called as he went towards the door. 'Bring me something. A little tea or something. Whiskey . . .'

Five minutes later Pat returned. He brought with him a mug filled with whiskey, hot water and sugar. He found his daughter asleep.

He touched her shoulder and called her name but her eyes remained firmly closed.

Poor Bridget, he thought. She oughtn't to have been out at all and no coat.

He returned to the hearth. He draped her wet clothes over the clothes-horse and put it in front of the fire. Soon her things were steaming nicely in the heat. He moved the horse back in case anything scorched, sat down and drank the mug of whisky himself.

Cycling home from work in the darkness, Michael recognized Mr Hagan's cart coming towards him, and stopped.

'Greetings,' Mr Hermann called out to him.

'And good evening,' added Mr Hagan, pulling the reins.

The cart rolled to a halt.

'Hello,' said Michael looking up at the two men. 'How's my wife?' he asked.

'Never better,' said Mr Hagan.

'What about money?'

'Money,' laughed Mr Hagan, 'I gave her lots and lots of money.'

'Then I'd better hurry home and make certain she hasn't it all spent on fineries,' joked Michael.

Mr Hagan and Mr Hermann laughed. Week in, week out, when they met Michael on Thursday evenings he always made the same observation without fail. Indeed, if Michael had not made the usual crack about his wife's capacity to spend money, they would have thought something was wrong.

'Nice enough day,' said Mr Hagan.

Michael agreed and ran his hand over the warm flank of the horse. He liked the smell from the animal's coat. It was a smell of oats and blanket, and there was another smell as well. What was that?

'But, of course, you don't have to concern yourself with such dull matters as the weather, do you, Michael?' Mr Hagan continued. 'In the workshop all day, every day, snug and warm and out of the rain.'

Michael smiled and nodded. Of course, he thought, the

other smell was the carbolic in the saddle soap that Mr Hagan used to clean the tackle. It was a sharp, acidic aroma.

'That was some wind earlier,' mused Mr Hermann. 'It blew open the door of the piano room, sent all the sheet music flying. Sister said it was "mighty".'

Mr Hermann's imitation of Sister's Cork accent was appalling and Michael winced inwardly.

'But it wasn't anywhere like that wind when we were with Bridget,' said Mr Hagan, and looking at Michael directly he said, 'You'd have had to see it to believe it, Michael.'

'Why?' Michael wondered abstractedly. He loved the way, as he stroked the horse, that the coat rose and bristled beneath his palm.

'We were at the junction where your lane meets the road – Kilnagranagh. All quiet and suddenly, this huge gust comes, leaves, twigs, blowing everywhere and off goes Bridget's basket.'

'Any eggs in it?' asked Michael.

'No.' Mr Hagan shook his head. 'Anyhow I give chase, everything's blowing, grit and leaves are getting in my eyes and I'm not as young as I used to be. Anyhow, I draw level at last, at which point the old money pouch, the flap not having been securely fastened by Yours Truly, decides to empty a pound's worth of coppers on to the road. Hagan's a fool! Or what?'

What was he telling him the story for? Michael wondered. Something happened to old people. They became boring. Old Pat was much the same. Michael raised his hand. 'I'd better get home to Bridget,' he said. 'And Pat, I suppose,' he added.

'Good night, Michael,' said Mr Hagan. He jigged the reins. 'Walk on,' he said.

The cart moved off and Michael disappeared behind Mr Hagan and Mr Hermann into the darkness.

'He's a funny man,' said Mr Hagan quietly. 'I always get the feeling he's getting me to spy on Bridget.'

94

'Yes,' agreed Mr Hermann. 'Did I tell you I saw him one day in a pub, in Clonmel, quite sober, drinking a cordial, I think. The landlord had a dog, a little terrier, and it kept growling and snarling at Michael. So, suddenly, he just picked up his stick, no warning, and whacked the animal right in the face, hard as he could. Split one of the dog's teeth, blood everywhere. Naturally, the landlord was furious. He came out from behind the bar.

'"What do you think you're doing?" he said. "You've just struck my dog!"

'"That dog was trying to blink me," Michael replied, "and he's been giving me the evil eye ever since I came in."

'"You've cracked," the landlord said to Michael. "Get out." So Michael left. He's very strange, so loving and devoted to Bridget and yet it is funny the way he asks his questions.'

Mr Hermann fell silent as the cart swayed forward.

'I don't know whether I like him,' said Mr Hermann, 'I can't decide.'

'No,' agreed Mr Hagan, 'nor can I.'

It was dark when Bridget opened her eyes. Someone was moving around the room.

'Who's there?'

Michael came forward. He smelt of the cooper's yard, of glue and wood and sweat. The bedroom door was open and the oil lamp on the kitchen table was casting its pure white light into the room.

'Hello, Bridget. Do you want anything?'

Michael, she thought groggily, home from work. Her throat and body ached, and her skin was hot. But worst was her head. It was as if the skull had been split open, hot coals shovelled in on top of her brain and then the bone stapled back together.

'I feel terrible,' she whispered. 'I don't know what's wrong with me.'

95

She looked past Michael towards the lamp on the table in the kitchen. It was as if needles were flowing along the beam and into her eyes.

'Don't worry,' Michael whispered back, 'we'll get you better, Pat and I, don't you fear.'

CHAPTER FOUR

Bridget opened her eyes. It was still dark and no light showed around the edges of the shuttered window. From the small bedroom on the other side of the wall, as she had every morning for the two weeks now that she had been lying sick in bed, she heard the sound of her father stamping his feet on the ground. He always did this to get his boots on. Now quiet followed, and she knew that he was tying his long leather laces into neat double bows.

She knew this because as a child she had slept in the kitchen at home and she had seen the same ritual performed every morning. In those days, she now remembered, her father had referred to the bows into which he'd tied his laces as 'butterflies'.

'Butterflies, they're not butterflies,' she had always shouted back at him.

'Oh, yes they are,' he had always replied.

Then he would tell her – and he never tired of repeating this – that at night the laces magically transformed themselves into complete butterfly wings, and flew the boots away to a distant hill where they were polished by the fairies . . .

The bolts on the front door shot back and she heard Michael going out. She heard him passing her window and then along the gable wall.

Now she was more fully awake, she began to wonder how she felt. Her chest, she sensed, was aching. She touched her forehead. It was hot and there were beads of sweat bubbling up just below the hairline. Gingerly, she cleared her throat and found it was still sore. It hurt to swallow. She coughed gently and again more vigorously. Her head throbbed. The pain was excruciating, both behind her eyes and in the top of her chest.

Michael clumped back past her window and banged in through the front door. She guessed he had filled the basket with sods of turf, first task of the day, and now he was going on to the second. Sure enough, a moment later, she heard the characteristic rattle as the dry sods crashed against the metal bars of the grate.

The sickroom door swung open.

'Good morning.'

Michael was cheerful and smiling. He put the oil lamp beside her bed and returned carrying the enamel bowl with the pink rim. It was half filled with hot water and steam rose about his face.

'How's the patient?'

He set the bowl down on the orange box beside her bed.

Bridget shrugged. 'I'm no better. Really, we should call Dr Crean.'

'What Dr Crean can do is less than useless.'

Michael wrinkled his nose.

He lifted back the covers and helped Bridget to pull her nightdress off. She lay back naked on the bolster.

'Don't you trust Dr Crean?' Bridget wondered.

Michael, soaping the flannel in the water, said, 'Umh.' He was thinking what to say.

He began to wash her hands, first the palms and then between the fingers.

'I don't know,' he said.

Now rubbing Bridget's forearms he noticed the way the fine downy hairs were pushed back by the flannel, and then, when it had passed, how they lay back the way they were. Just like a horse, he thought.

'You should be better by now,' he said.

'My head hurts,' she replied, lifting her arms behind her

head. Michael washed in the hollow around the small tuft of black hair under her arms and then moved the flannel across to her breasts. They were small and pointed and the nipples were brown.

'I'm going to get better,' she said.

Michael moved the flannel down the middle of her chest and over her belly. She let her legs flop apart and he washed over the pubic bone.

She closed her eyes. The first time Michael ever washed her – this was in the early days of their marriage – was when she was bedridden for a fortnight with scarlet fever. Her face had gone bright red and her stomach had churned that first time. But now she felt at ease with him, and if she were well she would have asked him to climb in beside her.

She felt Michael's mouth on her belly-button kissing her and then his mouth on her left breast, kissing again.

'I will get better,' she said.

'I don't know,' said Michael.

It was raining when Michael set out from home on his bicycle in the darkness, and it was still raining when he arrived forty minutes later at the workshop in Clonmel.

'How are you?' he heard a young voice say as he wheeled his dripping bicycle through the workshop double doors.

'Bad old morning.'

The freckled face of Liam, the fourteen-year-old apprentice, stared towards him from the corner. The door of the stove behind him was standing open and the coals in the grate were glowing. They were the only point of light in the room.

'Mind your own business,' Michael scowled at the youth.

He took off his sodden coat and hung it on a hook by the stove to dry. Then he took off his boots. The leather was slimy with wet. He padded across the room, his wet socks making footprints on the pine floorboards. He opened the cupboard where Liam kept the kindling and took an old copy of the *Nationalist* from the pile inside.

Returning to the stove, he tore out a page and was about to crumple it up when his eye fell on the heading, 'Irish playwright triumphs':

An Ideal Husband, by Oscar Wilde, opened at the Theatre Royal, Haymarket, London, on 3 January 1895, before a rapturous audience which included the Prince of Wales, Arthur Balfour and Joseh Chamberlain.

Michael knew of Wilde. He had even been to see one of his plays with Bridget – *Lady Windermere's Fan* – when it played in Clonmel. They had laughed a great deal, and after the performance, it being a warm summer's night, he and Bridget had made love in a wood on the way home, a wood where they had sometimes gone when they were courting.

Staring into space he remembered now the particular glistening, shining quality of Bridget's skin that night, as she lay stretched out naked on the ground, and the way her hair smelt of scent, not only her own but the scent which it had seemed that all the other women in the audience in the hall had been wearing that night.

The reverie lasted a few seconds, then Michael cut it short with a shake of his head, crumpled the sheet of newspaper and stuffed it down into one of his boots. There was no point thinking about such times, he rebuked himself, because it only made the present worse. Bridget had been sick for two weeks now and there was no sign of recovery. Ganey was the answer, he thought, except he was going to have to do a whole damned day's work before he could go and see him.

A few minutes later the master cooper, Mr Corrigan, arrived at the workshop.

'Hello,' he said, pulling off his coat and waistcoat and pulling on his brown leather apron.

Michael, saying nothing, turned away to his bench to begin work.

Joanna Burke opened the back door of her house in Rathkenny. It was a dismal morning with the rain falling in what seemed like thick sheets which were stacked one behind the other for as far as her eye could see.

She closed the door and skirted the gable. On one side loomed an untidy pile of dripping sticks and logs. The cat was somewhere underneath, miaowing mournfully.

On the other side stretched a sodden square of lawn which they grandly called their garden, with the monkey-puzzle tree growing in the middle. Beyond this lay a low wall, and behind was the ditch where they threw their old bottles and tins and ash from the fire. Usually there was a coating of ash on the surrounding vegetation; however, this morning, the rain was so heavy, every grass blade and leaf was washed clean. The only exception was the monkey-puzzle tree, where the ash had managed to jam itself into all the crevices and fissures in the bark.

To her left, a little further on, stood the shed. The end was open and she could see it was crammed with rusting machinery, disintegrating creels and broken pieces of furniture. On a *chaise longue* that was oozing its grey stuffing, their two mongrel sheep-dogs lay stretched out asleep.

She moved down the lane. Ruts and stones were embedded everywhere in the wet ground. The wind was blowing the rain into her face, stinging her skin. She pulled her hat down, then drew her shoulders tighter together under her coat. The countryside around her, in the dismal light of a grey morning with rain pouring, was drained of most of its usual colour. The rippling puddles on the road were gun-metal; the hedgerows bordering the fields were brown and dark with wet; and beside every gateway there was a black mess of mud . . .

At last the grey shape of Bridget's house appeared ahead, separated from the lane by a grey, damp wall. The slates on the roof were glistening, and behind the glass in small brown windows there was a haze of condensation.

Joanna swung the gate open and went up the path. By the front door she put her face to the window. She was able to make out the shape of a figure sitting inside at the fire.

It was Pat, she thought, rapping on the glass to warn him she was there and about to come in. Inside, the ill-defined and ghostly, blob-like shape rose to his feet and moved towards her.

A few minutes later, Joanna set to work. She emptied the night bucket and cleaned it out with sand and earth. She fetched water from the well, boiled it up and laundered two shirts and a nightdress. She hung the clothes to dry on the line in the turf shed. She swept the hearth and scrubbed down the kitchen table. She opened the windows to air the house. She fetched two baskets of turf and banked up the fire. She made two cakes of bread, and while they were baking, she made broth with chop bones and onions. Bridget woke and Joanna brought her a slice of warm bread with butter melted on it. Bridget took a mouthful and then handed the plate back to Joanna.

'My throat's so sore,' she said, 'it hurts to swallow.'

As the morning progressed, the sky slowly lowered itself like a lid towards the earth, until by twelve it was so dark in Michael's workshop they had to light the candles and the lamps.

In the middle of the afternoon it was the custom to stop work for a few minutes, and for the half-dozen employees to gather round the now red-hot pot-bellied stove at the back of the workshop, and drink tea. But this afternoon, as the men assumed their customary circle, Michael, tin mug in hand, took himself off to the barrel by the double door, clambered up on to it, and started staring gloomily outside.

The sky, it seemed to him as he gazed out, was grazing the roof slates, and if it came any lower it was first going to flatten the houses of Clonmel, and then crush everyone in town to death. Meanwhile, the rain, of course, was still pelting down and bouncing off the cobbles in the yard. If the sky didn't get them, everybody was surely going to drown.

'Come over and sit with us, Michael,' called Mr Corrigan, but Michael went on staring through the door. Was there ever a day as miserable as this? he wondered. None that he could remember, he decided.

'Charming response,' Mr Corrigan said, turning back to the circle of workmen, 'charming,' and Liam and the others laughed.

After tea was finished, the workmen opened the stove door and threw their slops into the fire and the workshop was filled with the sounds of fizzing and hissing. Meanwhile, Mr Corrigan walked across to Michael.

'How's Bridget, Michael?'

'Improvement is slow, Mr Corrigan.'

'Why don't you go home,' he said. 'Go home early, before it gets dark.'

Michael thanked him and went and found an old sack. He tore it down one side to make a crude hood, which he then put on his head.

Michael cycled quickly through the town, past shops with steamed-up windows, lit up within by lamps whose light seemed smeared against the glass, and out into the countryside. Overhead the cloud turned from dark grey to charcoal and the trees along the road, as the light faded, seemed to stand out with extraordinary clarity, as they never did in daylight. On the road below, Michael heard the tyres squelching in the water which was spreading across the road in a thin sheet.

He stopped and pulled the sack forward to better shield his

face from the freezing rain. He was just able to make out the little brown flecks of hessian which were being carried under his cuffs by the rainwater. It reminded him of a river in flood, debris bobbing along.

He pedalled on for a while and stopped again under an oak at the side of the road. The thick trunk was covered with ivy, and the branches were stumpy and bare. He took off the sack and wrung it out. Water plopped on to the road at his feet. He was cold across his shoulders, where the rain had soaked right through to his skin, but under his arms and down his front he was still warm and dry.

As he put the hood back on, all wrinkled and prickly, Bridget appeared before his inner eye as he had left her that morning; she was ragged, pale, feverish. But not for much longer, he told himself. Two weeks in bed, sick, was two weeks too long. No wonder he was plagued with memories, like the time he lay with her in the wood. Now a different Bridget appeared to him. She was smiling and her eyes were shimmering, the way she looked when she wanted him to come to bed.

In the distance he heard the roar of iron-bound wheels. He looked up and saw Mr Hagan's cart approaching. It was early this evening, just like he was, probably on account of the weather. The cart pulled up beside him. Mr Hagan and Mr Hermann, hunched up on the seat at the front, were dressed in oilskins and bowler hats, all glistening with wet.

'It's a dreadful evening to be out, Michael,' said Mr Hagan.

'Now I know what the drowned rat feels,' replied Michael grimly.

'Still no improvement with the patient?' asked Mr Hagan. This was now the second Thursday in a row that Bridget had missed her appointment with him below Kilnagranagh.

Michael shook his head. 'No better.'

'But, no worse either?'

'No worse either,' agreed Michael.

'Have you had Dr Crean out?'

'No,' said Michael. 'What does Crean know? He's just a doctor. All doctors are chancers.'

'That was some downpour she was in,' said Mr Hermann quietly. 'It was terrible that day, don't you remember? She must have got soaked walking home.'

'Yes,' agreed Michael.

'It was a mad, mad day,' continued Mr Hermann, 'don't you remember the wind? Bridget's basket blowing away.'

'Fortunately,' said Michael, 'there are other doctors as well besides the likes of Crean.'

A rapt expression appeared on Michael's face, reminding Mr Hermann of the faces in line waiting at the altar rail to receive Communion. But the next instant, he felt Mr Hagan wriggling on the seat beside him, and the thought vanished. Mr Hagan was obviously anxious to get on and home.

'Goodnight,' said Mr Hagan. 'Let's hope that next time we meet it will be under better circumstances.'

Mr Hagan shook the reins and the cart careered away down the road. Michael turned and watched the red light on the back swinging wildly from side to side. The light grew smaller and smaller and finally vanished as the cart went round a bend.

In the distance, Mr Hagan cracked his whip twice and then the only sound Michael could hear was the rain falling in the hedgerows alongside him.

Michael cycled along the road, heading north and east towards home, but after a few miles branched southwards and headed towards the rounded shape of Slievenamon.

When he reached the foothills the rain eased off – which he took to be a good omen – and then he found the road leading up the side of the mountain. He dismounted and began to push the bicycle. There was mud all over the road, washed there by the rains, and the flat leather soles of his boots kept slipping on it

There was only one way to stop himself falling. This was to hold on to the handlebars and use the bicycle like a crutch.

At last – and despite the dark – he reached the track that he was searching for, which he took to be another good omen. He could see Dennis Ganey's cottage in the distance. It was a tiny dwelling, built in a depression and surrounded by pine trees. There was a light in the window.

He bumped down the track and left his bicycle at the bottom under a lean-to. He went to the door and knocked.

'Who is it?' a voice sounded within.

'Michael Cleary, Michael Cleary from Ballyvadlea.'

'Come in, Michael Cleary.'

He pushed the door and found himself in a dark room, half panelled with wood. There was a smell which he was not able to identify and which he guessed was a herb. There was a small fire spluttering in the grate. A red-faced man sat in the only chair, his body bent double as he leant forward.

'Come in.' The man was Dennis Ganey. He waved Michael forward. 'I was expecting you.'

Michael took off the sacking and rolled it up nervously. He was puzzled. How did Dennis Ganey know that he was coming?

'Hang your wet things up there.' Ganey indicated a nail in the chimney breast.

Michael unrolled the sacking, walked over and hung it up.

'How did you know I was coming?' he asked.

Ganey pointed at the box on the other side of the fireplace. Michael sat down.

Ganey touched his nose and smiled. 'I know what I know.'

Ganey stared across the hearth at Michael. For a few moments Ganey's look seemed friendly. Then he went on staring and Michael felt himself growing uncomfortable. He had never been much good at staring matches at school. Now Bridget, on the other hand, Bridget was able to outstare him or anyone.

Michael smiled weakly. He was hoping Ganey would look

somewhere else. But Ganey appeared not to notice and simply went on staring. Michael shifted in his place and began looking round the room.

It was small and square, with crooked windows front and rear, and an old black mantelpiece with clean, empty bottles lined along it. The walls were blue and dirty, and there were cobwebs in the corners. Opposite the hearth there was a small unevenly shaped door – Michael presumed it led to a bedroom – but otherwise there was nothing in the room. No dresser, no table, not even a St Brigid's Cross. Michael had never been in a place quite so desolate and so cold, and he wondered why a healing doctor lived like this.

Ganey coughed. Michael looked across at him. The fairy doctor had produced three short pieces of hazel – Michael assumed he had taken them out of his pocket – and he was holding them in a fan, like playing cards, while staring at Michael intently.

'For the fairy stroke,' said Ganey, holding up one of the rods. He took a knife out of his waistcoat pocket and marked it with a groove.

'For the fairy wind,' he continued, and marked the second with an 'X'.

'And for the evil eye,' he concluded, and he marked the third by making a hole in the side. 'From these I will ascertain from which of the three evils you suffer.'

'My wife, I've come because of my wife,' said Michael hastily. 'My wife is sick. That's why I've come.'

'I know.'

Michael looked at the uneven floor of dark earth.

'Who is your wife?'

'Bridget.'

Ganey stared into the fire, the three short hazel rods still in his hand. Michael listened to Ganey's breath, slow and wheezy. There was a dog barking a long way off, and the wind was moaning in the trees outside.

Several minutes passed while Ganey sat and pondered. What was happening? wondered Michael. Why didn't he just do the business? Fairy doctors had their ways, he didn't doubt, but this sitting was getting them nowhere.

Finally, he could stand it no longer. 'She is very unwell,' he said. 'My wife is very unwell. I am frightened she won't get better.'

'She has a good name,' said Ganey. Much to Michael's astonishment, the doctor appeared to be continuing the conversation of several minutes before.

'Hers is a holy name,' said Ganey, and sighed.

He bent slowly forward and began to undo the laces of his boots. He pulled them off his feet and put them neatly on the floor beside his chair. Then he pulled off his socks. They came off inside out and Ganey reversed them carefully and folded them over his boots. The smell of leather and bare foot floated upwards. Michael noticed there was dirt between the doctor's toes. Then he quickly looked away in case Ganey saw that he had noticed. The fire crackled and coughed.

Ganey stood and slowly took off first his jacket and then his waistcoat. He walked across the room and hung them on another nail banged into the back of the door. Then he slowly rolled up his sleeves. At last the cure was under way, thought Michael, and he felt his impatience gradually dissolving.

Ganey padded back to the fireplace and lifted his face towards the ceiling. He crossed his bare forearms over his chest and began to pray.

Michael listened, trying to follow what was being said, but Ganey spoke too quickly, like Father Ryan at Mass. After a few moments, Michael abandoned trying to make sense of what he was hearing. He gave himself up instead to the sounds as they tumbled out of Ganey's mouth. Sitting there, he gradually felt the same sleepy stillness which he sometimes got in church slowly stealing over him. He felt safe and secure, and Bridget's sickness seemed suddenly far away, and not so terrible as he had thought or feared.

Then, suddenly, it occurred to him that for the first time in two weeks he was free from panic. Therefore, he reasoned, he was seeing Bridget's sickness for the first time as it actually was.

It was just a fever, he thought, and this struck him as a revelation.

He also saw that she was young and that she was strong, and now he felt quite certain she would soon be well, and it would be the fairy doctor who would make her better again.

Ganey reached a saucer of water down from the mantelpiece and set it before the hearth. He knelt and carefully laid the hazel rods side by side in the fire. Then Ganey stood, tilted his face towards the roof and crossed his arms over his chest once more and he continued muttering his prayers. Meanwhile, in the fireplace, the hazelwood rods slowly smouldered and blackened.

Several minutes later, Ganey knelt again and rotated the rods, moving the unburnt parts into direct contact with the heat. He stood and said more prayers. In the fireplace the rods went on charring slowly. Finally, a tiny trickle of smoke began to rise from them. They were black all over and about to catch fire.

With the tongs, Ganey lifted the rods out of the fire with extraordinary care and laid them on the hearth. After a minute or two, he picked up one of the rods and carefully drew a charcoal circle on the floor around himself and the dish of water.

Up to this point Ganey had been praying continuously, but now he fell silent as he took the hazel rods and dropped them one after the other into the dish of water. Then, as they floated, little flecks of black coming away from their sides and slowly discolouring the water, he stared down at them intently.

'It was the whirlwind,' he said finally. 'The fairies on the move in a great rush brushed against Bridget and that is why Bridget is sick.'

Yes, thought Michael, yes, of course. He remembered Mr Hagan's story of Bridget's basket being whisked away and bowling along the road as leaves and twigs and debris tumbled and spun through the air. Why had he forgotten what he had been told just – what – two Thursdays before, and which had been repeated to him just a few hours earlier? There was the reason for Bridget's illness, only he had been blind to it until now. He had been a fool.

'Yes, yes,' Michael agreed, 'Below Kilnagranagh, two weeks ago. A huge wind passed her. Her basket blew away. I had forgotten. You have reminded me. I don't know how I could have forgotten.'

'Do not speak,' interrupted Ganey. He spoke gently.

Of course, Michael immediately thought to himself, I must not interrupt. In church he did not talk, so why should Ganey's house be any different?

Ganey disappeared out through the side door and returned with a small grinding box. He put in one of the rods and turned the handle. When he pulled out the drawer at the bottom, it was filled with black dust.

Using a funnel, he carefully decanted the powder into one of the bottles on his mantelpiece, then he picked up the saucer of water with the two hazel rods still floating in it. All the while, Ganey took care to remain within the charcoal circle he had drawn on the floor.

Ganey removed the other hazel rods and threw them into the fire. Then he tipped the saucer over the funnel. As the water poured into the bottle, the speckles of ground hazel in the bottom turned and tumbled. It struck Michael that their movement was not unlike that of leaves blowing through the air.

When the bottle was full, Ganey corked it. Then, holding it

tightly between his clasped hands, he prayed. Then, he set the bottle down and went away into the other room again, carefully closing the door after himself.

A long time now passed and the fire began to shrink and splutter. Michael looked around. There were turf sods on the floor beside him but Michael felt oddly constrained in Ganey's house. He felt just the same, in fact, as he felt in church. He looked up at the mantelpiece. The speckles of hazel dust were slowly floating to the bottom of the bottle and forming a layer of black sediment.

At last the door opened and Ganey reappeared.

'Don't let the fire out,' he ordered.

Michael crouched and threw on half a dozen sods. His action sent sparks flying up the blackened wall at the back of the chimney.

Ganey coughed.

Michael stood.

Ganey beckoned.

Michael stepped into the charcoal circle.

'Your wife was touched by a fairy blast. That was the fairies as they passed in a whirlwind. The hazel rod told me. That was the day the basket blew off.'

Ganey handed Michael something wrapped in a piece of newspaper.

'Take these home. These are herbs. They will make Bridget better. Boil them with milk. She must take them three times. She may be reluctant but they are for her own good.

'But it might annoy them when she gets better,' he continued, 'and they may return and give her the touch or the evil eye. I have heard of this. And now they have seen Bridget is young and beautiful, they might take her away and leave a changeling in her place.'

Ganey held up the bottle of ground hazel and water.

'But with this charm she will come to no harm.'

III

Ganey wrapped Michael's hands around the bottle, then wrapped his hands around Michael's.

'Let no one see you have this as you go home. Talk to no one as you go home. And when you arrive at home, hide it. Do not tell anyone about it.

'Then, once Bridget is well, you take this bottle. You go outside the house at midnight. Nobody sees you. You walk around the house, clockwise like this.' Ganey indicated the direction with his finger. 'As you go, you sprinkle the potion in the bottle on the ground. When it is empty you face west; you say the Lord's Prayer three times and then you throw the bottle as far as it will go. This will guard your house against any passing fairy host and stop them coming in.'

It was time to pay, Michael thought. The custom, as he knew well, was that for a bottle of magic water no contribution to Ganey was necessary. However, if the fairy doctor handed over a herbal cure, a contribution was necessary and it had to be in silver.

Michael had his sixpence ready. He had got it out while he had been worrying about the fire going out, and because he had been holding it anxiously for several minutes, it had grown warm and sweaty in his hand.

'I want to leave a small contribution,' said Michael shyly.

Ganey pointed over Michael's shoulder.

Michael turned. On the ledge of the tiny window by the door, which he had not noticed either when he had come in or when he had been looking round, there was a money box. He noticed it was attached by a chain to a ring in the wall.

Michael went over and dropped his sixpence through the slot. Hearing it clink on the bottom he wondered absent-mindedly what other coins were inside. Then, wiping his hot, sweaty hand on his trousers, he retrieved his bit of sack from the nail, said goodbye and stepped through the door.

Outside, it had stopped raining but the ground underfoot was sodden.

He closed the door and went over to the lean-to where he had left his bicycle. To his great surprise he found two women squatting inside.

As the two women both got to their feet quickly, they blessed themselves under their shawls. Then, speaking simultaneously, they asked in high-pitched wavering voices, 'Is Mr Ganey ready?'

As Michael opened his mouth to reply he remembered the instructions that he was to speak to no one and closed his mouth again.

He smiled and nodded.

The women came forward, throwing back their shawls from their heads.

'Mr Ganey, sir, he is at home?' they repeated, again in unison.

They were identical twins with pointed noses and long sad faces. They were both in their forties.

Michael knocked twice on the door for them.

'Who are you?' Ganey called from inside.

'We are Margaret and Jane Boyle,' the twins shouted back.

Michael smiled as he opened the door for the two women.

'Come in, Margaret and Jane, I was expecting you,' Ganey shouted.

The twins hurried through and Michael closed the door after them. Then he turned, and with long eager strides he started to push his bicycle up the track towards the road.

From Slievenamon, Michael cycled north; then he took the back road through Tullowcassan. He whistled as he cycled, and the hedge to the side, lit up by his small paraffin-oil bicycle lamp, streamed past.

Rounding a corner, he saw a figure ahead of him on the road. A moment later the figure turned. It was Mary Devlin, a neighbour. She lived down on the main road, near Cloneen.

'Michael,' she called out.

He pointed at his mouth as he passed, in that way hoping to communicate that he could not speak, and sped on.

A few minutes later his house came in sight. He saw threads of silvery light showing around the edges of the drawn shutters. This was the lamplight inside seeping out.

He pulled on the brakes and put his feet down. His mood was benign. He touched the bulge in his jacket pocket. These were the herbs, wrapped in newspaper. He had put them there before leaving Ganey's.

He dismounted. Wheeling the bicycle forward, he heard its characteristic clicking beside him in the darkness.

At the gate he stopped. He touched the bottle. It was in his inside breast pocket against his heart. Years earlier, he had heard it said that their house was built on the site of a rath. A local farmer, he had been told, greedy for the few extra yards of land, had cleared the site one night. A week after the farmer was found drowned in a cesspit. Bad luck, ill health and injury dogged his descendants. In consequence, they had eagerly sold the site to the Cashel Guardians when the chance came up. The land was ill fated and they wanted rid of it.

All this was hearsay of course – none the less, Michael was not inclined to disbelieve it. In fact, in his heart he suspected Bridget's illness was not just because of the wind which had caught her, but was also connected with this original error.

However, with the herbs he was going to make Bridget better; then, with Ganey's potion, he was going to put a magic circle around the house. Fairy power would never hurt them again.

He put his bicycle away in the shed, wrapped Ganey's bottle in several old rags and hid it at the bottom of his toolbox.

Michael came out from the shed and walked along the side of the house. At the same moment Mary Devlin was passing along the lane on the other side of the front wall.

'Hello, stranger,' she called out from the darkness. 'Are you not talking to me?'

'No,' Michael laughed, 'no. I was just in a hurry.'

'I'm in a rush now myself,' she jested, 'and I can't stop and talk either.'

'Mary,' he called. He had reached the gate.

She turned and took a step back towards him.

'Would you leave a message for me?'

'Certainly.'

'And I promise I'll never not speak to you again.'

The old woman smiled.

'Call in to John Dunne, would you, and ask him to come up here to the house. I need his help with something tonight.'

'Certainly,' she said, and continued on her way.

Michael turned and walked back along the path. That was fortunate, he thought, Mary passing just then.

He opened the front door and went in. He found Bridget's cousin, Joanna Burke, sewing at the kitchen table.

'Hello, Michael,' she said, looking up. 'Where have you been?'

'Oh, round and about,' he said vaguely.

'You're late.'

He took the piece of sacking which he had used as a hood out of his pocket, unrolled it and hung it on the nail banged into the back of the door.

'I've been to see Ganey.'

'Oh.'

'I thought it was time. This has been dragging on too long.'

'What about the doctor?'

'Pah.'

Michael strode over to the fire, rubbed his hands in the heat, and then turned his back to it. Pat was snoozing in a chair under the mantelpiece.

'Bridget asleep?' asked Michael, nodding towards the bedroom door.

'Yes.'

'How's she been?'

Joanna rapidly rocked her head from side to side, her standard means of equivocation.

'Very hot. Very sore. Slept a great deal. Took a bite of bread and later some broth but nothing since.' She pushed the needle through the hem of the tablecloth she was working on, and pulled the white thread through after it.

'This fever has knocked her right down.'

She heard Michael grunting and she pushed the needle through again. Her father always used Ganey's cure for swine fever, and once, she remembered, she was treated by the man himself.

Aged ten her gums went bad after a tooth was pulled; her mouth ached and pus oozed, imparting a permanent taste of rotting metal to her tongue; and she had burned with fever. Her father took her up Slievenamon on the back of his cart. She lay on the boards on a pile of sacking. With every jolt her jaw throbbed.

Ganey's cottage was small and smelt vile. The herb doctor looked in her mouth and gave something to her father.

They went home and her mother boiled it up in a pot of water. It smelt like fish gone bad but it tasted worse.

'I'm not having that,' she shouted after spitting out the first mouthful.

Her father pinned her in the chair while her mother prised her teeth open with a spoon and then he tipped a cup of the concoction into her mouth. It was lukewarm, fishy, with bits in it. The taste filled the back of her throat and her nose. Her stomach retched and the food inside her rose. Her throat opened to let the vomit up and meanwhile the herbs coursed down, the two meeting half-way.

A moment later she was spectacularly sick, the porridge – which was all she had been able to take with her gums being so sore – coming out in a great white spear and shooting into the fire, where it hissed and sizzled.

Later, she fell asleep, and when she woke up she was cool and the ache in her gums was gone.

'These are they,' said Michael beside her.

He had sat down and was carefully opening a crumpled piece of newspaper on the table. The herbs inside were deep brown, nearly black, shrivelled and dry. Joanna pushed the needle halfway into the hem, put the tablecloth down and reached into the middle of the pile. They were small dry leaves, very thin to the touch and crinkled like fern.

'What are they?'

Michael shrugged.

'I went to Ganey once,' she said.

'And?'

'I can't remember. I was a child.'

She lifted a brown leaf to her nose and sniffed.

'Uhhhh! They smell terrible.'

Michael took a leaf himself.

'Yes,' he agreed, 'but maybe that's why there's such a cure in them.'

'Maybe,' Joanna agreed, returning her leaf to the pile. 'The herbs I had made me sick. But I got better,' she added.

Pat murmured as he slept in the nearby chair.

'What do you do with them?' Joanna asked. Her hands were in the pile again turning the leaves over.

'He told me to boil them in milk. I thought to make a start tonight. I asked John Dunne to come up and help. I wouldn't if I'd known you were here.'

'Bridget's sleeping, you know.'

'I'll go in in a moment and see the lie of the land. I think it would be good to begin.'

'You don't need Dunne. He's like having two left hands, that man.'

Joanna took the needle and resumed sewing.

'He knows things,' said Michael.

'What things?'

Joanna put her head down; she didn't want Michael to see her expression.

'Put on the milk and I'll go in,' said Michael. He stood up slowly and moved away towards the bedroom door.

Bridget opened her eyes, then realizing her husband had come into her room and was moving around she murmured, 'A drink, please, Michael.'

'Why didn't you tell me?' Michael said aggressively.

From half-asleep and befuddled, Bridget was wide awake in an instant. She lay still, her heart racing, while in her stomach there was a curdling sensation, like milk when lemon juice is added.

'Sorry,' said Bridget tentatively, 'why didn't I tell you what?'

She had vomited earlier and the sick bucket was under the bed. Her father had washed it clean, yet the sour smell still drifted up from it.

'It was a fairy wind.'

'What?'

'Thursday, a fortnight back, when you were doing your business with Hagan. Everything blowing about, your basket takes off, Hagan chases after it, loses his money because he's forgotten to do up the clasp – you remember?'

'Yes.'

'You didn't tell me.'

'I did.'

'No. You told me, you went up to Kilnagranagh to meet Hagan.'

Sick as she felt, Bridget sat up, alarmed.

'It rained,' he continued, 'you had no coat, you were soaked, you got sick.'

His words poured out pell-mell.

'Yes. It was dry when I left. I forgot my coat. I got wet.'

'You wanted to be sick?'

'Michael, my head and every other bit of me hurts. Nobody would want that.'

'It was very convenient forgetting your coat. That way you didn't have to say the real reason.'

'You're not making sense.'

'It's a bad place to hang around.'

'Where is?'

'Kilnagranagh.'

She had to stop this, now, immediately, at once. She had to get out of bed, and go over and calm him.

'Why is it a bad place?'

She threw back the covers and swung her feet down on to the floor.

'You know why.'

She stood up. She was going to go over to him. She was going to put her arms around him. This scene had to stop.

'Don't. Stay in bed,' he shouted.

'What is it, Michael?'

'You won't trick me. Into bed. Into bed,' he ordered.

'Then you come here,' she said gently.

She looked closely at him, and at the same time beckoned him with her hand to come forward. Michael took a step towards her. She beckoned again.

'Will you help me, Michael?' she asked. Her voice was very smooth and quiet. This was the voice she always used when she was calming him down.

'Will you help me, Michael?' she repeated. 'I can't manage to get into bed unless you help me.'

Asking for his help was an infallible way of soothing him.

Michael came up to the bed, pulled the bedcovers back for her and smoothed the bottom sheet.

'What is going on?' she asked, as he lowered her gently into the bed. 'What's this about Kilnagranagh? Why's it a bad place? It wasn't last month, was it? Or last year?'

Michael lifted the covers and placed them carefully over her. He tucked them under the mattress.

'I know something,' he said. 'Nothing is certain.' Then he muttered ambiguously, 'You can't be too careful. You can't trust anyone.'

She sneezed, twice, wiping under her nose with the cuff of her nightdress.

'Michael?' she asked, and in a moment he had found the handkerchief she needed and was handing it to her.

He sat down on the edge of the bed.

'It was a fairy wind.'

'Michael, listen. When you were a young boy, your mother was taken. A fortnight ago was different.

'When I got up I didn't feel well,' she continued. 'I came and woke you and you put your hand here. Do you remember?'

She took his hand and lifted it to her burning forehead.

'You said I was to be careful. Remember? Here, in this room, that morning.'

Michael was staring through the doorway into the kitchen. Why did he not answer? she wondered. Why was he acting as if none of this had happened?

Michael lifted his hand from her brow and laid it beside the other on his lap. He clenched his fingers into a fist and then unclenched his fingers.

'I've been to see Ganey,' he said. 'Everything's going to be all right.'

In the kitchen Joanna fetched the milk jug from the dresser and went over to the hearth. It was set into the wall. There was a mantelpiece above. This was thick and heavy and cluttered. Among the objects lined along it were several old bottles, three broken cups, two empty jam jars, a box of marbles, the wrapping paper from a bar of soap, the black-handled knife, a twist of catgut and a dozen candle stubs.

The grate below was cast iron. It was heavy and black, with thick legs beneath, and flat ovens on either side where food and crockery was put to warm.

On the right of the fireplace was the crane. This was a heavy metal column hinged in the floor, with an arm sticking out at right angles from the top.

Joanna now hung a small pot here, poured in some milk and swung the arm over the fire so that the pot was just above the embers.

Waiting and staring into the dark mouth of the pot, she heard Michael and Bridget talking in the bedroom behind the closed door.

After some minutes, bubbles began to rise and she heard the rush of milk about to boil.

'Ready, Michael,' she called, pulling the arm back from the fire, the pot swinging from the end.

Michael left the bedroom and came over to the table.

'How much do you reckon I put in?' he asked.

'What did Ganey say?'

'I can't remember. Maybe he didn't say anything.'

'A handful,' Joanna suggested.

Michael got a small fist's worth and threw it in. The leaves floated on the surface at first. Joanna pushed them down with a spoon. The milk went an olive colour. She swung the pot back over the fire. The milk began to bubble and the room was filled with a bitter, metallic smell.

'Strong,' exclaimed Michael, holding his nose and backing away.

'Yes.' Joanna stirred the concoction while breathing shallowly through her mouth. 'That's some smell. And look at the colour of the milk.'

Joanna swung the crane back again. Then, with Michael at her side, she stared down. The sides of the pot were only slightly blacker than the black liquid in the bottom.

'I suppose there's some cure in there,' said Michael.

'I'd say there's some truth in that,' Joanna agreed.

Everything from Dennis Ganey was horrible, she thought, but if Bridget took a drop, no matter how bad the taste, it would make her better. This was what Joanna hoped, anyway . . .

However, Bridget was only able to manage a taste that evening, before she was violently sick. After she had finished vomiting, Michael asked her to try some more of the cure. Bridget refused. Then John Dunne arrived, and told Bridget not to be so defiant. She remained adamant, however. She would take none of the cure that night, she said, although she might another time, if she felt up to it.

Bridget went to sleep; Joanna went home; Pat went to bed; Michael was left alone with John Dunne.

'How are you, Michael?' asked John Dunne.

Michael was silent.

'It goes hard with you,' said John Dunne.

Michael stared sullenly into the flames and nodded. Bridget had been sick for over two weeks. He was worried and troubled.

'I was banking on Ganey's medicine,' he said.

'Bridgie wouldn't have it.'

'She will. She said as much at the end now.'

'What did Ganey say?'

'About what?'

'Her sickness.'

'A fairy blast.'

'Oh, yes, you said earlier. You know I saw that wind. I was watching from my cottage. It blew her basket away. It was fierce.'

Michael looked across. John Dunne held his head inclined to the side and his eyes were very bright in the firelight.

'You think Ganey's right?'

'I believe him,' said Michael. 'Why do you ask?'

'There's some cure in those herbs.'

'If she'd have them.'

'How do you know it is her?' said John Dunne quietly.

He tumbled his hands.

'It could not be Bridget,' continued Dunne.

'What do you mean?'

'Nothing,' said John Dunne, 'nothing at all. I just wanted to know what you think. You know her better than anyone else. It's Bridget. We agree.'

For a moment Michael thought he heard laughter outside but then it vanished. He looked down at the floor. He remembered again that his house stood on the site of an old rath. Bridget must take her medicine and get better, he thought, and then he would throw Ganey's charm around them as protection from all further harm.

PART II

CHAPTER FIVE

Bridget was woken one night, during her third week of sickness, by cold water sprinkled on to her face. She opened her eyes, heart racing. Michael stood by her bedside.

'What are you doing, Michael?' she exclaimed. 'What is this?'

She wiped herself with the cuff of her nightdress.

'To make you better. Holy water.'

'Stop it,' she said.

It was not as cold as rain yet it was more stinging on the face.

'Stop it.'

'I have only a drop. You can stand it.'

By the light of the candle beside the bed, she saw he was holding a cup, and that he was using a wooden spoon to flick the water at her.

'I said stop!'

Michael drew himself up to his full height.

'This is for your own good.'

'The doctor will make me better.'

'What does Crean know?'

'We'll see when he comes tomorrow.'

'Why did you ask him?' he demanded.

He had only learned that evening that Joanna, on Bridget's instructions, had been to the dispensary and asked Dr Crean to call down.

'I need him.'

Michael flicked another spoonful of water.

'You were hit by a fairy blast, and you haven't got out of

your bed since that day, which is three weeks on Thursday.'

'If you want me on my feet, then let me back to sleep,' she said. 'Strength is what I need. Not being woken like this in the middle of the night.'

'I know what's best.'

'You don't.'

'We must fight with everything we have.'

His words came to her from the darkness, certain and resolute.

'Are you all right?'

Michael cackled for a moment, the skin under his chin wobbling in the candlelight like a turkey's neck, then he fell silent.

'Don't ask me. Ask yourself.'

'I feel wretched. My throat hurts. I ache all over. I have a fever.'

'You will be better, I promise you. I know what to do.'

It was Michael standing beside her, yet he was talking in a voice that was sonorous, booming and solemn. It was not his own voice.

'What made you come in here?' she asked.

'To make you better.'

Another spray of droplets hit her face.

'Were you asleep? Did you wake up?'

'I was upstairs,' he said, alluding to the tiny loft where there was a mattress and a blanket. He had been sleeping there since she had fallen sick. 'I thought I heard something moving outside,' he continued. 'I dressed and came down.'

'It was probably an animal.'

'It might have been, but again it might not.'

'You miss me, don't you? You miss us,' and here she hesitated. No husband could be happy with that, she thought.

'Do you know what was here before the house?' he interrupted.

'No.'

He tipped the cup upside down. A single drop plopped into the spoon.

'A rath,' he said, flicking the spoon at her, 'and it was pulled down.'

He turned and marched away.

'Goodnight,' he said, and closed the door behind.

Their holy water came from the clear bottle which lived on top of the dresser, while in Drangan church the water was in the font just inside the front doors. Holy water was always cold when she took a dab before Mass. But the spot on her forehead soon warmed as she walked forward, the hollow church sound of feet on stone, the whisper of the waiting congregation, and the smell of burnt incense rising about her. In church it was friendly and safe, but in the bedroom it hurt her face and she had to wipe it away.

Unbidden thoughts, they wore her out. She heartily wished she could close her eyes and fall asleep, effortlessly, immediately. Her hair, she noticed, was lying damp on the pillow beside her.

'It's to make you better,' she remembered Michael calling from the darkness, and the cold shock of the droplets.

'You were hit by a fairy blast.'

Ganey put the notion in Michael's head. Yes, except her husband might as easily have come up with it himself, of course. She might even, for she had heard tell of it from her mother.

But in this instance, it was not what had happened.

In her mind's eye she saw her basket bowling down the Drangan road that morning three weeks earlier. She wished Michael could see it. Then she recalled the cold rain which had drenched her that morning as she made her way home, and yet how hot she had been with fever.

She swallowed. Her throat was sore. She was alone in the darkness. Michael was climbing the stairs next door to the attic, to his mattress. She was hot and she hurt, under her arms, on each side of her neck, in the joints of her knees and elbows.

When Michael had asked did she know about the rath which supposedly stood on the site of their house, her stomach had trembled and shrunk.

Her daddy or someone had told her years before. It happened when he was a child. Or perhaps it was when his daddy before him was a child.

Her answer was no, but did Michael believe her? He was not so inclined, she thought.

She would have to get better.

'Better,' she said, 'better,' her lips moving.

Michael did not know what was the matter with her, so he had gone to Ganey for his answer. Damn it. After Dr Crean she would summon Father Ryan. She must have someone to talk to.

She turned on her side and fell asleep.

She was in a clean nightdress and shift. She lay with her head propped up by the bolster.

Her sickroom was small and oblong, about twelve feet by eight. The door and the window were painted brown, and the walls were blue, except around the window which was covered with plain whitewash. The blue ran out when Michael was painting the room, and this was all there was to hand. The only decoration was a border which ran right round the room. This showed a robin redbreast on a branch with a berry in his beak.

She stared at the white wall by the window. She had been staring at it now for nearly three weeks, and she could effortlessly read the pictures hidden in its uneven surface.

Most prominent was the face of a man; he was young, handsome, and he wore a top hat. Beside him there was a wheel, with a crowd of children's faces floating below it.

Lower again, there was a tree and a river flowing past a mountain.

Bridget moved her eyes slowly to the window. On the wall which bounded their front garden, a blackbird with a bright yellow beak was capering along the parapet. On the other side lay the lane, and beyond that lay fields and meadows which stretched to Slievenamon. The day was dismal and overcast. The clouds appeared to be resting on the upper slopes of Slievenamon. At this distance it looked as if the mountain were on fire, while the hillsides below were black, as if they had been scorched.

Next door her husband was talking.

'Cook the egg,' he was saying, 'for five minutes.' Her husband and her father were discussing her lunch.

The door flew open and Michael came in. She closed her eyes and felt his lips, first on her cheek, then on her mouth. Under the covers he squeezed her elbow passionately.

'Goodbye,' he whispered. It was as if what had happened in the middle of the night had never been.

Seconds later the front door banged. She heard him manoeuvring his bicycle out of the gate and cycling away. He had overslept. He was late for work.

Bridget dozed off and when she woke up her father was sweeping the floor next door. The brush was new, the bristles stiff. They made a scratching noise.

'Dada,' she called.

Pat appeared in the doorway, his wiry body stooping and doubling. He was coughing. His face floated forward, the skin creased by lines, the eyes dark brown, black nearly.

Another cough from deep in his chest. His shoulders rounded and his body shook.

'You're getting what I've got,' said Bridget gently.

'No, darling,' he wheezed, 'I'm just old and it's winter.'

'How's the enemy?' said Bridget, which was the family shorthand when asking the time.

Pat turned and squinted at the alarm clock on the mantelpiece.

'Ten, near enough.'

'Time is slow,' she said, and added, 'Dr Crean said he'd be up sometime this morning.'

'When you're waiting it's slow, but when you're happy there's never enough time. Tea or something?'

She shook her head.

'Were you happy?'

'Was I happy?'

'With Mam?' continued Bridget.

'I was happy.' He looked down at his shiny, polished boots.

'Did you quarrel?'

'Yes.'

'Why?'

'Money. Or love. That's all anyone fights about. We didn't speak once for three months, although why I can't now remember.'

'I never knew that.'

'Oh, we spoke,' he explained. '"Hello", "Good Morning", "Cup of tea?", "No, thank you", that sort of thing, but that was all.'

'What happened then?'

'Then?'

Her father came forward slowly. She shifted her legs under the covers making room for him, and he sat on the end of her bed.

'What happened then,' he said, 'I'll never forget what happened then. It was March. Near enough this time of the year. The daffodils were out. I picked a bunch and brought it home. Handed them over. Still not a word from her. She just took them and turned away. I felt angry but I said "Whoa! Pat."

'Your mother got a jug of water and set it on the table. She had her back to me. I couldn't see her face. Silence in the kitchen as she arranged the flowers. You could have heard a pin drop.

'What do I do? Do I go? Do I say something? I'm standing there trying to make my mind up. I'm looking at her. I see your mother's apron strings, her skirt, her boots, and beyond her, the pine table. Do you remember the one?'

Bridget nodded. She remembered the table in the old house. When he moved to Ballyvadlea her father sold it. It was too big to bring with them.

'Your mother washed it every day, scoured that surface. The wood was pale and it went dark when it was wet. Suddenly, I see a dark circle on the table, this size.'

He made an 'O' with his finger and thumb.

'Like a five-shilling piece,' he continued. 'Then a second and a third. These are her tears, I realize, and they are falling silently. So I go up to her and I put my head on her shoulder and I tell her I am sorry and I love her.'

'Why did you never tell me that before?' asked Bridget.

'I don't know.' He shrugged and looked at her with his brown moist eyes. She saw he was puzzled himself as to why he had never told her.

'Did you ever feud again?'

'Oh, yes. It's never once bitten, twice shy. But we were never as bitter again. When we rowed after that, the pine table and the tears were always at the back of our thoughts.'

'You were happy?'

'You're full of questions this morning.'

'I've been lying here for weeks. It's good to talk.'

'Are you improving?'

Bridget shrugged and shook her head.

'So were you happy?' she repeated.

'Yes.'

'What was the key?'

Pat leant against the end of the bed and looked up at the ceiling. Bridget looked up as well. It was tongue-in-groove, brown as well. There was a flypaper near the window, with insects like old currants stuck to it. Finally Pat said, 'Patience.'

'That's how you got through?'

Pat nodded.

'So when life is hard, in times of difficulty, you just sit it out.'

'If you don't want tea I could get you milk,' he said, nodding.

'Why did you never tell me that story before about the daffodils?'

'I never took the notion,' he said feebly.

'You learn something every day,' she said.

Pat squeezed her knee.

'Are you all right, darling?'

'I want to be better.'

'What about Ganey's medicine?' he asked.

'I only had it the once. I was as sick as a dog.'

Pat looked down and touched the hem of the counterpane with the tip of his boot.

'Ganey's usually good.'

'Joanna said that.'

Her father made a strange face, a mixture of the puzzled and the displeased, she thought.

'Was Michael down here,' asked Pat abruptly, 'in the middle of the night?'

'Yes,' she said, and added quickly, 'he came down to make certain everything was all right.'

'We all await Dr Crean then.' He coughed.

'I want you to be better,' continued Pat. 'I do. This is not how I like to see you.'

Pat stood up nodded, and sauntered out of the door. She heard him taking up the brush and the scratching of the bristles on the floor again. He began to whistle quietly through his front teeth.

Bridget licked the sweat off her upper lip. How had she lived twenty-six years, yet never known about the huge row and her mother's tears staining the table?

The glands in her neck were throbbing. She touched them gingerly with her fingertips.

No matter how well one knew someone, there was always something else, it seemed, to discover about them.

Her lungs felt tight. She imagined plugs of mucus blocking the tubes inside, stopping the air rushing in. The bottom of her spine was numb, she noticed, from lying on it.

A picture of Michael the night before, standing by her bedside, now sprang into her thoughts. Michael believed she was sick, obviously; hence the holy water. And maybe she was so unwell that Doctor Crean, when he came, would order her to be taken away to hospital.

However, no sooner did the idea cross her mind than she was filled with a sense of panic. She pictured the fever hospital. She had passed it every day when she had worked in the drapers. It was a dark, soot-covered, forbidding building, more like a mill than a hospital, with its long rows of identical windows and its big chimney. Once, she had watched a man on crutches bobbing his ungainly way along the whole length of the second floor and back again, his face glistening with tears. Someone told her he had just lost his leg. And the outstanding memory from her one ever visit inside was a silvery bowl filled with blood, which she had glimpsed on a shelf in a room like a pantry. And the whole place, she remembered now, had stunk of pee and privy . . .

No, she thought. She did not want to be so sick that she was taken away. No, all she wanted was to be better. All she wanted was to be on her feet, and to be preparing for spring and then summer.

Now vague images of summers past began to flood into her mind.

. . . Michael in the evenings returning from work, his hat

filled with buttercups and celandines, cuckoo flowers and cow-slips; holding his hand when they were alone by the fire after her father went to bed; slipping off her nightdress in their bedroom and the summer night's breeze coming through the open window, and Michael kissing her behind the ears. Then, later, looking out past the opened shutter at the black sky, with silver stars threaded across it . . .

Please, she thought closing her eyes, let the doctor come, let this end, let me be happy.

Opening her eyes, she found Dr Crean was standing beside the bed.

'Good morning, Mrs Cleary. How are you feeling?'

'Not very well.'

He took his stethoscope from his Gladstone bag, then nodded to Pat standing in the doorway. Her father stepped back and closed the door.

'Can you lift this?' Dr Crean indicated her nightdress.

She bared her back and when the cold disc of the stetho-scope touched her spine she let out a cry.

'Always the worst moment,' Dr Crean said amiably.

Dr Crean placed two fingers on her shoulder blade and tapped them with his free hand. She registered the vibrations inside her chest. She felt sick.

The fingers moved across. He tapped again, producing a dull sound.

'Blocked,' he murmured.

She undid the buttons on her neck and pulled her nightdress open. The cold disc went on to her breast.

'Breathe. In, out. In, out,' he instructed.

She heard her lungs wheezing as she pulled the air in and pushed it out, pulled it in, pushed it out.

'How's that?'

'Hard,' she said, breathless from the effort.

'Again,' he ordered, 'big breath.'

Inside her ribcage she felt her lungs wobbling and juddering.

'How long have you been like this?' asked Dr Crean.

She looked up. He had a wide freckled face and sandy hair, but surprisingly, she thought, the beard on his face was black.

'Not last week, not the week before, but the week before that, Thursday, I went out, down to the Drangan road, no coat,' she explained.

'Oh dear, open wide, say "Ahh",' said Dr Crean.

Her teeth were furry and bringing her swollen tongue forward, she expected Dr Crean to grimace at the smell of her breath. However, instead of recoiling, he stooped and looked down her throat.

'I see. No coat. Say "Ahh".'

'Ahh.'

'Very good.'

'I didn't feel well anyway. Then I was caught in a storm. By the time I got home I was wet and also feverish. I went straight to bed, since when I haven't been up. I have a cough. My head aches. My eyes hurt. I can't get out of bed. If I eat, I am sick. And I don't know what's the matter.'

'Why didn't you call me out before?'

'I don't know. I thought I would get better by staying in bed.'

'But you haven't.'

'No.'

'Have you taken any medicine?'

Did she mention the herbs which Michael had got from Dennis Ganey? Yes, she ought to, she decided. At the same moment, however, she heard herself tentatively replying, 'No, not what you would call medicine, no.'

Dr Crean wrapped the stethoscope around his hand and let it uncoil.

It was more than likely, she thought, that Dr Crean

137

disapproved of Ganey. However, it was always better to tell the truth, especially to a doctor who was trying to help one.

'Uhm,' she started, while in her mind she searched for the words to describe Dennis Ganey.

'No quack medicine, I trust,' Dr Crean muttered, and her resolution fled like a fish startled by a shadow.

'No,' she said.

'No,' he repeated. 'You don't sound certain.'

'I am certain.'

'Mrs Cleary, can I talk to you frankly?'

'Yes,' she said quietly. In her stomach she felt a tightening.

'Is there something the matter?'

'Yes, I've been sick for three weeks.'

Dr Crean glanced sideways, just the faintest sign of concern on his face.

'I know, but is anything else the matter? You seem very on edge. Is there anything causing you to be anxious?'

'No,' she said forthrightly. She might have consulted Dr Crean three or four times in the preceding six years, she thought, but that did not give him the right to ask such questions. Then she said emphatically, 'I have no troubles, I assure you.'

Dr Crean stared down. He was not blinking.

'You can speak to me in confidence,' he said.

'I don't have anything to speak about.'

To think, she thought, she might have blurted out about Ganey. It had been a close escape and now all that remained was to stop Dr Crean's questions. She looked up at him and smiled.

'Thank you,' she said, 'there's nothing worrying me except my health.'

For a moment or two he seemed uncertain. Then he smiled himself and she saw that his doubts had vanished.

He pulled the chair from the corner and sat down near her by the bed.

'You've got bad catarrh, and some bronchitis,' he said.

Dr Crean lifted his Gladstone on to his lap and opened it.

A picture of the gaunt fever hospital sprang up before her mind's eye. 'Is that bad?' she asked.

'It's not good, if that's what you mean,' he said, 'but there's no reason why you won't get better. Not if you take this anyway.'

He pulled out a brown ribbed bottle with a cork stuck in the top. A label followed from the bag. He licked it and stuck it on. Then he took a fountain pen out of his pocket and began writing on the white empty surface.

'Take this, three times a day, a teaspoon at a time. In two or three days, a week at the most, you'll be on your feet again.

'Am I sick?'

'Yes.'

'How sick?'

'Anything could be worse but you're going to get better.'

She felt his eyes scrutinizing her again.

'You're certain, you're not worried about anything else?' he repeated.

'Yes,' she said.

Dr Crean stared at her intently for a moment or two, then stood up and put the bottle on the window-sill.

'Certain?'

'Certain,' she repeated hesitantly.

'Good morning then.'

Dr Crean walked out, spoke briefly to her father in the kitchen, and left the house by the front door.

A moment later, Pat came to her doorway and asked, 'What did he say?'

'Bronchitis,' she said gloomily. 'Bring me a spoon, Dada.'

She stared out of her bedroom window at the cowl of the wall. The doctor on his horse slipped past, his boots and trousers spattered with mud.

Bronchitis was not far from pneumonia and was rightly

feared in the country. She scraped her upper teeth over her bottom lip. Pat returned with the spoon.

The parochial house stood outside Drangan. It was separated from the road by a stone wall that was spiked with glass. The gates were metal and painted white, set between imposing stone piers. The small driveway behind ran past trees and bushes and curved round to the house itself. It was a plain, square but not unattractive dwelling with a short flight of granite steps leading to the front door. These were flanked by casement windows on either side. Above this were the bedroom windows. It was like the house that a child might draw.

It was early afternoon. Father Ryan, the parish priest, was eating alone in the dining room at the dark mahogany table. The ugly chairs were covered with a fabric decorated with a humbug stripe. The heavy sideboard was to his left, the door behind, and the window ahead. Beyond the glass the sky was grey.

Father Ryan cut a piece from the chop lying across the plate and put it in his mouth. He began to chew. The pork was dry and dense. From the corridor outside came the sound of approaching feet. The door opened and Nora came in.

'Father,' she said apologetically.

Nora came forward to his side.

His housekeeper's forehead was wide, her eyes very blue and her chin tapered to a point. She was fifty-four years old. She always seemed to him to smell vaguely of flour and sweat.

'There's someone here with a message. Mrs Cleary in Bally-vadlea is sick and she wants you.'

Father Ryan stared at the tiered plates in the middle of the table. They had gold rims. In his mind's eye he tried to conjure up a picture of this parishioner. However, as he concentrated, what came to him instead of Mrs Cleary was the husband, Michael Cleary. He was a thin-faced, angular man, Father Ryan remembered, all elbows and knees. And he was always in a hurry.

Father Ryan put down his knife and fork.

'You haven't eaten your cabbage,' said Nora.

She was at the sideboard. He turned and saw she was holding the lid of the vegetable dish. Inside the bowl, as he knew well, there was a heap of cabbage. It was grey and furthermore, the butter which had melted had now set hard again, and formed a white rim around the edges.

'No,' he agreed. 'I didn't.'

The truth was he did not like cabbage. However, having failed to say so at the start of their relationship some years earlier, it was now too late.

'It'll do for tonight,' said Nora breezily. She would fry it with potatoes, he imagined, which was the only way he was able to manage anything green. 'What time will I say you'll go to Mrs Cleary?'

'Just say to expect me.'

At half past three Father Ryan dismounted in front of the Clearys' cottage. Leading his horse through the gate, he was filled with a faint sense of dread. It was the husband who unnerved him, with his bright blue eyes, and his fast, ugly walk.

Coming into the yard at the back of the house, Father Ryan met Bridget's father, coming from the hen shed. He was clutching a tin of fresh eggs. There were feathers stuck to some, Father Ryan noticed, while others were stained or mired with chicken dung.

Pat nodded and took the reins of the priest's horse.

'Thank you, Pat.'

Father Ryan unclipped his bag from the saddle, circled the cottage and went in through the front door.

In anticipation of his visit, Bridget's room had been prepared and the sick-call set had been laid out: two candles in candle-sticks, a crucifix and a saucer for the holy water.

Father Ryan heard Bridget's confession, gave her absolution, performed the Blessing of the Sick and prepared the host.

'This is the lamb of God who takes away the sins of the world,' intoned Father Ryan.

As the wafer went on to her tongue, Bridget held her breath. She did not want the priest to smell her breath. She closed her lips and exhaled slowly through her nose.

The host was swelling on her tongue and, for a moment, she thought she was going to choke.

She opened her eyes. Under the white tips of Father Ryan's nails there was not a speck of dirt to be seen. She looked up and saw Father Ryan staring down at her.

'Mrs Cleary, are you all right?'

She nodded and swallowed.

The wafer was dissolving, the solid turning into liquid and sliding down her throat. It left a faint aftertaste. She had often noticed this but never found the words to describe it. Now she had. The taste was like paper.

Father Ryan wiped the chalice and put it in the bag. Then he slipped the wafer case into the special pocket inside his cassock.

'Mrs Cleary, how are you?' Father Ryan now enquired as he sat down on the chair. His formal, priestly tones had given way to his informal voice that was quick and warm.

'Not the best,' she said.

'No, I see.'

'Dr Crean was up.' She pointed at the bottle of medicine and the priest nodded.

'Why did you ask to see me?'

There was a long pause.

'You can talk to me, Mrs Cleary.'

Silence.

'You seem very agitated.'

Another long silence.

'How are relations with your husband?'

Several thoughts raced through her mind, some of which left her with a faint sense of dread.

'I'm not certain I know how to explain,' she began. 'He's very angry with me.'

'Why?'

'Because I am sick.'

'Why?'

'He says it's my fault,' she said, but as the words tumbled out she realized this was not what she really wanted to say. It was actually Michael's belief in the fairy blast which was troubling her. She did not believe it herself. It was Ganey who had put the idea into his head. However, if she was to tell Father Ryan, how was she going to put it? She knew that Father Ryan disapproved of herbs, just like Dr Crean. But could she lie? she wondered. No, she could not. She was going to have to tell the truth in some way, even if that meant Father Ryan might be angry.

She blinked. The whole subject was not only so complicated, it also left her feeling anxious. Apart from the herbs, was Father Ryan going to be cross for any other reason? What was he going to think of Michael? Was the business with the holy water the night before going to make Father Ryan think badly of him? She did not want that. Michael loved her and she loved him. There was no doubt about that. However, for those few minutes he had been standing by her bed the night before and flicking holy water at her, he had been a different Michael from the man she married.

'Mrs Cleary,' Father Ryan interrupted her thoughts. 'I wouldn't want you to feel that you have to hold back. I have known you for some years. You may talk frankly and in the strictest confidence, and it might even be that I can put your mind at rest.'

'My mind is troubled, Father.'

'Are you in conflict with your husband?'

'It's just that sometimes he seems to be not what he is for the rest of the time.'

'Does he drink?'

'No, not really. He might take the odd glass of beer, the very occasional whiskey. Other than that, no, he really doesn't drink very much.'

'You're saying his character changes?'

She nodded.

'Under what circumstances?'

'At the moment. With my being sick and in bed.'

'Is he bad-tempered? Is he short with you? Does he resent your being in bed all day? Is that it?'

'In a way, it's something like that.'

'Something like that,' echoed Father Ryan, and he continued, 'Sickness, of course, is a time of great anxiety. You must understand that it is troubling to Michael that you have been laid up for three weeks.'

'I understand that.'

'You've had the doctor, of course, but the very fact that I have come must add to Michael's anxieties.'

'Oh, why?'

'I have come to see you in just the same way that I go to see those who are dying. Now, you are seriously unwell, yes, but I would suggest you are not going to pass away.'

'No, I'm not.'

'Michael knows that and there is no doubt about it and yet here, at the back of his mind,' and here Father Ryan touched his head, 'he must be fearful although he'd never say so. In some part of himself he must be thinking that you are going to die – even though he also knows that you're not going to die – and it must terrify him.'

'I see what you mean,' she said. She had never thought of it like this before. However, now Father Ryan had helped her to put herself into Michael's shoes, she saw that she had not seen something which was perhaps very obvious. Yes, she thought, now she came to think of it there was sense in what Father Ryan said. Of course, the fact that Michael was worried sick explained why he had gone to Ganey as well as his visit the night before.

A smile spread slowly across her pale face.

'I think I understand you,' she said.

'It's very difficult, when you're stuck in the middle of something,' said Father Ryan, 'to see how someone else is seeing the same event. They might have a completely different view of a situation to the one that we have, and we don't know what that is and we never will, unless we stop and think ourselves into their shoes.'

'Yes, yes,' she agreed.

She felt a sense of balance and calm certainty spreading through her.

Father Ryan stood.

'I am so glad we have had this talk,' he said. 'I hope I have been able to help you.'

'You have.'

'That gives me great pleasure. Goodbye,' said Father Ryan, and he left the room.

In the yard, Father Ryan found his horse tied to an iron ring.

'Hello, Pat,' he said, greeting Bridget's father. The old man had clearly been sitting there waiting for him.

'How is she?' asked Pat. He bent and untied the reins.

Bridget was not dangerously ill at that moment; however, Father Ryan did not discount the possibility that she might worsen. Brain fever, he imagined.

'Will my girl be all right?' asked Pat.

Well, thought Father Ryan, she was troubled and fearful as he had noticed the moment he had entered her bedroom.

However, in reply to his questions, she had told him quite categorically that she had no spiritual worries. And when he had asked how things were with Michael, she said little, only shrugged. She would not be drawn on the subject of Michael's worries, and he had left the room none the wiser as to the precise origin of her anxieties.

None the less, Father Ryan now produced his most reassuring smile. It was not his intention either to share his fears about brain fever or to discuss any of these other matters.

'She will be all right,' he said.

He attached his bag to the saddle. Pat led the horse out to the lane. Father Ryan took the reins.

'Good afternoon, Pat,' he said. He heaved himself up and trotted away. When he rounded the corner at Simpson's place, a hundred yards down the lane, Father Ryan felt a great wave of relief at having left the Cleary household behind.

Bridget was staring through her bedroom window. Outside, the light was draining away. The alder trees and the hawthorn bushes on the far side of the lane were no longer distinct. They had merged to form a single dark shade. It was like a dog, crouched, waiting for his master to come home. She liked to think that his tail was wagging.

The reassuring smell of turf smoke drifted through from next door. Her father was coughing in his chair. Afterwards she heard him spitting into the fire.

Now she closed her eyes and remembered her father bringing the same chair home when she was a child. It had been pouring with rain and he had carried it upside down over his head. However, as he had come out from under the trees and headed towards the house, she had not seen it for the chair that it was. She had seen it as a monster, with the chairlegs doubling as spikes and the chairback as its shell. As the monster scuttled towards her house, Bridget had been frozen sick with terror for several seconds. Then she had realized what she was seeing.

She was over-sensitive, she thought, and always had been. She also had a great ability to remember detail. It was admired by others but what did it produce except memories, she thought, which overwhelmed and burdened her? Like now, listening to the chair creaking and groaning, she was remembering her childhood terror as if it were only yesterday.

Her feet were warm and she stretched them down into the cold corner at the end of the bed. With her inner eye she saw the scene again, her father with the upturned chair over his head, coming out from under the chestnut tree and sprinting through the rain.

Right way up a chair was a safe thing which took your weight and allowed you to rest. Upside down, however, chair and man became a monster with barbs which were probably poisoned. It was just a matter of how one looked at things. Father Ryan was right there.

Later, she heard the tick of a bicycle chain, the shed door squeaking open and shut, and finally the front door handle groaning as it turned. It was Michael and the way he made these sounds were as unique to him, she thought, as the colour of his eyes. Her heart began to race.

Michael burst in.

'How are you?' He stared with his blue bright eyes.

'The doctor was up.' She glanced in the direction of the brown ribbed bottle.

Michael picked it up and squinted at the label.

'What's this written here?' he demanded brusquely.

'It's a prescription for bronchitis,' she explained.

Michael was not able to read as well as she was.

He sat down on the bed beside her. She closed her eyes and his hand came to her forehead. She could smell the glue which they used at work. It was in his clothes and in his hair. When she was well, there was always water boiled and waiting for when he got home, and he always washed straight away to remove the work smell. Those days seemed very far away, she thought, although they were not really.

Michael began smoothing her forehead, flattening it in the direction of one temple and then the other, as if he were smoothing creases out of paper. His movements were firm and regular, and she could feel the callouses on his palms as he stroked her. On Saturday nights, she used to rub them with a pumice stone until they were gone, leaving the palms soft and white. That was something else which seemed suddenly as if it were in the distant past.

Michael was calm. She would say little or, better still, nothing. The last thing she wanted was a scene like the one the night before.

He had been very kind to her that Wednesday morning. However, when she heard him leaving, she was relieved. It was not that she never wanted to see him again; it was just that she had sensed it was going to be easier with him away.

Now he was home again, and despite the talk she had had with Father Ryan, she felt a sense of anxiety creeping back. Perhaps she would send her father to ask her aunt, Mary Kennedy, to come up. Or maybe Joanna would call by. She hoped so, anyway.

CHAPTER SIX

On Thursday Joanna Burke opened the back door of her house and stepped outside. The day was grey. There was a wind. She was off to see Bridget again. She had been over at Ballyvadlea only the night before with Mary Kennedy, and Bridget had made her promise to come back this morning.

She followed the path along the side of the house. This morning their cat was lying on top of the woodpile. He was stretched across a white, bleached log. As she approached he stood and arched his back. She reached forward and began to stroke him. She felt the bumpy shape of his spine under the fur. Their cat was called Harry.

She walked on. The wind gusted, lifting ash from the ditch on the far side of the lawn. The brown stalks of the nearby brambles were white again with the dust.

She passed on, skirting their shed. Two sheets were hanging from a rope stretched between the rafters. They looked damp and forlorn. Would Thomas, her husband, bring them in? She doubted it. She was feeling morose suddenly. She had left her kitchen untidy, she remembered. Now the sheets. She never did like to leave tasks undone, but why, she wondered, should it upset her particularly this morning? Probably she was just tired, she decided.

She moved up the lane. The wind gusted again. She felt cold. She drew her shoulders together under her coat.

March was a depressing time of the year. She had always thought so. Yes, there were other times when it was wetter, colder, and when the days were shorter. And yes, there were signs of change. On sheltered banks snowdrops had forced their way through the rotting leaves. The sycamore trees near the privy at the back of her house were showing green buds. She had even noticed a starling swooping around the shed just now. It had not been there the week before. The world was getting warmer, the days longer. But it was not yet warm enough, or bright for long enough, to believe it was spring yet. March was a time of promises which were not fulfilled.

When she arrived at Bridget's house Joanna was tired. She stopped for a moment in the lane and looked at the slate roof, the small brown windows, the brown front door. Bridget's home was a labourer's cottage, recently built, drier than her own house and a good deal more comfortable. The Clearys were very fortunate to have secured it, she found herself thinking glumly.

At the gate she stopped and she peered in the direction of the yard. There was no sign of Michael. As she had thought, he had left for work.

Joanna was not exactly disappointed. She liked Michael but there was no pattern with him. One moment he would be fussing over Bridget, the next he would be angry. Only the night before he had wanted Bridget to try Ganey's herbs again. When Bridget refused, Michael's eyes widened, his jaw came forward, his fists clenched. It had seemed to her that inside his body a spring was compressing.

For the next hour he had sat grumbling in the kitchen while she listened patiently. Then Bridget called him to her and kissed him, and as suddenly as it had come, his mood now passed. His eyes lightened, his jaw relaxed, his fists unclenched, and the inner spring released.

Joanna liked her unpredictability to be predictable, as for instance with her brothers and their drinking.

Sober, Mikey, William, James and Patrick were reasonable and God-fearing; drunk, they were wilful and violent: they attacked each other with chairs and bottles, or they smashed windows in the streets of Fethard and Clonmel.

Enter the peelers, who would admonish and caution them; and if they were very far gone, they would cart them off to the cells.

Come the morning they would awake with sore heads. They would be ashamed and apologetic. They would vow never to drink again.

But within a month they would break their promises and the cycle would start again.

Joanna swung the gate open and went up the path. She found her brothers unpleasant when they were drunk; however, at least there was a rhythm to what they did. Her brothers were like clockwork; Michael, on the other hand, was a wild card.

Joanna rapped on the door, turned the handle and went in.

Bridget heard the door opening and called out, 'Hello.' Her cousin came straight to the bedroom.

'How are you?' she heard Joanna asking her.

Bridget shook her head and described her symptoms. She felt neither worse nor better than the day before.

'Well,' said Joanna when she finished, 'you did say Dr Crean said a week.'

'Will I ever get out of here?'

'Of course. But now,' she continued brightly, 'to work.'

Bridget lay back and listened now as Joanna swept the floor, washed the table, cleaned the ashes from the fire; brought in two baskets, one filled with turf, the other with sticks; fetched the chemise and the towel she had washed the night before from the shed where she had hung them to dry, and draped them over the clothes horse in front of the hearth; made Pat's bed; washed Pat's vest and long-johns and draped them over a bush outside to dry; polished Pat's Sunday boots; washed the windows in vinegar, inside and out, and afterwards wiped them down with old pieces of newspaper.

Finally, she heard Joanna taking Michael's jacket – a

button had come off it – fetching the sewing box and coming into her room. Bridget moved her legs and her cousin settled herself down on the end of her bed.

'Any better?' she asked jovially, licking the end of a thread and wiggling it through the eye of a needle.

'Not since an hour ago.'

Bridget puffed out her cheeks and exhaled loudly.

'Am I ever going to get better?' she continued wearily. 'I am heartily sick of being laid up like this.'

She watched as Joanna evened out the ends of the cotton and tied them deftly into a knot.

'Of course you are,' she said peremptorily. 'Don't be so gloomy.'

Bridget gazed through the gleaming window. The cloud spread across the sky was more white than grey, she noticed. The sun behind, she thought, was obviously striving to show through.

'Anyway,' she heard Joanna continuing, 'you've Dr Crean's medicine. And by the way, did you take it this morning?'

'Of course I did,' she said.

'What's it like?' Joanna wormed the needle up through the worsted of the jacket, then through one of the holes in the button.

'Better than Ganey's muck, anyway,' Bridget murmured, continuing to gaze at the sky outside, 'which was disgusting.'

Bridget shifted her gaze back to her cousin. Joanna stretched her arm out full as she pulled the thread, then forced the needle through another hole in the button and out the other side. This was what she hated about buttons, she thought, this first bit, getting the button in place. At least there was this to be said in favour of her situation; Joanna did the chores she detested.

'I know Ganey's stuff was horrible,' Joanna began. The needle came back and her arm stretched full again. 'I had some myself.'

'Yes,' Bridget said, 'when you were ten.'

'It tasted disgusting. I was sick in the fire.'

'I was sick too, you may remember,' said Bridget tartly.

'I know you were, but will you listen to me?'

Bridget looked at her cousin, who she saw was staring back at her intently.

'Yes,' she said, tentatively.

'You didn't give it a chance.'

'I did.'

'You spat it out. Now I was the same. But my parents made me swallow the stuff and I got better.'

'What was wrong with you?' Bridget asked quietly.

'Blood and what's like blood but it's white and was coming out of my gums.'

'I remember. And Ganey's herbs, you say, made you well.'

'Yes,' she heard Joanna agree.

'How do you know?'

'I was sick before and I was better after.'

'Are you saying to me I need Ganey's concoction?'

'Maybe if Dr Crean's doesn't work you should give it a proper chance.'

'I can't swallow it. That's why I wouldn't have it.'

'I know.'

'Michael thinks it's a fairy blast I have,' she heard herself saying quietly. 'That's why he wants me to have it.'

The thread whispered as Joanna pulled it through.

'But once it's down and in, Ganey's medicine gets you better quickly,' said Joanna.

As she thought this over Bridget gazed again out of the window. That was when the green-uniformed figure of the police sergeant pushing his bicycle passed outside. She let out a little cry which was followed almost immediately by a wince of pain from Joanna. Looking across, Bridget saw Joanna staring at her finger end where a bubble of blood balanced precariously. Joanna, she realized, had pricked herself.

153

They heard the policeman clumping through the gate and coming up to the front door where he banged smartly, three times.

'God,' said Bridget quietly, 'what can it be?'

'I'll see.' Joanna hurried out and returned a moment later with Acting-Sergeant Egan behind.

There were a few moments of uneasy conversation and the policeman broke the news. Michael's father was dead.

'He's dead, you say,' said Bridget.

'I'm afraid so.'

His nose, she noticed, was very rounded and large, while the eyes above were smallish and close-set. His chin jutted forward, yet when the policeman spoke it was stationary, only the lips appearing to move. His mouth was small and rounded.

Dead, she thought, and what was like a bubble rose from within and broke. She began to cry, the tears running quickly down her face. What a time to be in bed, sick. Joanna, her head bowed, rested her face on her hands. Acting-Sergeant Egan, standing by the window, his hat under his arm, was staring out as he waited.

Poor Michael, Bridget thought, poor, poor Michael. She pictured the father. In later years, as he had thinned and aged, Michael's father's face had lost its uniformity and become crooked, the eyes wild-looking and the mouth uneven. Death was inevitable, she admitted, and furthermore it was also the case that Michael and his father were not close. Since he had left Ballynure at seventeen, her husband had only been back infrequently. But the news would hit him hard, she thought. Blood was blood. She also felt a vague uneasiness that she was first to hear, while Michael was still working away in the cooperage, blithely unaware of what had happened.

She wiped her face. 'Sergeant Egan,' she said 'as you see, I'm indisposed.'

Bridget smiled at him weakly.

'Can a message be got to Michael?'

'I'll do it myself,' she heard the policeman saying.

A moment later he appeared once more outside her window. He mounted his bicycle and set off, this time in the opposite direction to the one in which he had come, towards Fethard and Clonmel.

'Poor Michael,' Joanna whispered. Bridget saw the blood had been flowing as she wept. It had travelled along her finger to the knuckle from where it had then dripped down on to her white apron and formed a red disc. What was curious, Bridget thought, as she stared at it now, was the speed with which blood dried and the colour that it went when it did. On the apron it was brown, russet, almost rust coloured, whereas at the point where it flowed freshly, it was crimson.

'Oh good God,' murmured Joanna, her face still averted.

'You know,' said Bridget, 'from the moment you pricked your finger, I knew there was going to be bad news coming into this house. I just knew it.'

Michael looked up from his bench in the workshop and saw the policeman standing in the doorway.

He was talking to Liam. The policeman was a tall fellow, over six foot and with a black moustache. On his arm he wore the stripes of a sergeant.

Liam raised his arm. Surprisingly, Michael noticed it was towards himself that the apprentice was pointing. Obviously there was a mistake, he thought. It had to be Mr Corrigan whom the sergeant was seeking.

Without thinking Michael turned. He was expecting to see the bald-headed bowed shape in brown apron who controlled his working life. However, amazingly, Mr Corrigan was nowhere to be seem in the dim, shadowy recesses of the workshop.

Turning back to his bench, where he had a length of

English oak trapped in the mouth of the vice, Michael was astonished to see that no less a figure than the foreman himself had now joined the apprentice and the policeman where the double doors were thrown open to the sky outside.

Michael watched as now Mr Corrigan nodded at the young Liam. The boy's dismissal from the world of adult conversation was unmistakable. However, instead of walking away, Michael saw that Liam was now staring along the workshop towards him.

Michael, his plane travelling along the oak automatically, raised his eyebrows as he and Liam met one another's glances. Something was afoot and Michael's hope was that the apprentice, with a nod or a shrug, would indicate the object of the policeman's quest.

But instead, Liam simply stared, and his broad freckled face, bordered along the top by his shorn fringe, almost seemed pitying to Michael for a moment. Pitying of him.

What was happening? he wondered, with a faint undertone of irritation as he asked himself the question.

He scoured the plank edge with his blade, and watched as the pale, white sliver of wood which he had just skimmed off fed through the slit and curled up towards him like a tongue.

With his bare hand he now tested the edge for smoothness. then he looked up. He saw Liam slipping around one of the doors into the cobbled yard, shaking his head as he went.

Corrigan, his head cocked to the side like a bird, now offered his ear to the moustachioed mouth of the policeman. As the sergeant talked, Mr Corrigan shook his head slowly.

Glancing around the workshop, Michael saw the other workmen had also noticed something was up. Just as he did, they were glancing up from their benches now and again, and then going back to work. Every one of them was adept at maintaining the impression that they were working.

Michael shook his head, cleared the debris from his plane, and pushed it once again along the wood. What would bring

156

a policeman to the workshop, he wondered, and why would he speak at such length to the foreman?

Perhaps it was about Bridget, he answered himself.

He swallowed and gulped and glanced again. With the light coming from behind, the profiles of the two men standing in the doorway stood out with extraordinary clarity, but from where he stood he was not able to read their expressions.

Damn them. Why didn't they turn towards him? But of course, the thought struck him then, the subject of Bridget would not cause the two men to talk so intensely and intimately. Therefore, his worries on that score, at any rate, were unfounded.

Consoled by this thought, Michael released the vice and turned the plank over. He ran his fingers along the newly upturned edge, feeling the coarse surface of the wood, noting where it was knotted and splintered.

He ran the blade over the wood, gently testing and rehearsing his stroke, then with a single sweep he ran the plane from end to end, the white tongue of wood shaving unfurling behind his blade.

He cleared the plane. This time he did not even bother to look up. Obviously it was a small matter – otherwise why was there only one policeman – and obviously it was a criminal matter – otherwise why else were they talking for such a long time?

It was probably Flynn, he hazarded, sweeping the plane along again from one plank end to the other. Michael remembered, bringing all his chisels in to work two years earlier. His intention was to sharpen them on the revolving whetstone which was worked with a footcrank. However, when he went to his toolbox, he found that his favourite one-inch Derby chisel had disappeared. He asked his colleagues if any of them had borrowed it. None of them had.

Then, a year later, he found his one-inch Derby in Flynn's toolbox. He could still make out the initials – MC – which were carved in the handle, although there had been some attempt made to sand them away.

Confronted with the chisel, Flynn smiled.

'Michael,' he said, 'if I had anything to hide, would I have asked you to fetch a mallet from my box?'

While Michael tried to frame his answer, Flynn continued in his reasonable and plausible manner, 'Anyone could have put your chisel in with my things, Michael. And you know, you'll probably find the things of half the men in this workshop in someone else's toolbox, if you cared to look, for our belongings all get mixed about, don't they?'

It was a masterstroke on Flynn's part to imply that Michael was just as likely to have the possessions of others as he was. Michael literally found himself at a loss for words. How dare he, was all he could think. The cheek of the man. But while he flushed with anger he lost the initiative. As he was trying to think what to say, Flynn simply turned and walked away.

From that day on, at least between himself and Flynn, the subject was never again raised. But objects continued to go missing, though mercifully none of his. Flynn was never caught again. However, everyone believed that he was the pilferer.

So of course, Michael thought now, it was Flynn. Had to be.

Lifting his eyes from his workbench he glanced into the corner where the thief worked.

Flynn was a fellow in his middle fifties, with fine hands and small feet, and a surprisingly ample waist. His trousers, lifted almost to his chest, were held in place with a brown belt. Flynn was planing as well, and in between each stroke, Michael noticed, he too lifted his head and glanced nervously towards the policeman as he talked into Mr Corrigan's ear.

Michael smiled gently, running his hand again along his wood. Flynn had it coming of course, and now he was going to be arrested in front of his workmates.

He turned the plane upside down and picked at the white strip of wood shaving which had stuck behind the blade. As he did this, a picture of Mrs Flynn, who collected her husband from work each evening at six-thirty, appeared before his mind's eye.

Like her husband she was large. She often wore a cream dress and a bonnet decorated with silk flowers.

He pictured her sailing in and finding Flynn's workbench empty. He pictured Mr Corrigan going forward and whispering to her. He pictured the blue eyes of Mrs Flynn filling with tears.

He tugged at the sliver of trapped wood. The piece snapped and the end which was left behind was trapped behind the blade. He jiggled the plane upside down and back again in order to dislodge it. Nothing happened.

He found a piece of wire and began trying to poke the piece out. Did Mrs Flynn deserve the fate he had imagined? he wondered. Of course not. She didn't deserve to be punished for what her husband did. Flynn's folly was his own doing.

Success. The wooden strip dropped out. He turned his plane upside down and watched it flutter towards the floor that was strewn with shavings and sawdust.

Mr Corrigan, he saw, was stepping back now from the policeman. The conversation was over and each man, judging by their expressions, was resolved to do something which was quite unpleasant.

Now a twinge of sympathy ran through Michael. It quite surprised him. He detested Flynn and had done since the business with the chisel, and yet at the same time he found himself feeling sorry for him. Yes, he thought, it would have been more discreet to have arrested Flynn at his house.

Anyway, Michael decided, as he bent towards the plank again, he wasn't going to stand and stare like the rest of them. He explored a knot with his finger, then bent forward and pushed. The blade skimmed and he noticed, with some pleasure, the wood ribbon curling and growing behind.

'Michael,' he heard.

'Yes,' he said mechanically, still advancing the plane slowly.

'There's someone to see you.'

It was Corrigan. What did he want?

Michael looked up. The policeman with the whiskers was at the foreman's shoulder. He was staring at him. Michael felt his stomach trembling and the faintest quaking in his knees. At the same moment he could not help but notice that Flynn was working feverishly. He was throwing his plane along the wood and producing, with each thrust, a great coiling snake of shaving which then flew some feet through the air before landing on the floor. Everyone in the workshop, in fact, was working feverishly.

'Mr Cleary, I wonder if I might speak to you?' the sergeant asked. His tone was polite.

'Is it Bridget?' Michael asked, nodding and nervously running his thumb over the blade. 'Is she all right?'

'Mrs Cleary is at the house. I've just called to her,' said the sergeant. Now that Michael was able to see him properly, he realized the policeman was a local man. He was from the Drangan barracks. He had even called up to the house once. It was the time they had had that trouble with the young bloods who eavesdropped when he and Bridget were alone in the house. The policeman's name was Egan.

'So it's not Bridgie,' said Michael. 'Nothing's wrong in that department.'

'No,' agreed Acting-Sergeant Egan. 'However I wonder, Mr Cleary, if you wouldn't mind stepping out into the yard with me, for a moment.'

The trembling in his knees was now so great, Michael thought he might fall over. Meanwhile in his stomach, he felt the congealing sensation which he recognized as pure panic.

'What's the matter?' he blurted.

'I think you'd better come outside,' he heard the foreman saying. Mr Corrigan had fixed him with a look which he had never seen on the foreman's face before. He recognized it as sympathetic.

Michael followed them through the workshop. All the men were banging, hammering and planing furiously. Despite his terror, Michael recognized the energy of those who knew they had been spared.

They passed through the double doors and out into the yard. In the corner, a huge barrel was being fitted with a red-hot metal collar. As the metal closed around the wood it smouldered and hissed.

Together, the three men walked to the gateway at the end of the yard and stopped.

'Mr Cleary,' said Acting-Sergeant Egan, 'I've had a communication from Carrick-on-Suir police station, who've had a communication from Ballynure.'

'Yes.'

Michael watched as the policeman's gaze visibly softened before his eyes.

'Look,' he said, the tone of his voice audibly softening, 'I don't want to keep you waiting. As you've probably guessed, since the news is from Ballynure, it concerns your father.'

'Yes.'

'I'm afraid I have to tell you that your father died last night, and it's fallen on my shoulders to break the news to you. I'm very sorry, Mr Cleary.'

'You say my father is dead.'

'Yes, Mr Cleary. A neighbour, we gather, found him in his bed this morning. He died sometime in the night.'

'Come and sit down, Michael, come on,' Mr Corrigan whispered emphatically.

His whole body was jerking.

He felt that each of them had taken hold of an arm. Now they were guiding him over the cobbles. At last they reached the steps which rose up to the green water-pump which stood in the middle of the yard.

Michael slumped on the second step from the top. He sensed he was breathing heavily. He was also expecting tears. Surprisingly, however, none were flowing.

'Daddy is dead,' he heard himself saying in a quiet, small voice.

'Sit still, Michael, don't trouble yourself.'

The sky was bright behind Mr Corrigan and so his face was blanked out and featureless again. He felt Mr Corrigan squeezing his shoulder.

Daddy was dead, he thought, so there was going to be a funeral. He pictured the kitchen at home, the table covered with clay pipes and crocks of whiskey, uncles and aunts around the fireplace, the door open to the bedroom, the coffin lid standing against the wall, like an extra mourner almost, the coffin on the bed and his father lying inside, his eyes closed, his arms crossed, and his best suit on him, his best white shirt as well, fastened at the collar with his ivory dress stud.

Michael stared down and sideways. Acting-Sergeant Egan's laces were leather and the eyes of his boots were shining brass. Daddy was dead. First there was going to be a wake; then a funeral; then they were going to put his daddy in the graveyard beside his wife, Michael's mother.

He saw the place in his mind's eye now. It was a lonely, sloping, hillside plot, strewn with paths, tombstones and crosses. As a child he had never cared for the graveyard. He didn't like to play there like some of the other children. He had only ever gone there for burials. But come the following Sunday or Monday he would be there in his suit. He would follow the coffin to a muddy oblong. Then he would watch as the coffin was swung down on ropes into the hole.

Still no tears, yet inside he was quivering. Mr Corrigan and Acting-Sergeant Egan meanwhile were motionless on either side of him. They were waiting for his tears just as keenly as he was.

Now, at the back of his throat, he sensed the rawness that had always come before tears – at least when he had been a boy and he had cried then. An instant later, a single orb rolled out of each eye and trickled down his cheeks. They left the skin over which they ran feeling momentarily hot. But then the wind blew and his skin felt cold again.

His head dropped forward and he swallowed. The rawness was growing stronger and he knew he was about to burst out crying. He lifted his hands to his eyes just in time. The next instant his body juddered, something in him choked and his skin was wet all over in an instant, and his mouth was filled with the salt taste of his tears.

Now, as he cried, pictures of the kitchen at home, his father laid out for waking, and the graveyard on the hillside, flashed again through his mind. However, this time they were jumbled up with recent memories of his wife. For instance, he saw her as he had seen her that morning, lying in her bed and wheezing painfully, her pale, worn face framed by her lank hair. A great sob flew from his mouth.

Damn it, why hadn't he been to Ganey earlier? Why hadn't he been to the herb doctor years ago and put a protective ring around his home?

'My wife is sick,' he mumbled. Acting-Sergeant Egan and Mr Corrigan responded with gentle nods. Michael wanted to signal in return that he appreciated the gesture. However, his face felt as stiff as if it were frozen. Then he forgot about the present as his thoughts moved back in time. To a winter's night when he was a child . . .

He was eleven or twelve. He was kneeling at the trapdoor of his attic room. He could see the ladder dropping down below him. His parents were sitting at the fire. It was the local herb doctor. Quinn had acquired his powers by spending a whole night in Kearney's rath. Quinn both impressed and terrified Michael.

'Listen,' he heard Quinn saying quietly. Michael drew

closer to the opening to hear what the man was saying to his parents.

'There was once a man died, and at that time his wife was already sick. It was the evil eye she had. The fairies had laid it on her because she stole from them.

'With her husband gone the wife, her name was Philomena, naturally she got out of bed of course – well, what else could she do? – and the husband was laid out in the bedroom ready to be waked. But do you know what happened then?'

Michael, listening above, ached both to know and not to know.

'The relatives and friends came into the house but there were strange noises in the air, and then the seed potatoes in their sack in the corner, they began to ooze blood, to bleed.

'And the next day, when the time came to close the coffin, wasn't the dead man gone? He had vanished. Just like that.'

Quinn snapped his fingers.

'But he wasn't vanished. For the next forty days and nights, he was out on the little roads and lanes around the house, crying and moaning and whimpering and startling everyone who passed, until at last all the people of the district had fled, and it was emptied of every living soul. Well, almost, almost . . .'

Quinn paused.

'Because some say the husband is still there, alone on the roads, screaming and shouting and pleading. But he is barred for ever from heaven, you see, because the sickness of his wife when he died, it dirtied his house. That's what a fairy sickness does. It's like a rotting sheep in a well; it poisons the water . . .'

'I must go home,' said Michael abruptly. He jumped to his feet. The violence with which he moved and spoke was a surprise to Mr Corrigan and Acting-Sergeant Egan.

'Yes, indeed,' Mr Corrigan agreed and smiled at him.

164

'Get your bicycle, Michael,' said Acting-Sergeant Egan softly, 'I'll go with you.'

'I'll go alone.'

'As you wish.'

Feeling dazed and light-headed, he wandered back towards the workshop.

Someone was singing inside. He recognized the piece. It was a sentimental song about a girl called Mary and her love for a dragoon.

He reached the door and stepped in. To his surprise Michael saw the singer was none other than Flynn. The man was happy, Michael supposed, because he had escaped. In contrast, however, he who had had nothing to fear when the sergeant arrived, was now crushed by the news which he had been brought.

It wasn't fair. Nothing was fair. Not one bloody thing. But most of all, it was unfair that his father should die at this time. It was plain bloody rotten luck. That was what it was. It was plain bloody rotten.

His bicycle was at the back. He went forward. The workshop was noisy and dark.

Flynn broke off his song and called over jovially, 'What's up, Michael?'

Michael crossed over to Flynn and stared into his face.

'What did that peeler want, Michael? Not come to take you away?'

'No, my father just died,' said Michael quietly.

Flynn's eyes widened, his mouth opened. Michael saw that a little thread of white saliva stretched between his lips.

'And if that isn't enough,' Michael continued, 'my wife is sick, very sick as it happens. This is not a very good day to be making your cracks, Flynn. And by the way, everybody here knows that you're our thief. I hope the sergeant takes you away the next time he comes.'

Michael fetched his bicycle and left.

Pedalling home along the small roads, the brown hedgerows flashing past, Michael's mind was filled by one thought alone. When he got home, Bridget was going to take Ganey's herbs. She was going to get better. Once she was better, he would be able to go to the wake. But not before. He didn't want any fairy sickness going into the house in Ballynure, trapping his father on this earth. It was the very least, as his son, that Michael could do for him.

When he got to his house he did not stop. He hurried on instead. He went past Simpson's house on the corner. He carried on down the lane to the end. Here, he turned right on to the Drangan road. When he got to John Dunne's cottage, he threw his bicycle against the wall and ran to the door. His friend would help him. He banged on the wood. The door scraped back. His friend stood before him.

Dunne's nose was pointed and his mouth was small. He was almost completely bald except for the little hair growing at the back. His face was very red.

'Hello, Michael.' Dunne smiled, his blue eyes seeming to shine. Then he removed the smile, quite consciously it appeared to Michael, and changed his expression to one of tenderness.

'I heard your news, Michael.'

Michael nodded.

'Listen.' Michael wiped his face with his sleeve. 'I'm going to give Bridget the herbs tonight. She has to have them.'

Dunne nodded and smiled vaguely.

'Will you come up?'

'I'll be up presently.' Dunne rubbed his hand over his chin. 'I want to have a shave, make myself look presentable to Bridget.'

It was a curious remark, thought Michael, as he made his way back to his bicycle. However, he quickly forgot about it as he hastened back up the road and turned on to the lane.

A few minutes later Michael reached his house. He opened

the gate. He was sweating. His shirt was sticking to his skin. The wind blew and he felt the perspiration cooling. He threw his bicycle against the wall and hurried inside.

He went straight into Bridget's bedroom and closed the door. His wife put her arms around his neck. He felt how thin they were after three weeks in bed.

She kissed him. Her mouth was hot and her skin was dry and rough, like a cat's tongue against him. Her breath smelt. He wanted to pull away. But that was going to cause offence. He would wait until she finished kissing him.

Inwardly he started counting, One, two, three . . .

At nine she released him.

'Michael, dear poor Michael,' she said.

She smoothed the hair back from his temple.

'You're wet. Was it raining?'

'No. It's just I'm hot.'

She wrinkled her nose and raised her eyebrows, her habitual response to his sweat.

'Bridget, will you have Ganey's cure tonight, please?'

She assumed a look of astonishment.

'I want you to,' he said quietly. 'You must.'

He looked intently at her. She looked back at him. He felt himself trembling. Bridget's eyes were normally blue, but the eyes in the face staring back at him were grey. How could this be? he thought.

He lifted the candle across. The yellow light fell softly on Bridget. Yes, they were grey.

He let his eyes rake up and down her face. Observed closely he saw that it wasn't Bridget, it just looked like her, very, very like her, so like her, in fact, as to be indistinguishable – well, almost that is, for he could see this was a counterfeit, a fake.

'What is it?' Bridget asked, smoothing her face and then her hair as she stared back at him. 'I must look terrible. Do I?' she asked.

The angle of her face in the light had shifted and now he

saw he had been wrong. It was Bridget. The skin was the skin of his wife. The eyes were the eyes of his wife. The mouth was the mouth of his wife.

He could feel his heart beating. One moment it was Bridget in the bed, the next moment it wasn't. He took a deep breath. He was going to have to be very cunning and under no circumstances was he to let on what he suspected. Quietly and stealthily he was just going to have to carry on with the business of the herbs. If she took them, then obviously it was Bridget that he had. And if she didn't, then John Dunne had been right about the changeling. But, thanks be to God, they weren't there yet. No. The cure was the answer, if he could only get her to take it.

Bridget lay in bed. The door was ajar and she heard their voices in the kitchen, her father's, Michael's, Joanna's and John Dunne's. Why on earth had Michael asked him up? He was a horrible, vile man. When all this was over, she might just tell Michael what happened the day she was reading *Kidnapped*. She heard the squeak of the crane swinging over the fire.

They were making a concoction. If she could just manage a mouthful, that was all, Michael said. A little cup's worth and he would be happy.

The unmistakable herb smell wafted through. She was trembling and shaking. Just one mouthful. Surely she could manage to get that much down and keep it there. One swig and it would be over.

Think of it like the cod liver oil, she told herself, that she had when she was a child. It had a hideous flavour but, once swallowed, that was it – over. It always came presented on a big spoon which was kept in the house expressly for medicine. The handle was long and freckled, the end of the spoon lightly buckled and the rim sharp. There was always a taste of metal on the tongue as it went in, and if she kept her mouth too closed when the spoon was withdrawn, it sometimes cut her lip.

The burnt herb smell was growing stronger. It reminded her of something, she thought. No, that was a useless way to think. She had to push her mind in a different direction. She most not think bad. She must think good. She remembered her conversation with Joanna in the afternoon. That was better. Maybe her cousin was right. She hadn't given the herbs a chance before. For all she knew they were a miracle cure. One go and they might restore her completely. Wouldn't that be wonderful?

In her mind's eye she saw herself the next morning . . . She awoke. She stretched herself in bed. There was no pain, not in her arms, her elbows, her knees, her throat. She coughed and her throat was clear. She touched her upper lip. It was dry. Then her forehead. It was cool. She threw the covers back and reached her legs on to the floor. Slowly she stood. She felt strong and light. She was better. It was over.

They came through the door now, Dunne first and Michael following. He was carrying a saucepan over which he was cutting the sign of the cross in the air.

'Where's Joanna?'

'She'll stay outside,' Dunne murmured.

'This room's too small,' said Michael.

Dunne closed the door. Old Boot Polish was freshly shaven and his fifty-year-old face was pink and glistening. However, it was only a matter of seconds before his sour smell was all around her, mixed with the herbs. The time she looked after him when he was sick, she remembered, she had had to burn a good many of his clothes because they were too filthy to wash. Michael set the saucepan down, produced a cup from his pocket, dipped it in.

He lifted the dripping cup out slowly. Dunne wiped the edges with a cloth.

One cupful, that was all, and then it would be over, she told herself.

She reached forward. Michael put the cup into her hands. The porcelain was warm. She looked down. The liquid was black with bubbles and bits floating.

One cupful, she could knock it back in a gulp.

She swallowed and exhaled. That way she kept the odour at bay.

They were watching her, their eyes bearing down.

Slowly she raised her arms.

The rim was at her lip.

She dropped her tongue down to make a space behind her teeth.

Think of it as a raw egg. Hadn't she had plenty of those in her time?

She counted inwardly. One, two, three.

This was it.

One, two . . .

She tipped her head back and threw in the liquid. For a moment she didn't know what was happening. Then she had this overwhelming sense of the concoction being everywhere – up her nose, down her throat and in her mouth . . .

It was like the one time she went to the sea and she went into the water. A wave smacked her in the face and there was salt suddenly everywhere, the bitter, bitter taste of salt as she had never before tasted it. It was in her mouth, up her nose, in her eyes in her ears, in every nook and cranny of her head and body. It overwhelmed her.

Dazed, panic-stricken, grimacing, spluttering, retching, she tried to stagger towards where she thought the beach was. Then, bending and falling forward, she went on coughing and gasping while a length of mucus dropped from her nose and she spat with all her vigour. None the less, the salty taste remained for minutes afterwards . . .

But this was not seawater, cold and at least clear. This was warm, with solids in it which were slimy, and it was not going to go over the back of her tongue, it was not going to pour down her throat. It was a filthy brown-black mess, in fact it was privy mess, she thought, and as she made the fatal connection she spat forward with all her might. She immediately felt the milky stuff through her nightdress. It was warm for a second but then it quickly went cold. Then she heard the cup landing and smashing on the floor.

Blinking through the tears in her eyes, she glimpsed the towel Dunne had draped over his arm. She lunged and pulled it to herself and started dragging its rough bumpy surface over her lips and her tongue. She wanted to scour away the taste of the concoction which remained.

'Bridget,' Michael shouted. 'What have you done?'

Joanna was suddenly at the door.

'Go out, Joanna,' he said.

'Stay,' she called. Her voice was muffled through the towel. She saw Dunne was pushing her cousin away and now he was closing the door.

'There's a whole pan here,' said Michael. 'You will have it.'

'I can't. I won't,' she said angrily.

'You will.'

'I won't.'

'You must,' said Dunne solemnly.

'I won't,' she shouted back at him fiercely. She rubbed the towel against her tongue. The damn concoction was like a stain; she would never get it out.

'Give me water,' she said. 'Give me a drink of water for God's sake.'

'Get a spoon,' she heard Michael saying now.

What was this? she wondered. Oh yes, she thought, that old trick. That was the way Joanna's parents made her take Ganey's medicine for her sore gums, wasn't it? Well, they weren't going to get her with that one. No way.

'Yes,' she heard Old Boot Polish replying, eagerly if she

171

wasn't mistaken, and then she followed the sound of his footfalls as he turned and moved from the bed.

Opening back the sickroom door and stepping into the kitchen, the first thing John Dunne saw was Joanna Burke sitting at the table.

'What are you doing?' he demanded. He was intentionally abrupt. This was, he thought, the only answer to the brazen manner in which she was staring up at him.

However, then, which was typical, she ignored the question and called past him through the doorway, 'Are you all right in there?' to Bridget on the bed.

'Joanna,' Bridget called back to her but before anything further could be said, he slammed the door smartly behind himself and scowled.

'Hello, John. How are you? How's Bridgie doing?' Joanna asked cheerfully.

He shook his head and thought to himself how very disagreeable he had always found Joanna Burke.

He strode over to the hearth, nodded to Pat sitting there in his chair and thrust the poker into the middle of the hottest embers in the grate. As he squatted he felt the heat on his face and on his eyes. It was even in his mouth as he breathed in.

He riddled the poker from side to side. Red coals dropped silently through the grate and plopped into the grey ash below, glowed momentarily and lost their colour.

John Dunne resented Joanna Burke. Bridget would have been his friend, he thought, but Joanna was jealous and would not let her. As he stared into the fire, he remembered the winter he was sick and how Bridget came down to him once and sometimes twice a day. She made the fire; she washed the sheets; she cleaned the house and trimmed the lamp; she fed the chickens; she fetched the eggs; she made him soups and broths; she read to him. He could tell that she liked him. Then, one day and for no good reason, Joanna appeared down at his house with Bridget and from that day forward he was never alone with Bridgie again. That was when he realized Joanna was jealous of him.

To thank Bridget for caring for him when he was sick he had bought her a pair of ear-rings. They were the long, dangling type – a gold hoop and a piece of glass etched with the profile of a young woman. Bridget was shy and awkward when he presented the small package wrapped in brown paper. However, she touched his hand after she opened the box, and he could tell she was pleased.

But he never saw his present again after that. Once, he asked Bridget about them; this was one evening when she was outside her house, returning with a basket of turf, and he had gone out to help her. She told him they were lost. She even added some nonsense about fairies, he remembered now, staring at the sooty chimney-back and the sparks floating upwards.

He knew that it was Joanna who had turned Bridget against him. But then, given her jealous and possessive nature, he told himself, it really should come as no surprise to him that she acted like this.

He jiggled the poker again. In the middle of his palm he felt how the handle was starting to warm up. It was a good fire all right.

His thoughts turned to Bridget lying inside on her bed. When he was sick she cared for him and now he was repaying her for looking after him. And when she was restored, she would thank him and Michael for helping her to get better, and maybe this time she might even buy him a gift.

The next thought followed and, as it did, he smiled. Oh no, she would not of course thank Joanna, because her so-called best friend was doing nothing.

Involuntarily, he glanced over his shoulder at Joanna. She had remained sitting at the table. As usual he saw she was wearing her long mournful face, her large cow-like eyes were dull and she had adopted her usual slovenly position, elbows on table, head lolling on her hands. And she was waiting to complain about what he and Michael were doing to help Bridget. He just knew it.

John Dunne turned back to the fire. She did not like him and he felt quite entitled to dislike her in return. She was an irritating, nosy busybody, and he would have been very happy never to set eyes on her ever again. Indeed, just the idea of staying in the kitchen with her for even one second longer was repulsive.

He hurried back across the floor towards the sickroom.

From her bed Bridget saw the door swinging open and then John Dunne's flushed face. He looked furious. His red skin looked as if it were stretched as tight as the skin of a drum over the bones of his face. It was obviously something Joanna had said. She would ask her later. It was funny that. She was frightened and angry, yet somewhere within, there was a part of her that was calm. She was watching, thinking, calculating how to get through this.

'I won't take Ganey's stuff,' she bellowed.

Her father would hear that, she thought. And Joanna too. It was about time they stirred themselves. But then she heard the door closing. What were they doing out in the kitchen?

'Yes, you will take it,' she heard Michael shouting now. 'If I bring sickness into my father's house, he'll never leave this earth.'

What was he going on about? She was the one who was sick. Not him. She was the one who was sick and she was not going. No, she couldn't, of course she couldn't, feeling as she did, hot, weak, feverish. She could barely cross the room, let alone make the – what was it? – eight-mile journey to Bally-nure. Wasn't that obvious? she wondered.

'But I'm not going,' she shouted up at him.

'Yes, you are,' he shouted back. His voice was steely. They

were talking at cross-purposes now. She meant the wake but he was back on the herbs again, she realized. Anyway, no, she wasn't taking them. She had tried the concoction and it was revolting. No one could swallow muck like that. Well, children maybe, ten-year-olds, like Joanna, who were made to, she thought. But not her. She simply could not. It was impossible.

'Did you get the spoon?' Michael's chin floated above her as he spoke across the bed.

She swivelled her eyes right. John Dunne's shining red chin, mirror of Michael's, pointed back from the other side of her bed.

'The spoon, sorry,' she heard Old Boot Polish apologizing. 'I forgot.'

The sickroom door scraped back and John Dunne went out again.

'Where do you keep your spoons, Pat?' His voice coming from the kitchen was oily, she thought. He sounded polite but that was just put on to impress her father.

'In the base of the dresser,' came the voice of her father. He was suitably impressed of course and his usual obliging self. Why didn't he lie? she wondered. And what had he been doing for the last half an hour?

Sitting in his chair by the fire, she told herself.

Well, get up, Pat, she thought. Get up. Get in here.

No, that was a ridiculous hope. He was an old man, frightened and cowed.

But what about Joanna, her cousin and her friend? Why didn't she do something? Where was her courage?

She held her breath and she strained her ears. Come on, Joanna, she thought. But there was only silence. Not a word from her.

Now she heard the sound of a hinge creaking. That, she guessed, was the dresser door opening. Now sounds of rummaging followed, then the door banging shut. Old Boot Polish had found the spoon. Any second he would be back in the room and the whole business of the cure was going to start again. She had to prepare. She had to close her mouth as firmly as it would shut.

'Hey!' she heard. That exclamation was in Joanna's voice. At last, her cousin had spoken.

'What's going on?' she heard Joanna continuing. But that was not Joanna's normal, angry voice, she thought. Her cousin sounded – what?

'What do you think you're doing?' She heard Joanna again, louder than before.

Yes, now she had it. She knew what it was. Her cousin sounded frightened. So what was happening? Was Old Boot Polish hitting her?

She listened but there were no sounds of blows exchanged or screams of pain. No, all she could hear were hurrying feet, and the noise of bodies in motion.

Now Boot Polish was at the door. He got in and slammed it behind himself. Then she heard the key turning in the lock.

A second later Joanna was on the other side of the sickroom door. She was kicking and banging and rattling the handle.

'Open this door,' she heard Joanna shouting.

'Go away,' said Old Boot Polish gruffly, but with what sounded to her like a smirk in his voice.

'Unlock this at once.' It was Joanna again. 'Don't worry, Bridget. I'll be in there in a moment.'

'No, you won't.' Dunne was laughing now.

Ferocious banging on the door continued as Joanna shouted, 'Let me in. Let me give Bridget the herbs. You know it'll be a lot easier if I do it. She'll take from me what she won't from you.'

That's it, you tell them, Joanna.

'Leave us to our business, Joanna.' It was Michael speaking this time.

Now Old Boot Polish was turning from the door and she suddenly understood her cousin's tone of voice. In one hand

176

he had the wooden spoon but in the other he was carrying the poker.

Oh my God. Her heart trembled. What was he doing with that thing in her bedroom?

'Look at this, Bridget,' he said.

The black tip of the poker was waving in the air. Then suddenly Old Boot Polish jabbed it against the orange box in the corner. She heard the wood hiss as it blackened and saw a coil of smoke rising.

It was hot. Oh God. Her heart raced faster. The poker had been in the fire and he had gone back to fetch it with the spoon. Oh God. Old Boot Polish was mad. Michael too. What possessed them? She was suffering from a fever, for God's sake. She was sick with bronchitis and they were . . .

No, she interrupted this thought. She had to remain calm and keep her thinking cool. She had to avoid the end of the poker. Absolutely. At all costs.

Old Boot Polish came up to the bed. She watched as he passed the wooden spoon across and then as Michael dipped it into the saucepan.

'One drink, Bridget, and then you'll be better.'

The spoon was slowly floating through the air towards her. It dipped below the level of her chin and she could see the black concoction delicately balanced in the bowl at the end of the handle.

Joanna was banging again outside. 'Let me in. Do you hear me?'

'I wish she'd shut up.' It was Old Boot Polish this time. She saw his knee coming up over the side of the bed. It came down on to her chest and he started pushing down on her. She felt herself sinking into the mattress.

She started to wriggle. If she could get under the bedclothes she could get away from the spoon and the poker. But movement was difficult. The knee was pressing down on her chest very hard. Very, very hard.

177

'See this?' Dunne was shouting at her.

She saw it all right, the point of the poker hovering six inches from her face.

'If you don't cooperate, you're going to get a taste of this.'

She had to keep wriggling. The spoon was getting closer. She had to struggle, to wriggle. Dunne's knee was pressing down harder than ever. But she could feel her strength coming. God knows where it's coming from, she thought, but yes she could feel her body was slipping out from under Dunne's knee. If she could get out from under Old Boot Polish, and then pull the covers over her head and shove herself down into the bottom of the bed, she'd be safe for a while. They would have to drag her back up.

'I'm warning you,' she heard Dunne shouting. He lowered the poker another inch. His eyes were gleaming. She had seen them gleaming like that before. Knew them only too well. She should have told Michael what had happened when she was reading *Kidnapped*. If she had told him, Old Boot Polish wouldn't be here in the house now, let alone in her bedroom. It had been cowardly. She should have spoken. If Michael knew what she knew, then he'd understand what Old Boot Polish was up to. He wasn't there to give the herbs. Damn, why hadn't she told Michael? Well, it was too late now and there was no point in fretting. She had to concentrate. She had one objective and one only. She had to get away from the poker.

She wrenched downwards, almost escaping from under Dunne's knee. However, then he caught her neck and started pushing down there. That hurt even more than when he was pressing on her chest.

Suddenly, the poker point was right in front of her eyes. She could feel the hotness of the metal on her face.

'I'm warning you,' she heard.

It was coming; what she dreaded and feared, it was happening. She opened her mouth. Her intention was to shout

'Joanna, Joanna.' She was going to shout with such urgency that her cousin would have to break down the door. That was when she felt it, the poker point on her forehead. It was like a drop of hot lead plopping on to her skin. For a second there was no pain and then the pain started. She opened her mouth. She heard a scream coming out. It was the loudest scream she had ever screamed. 'Joanna,' she screamed at the top of her lungs, 'Joanna, Joanna . . .'

From the other side of the door in the kitchen, Joanna heard Bridget calling out 'Joanna, Joanna . . .' Then she heard the bed-head thumping against the wall, the bed-springs groaning, a chair crashing, and finally a wordless scream . . . This all happened in a matter of seconds.

'Open this door,' Joanna shouted, beating her fists on the door.

She put her eye to the keyhole. Blocked. She plucked a hairpin from the back of her head and frantically poked with it.

'Get a cork,' Michael shouted inside, 'to hold her mouth open.'

'The cork'll be useless,' Dunne argued back, 'she'll just bite on to it and stop us getting the herbs into her.'

The barrel of the key slid back, the key dropped and at last Joanna saw inside. The bolster had split. Feathers were floating about. Bridget was somewhere hidden in the tangled bedclothes. Michael, holding spoon and saucepan, was towering above her. Dunne was on the bed, brandishing the poker, his knee across Bridget's neck.

Dunne turned. She saw him staring back furiously at her eye. Then with a horrible cry he leapt from the bed and sprang towards her. He was like a wild animal. Joanna jumped up, terrified, and fell back on to the floor.

'It's kill or cure. Do you understand, Joanna Burke?' John Dunne shouted at her through the keyhole. She heard him

179

ramming the key back in and twisting it half a turn. He did this, she realized at once, so that she could not poke it out again.

'You're animals,' she shouted back through the wood as she struggled to her feet. 'This is no cure!'

She snatched her coat from the hook where it hung. She saw Pat was still sitting in his chair, crying quietly now into his handkerchief and moaning.

She bolted out of the door and through the gate and hurried on down the lane.

Joanna half-walked, half-ran through the darkness. By the time she arrived home her face was red and her stomach was churning.

'I heard about Michael's father,' said her husband Thomas, as she came into the kitchen.

He was sitting at the head of the table peeling a turnip.

'They've taken a p-o-k-e-r to Bridget,' said Joanna, spelling the offensive word so that Katie, who was also at the table, would not understand.

'What?'

Thomas pulled a face, a mixture of disgust and astonishment, and a grubby coil of turnip skin tumbled into the pig's bucket between his feet.

Joanna recounted everything she had seen, or not seen but heard. Her emphasis was on John Dunne's nastiness.

'How strange,' Thomas commented when she finished. 'Don't you remember when he was ill how mad he was for her? Kept asking when was Bridget coming to feed him. It was probably the first time he'd ever known a woman's kindness.'

'It was more than just kindness he wanted from Bridget.'

Thomas laughed quietly. 'I don't think he'd much hope there.'

Joanna was shaking. He moved to the chair beside her. He took her hands and rubbed them gently.

Suddenly Joanna stood up.

'I'm going for the peelers.'

'Wait a minute.'

'I shall tell them what's been going on.'

'What? Michael's been giving her herbs from Ganey, and you think Dunne's hit her with a hot poker but you can't be sure.' He laughed. 'That's hardly something to report.'

'The herbs are being given against her will.'

'You've nothing worth telling. What passes between a husband and his wife is no concern of theirs. Or ours, Joanna.'

'Or Dunne's,' she added.

'You threw the teapot at me last summer,' he said, 'and it was full of scalding water. You might have meant to hurt me for a second but you soon regretted it. But what if Katie here,' he waved at his daughter who was assembling her coloured wooden bricks into a wall, 'had gone to Drangan barracks and reported it and you'd been hauled away. What would you have felt? Tell me. Go on. You know. You'd have felt outraged. You'd have felt angry. And all because the police were sticking their noses where they had no place to put them.'

'I could go for the priest,' said Joanna quietly.

He shook his head and smiled.

'Father Ryan's not exactly a man who knows about men and women, is he? He's a book reader. But that's by the by. If they want the priest, it's for the Clearys to call him in themselves, not us.'

'I'm Bridget's best friend.'

'Be her friend then. Go, look after her. Cheer her up.'

'Shall I go back tonight?'

'Of course, go back tonight.'

Joanna slowly sat down again.

The front door went several times and Bridget heard her father admitting first her aunt, old Mary Kennedy, then

Mary's four grown sons, William, James, Patrick and poor Mikey, and lastly, William Ahearn, the sickly son of a neighbour and a friend of them all.

The men were for the wake, they said, but then she heard Michael whispering to them. The next thing three of her cousins trooped through and her tiny room was suddenly crowded.

'Get out,' she said to the boys.

'Get hold of her,' said Michael.

She felt William grip her around the ankles and push her legs together. The other two took her by the arms and shoulders. She felt their fingers digging into her skin.

Dunne began to twist her ears. By doing this he made her face forward.

Her cousins, she observed, had a rustic smell. They smelt of sweat and cowshed and the flour sacks they slept between. The smell of John Dunne, in contrast, was chemical. It was the smell of something sticky, slimy and permanently staining.

This was a clear distinct thought, for much as she was in pain she was not terrified; she was lucid and observant.

'Steady her,' ordered Michael, sliding from her sight.

She tried to swivel her head to watch him go out the door, but Old Boot Polish was holding her ears so tightly, it was impossible to move.

Why was she so kind to this man when he was sick? she asked herself. Because he was a neighbour and because she was asked to, came the answer.

His little mouth and crooked teeth hovered a foot away from her. She saw his lips were trembling, just the same as they had earlier, when he was waving the poker about.

I hate you, John Dunne, she thought.

She heard Michael coming back through the sickroom door. She tried turning her head again. John Dunne was still holding her so tightly, any movement was impossible.

'Let me go,' she shouted into his red face.

'No chance.'

But she sensed Dunne's grip faltering. She wrenched her head sideways and glimpsed beyond the door the heavy figure of her dear aunt. Surely Mary would stop them? She wouldn't run away like Joanna.

'Mary,' she exclaimed. But an instant later, Old Boot Polish had a hand clamped over her mouth.

'Stop being silly now,' he sneered.

Michael slid into view above her, saucepan and wooden spoon in hand.

Oh no, she thought, it was about to start again, the herbs. Why couldn't they understand? Ganey's cure was pure poison, impossible to take.

'It's too dark in here to work properly,' Michael shouted, 'I want someone to hold a light or we'll end up spilling this stuff.'

'Ahearn, get in here,' ordered John Dunne. Oh, how he was enjoying his power, she thought. It was enough to make you sick.

She heard footfalls. Mary maybe? Then she saw the large white forehead and the lank black hair that were unmistakably Ahearn's.

'Take the candle.' Boot Polish gave the order this time. By the sound of it he was enjoying himself. Of course he was. He loved lording it over her and everyone else. He loved it. Well, she was going to tell Michael when this was over. The whole *Kidnapped* story. That would cook his bacon. Old Boot Polish would never darken their door again.

Ahearn had the candle. The yellow trembling flame was gliding towards her. She saw gigantic shadows moving on the ceiling overhead.

Michael leant forward and into view.

'One sip,' he said.

He dipped the spoon and carefully lowered it towards her.

'Hold her steady. Too much has gone on the floor already,' he said.

'I won't take it,' she shouted up. 'I won't.'

'Come on. Don't be like that.'

The spoon was inches away. She tried to wriggle away but Dunne was tightening his grip.

'Come on now.'

The rim was against her lips. The horrible odour drifted up into her face. She clamped her teeth shut and closed her eyes.

But a hand was digging under the back of her neck and attempting to lift her. Old Boot Polish had let go of one of her ears and was trying to make her sit up, she realized.

She pushed back against the hand beneath her with all her might. She was not having one drop.

The edge of the spoon was through her lips and against her teeth.

'You're making me angry,' Michael was shouting.

He was worming the spoon between her teeth, trying to lever them apart.

Then suddenly the hand that was holding her ear slipped.

Turning her head sideways she shouted up, 'Leave me alone.'

'You'll take it in the name of God.'

She felt Dunne taking her ear and manhandling her forward again. Then the spoon was against her mouth once more. She felt the grey cold concoction dribbling over her lips, running down her chin and wetting her nightdress.

'If this lot goes on the ground you can't be brought back from the fairies,' Michael threatened.

'Pull her, boys. That's the way to get her to take it,' said Dunne. Now Michael had his hand over her mouth. That way she couldn't spit. The concoction taste was on her lips, and her tongue. It was hard to breathe.

'Come back, Bridget Cleary, in the name of God,' she heard Michael shouting.

'Didn't I say pull her, boys?' Dunne was saying again.

Michael took his hand from her mouth and her cousins began to pull her, first one way and then the other. She took a great gulp of air and tried to scour the taste off her tongue by scraping it with her teeth.

'Come home, Bridget Boland, come home,' the men called in unison as they jerked her one way and then the other.

'Leave me alone. I'm Bridget,' she shouted back.

So, it wasn't just that they thought she was sick from the fairy blast any more and they were trying to make her better with Ganey's herbs. No, she saw that it was much worse now. Much worse.

What was it Old Boot Polish had been shouting at Joanna before she fled. 'Kill or cure,' she remembered, 'kill or cure.'

They didn't think it was her any more. They thought it was someone else. Or something else. She didn't want to even let herself think the word but it came hurtling into her thoughts none the less. A changeling. That's what they thought, or Dunne at any rate. Yes, Old Boot Polish, he was the one who probably said it first. Seared the idea into Michael's mind. And what an ideal time, after all, to do it. What with the news of Michael's father's death, fresh that afternoon. It was all Old Boot Polish's doing and he was having his revenge because she'd spurned him. She saw it all suddenly, instantly. It was horrible.

As for Michael, he was simply stupid and gullible.

And the Kennedy boys, they were just falling in with what was happening. They were just doing what they were told. As young men did. But there was not one single person there to whom she could turn. Not one single person to whom she could say, 'Am I Bridget?' and whom she could guarantee would reply, 'Yes, you are.' Not one. There was not one. Joanna was gone, and even her cousin she doubted. Or at least she couldn't be sure she would speak up for her.

Since there was no one to whom to appeal, she told herself to pray.

Dear God, she began, do not forsake me. Please, let this end. Let them go away. Please. My arms are hurting. My legs are aching. I cannot go on . . .

It was ten o'clock, very cold and pitch dark, as Joanna walked back along the lane towards the house in Ballyvadlea. Katie was squeezing her hand and skipping beside her as she talked.

That morning, Joanna heard, Harry the cat had fallen into a barrel that was half-filled with rainwater. He had gripped the inside with his front claws, but he had neither been able to climb out, nor had he let anyone pull him out. Finally, her husband had had to lift him out on the end of a spade, and Harry had spent the rest of the day curled up in the hay, hissing and miaowing to himself.

Hearing footsteps, Joanna peered ahead. She saw two dark shapes were hovering outside Cleary's. Drawing closer she saw it was the Simpsons, the caretakers from the farm next door to Cleary's.

William was a stocky man with a broad red face, heavy jowls and a snub nose which reminded her of a lump of putty. He always wore a bowler hat. Their acquaintance was now a nodding one although it had not always been so.

The year before, Joanna's sheep-dog, Lucky, had disappeared and she had wondered aloud in William's presence if a shepherd who had complained that Lucky chased his sheep might not have had something to do with this.

She had spoken in confidence to Simpson but this had not stopped him reporting the shepherd to the police. She tackled him and he swore he had only had Joanna's welfare at heart, whereas, as she knew full well, the shepherd in fact owed Simpson a large sum of money.

The police interviewed the shepherd and the following day

Lucky turned up. He was floating face down in her well, and for good measure his throat had been cut. The shepherd never spoke to her again.

'How are you, Joanna?' came the voice of Minnie through the darkness. Simpson's wife was smallish. She had a lovely shaped mouth and bright eyes, Joanna had always thought.

'Isn't it a terrible thing about Michael's father?' said Simpson formally.

Joanna nodded mechanically, although actually she had forgotten all about this. It was what she had seen earlier that evening that filled her mind.

'What are we hanging about for?' Simpson asked jovially.

He walked down the path and knocked loudly on the front door.

'No one will come in yet,' boomed Cleary suddenly, from inside. His voice gave Joanna a fright.

There was a great deal of confused shouting in the house and then coming through the confusion Joanna distinctly heard, 'Take it, you bitch, or we'll kill you.'

She recognized John Dunne's voice.

The four of them in the darkness turned now to the window nearest the door. Light was leaking around the edges of the shutter of Bridget's bedroom but they were not able to see in.

'Take it, you strop.'

Incredibly, Joanna realized, she was hearing the voice of Mary, her mother.

She gripped Katie's hand and felt the child shifting from foot to foot beside her. Katie was cold, Joanna assured herself. After all, it was a freezing night.

There was more shouting inside. It was incoherent this time.

'Stay here,' Joanna whispered to her daughter.

She let go of Katie's hand and slipped round to the back of Cleary's. The old bucket, as she had remembered, was on the wall behind the turf shed.

Joanna carried it back, set it under the window and used it to climb up on to the ledge. She put her eye to the small crack at the top of the shutter. However, because of the angle at which she was looking down and the smallness of the gap, all she was able to make out were slivers of the arms and shoulders of several people milling around inside. It was impossible to tell what was happening or who was in there.

Joanna jumped down, went to the door and knocked loudly again. Nobody answered.

'I don't like it here,' said Katie, taking her mother's hand.

'Sssshhh!' said Joanna. William Simpson began to whistle through his teeth in the darkness beside her.

A few minutes later, Joanna heard the sound of the key being turned inside and the bolts being drawn. The door jerked back and she saw Michael Cleary standing in front of her. He was holding a wooden spoon in one hand, the wretched saucepan in the other. Joanna assumed this was filled with Ganey's herbs.

'Away she goes. Away she goes,' she heard several voices calling from inside, and Michael looked up as if he were following the flight of something out through the door. Joanna involuntarily found herself following the line of his gaze, but there was nothing to see, only the dark shapes of the trees around the house and the black night sky.

Michael Cleary was smiling as she turned back to face him. 'Come in,' he said, 'come in.'

With Katie's hand in her own again, Joanna stepped past Michael and into the house. 'Uhhh!' she heard Katie exclaiming, and her daughter wrinkled her nose.

It was the herb smell. It was unpleasant, it was true; however, Joanna didn't want Michael taking offence so she said to Katie, 'It's medicine,' loud enough for him to hear.

Joanna took off her own and Katie's coats and hung them

up. There was a fire burning brightly in the grate and the plates on the dresser were reflecting the firelight.

Michael was still standing at the front door, his back to the room. Now Michael wheeled about suddenly and, staring oddly at herself and the Simpsons, said, quietly, 'All that's inside must stay inside, do you hear?'

'Of course,' Joanna agreed.

Then Michael slammed the door so hard it made Joanna start.

'Of course,' she repeated.

While the Simpsons crossed behind her to the fire and sat down without saying a word, Joanna moved into the centre of the room. While she had been away at home, her mother had arrived, and Mary Kennedy was now, Joanna saw, sitting on a bench talking to Pat Boland. Joanna also saw that her youngest brother, Mikey, was sitting at the kitchen table.

'Are you going to the wake, boys?' He directed his speech to the door to Bridget's bedroom. Looking in, Joanna saw that her other three brothers were in the sickroom. Presumably this explained all the shouting she had heard earlier coming from in there.

Patrick and James were standing at the head of Bridget's bed and each was holding their cousin by an arm, while her third brother, William Kennedy, was at the other end of the bed, sitting on Bridget's legs. William Ahearn was also inside, holding a candle and looking nervous, while John Dunne, head bowed and face resting in the palms of his hands, was sitting slumped in a chair as if exhausted. Bridget was a small shape hidden under the tangled bedding.

'Are we going to the wake?' repeated Mikey.

The wake for Michael's father, remembered Joanna. It was happening eight miles off in the home of the dead man in Ballynure. Her brothers would want to go of course. They would have come to collect Michael. That explained their presence.

'Are we going?' said Mikey again. His tone was faintly irritated.

'I don't know,' replied William from the end of Bridget's bed, where he remained sitting on his cousin's legs. 'We'll go when we finish, I suppose.'

Mikey caught Joanna's eye, shook his head and made a face.

'I want to go now,' he mouthed to his sister. As always, Mikey was trying to get her on to his side. Joanna, however, remained expressionless. No, she was not going to take sides in this, especially given the mood Michael was in. She could see Michael out of the corner of her eye, moving into the room.

Now Joanna wondered if her brothers in Bridget's bedroom were drunk. Judging by their appearance she decided they were not, which was good; there was a better chance of controlling Michael if they were sober.

She swivelled her gaze to Mikey. Ominously, because of the way he was holding his head in his hands, it did seem to her as if he might have been drinking.

'Let's make a start now. It'll be a good two-hour walk to Ballynure,' Mikey called to his brothers, slurring faintly, and confirming her suspicions.

'No,' her brother William called back, 'Michael says we're not finished yet.'

Bridget, as if suddenly waking up, began to jerk under the bedclothes.

'You have finished. Leave me,' Joanna heard her cousin's muffled voice in the sickroom.

Bridget tried to sit up and Joanna saw her two brothers at the head of the bed shove her back down again.

'Don't be so hard,' Joanna remonstrated. When they appeared to have loosened their grip, she moved over to the fireplace where Michael Cleary was emptying his saucepan. Her next move would be to speak to him. However, before she was able to do this, Mikey got up from the table, crossed in front of her and touched Michael on the elbow.

'Aren't we going to make a move soon?' her younger brother asked impatiently.

'No! We are not,' Michael replied, shrugging Mikey off and tipping the remnants of the herb medicine into the fire where they hissed and spluttered.

'When are we going to the wake then?' Mikey persisted.

'I don't know.'

'You have to go. It's your own father's wake.'

'I am not going.'

'Why?'

'Because I don't give a damn whether he's dead or not. And none of you will be going either until I finish this business.'

Here, thought Joanna, was her chance.

'And what is that business?' she said, quietly, politely.

With the gallon milk-can Michael refilled the big pot. Then he swung the crane with the pot on the end over the fire.

'Wait, boys, until you see what I will put out the door,' he called over her shoulder to her brothers in the bedroom.

'What will that be?' asked Joanna.

'I haven't had Bridgie these six or eight weeks, since before she was sick.'

'What was that then by the door?' Joanna asked. 'It flew out then, didn't it?'

There was no alternative but to humour him.

Michael smiled and turned his head away. His face looked grubby and wild to her and his eyes had a strange brightness about them.

From long experience she knew that Michael was abrupt, unpredictable and difficult, but this evening he was worse than normal. Although at first sight it didn't seem like it, she believed it was the death of his father that was the cause, although at the moment Michael seemed indifferent to this. But if Bridget took the cure just the once, then he wouldn't have his wife as an excuse any more and the death could assume its proper place in Michael's life.

Yes, decided Joanna, it wasn't such a bad thing after all that her brothers had turned up, for they might just get Bridget to take the herbs . . .

While Joanna was thinking, Michael remained at the hearth, his back to her. When the milk boiled he took a handful of herbs from the opened-out newspaper on the mantelpiece and threw them in. Within seconds the bitter smell which suffused the kitchen became even stronger.

Michael let the concoction stand for some minutes, then transferred the mixture from pot to saucepan; then he carried it through to the bedroom, all the time cutting the sign of the cross in the air.

The bedroom door closed.

'Are you Bridget Cleary?' Joanna heard Michael asking inside.

'Yes, I am,' Bridget replied. Her voice, Joanna judged, was strong and certain.

'You're not,' Michael shouted suddenly.

'Yes, I am!'

'One of you in the kitchen,' Michael shouted, 'get the chamber pot.'

Joanna, standing with her back to the fire, saw that nobody in the kitchen was moving, neither Pat nor her mother, Mikey or the Simpsons.

'Are you deaf out there?' continued Michael. 'Did no one hear me? Will someone get the chamber pot or do I have to get really angry!'

Joanna saw the chamber pot was on the far side of the room. It was on the floor in the corner by the dresser. It was white with a handle and a heavy lid. At the same moment she heard someone standing. It was her mother.

'I'm coming,' Mary Kennedy shouted at Bridget's bedroom door.

'This will be all right,' her mother whispered as she passed. 'I saw this work once many years ago.'

Her mother picked up the chamber pot and carried it through the doorway into Bridget's room. Inside, Michael took it from her, saying nothing. He was not able to speak for he had the wooden spoon clamped between his teeth. He took the lid off and put it down.

The bedroom door swung and shut fast.

After Michael took the chamber pot Mary Kennedy turned and peered at Bridget. Her niece was being held down by three of her sons. The bedclothes were all tangled but she was just able to make out Bridget's face. She was peering out from behind the corner of a sheet.

'Mary,' she heard Bridget crying, 'help me. Don't let them.'

How harsh that voice sounded, thought Mary, and how wild Bridget looked. Her eyes had shrunk to the size of sixpences, Mary estimated, and the fine down on the upper lip glistened with sweat. No, she thought, shuffling past her son William, who was sitting on the edge of the bed, this was not the pretty niece she knew and loved. It looked like her but it was not her.

'Mary, Mary,' she heard it calling, but she did not turn.

Yes, she thought, opening the door and closing it after herself, Bridgie was stolen. That was as clear as a hand in front of the face. And a parasite had insinuated itself into her place, and God only knew what was happening to poor Bridget, wherever she was. Kilnagranagh probably, or some place like that.

Poor Michael, she mused, smiling now as she passed her daughter Joanna and little Katie, who were both in the kitchen. How awful to have lived as he had lived, sharing his house with a stranger night after night.

The next half-hour was going to be hard, but Bridget would thank him afterwards. They would all thank him.

Mary resumed her place on the bench and stretched her feet out towards the fire. This was rather nice, she thought, knowing she was going to have company all night and right through to the morning.

Please God, please let this end, Bridget prayed.

Michael was standing over her, supporting the chamber pot with one hand and holding the wooden spoon in the other.

He dipped the spoon into the bowl and flicked it at her. Droplets spattered on to her face. What had she done to deserve this? By God, they were mad. Not just Michael, but the Kennedy brothers, her Aunt Mary, Ahearn, her own father for all she knew, and perhaps even Joanna.

She felt a great rush of anger and energy. She wrenched sideways, keeping her neck rigid. Miraculously, Old Boot Polish lost his grip on her ears. She went on turning sideways. The next splash of urine landed on the side of her nose, wetting an eyelid and her cheek.

'Keep still,' Michael shouted.

Her closed eyes were stinging, and she smelt the salty, brackish odour of the pee.

'I won't. Go away,' she screamed.

Her hair was now being twisted and tugged and she felt the pain of it surging all round her scalp. That was Old Boot Polish, trying to get her facing forward again. Well, she wasn't, no matter how much the top of her head hurt. He could pull the hair out by the roots for all she cared.

'This'll bring you to your senses,' said Michael.

The entire contents of the chamber pot hit her. The urine was cold and made her gasp. She felt it running into her ears and up her nose, through her hair and down her face, on to her flannel nightdress and through to her skin.

'More, get me more,' shouted Michael.

He was holding the chamber pot over her head and emptying the very last drops out of it.

'There isn't more,' Mary Kennedy called back from the kitchen.

There was a terrible brackish taste on the back of her teeth and on the tip of her tongue. The urine was soaking through the bolster and the mattress. They were cold and wet beneath her. She closed her eyes. It was the only protest which was left to her.

'Come on now, wake up, stop acting the fool.'

Michael was slapping her hands. Michael would not touch her face, she realized, only her hands because there was no pee on her hands and they were dry. But she would not allow him to do this without him knowing that she knew.

She opened her eyes slowly. They stung.

Now her father Pat appeared by Michael's side. He lifted her head, bringing it close to his.

'Are you my daughter, in the name of God?'

'Yes.' How many times was she going to have to answer this same question? 'Yes.'

The taste was all through her mouth.

'Are you my daughter?'

Louder this time, 'Yes.' She would convince them.

Perhaps she could get one of her arms free and lift her cuff to her face and wipe it.

'Are you?'

'Yes,' she shouted.

She tugged at first one and then the other arm, and in turn the Kennedys tightened their grip.

Her father dropped her head back on to the wet pillow and fastidiously began to wipe the moisture from his hands on to the bedclothes.

She heard John Dunne behind her head saying, 'She will keep you there till the hour is up, till twelve o'clock.' He was

195

holding her by the ears again. 'Make down a fire,' he added grimly, 'and she will answer quick.'

She had tried reason. She had tried prayer. She had tried resistance. Only magic was left. Maybe if she could make herself invisible she could save herself. They were all readying themselves to lift her and, as they did, she felt herself going very still.

Outside in the kitchen, on the other side of the sickroom door, Joanna could hear Bridget being questioned inside in the bedroom. It was her sense that the main business of the evening was over and that at any moment her cousin and all the others were going to emerge through the door.

Then Joanna noticed that the fire was low. It had shrunk to being just a small layer of embers lying in the bottom of the grate. With all the commotion going on, no one had remembered to keep it going.

She knelt down on the hearthstone and pulled the wood basket over. It was filled with short lengths of ash. They were thin and – as she found when she tried to break the first one – springy.

With difficulty Joanna broke several pieces in half. She laid these across the embers and then put other lengths on top of these until she had built a platform in the fireplace which was some inches below the two hobs; these extended on either side of the grate and ran to the back of the chimney. Usually these were crowded with pots and pans or food which was being kept warm, but this evening the hobs were empty.

Joanna decided now that everyone was going to want tea. She lifted the huge black kettle from its place on the floor and hung it on the end of the crane. Then she filled it with well-water from the bucket. Then she looked at the fire.

There was smoke moving upwards against the sooty back of the chimney but the sticks she had just laid down had not yet caught and there was no point in swinging the kettle into place until there was a good fire going.

Suddenly, there was a considerable noise behind her.

Joanna turned and saw, emerging backwards from the sickroom, her brother William Kennedy. He was carrying Bridget by the feet.

Her other two brothers, Patrick and James, followed behind. They were each holding one of her cousin's shoulders.

John Dunne was next. He was holding up Bridget's head, supporting her by the neck.

Following behind were Pat Boland and Michael Cleary, and last to emerge was William Ahearn, who immediately went and stood in the shadow at the side of the dresser. He looked extremely ashamed of himself, Joanna thought.

All the others kept moving slowly forward, until they came to the middle of the kitchen where they stopped.

'Who are you?' asked Michael.

Bridget's eyes, Joanna saw, were open, but she did not reply.

'Are you Bridget Boland from Ballyvadlea, in the name of God?' asked Pat Boland.

Bridget remained silent. There was a salty smell of urine, Joanna noticed.

'Come on, let's not be losing time,' said John Dunne. 'It's near the hour of midnight, and if we don't do it soon she'll be lost for ever in spite of us.'

Bridget, who had seemed until now to be insensible as far as Joanna was able to make out, suddenly lifted her head and looking her cousin in the eye called out to her, 'Oh Han!'

Joanna felt Katie at her side taking her hand. She was uncertain about what she ought to do. She turned to William and Minnie Simpson, but she found them obviously as confused as she was for they were both staring at the floor.

What about her mother? Joanna thought.

She looked across the room in the other direction. Mary

Kennedy was not sitting on the bench any more but had got up and gone to the linen trunk which stood against the back kitchen wall. She had removed clean sheets and a bolster and was now walking towards the sickroom. Clearly, her mother's intention, Joanna realized, was to change the soiled bed.

As her mother passed, Joanna's eye fell on her fourth brother, Mikey Kennedy. He was back at his place at the table, staring at the oil-cloth and running a finger up and down. He was going to be no help either.

Lastly, there was William Ahearn. He remained as before, in his dark corner, staring up at the ceiling now.

'Are you going to make a herring of me?' Bridget shouted suddenly. 'Give me a chance.'

Her cousin's words made Joanna jump and her heart began to race. The kitchen was quite silent. When at last John Dunne spoke it was almost a relief.

'If you do not answer your name three times,' he said matter-of-factly, 'we will burn you.'

Joanna watched as her three brothers, Patrick, William and James, placed her cousin sideways in the fire, with the hob on one side supporting her neck and shoulder and the other hob under Bridget's knees.

Still nobody stirred or spoke. The only noise which Joanna could hear in the house was her mother stripping the bed in the sickroom.

Then there was a crack from the fire. That was one of the sticks of course but they hadn't caught yet, she thought, no, they were far too green . . . There was no fire to burn Bridget. Not yet. And they wouldn't blaze, the ones she had put on, not for ages. And by then Bridget would be off the grate. It was only to frighten her that they were holding her over the fire. Of course. But she couldn't stay, oh no . . . She couldn't watch . . . But how could she get out? Oh yes . . . She would help her mother . . .

Pulling Katie after her, Joanna fled through the bedroom door.

'Oh Joanna,' Bridget called after her.

Silence.

Why didn't her cousin reply? The fire was crackling. Joanna had just laid down some sticks. Oh, unfriendly deed. Maybe they were green and wet on top, but underneath the fire was burning.

Think! she told herself. She had to make herself very still. She had to tell them exactly what they wanted to hear. There were others in the room, and they would be her witness when she said that she was not what they thought but was Bridget like she said.

'Give me a chance,' she begged.

The ceiling sweeping overhead. The ceiling was wooden with the shadows from the candles and lamps playing across it. She could feel the heat of the fire rising.

'If you do not answer your name three times, we will burn you,' John Dunne was saying. That's what he had said before, hadn't he?

The hob on one side was pressing into her neck, while the other hob on the other side had caught the back of her knee. The right side of her body was lying in the grate and she felt the sticks underneath digging into her. And on the hip and thigh that were in the fire, she could feel the heat that was rising from below. She wanted to scream but maybe that was what they were expecting from a fairy. She bit her lip hard and shut her eyes tight. She wanted to be able to block out the pain when it became unbearable, as inevitably it would. Yes, she would just have to tolerate it. So count, she told herself . . .

'One, two, three . . .' she began.

Into her mind came a memory from her schooldays. The bully, Carmel McBride. A nasty, spoilt child. Also rough and strong.

A pain shot through her side, interrupting her memory. She wasn't burning, was she? No, not yet. But she mustn't scream, she thought, must not. No.

In her mind the memory drifted back. It was like something blurry coming into focus . . . It was after school. McBride was waiting for her at the gate at the end of the schoolyard. She approached, heart thumping, kept walking. After she passed, McBride whipped out the steel ruler which she carried in her satchel, and whacked the edge hard into her head above the ear. It hurt. Ow. Yes.

The next evening Carmel was there again. And the third.

After this, her tormentor grew emboldened. Carmel struck her in the toilets. In the corridor. Once she even struck her in the classroom. Mrs Leary did not see this because she had her back turned.

Bridget told Pat but her father just laughed. He told her to stay away from Carmel. But she couldn't. How could she? Carmel sought her out. More and more. All the time. On the way to school, during school, leaving school.

And the more Carmel bullied, the more fearful she became. And the more fearful she became, the more Carmel bullied.

At last, she decided to fight back. Carmel was at the gate. She approached, heart thumping, but her hands rolled into fists. The gap narrowed and narrowed and finally they were only a couple of paces apart.

Suddenly she rushed forward and threw her punch. Carmel looked surprised and dodged. Bridget caught Carmel's shoulder.

The next second the ruler was out. It flashed through the air. Carmel whacked her on the knuckle, in the crevice between her ring and her little finger. The skin split. Blood began to spurt. Carmel was laughing. Carmel was excited by resistance. Bridget was giving her what she wanted. She recognized the mistake at once as Carmel threw her to the ground. Carmel began to beat her legs. There was no alternative. Bridget gave up. She stopped caring. She stopped responding. She stopped all feelings. She stopped pain, fear, the lot. And in their place came a lovely, quiet, hovering, slightly above things feeling . . .

Which produced the desired result. Carmel grew bored. Carmel lost interest. Carmel drifted off to pick on someone else . . .

Now the heat again and the pain and talking somewhere . . .

'Call your daughter in the name of the Father, the Son and the Holy Ghost,' her husband's voice came to her, 'and I will have her in spite of the world.'

Michael was beside her father, Pat Boland, squatting on the floor in front of her.

Or was that Michael? It seemed that it was but then it was not him also. He was not himself. He was another. Something had happened.

Was it Michael's daddy, his dead daddy? Well, now, was it? A good question. He said he wouldn't go to the wake because of her. First, he said it was her and the fairy blast, he said that it was going to pollute the Ballynure home.

'But I'm not going,' she had said.

Then, some way, how did it happen? The situation changed. He said she wasn't Bridget any more. Stood at the door. Told Joanna and the others something was flying away. A fairy, he said. Her. Preposterous, of course. It was her there in the house. They all knew her. Had done for years. But now, how to prove it to Michael and everyone else? Their heads were filled with crazy ideas.

Now Michael's face was hovering right in front of hers. His eyes were very small. Tiny. He was mad, obviously he was mad.

But maybe so was she. Why wasn't she screaming? Why was she so still? Maybe it wasn't a hot fire. No, wrong. It had to be burning her. She could smell her nightdress burning. It

201

was giving off that 'brown smell', as they called singeing when she was a child. My God! Why didn't she shout?

'Call your daughter and I will have her in spite of the world,' she heard Michael Cleary ordering.

Same words every time, over and over again, no change.

'Are you Bridget Boland my daughter, in the name of God?' her father was intoning now, squatting in front of her.

'I am, Dada, I am.' She was calm. That was right. That was good.

'Are you Bridget Boland, in the name of God?' Pat was intoning.

She could not believe this.

'Yes, I am, Dada.'

The smell of the scorch, for Christ's sake, it was overpowering. Yet every fool was staring at her like a rabbit. She was bunched up and jammed backwards into the grate, Old Boot Polish holding her head, the Kennedy brothers still holding her arms and legs.

Now why hadn't the Kennedys stayed at home this night? They could surely have managed without a drink just one night. Thirsty for the wake of course. Mikey, particularly, always smelt of the stuff. Idiots, all idiots. Well, the peelers would soon bounce them into the barracks, and so quickly their feet would hardly touch the ground.

'Are you Bridget?' Pat asking for the third time.

'Yes, Dada.'

She was feeling real pain now. And it wasn't just a question any longer of the nightdress singeing. It was her skin if she wasn't mistaken.

'Will they burn her?' William Simpson was asking someone.

As she awaited a reply to him the room starting swaying and swirling around her. Faces, she thought, stare at them. Focus. She looked now at her husband and her father, two faces side by side, hovering in front of her. They were growing brighter and brighter. This was not from the firelight, which was red and yellow, but from sunlight. It was flooding the room and everyone was growing whiter from it.

'We have her, yes, we do,' John Dunne, shouting.

'Certain?' Michael shouting back. 'I'd say so and it's not midnight yet. We've done it.'

A faint round of applause if she wasn't mistaken, rippling now around the room.

'Lift her, boys. Quickly now.' John Dunne was saying.

Their faces were shimmering like suns so bright, the features were disappearing, lost in light. The walls of the room were shimmering as well. They were lifting her out of the fire, the three Kennedys and John Dunne. They were lifting her out of the fire and they were carrying her off. They were moving crab-like towards the sickroom. Oh, blessed bed. Oh, blessed sheets, blankets and bolster. Mary had everything changed. Oh, thank you, good Mary, thank you, dearest aunt.

Room spinning, faster and faster, and the walls flashing and glistening like pieces of mirror reflecting sunlight. It was like when she was a child, and they signalled from one camp to another when they played war with pieces of mirror held up to the sun, she and Joanna, Mikey and James, Patrick, William and Ahearn.

But what was this? Turning her head she saw that it had happened. The very thing which had terrified her before. The nightdress was on fire. The chemise was on fire. Red and yellow flames were dancing up from her clothes towards the ceiling.

As they set her down on the ground she felt the floor underneath her body. The flags were cold and hard. They should have had linoleum. William was coming towards her. He was pulling his jacket off. He swiped at her. The jacket moulded itself to her body. It hurt her as it did. It was her distinct impression she could feel the buttons stinging her.

The flames were making a funny sound. What was it? Yes, a sort of warbling sound. And funnily enough they weren't hurting, were they? The flames weren't hurting, although she was expecting them to hurt. William swiped again. Ow! Now that hurt. Yes, indeed. He swiped again. Ow! Ow!

What was that? It was Mikey. He was on the floor just a few feet from her. What was he doing on his knees? Oh, yes, he was slowly keeling over. How peculiar.

The jacket whipped into her again. If she wasn't mistaken the flames were smaller than a couple of moments earlier. No, she wasn't mistaken. That was right. They were.

What was Mikey doing? He was stretched out now completely.

The flames were getting smaller. William swiped again.

Everything very fast before, but now slowing suddenly, slowing. Everything so slow now, movement almost imperceptible. Thoughts slow too. Very slow. Calm too. Coming from somewhere distant and slowly floating into her mind.

Joanna bending down beside Mikey and lifting Mikey's head. His eyes were open but iris and pupils had disappeared. Completely? Yes. Only the whites showing.

What was Joanna doing now? Interesting. Finger in Mikey's mouth and running it across his tongue. Of course. Mikey had fainted. Understand now, but understanding very far away.

Poor Mikey. From earliest age, feared and detested scenes. How old when it happened? Five, wasn't he? They'd stolen sugar. The four boys. Mikey, William, Patrick, James. All due to be beaten and awaiting father. Mikey so nervous, he wet and soiled himself.

William swiping the jacket at her again, the flames almost gone now.

'Come here,' Joanna calling, and Ahearn scuttling from his place in the shadows by the dresser.

'I want to go home.' Ahearn crying. 'My mother isn't very well. But the door's locked here. Could you have a word with the boss for me?'

'Later,' Joanna saying.

Lifting and dragging Mikey off towards Pat's bedroom. And what was this? Someone lifting her as well. Oh yes. Her cousins, the boys. Up, up, up she was going, ceiling now much closer than when she had been on the floor.

Passing now under the lintel of the door into the bedroom. It was brown but reflecting the firelight. Funny, in darkness, what a dark colour did.

Mattress underneath her now, yielding beneath her. Oh, lovely, lovely bed.

Her nightdress must be charred though. Horrible smell of burn about the place. Also pee and herbs. Her skin must be blistering. Must be very red. Ought to inspect. No, too, too tired.

Shadows on the ceiling. Faces coming into view, peering now down over her. Minnie Simpson and Mary Kennedy and Joanna.

'We have to change her,' Joanna speaking.

Yes, give me a clean nightdress, girls.

Standing on her feet suddenly. Room swaying. Close eyes. Eyelids lower. Listening for sound of breathing. Hardly, hardly audible. None at all? Dead, maybe? No, some, but faint. Hair, damp, dirty, dishevelled feeling about it.

'How's Bridget?' Katie the child whispering. Nice of her.

'Go outside.' Open eyes. See Joanna turning daughter round and propelling her towards the door.

Three faces of the women now staring as one at her. Something about a red mark on her forehead and a bruise on her neck. Angry feelings suddenly. That was John Dunne. Every right to feel angry with him.

Hands and arms in air and her chemise and her nightdress lifting off slowly. Naked before the three women who now are poring over body. Small breasts, fine wrists, otherwise nothing to see.

'But look,' voices exclaiming. Three faces staring now at

her bottom. What are the voices saying? Her skin is scorched red and there is a blister on her hip.

Next, standing in the basin and they are washing and sponging all over her, hair as well, then towelling, and then a clean nightdress dropping over her head and wafting floor-wards and the women saying she was all right, she was going to be all right, but mostly silent themselves as each faced conse-quences maybe, as perhaps each feeling guilty, maybe, maybe.

Somebody knocking, door opening, John Dunne appearing.

'All ready?' John Dunne asking.

'Can we come in?' husband Michael behind John Dunne asking.

Everybody in the house crowding in and ringing themselves about her in the bed. Atmosphere strangely reverent, hushed, churchlike, genuine sense of occasion, like her birthday, wed-ding day, and now somebody coughing.

'Do you know where you are?' Michael asking. Lifting eyes, daft question.

'Yes.'

'Do you know who this is?'

Michael pulling William forward.

'Yes.'

'Who is it?'

Daft question said yes already.

'My first cousin.'

'Who is?'

'William.'

'William what?'

'William Kennedy.'

'And this?'

'That's his mother, my aunt Mary Kennedy.'

Slowly Michael now bringing each one forward in the same way in small cottage bedroom and asking same question and she answering same answer person after person, until feeling tired and wanting to sleep, and eyes beginning to close.

'Do you think it's she that's in it?' Michael asking.

Oh, blessed question, at long last. Obviously it was her, wasn't it, wasn't she after answering right, identifying everyone right, and now time to stop, time for finishing, all over, everything, time for resting, sleeping.

'And we'd better have your answers now, otherwise there's still work to be done,' John Dunne saying fiercely, looking around at everyone. 'It's not yet midnight. We have time.'

Her breathing? How was it? Quite audible. Certainly louder than before.

No, she wasn't dead. She had died, almost, and left, but then she had decided not to go and come back.

'Yes, that's my daughter.' Pat, her father, speaking quickly.

A chorus of 'Yeses,' following, quietly to begin with but growing louder and louder.

'We'd better let her rest,' Joanna saying protectively. Thank you, Joanna, thank you for that.

Everybody turning and filing out. Thank God for that. Ordeal over, done with, survived. Dying almost, she had come back at the last moment.

'I'm dying for a cup of tea,' cousin James muttering, which was the other dying of course.

Tea, yes indeed, sweet and milky, but not too milky, for tea that was too milky furred up the teeth and the tongue but yes, please, lovely idea, tea coursing down her throat, washing everything away, all those tastes. No, don't think about them. Concentrate, concentrate, call out for tea.

But opening mouth, no words emerging, no words, nothing.

And now eyelids closing, so tired, eyelids heavy, heavy and falling, tumbling, shutting, darkness visible, darkness invisible, sliding down, down and finally out.

Michael Cleary watched horrified as Mikey Kennedy, recovered now from his fainting fit dug his spoon into the sugar, floated it over his cup, and tipped. It was his third.

The evening was costing him a fortune in tea and sugar.

'More milk?' Joanna was asking William as she held out the jug to him.

That was just typical, he thought, doing exactly as she pleased without so much as even asking him. Tea and bread all round. Make yourself at home, lads. Have as much as you want. And don't bother asking Michael, he's only the house-holder, after all.

'What about you, Michael?' She had turned and was address-ing him directly.

He shook his head.

'No, I don't want any more,' he said. 'At the rate your brothers are going through it, I can't afford to have tea myself.'

She bent towards him.

'These are your neighbours,' she whispered. 'You mustn't begrudge what they'd give just as freely to you. Besides which, you owe them a lot more than a cup of tea for what they've done tonight.'

'I'm grateful for what they did,' he agreed. He hoped with that admission that she would go away.

But no, instead of leaving she sat herself on the stool in front of him, leant forward, and brought her face close to his.

'I'm not certain that everyone here has just your interests at heart,' she whispered. Joanna glanced at John Dunne, who was talking to Ahearn on the other side of the room.

'I think you should be careful with him,' she said.

'Why?'

She touched his hand. 'He's trouble for you and Bridget.'

'What are you saying?'

'Ever since he was ill, when she looked after him, he's taken to bothering himself about Bridgie. Why should he do that? You just watch him when he's with Bridget, see how he behaves.'

Michael scowled darkly. He caught her drift. It was prepos-terous. John was twice Bridget's age.

'You're wrong,' he said firmly.

'Bridget doesn't trust him and nor do I.'

But Michael did. Apart from Bridget, only John knew his secret about his mother and, what's more, he had kept it to himself. Now, that was a sign of something. John was a man to be trusted, and over the preceding evening he had seen his trust had not been misplaced. Only John had believed him about Bridget. Only John had really helped him to save her.

Unfortunately, he could not tell Joanna anything about this.

He turned away to the fire. In this way he signalled that the conversation was over. To his great relief he heard Joanna Burke standing up.

She walked away, then came back into view. He watched her now as she moved across the kitchen floor. She was offering tea to everybody.

Mikey proffered his cup and a dark brown stream poured from the teapot.

Good God! That was the fellow's fourth. That made twelve heaped spoons of sugar, in all. That could be four ounces, a quarter of a pound, easily. Why on earth, he wondered, was he feeding and watering this local drunk and wastrel, when the boy could not even be relied on to help.

'How are you, Mikey?' he called across grimly.

But Mikey's response, amazingly, was to grin right back at him as he dug into the sugar bowl. 'I'm much better now, Michael. I just think it was the heat that got to me.' He began to stir his spoon. 'Are we for the wake now, Michael?'

Didn't the boy think of anything else? he wondered.

'No,' he said. 'As I told you earlier, I cannot go. I thought I made that clear.'

'You did, Michael,' said Mikey obsequiously.

Michael had forgotten his father entirely since Acting-Sergeant Egan and Mr Corrigan had broken the news to him, and for a moment he reflected on what an extraordinary thing that was. His own father dead, and he had not given it a moment's thought all evening. Of course, that was what happened when there was something as pressing and demanding as a fairy sickness.

But yes, he felt very sorry the old fellow was gone. He was going to miss him – well no, not exactly, it was the idea of James he was going to miss, the comfort of knowing that his father was at home in Ballynure if Michael was ever in trouble and should need to go to him, not of course that he had ever once done this.

In his childhood, his father had been a remote man who went out in the mornings, milked the cows, cut the turf, dug the potatoes, came home again in the evenings and went to bed. He had not talked much and had not seemed to have many friends, apart from Quinn the herb doctor, and Michael had always felt this was more to do with his father protecting himself – it was a mistake to get on to the wrong side of Quinn – than because his father had genuinely liked the man.

At the age of seventeen, Michael had left home and gone to Clonmel to start his apprenticeship as a cooper. He hadn't gone home much after that, and in fact, once he had married Bridget and established his own house in Ballyvadlea, he had never again slept at home under his own roof.

After that, he mused, his parents and he had sort of drifted apart, to the extent that on one famous occasion he had even failed to recognize his father one day, when the old man had greeted him in the street. Family loyalties hadn't disappeared but loosened, and in that respect he was quite unlike Bridget, who would never have considered living apart from her father. But when all was said and done he was sad too, he reminded himself, that his old father was gone; or he had been anyway, for the short space of time after he had heard the news from Acting-Sergeant Egan and before he had remembered Quinn's story.

'But won't you reconsider?' he heard Mikey now calling back across to him. 'It's eight miles and we'll make it in two hours, easy. Then a few hours there and we can be back for breakfast. Joanna'll stay. She'll look after Bridget. Won't you, Joanna?' he called.

Yes, his father was dead. Under any normal circumstances he would, yes he would, have wanted to be at the wake. Of course. However, these were not normal circumstances. The mortal soul of his Bridget was in peril, the wife he had promised to love, honour and cherish for the rest of her lifetime.

'I will of course mind Bridget,' he heard Joanna call back from the door of the sickroom.

It was unfortunate that his obligations to his wife and his father clashed, but there it was. A choice had to be made and he had done so. And because of present circumstances, he saw now with a clarity which surprised him, the grief which he ought to have been feeling had been postponed. He didn't actually mind not going to his father's wake, and not until he actually started mourning his father would he begin to resent the fact of not having gone, and this was months, perhaps years away.

'We might as well make a move then,' said James, rallying his brothers to go. 'Come on, Mikey, finish up.'

'Where's that you're off to?' he asked, in what he believed was a tone of sly humility.

'To Ballynure,' replied James quietly. The other Kennedys were ringed behind him in an arc.

'To my father's house?' He could hear the note of outrage seeping through his words; the question was, could they?

'Yes,' said James. Amazingly, judging by his tone, the boy clearly hadn't been listening.

'We thought we might as well stroll over there,' said James, and he added: 'And you ought to come too, Michael, it's your own father's wake.'

'Ought!' he exclaimed. 'Ought! I don't give a damn about my father, do you hear me?'

Michael was amazed, first by his shouting, and then by the way he punched the mantelpiece above his head and made the tea caddy on the end leap up into the air.

Silence descended on his kitchen. At long last, his message was getting through.

'You're not going now,' he said coldly. 'I've something in mind. You'll not start out from this house yet.'

'You're the boss, Michael,' ventured Mikey. The room remained quiet.

'And I say we wait,' Michael continued. 'We may have more business here yet.'

The brothers sat down obediently and began whispering amongst themselves. Meanwhile Michael sat alone, half-listening to their talk, at the same time half-ruminating on the curious twists and turns of his existence. Maybe everything in life was a matter of balance, he thought. One soul was taken, another soul was rescued. His father was gone, but Bridget was recovered.

The more he thought about it, the more sense the idea made, and the more the idea made sense, the more his feelings of anger and irritation were mollified, until at last he felt it was safe. Yes, they could go, and nothing harmful would travel with them to the house in Ballynure, and he heard himself saying to the Kennedy brothers, 'Well, boys, you'd better be off.'

Without a word, the four stood up immediately.

'But I won't be coming,' he added. No, he was going to stay. Bridget was going to have to be watched and there was no one else but himself to do it.

'Thank you, boss,' he heard Mikey calling. Then the front door opened, there was a draught of cold air, the door closed and the four Kennedys were gone.

He grabbed a chair and dragged it across the kitchen to the

corner where John Dunne and William Ahearn were sitting. John had dozed off and the youth was staring into the fire.

'Not going to the wake with those Kennedys?' Michael asked, prodding his friend John on the arm.

'What's that?' asked Dunne, sitting up and blinking in surprise.

'Are you not going to the wake?'

Michael could tell his friend was embarrassed that he had been caught napping.

'No,' replied Dunne cautiously. 'I think I'll turn in for the night.'

To which Ahearn added quickly, 'My mother's sick, so I can't go either.'

'She is,' Dunne agreed, 'and I must be on my way.'

The door of the sickroom opened and Joanna came out carrying the enamel bowl. It was filled with soapy water. She opened the front door and went outside. It was her intention, he guessed, to tip it away. Next thing his friend Dunne was whispering in his ear.

'I'm off now,' he said, 'but you keep your eye on Joanna.'

First Joanna warns him against John Dunne, and now his friend warns him against her. This was confusing. Why couldn't conversations and transactions be clear and straightforward?

'Come on, Ahearn, I'll walk you home,' said John.

Dunne led the youth away, leaving Michael to his thoughts. He felt suddenly muddled and worried.

What day was it? Thursday, he thought. Thursday night. He looked at the clock. No, it was half-past one on Friday morning. Father Ryan had been on Wednesday, hadn't he, and said Mass?

It was time, Michael decided, yes, it was time Bridget saw the priest again. Good insurance as well. For all he knew there could still be malevolent spirits floating about his house. They had a way, didn't they, of hanging around.

'Simpson,' he called out sharply.

Simpson was talking to Mary Kennedy. Hearing his name, the older man turned and looked at him across the room.

'I've a mind to walk over to Drangan to fetch Father Ryan. Will you see me on the way?'

Now he watched as Simpson glanced at his wife and she nodded.

How puzzling. However, before he had time to think about it he heard Simpson calling, 'Certainly.' He forgot his curiosity about the glance instantly and instead he found himself feeling pleased.

Company, even that of his fat, boring neighbour, was a fine idea on a country road in the middle of the night.

When they were in the lane outside the cottage, Michael asked Simpson to stop for a moment. The lace of one of his boots had come undone. He crouched down, and as he took the wet and muddy end of the lace, he heard Simpson breathing beside him in the darkness.

'It's cold,' said Simpson, stamping his feet.

Michael ignored the remark and glanced back at the dark shape of his cottage. The shutters were closed and silver lines of light were showing at the edges. His home looked strong and secure, he thought, but how misleading was such confidence based on appearance.

He wrapped the lace around his ankle several times and began tying it in a double bow.

Stone walls and wood had no power against fairy magic, and as he had seen with his own eyes, during the whole long exhausting evening, the power of mortal men and women was not much better against a wily adversary. However, he thought firmly, he had administered the herbs; he had tested Bridget in the fire; he would sprinkle Ganey's potion around the house in a day or so; but now he was going to bring in the

214

priest. He was using every means at his disposal and in the end he would win.

'It's very cold,' Simpson repeated.

Michael was now tying the other lace and he grunted in reply. Simpson, with the hedge behind him, was a broad, dark, round shape with a bowler hat resting on his head.

'The walk'll warm us up,' said Michael grimly. He stood and set off smartly in the direction of the Drangan road, swinging his arms briskly like a soldier.

It wasn't long before he heard Simpson trotting a few feet behind him and calling plaintively, 'Wait for me, Michael.'

Blasted slowcoach, he thought. Michael decided to ignore the fellow and continue.

Miraculously, Simpson suddenly appeared at his side, holding his bowler hat and running in his flat-footed way. It was rather like the way a woman ran, thought Michael.

'Why are we rushing?' he heard Simpson enquiring breathlessly.

He decided to say nothing, while wondering to himself if it really hadn't been a mistake to ask Simpson to come.

'Can't we stop for a moment? Please, Michael.' There was a note of desperation in Simpson's voice.

'No,' said Michael, 'you'll just have to keep up.'

By trotting forward, Simpson brought himself abreast with him again. This achieved, he switched to a rapid walk. However, after half a dozen steps, Michael noticed with a certain amusement, the old fool was, lagging again. None the less, seemingly undeterred, Simpson trotted forward until he was once more beside him. Then another half-dozen paces and he was lagging again. A rhythm was forming. Trot, walk, walk, trot, walk, walk . . . They were going very fast and Michael felt trickles of sweat running down his face.

'At this rate, we'll make Drangan in minutes, and it'll be too early to wake up Father Ryan,' Simpson finally ventured beside him.

This really was more than he'd bargained for.

'He'll wake up when he's woken and he'll do as he's told,' Michael muttered back.

'I'm not quite certain he'll be pleased with us, you know, waking him at such an early hour,' Simpson cautioned.

'He's the priest, isn't he? Isn't that what he's for?'

He felt Simpson's arm on his own arm, trying to stop him.

'Father Ryan is an important figure who deserves respect,' said Simpson, 'and I'm speaking not only as a parishioner, but also as his friend.'

Yes, Michael thought, you have spent two years trying to insinuate yourself into the priest's good books. He had noticed: everyone had.

He shook off Simpson's grasp but the impudent man immediately took hold of his arm again.

'Will you stop!' Simpson shouted. 'I'm trying to talk to you,' he continued.

Cleary turned and faced him. 'Say what you want then.'

'We're not running a race, you know. Let's go easy. Let's talk,' he heard Simpson saying in his reasonable voice. However, behind the words, Michael sensed there was something else pressing to come forward into the conversation.

'What else have you to say?'

Simpson opened and closed his mouth and shrugged his shoulders.

'You have something else to say, haven't you? I saw the way you looked at Minnie after I asked you to come with me, and I saw the way she looked back at you. I know you've something to say, so get it off your chest.

A few apologies from Simpson and then his story tumbled out. His post as caretaker on the farm down the road was going to end, inevitably – a source of terror to himself and Minnie – but one solution lay with Michael, his good neighbour. Cleary earned a good wage: in time he would buy his own place with a bit of land. Bridget often said as much. If

Michael recommended them to the Cashel Guardians when they left, it would secure the cottage for himself and Minnie. His wife was always on at him to broach the subject, but he had never found the right time. That was why he was taking this opportunity, he explained in conclusion, to raise the matter.

What a subject and what a time to raise it, thought Michael, when his neighbour finished. He was trying to save Bridget but all Simpson was thinking about was a roof over his head.

'I need the priest,' said Michael firmly, 'and I want him now.'

He turned and walked off down the lane. He was moving very fast. Perhaps he would lose Simpson altogether this time. However, within a few seconds, the heavy plump figure was at his side again.

'We'll be there well before five at this rate,' shouted Simpson, 'and that's far too early to wake the poor man.'

'You always were one for climbing into another man's pocket, weren't you? A toady, that's what you are, Simpson.'

Michael noticed he was angry; he was shaking and spitting as he spoke and punching the air in time to his words.

'I don't damn well care when we get there,' he continued at the top of his lungs, 'and, when we get there, he's damn well getting up.'

'Calm yourself.'

'Go to hell!' Michael shouted back.

'Well, that's settled then,' came Simpson's voice from the darkness behind him. 'I'm not coming with you.'

Good riddance, Michael thought, and turning he saw Simpson standing in the darkness in the middle of the road. He had pulled his fob watch from his waistcoat pocket and struck a match to read the time. For an instant Simpson's jowls were weirdly lit up from below and then the light went out.

'Be seeing you, Simpson,' he called, and laughing he turned again and disappeared into the darkness.

CHAPTER SEVEN

In his dream Father Ryan was a boy in a garden. He was with his mother. They were walking under a trellis together. It was covered with old roses. The blooms were deep creamy whites and lovely rich pinks. Father Ryan wanted to pick a flower. 'No,' said his mother. Father Ryan began to cry. He put his hand into his pocket. He had a handkerchief there. However, when he pulled it out, he found he was holding a telescope instead.

He lifted the eyepiece to his face and looked through. In the distance he saw a mill. The gigantic wooden wheel was turning furiously. He spent some time looking at it. He felt greatly excited. He was particularly captivated by the bright shapes which he could see flashing in the water. For some moments he stood amazed and puzzled. Then he realized what they were. They were fish and they were dead.

He started to cry. He lifted the telescope down from his eye. He was no longer a boy now but a grown man. He was still in the garden and his mother was gone . . .

From somewhere far away came the sound of banging on a door. Father Ryan opened his eyes in darkness. He sat up. Down below, at the rear of the house, he heard Nora pulling back the bolts. He lit a candle and looked at the alarm clock on the bedside table. It was four-thirty. Who on earth wanted him at this time of night?

He lifted back the heavy warm blankets and reached his woollen dressing gown from the hook on the back of the door. He was knotting the cord around his waist when Nora knocked outside.

'Yes, come in.'

She opened the door halfway.

'It's Cleary,' she said apologetically. 'He says his wife's had a bad night and he wants you to come.'

Father Ryan shivered.

'Did he say anything else, apart from that it was urgent?'

'No, only that it was a matter of kill or cure,' she replied and disappeared.

What a strange expression, he thought, pulling on a pair of socks and then his slippers.

He went down to the scullery. He could see the man Cleary through the window. He was staring up intently at the night sky. Father Ryan opened the back door and stepped out.

'Well then, Cleary,' he asked, 'what can I do for you at this time of the morning?'

'Will you please come now to my wife, Bridget. Please Father, straight away, say you will,' said Cleary, the words tumbling out of his mouth.

Father Ryan felt himself instantaneously growing impatient.

'Calm down,' he said. 'Wasn't I with Mrs Cleary just the day before yesterday?'

Starting again and speaking more slowly, Michael described Bridget's deteriorating physical condition, then implored Father Ryan to visit her at once.

'Yes, I will,' agreed the priest, when he had finished. Father Ryan was feeling cold now and he wanted to go back inside.

'You go home now,' he said in his reassuring voice, 'and I'll follow on as soon as I'm ready.'

'When, exactly?'

'Once I'm dressed and ready.'

He went upstairs to dress.

Meanwhile, in the kitchen below, Nora stoked the fire and put on the kettle. Then she woke the boy who slept in the tiny downstairs bedroom.

'Saddle Father's horse,' she said to him, as he sat up in bed rubbing his eyes. 'Then run over to Mr Shee's farm and tell him that after Father Ryan has been to Mrs Cleary, he'll be calling up for his breakfast.'

Father Ryan mounted the horse. The leather of the saddle was cold underneath him. He trotted down the short lane and turned on to the road. It was no longer night but not yet morning. The puddles were tarnished silver. Glancing over the ragged hedges, he saw the fields were wet, empty and still. He felt a little depressed and gloomy. He was hungry as well.

When he arrived at Cleary's he found one of the Shee sons sitting on the wall.

'Tell your father I'll be down presently,' he said. He led his horse into the yard.

A minute later he was stepping through the front door. Michael Cleary got up from the fire and hurried towards him.

'You got here,' blurted Cleary. He seemed surprised.

The priest noticed the old man, Boland, snoring in a chair, and Mrs Burke's daughter, Katie, lying under blankets in a corner. The mother, Mrs Burke, was sweeping the hearth.

'Good morning, Father,' she called to him politely.

He nodded and sniffed the air. What was that smell? he wondered. It was herbal, pungent and deeply unpleasant. He grasped the handle of the sickroom door. Cleary, he noticed, was standing close by his side.

'Wait out here, please,' said Father Ryan.

Inside he found Mrs Cleary sitting up in bed, leaning back against the bolster and pillows. He closed the door behind, then waited for the sound of Cleary's footsteps as he moved away outside in the kitchen. He heard Bridget's confession and administered the host. Then he asked, 'How are you?'

'Very faint, Father. I don't know what's the matter with me.'

The vile smell was in the room as well. Perhaps that had something to do with the way she was feeling.

'Do you think you should open the window?'

'Oh, the smell is the herbs and that'll go away presently,' she said. Then she looked away. She was embarrassed, he presumed, because she had let slip that she was taking a herbal cure.

'I am ill,' she stressed.

He could hear she was breathing in short, sharp breaths.

'Did you sleep last night?'

He noticed Dr Crean's medicine bottle on the window ledge.

'Barely,' and nodding in the direction of the door she continued, 'They hardly leave me alone.'

Her eyes darted from the window, to the corner of the bedroom, to the door, to his face and back to the window again as she spoke.

'Surely that's better than lying here all day and night on your own and being ignored, isn't it?'

That was when he noticed a mark on her forehead like a blister. There was also what appeared to be bruising around her neck.

'By the way, how did you hurt yourself?' he asked.

'I'm not hurt,' she said, seemingly uninterested in his question. 'But Father, I'm telling you they're always pulling at me, coming in and out, and they all know what's right, claim they do anyhow, even after the Doctor's been and I have his medicine.'

Father Ryan got to his feet, walked over to the window ledge and picked up the bottle. Holding the brown glass against the candle, he saw it was half empty.

He pulled out the cork, upturned the bottle on to his finger and then dabbed a spot of the medicine on to his tongue. The taste was a mixture of camphor and eucalyptus. He disliked the idea of the herbs; however, at least modern medicine was also being taken.

And furthermore, he thought, Mrs Cleary was just tired

and nervous because nobody would let her sleep. This left him with one remaining anxiety.

'You still haven't explained the markings,' he said again.

'I knocked my head when I fell and this on the neck came from having my scarf on too tight.'

Father Ryan returned to the kitchen where he found the others. Lit by the pale light seeping through the now unshuttered window, they were seated in a silent circle around the small fire. Were they sad? he wondered. Then he decided, no, they too were simply tired, like Bridget. Sickness was a terrible strain on a household.

'Cleary, can I have a word with you?' he said.

'Certainly, Father.'

He led Cleary outside, closing the door after them.

'Is Mrs Cleary receiving Dr Crean's medicine regularly?' he asked.

'I have no faith in it,' replied Cleary politely.

'This is a great pity,' he began crossly but then, remembering the news he had heard about the death of Cleary's father, he checked himself. Obviously his parishioner was upset, distraught even, which probably explained his odd, jumpy manner.

'To have gone to the trouble of calling out and prescribing, as Dr Crean did, and then not to give what he has left for the patient is perhaps foolish.'

Cleary listened silently.

'I'm certain the medicine is good and that you ought to give it to her as directed. I smelt it when I was in her room; in fact I tasted some. And I should think it would do her good. Also, I think Mrs Cleary needs a good deal of sleep.'

Father Ryan buttoned his coat, expressed his regret that Michael's father was dead, and went to the yard to fetch his horse. He was looking forward to breakfast.

In her dream Katie was in an orchard with a horse. There were apples all over the ground and the horse's hooves were crushing them into the mud. From the orchard gate she watched with horror. I'll never get an apple, she thought, they'll all be gone . . .

Then the bang of the front door slamming shut woke Katie abruptly from her dream.

Her eyes lifted and she was awake instantly, her stomach tight.

Through the window she glimpsed Father Ryan's brown leather boot as he went past on his horse. Next thing she saw Michael was at the door and she guessed he had just come in.

For a moment his angry face hovered on the far side of the room and then he turned and shouted in the direction in which Father Ryan was disappearing, 'The people have some remedies which have more effect than doctor's medicine.'

Then Michael began to pace angrily up and down the room muttering to himself.

Her mother, who was sitting by the fire, sprang up and sprinted over to Michael.

'Do you want some breakfast?' she asked.

Her mother had put on her gentle voice. Katie recognized it. Her mother only used it when someone was angry, like Michael was now.

Michael stopped. He looked at her mother.

'Don't you ever think about anything but food?' he said.

'I thought you were hungry.'

Her mother swallowed. Katie could see her mother's throat as it moved. Her mother was anxious. She didn't like anyone shouting, and she especially didn't like Michael shouting. Katie didn't like it either.

'You know,' continued Michael to her mother, 'you are a nasty, meddling, interfering . . .'

Katie felt her thighs shivering. The kitchen was silent and then suddenly Michael was laughing. Her mother always said

223

there was no rhyme or reason to him, and her mother was right.

Michael stopped laughing and he looked now at her mother.

'You've been a great help to me, Joanna,' he said, 'and I count you among my few friends, but I've still got a long way to go, and I want to know, now, are you with me?'

'Yes . . .'

While Michael sat and dozed in a chair her mother made his breakfast – eggs, rashers, toast and tea.

'Your food, Michael,' she heard her mother calling quietly when it was ready. Michael woke up and ate quickly, and when he was finished Katie heard him telling her mother that he was not going to work.

'You must be tired, I supposed,' was all her mother said.

Michael stared into the embers in the fire. When he went silent he was best left alone. Her mother always said this and Katie knew she was right . . .

A few minutes later her mother called her to the table for tea and bread, and after she had finished eating her mother told her to go and play outside. Her mother said she wanted to get on with cleaning the house, and she didn't want Katie getting under her feet.

She put on her coat and went out. It was cold that morning. She wanted to go back in straight away but she knew her mother would only send her out again if she did. She spent a penny behind the bushes and began to walk up and down the lane. A few people passed and said hello to her. She began to feel warmer; she began to feel better . . .

Towards midday she was standing on the wall and singing to herself. The sun came out and her mother ran out of the house carrying the big black scissors. She watched her mother run to the bank a little way down the lane where there were daffodils growing. Her mother cut a pile of flowers and came back with them heaped up in her apron.

'I'm the king of the castle,' she called to her mother.

'Get down, you dirty rascal,' her mother called back.

'Can I come in?' she asked.

'You can,' her mother said, 'but mind you leave Michael alone.'

She jumped down and ran after her mother through the front door, only to collide with Michael Cleary who was standing in the doorway of Bridget's room and staring at his wife as she lay sleeping in bed.

'What is it, Michael?' her mother said. Her mother was beside her. She could smell the bitter smell of the cut daffodils her mother was holding in her apron.

'I can see what you can't see, Joanna Burke,' said Michael to her mother.

He was in the sort of mood that always ended with talk of fairies. Katie knew this and she felt anxious again.

'What's that? What can you see?' her mother asked.

Michael was angry and her mother was speaking in her gentle voice again.

'I don't know whether you're to be trusted,' he said. 'I rather think you're not.'

Katie sensed her mother breathing deeply at her side.

'I don't know what you mean,' she said.

Joanna went away to the kitchen table and Katie followed her quickly.

Her mother tumbled the daffodils onto the oil-cloth and they began to arrange them together in the white and blue striped jug.

And as they did Katie heard Michael Cleary pacing up and down the kitchen floor again . . .

'I'm going out for turf,' her mother announced, and taking the creel, she ran out through the front door and round the side of the house to the turf shed at the back.

Katie didn't want to look at Michael, and she didn't want him to catch her eye, either. So she stared at the yellow blossoms of the flowers. They didn't have much of a smell, she noticed. She was frightened of Michael, but as Pat was by the fire it wasn't like she was alone.

Then she heard a noise outside. Katie couldn't quite make out what it was and Pat stood up suddenly and said, 'What was that?'

They ran out together, she and the old man, and they found her mother on the floor of the turf shed. She had fainted.

When her mother woke up they got her to her feet and led her back to the house. They met Michael coming out through the front door. He didn't ask about her mother; he just said he was going to Drangan for sugar and vanished . . .

In the afternoon it began to rain; Michael Cleary came home with the sugar and it was discovered there was no milk. Her mother said she would go to a farm nearby where they sold milk. Michael Cleary gave her a shilling.

Her mother dressed them both for outside, then went into the bedroom to say goodbye to Bridget. She was sitting up in bed, smiling, cheerful it seemed.

'Did Michael give you some money?' asked Bridget.

'He did,' her mother said.

'You're going to need a shilling. Are you sure he's given you money?'

'Yes, I'm sure.'

Her mother got the shilling out to show Bridget, and at the very moment Bridget was handing the money back to her mother, Michael Cleary burst in to the bedroom and started shouting.

'I want to know what's going on,' he said.

Bridget said, 'Nothing,' and her mother hurried out and she hurried after her . . .

When they got back with the milk they found Bridget and Michael were arguing.

'Come in here,' Michael shouted.

226

Her mother went into the sickroom and Katie went in after her. She didn't want her mother out of her sight. Katie felt tense again, the same as when she had woken up.

Michael was by Bridget's bed. He was trying to make Bridget drink holy water from a spoon.

'He says I rubbed that shilling on my leg like a fairy to make another shilling,' shouted Bridget. 'But I didn't. I gave it back to you. You saw everything, Joanna. Tell him I'm not a fairy.'

There was a lot of shouting which she didn't understand and then Katie heard her mother saying she would get the neighbours Tom Smyth and Francis Hogan.

'They've known Bridget since she was a child,' her mother said, 'they'll vouch for her,' and Michael agreed.

She went with her mother to the farms to collect the men and by the time the four of them got back to the house at Ballyvadlea it was dark.

When they came into the kitchen they found John Dunne and her mother's mother, Mary Kennedy, were seated at the fireplace.

Her mother went to Bridget's door and was about to knock on it when Michael said, 'Leave her alone. She's getting dressed.'

Mr Hogan and Mr Smyth sat down by the fire and lit their pipes. Bridget came out of her bedroom and sat down in the middle of everybody.

'How are you, Bridget?' asked Tom Smyth.

'Middling, my husband is making a fairy of me.'

As she said this, Bridget pointed at Michael, who was sitting alone at the kitchen table.

'Don't mind him and don't be afraid,' said Mary Kennedy to Bridget.

Mary Kennedy turned to Michael Cleary.

'Would you give your poor wife a drop of milk?' she said.

Katie felt her stomach moving. Michael's face was dark, as

it always was whenever there was talk of a fairy. She glanced quickly at her mother and her mother nodded back.

'No, I would not,' said Michael.

'Why not?'

'I'm busy. That's why not!'

'I never asked for any milk without paying for it,' said Bridget abruptly.

'Don't mind your husband,' said Mary Kennedy, 'You'll have your drink by and by.'

Now Bridget turned to her own mother, Joanna.

'Did I keep the shilling?' she asked.

Katie sensed her legs trembling again.

'No,' her mother said.

'Thanks be to God, there's no use in saying anything further.'

The room fell silent. Michael Cleary got up from the table and began pacing up and down.

Suddenly Bridget shouted out, 'There's no pishogues on me, thanks be to God.'

The door opened and William, James and Patrick Kennedy came into the house. They had come from the wake at Ballynure. They were very happy and smiling and she wondered if they would be able to make everybody else happy. The men smelt of tobacco and porter and they told everyone that their youngest brother, Mikey Kennedy, was still at the wake. No one, she noticed, seemed to be in the least surprised about this.

The three brothers removed their coats and sat with the others around the fire, and William began telling everyone about the wake. Suddenly Bridget pointed at the window and shouted, 'Our neighbour Jim Shehan's there!'

'What's wrong, Bridgie?' said Michael.

'And the peelers are at the window, mind me now.'

Tom Smyth and Francis Hogan stood up and said they

had to go. John Dunne stood up and said he would go with them.

Her mother said, 'Katie, help the gentlemen on with their coats.'

Standing in the doorway, Tom Smyth took a penny out of his waistcoat pocket and put it into her hand.

'You're a good girl, Katie,' he said, squeezing her nose between his index and middle finger.

He stepped outside and she followed after him crying out, 'Thank you, thank you.'

She was happy. In Cleary's no one ever gave her money, never before now anyhow. Watching the men walking away down the path, she wondered what she was going to buy.

Her two favourite sweets were butterscotch and humbug twirls. She liked bull's-eyes as well except the aniseed centres left the inside of her mouth feeling funny, as if it had been scoured. Toffee too was wonderful, she thought, and she remembered the brown, sticky block which was kept in the shop. She imagined Mrs Murphy scoring a line across the end with her special toffee knife, then snapping off a big piece for her.

The men called to her from the gate as they stepped into the lane. She waved and Tom Smyth waved back and then the men moved away, talking quietly. In a few seconds they had disappeared into the darkness.

She yawned. It was nice to be outside in the cold after the warm room, and she was waking up.

She put her hand into the shaft of light coming through the half-open door, and looked down at her penny lying there on her palm. She made out the face of Queen Victoria. She was an old woman with rounded cheeks and hair piled high under her crown.

Of course, she might buy a ribbon. Turquoise or red might be nice.

'Katie,' her mother called from the kitchen. Her mother came through the door.

Her mother had one eye that was smaller than the other, and gold studs in her ears reflecting the lamplight. Her mother was a worrier too: she worried about the corns on Katie's little toes; she worried about her chesty cough; and she worried when Katie's ears were pierced and the holes got sore and started to ooze just like Mrs McGoldrick said they would. The sores cleared up, of course, as Mrs McGoldrick also said they would, after Katie washed her lobes every night for a week with hot water and salt.

'You'll catch your death out here without your coat,' Joanna said.

Her mother's hand came to her forehead.

'Come inside.'

'It's too hot in there.'

'Just do as you're told.' Her mother put an arm over her shoulder and steered her back in. The heat of the room closed around her like a wave as the door shut behind.

Her three uncles, Patrick, William and James, along with Bridget, old Pat and Mary Kennedy, were sitting around the fire, while Michael sat alone at the kitchen table. In one hand he held the black-handled knife, while with the other he held a loaf of bread. He was poised, staring into the distance, like someone who had forgotten what they had started to do.

Katie did not like Michael. She did not like the way he blustered and shouted. She did not like the way he made Bridget take the terrible herbs. She did not like the way he was always looking at her in an angry, cross way, like she was a pest who was interfering and getting in his way. She had known him all the years he had lived in Ballyvadlea, and she had been in his house and he had been in her house, and yet never once had he given her a penny. She was not sure that she had ever really liked him.

'Go and sit down,' her mother whispered. Her mother did

not like Michael Cleary much either, or so she suspected. But her mother was always polite when talking to him, and at pains to please him. He probably frightened her mother, Katie thought, like he frightened her.

She decided to put herself in the corner behind Pat's chair. As she moved across, she kept her eyes firmly fixed on the ground. This was so that Michael could not catch her eye, and then scowl back at her.

She sat down on the floor. It was hot in the room and she rolled up her sleeves. There were little hairs on her arms, and it was funny the way they seemed to grow right out of the middle of her freckles.

Her mother was making tea. She watched Joanna hand a cup to her uncle Patrick. He started to drink noisily. She only liked tea if it was milky and heavily sugared, but in Cleary's she was never offered any. If she was thirsty, it was only ever milk or water that she got. This left her with the feeling that Michael and Bridget thought she was not old enough, and this made her mad.

The talk of the adults ebbed and flowed around her. To pass the time she thought about her penny again. Every so often she opened her hand, stared at it, then shut her fist tight around it. She really ought to give the penny to her mother to keep safe for her, but she was enjoying the feeling of the disc warming in her palm, and the coppery smell on her skin.

Katie began to feel drowsy. She put her head against the wall and drifted into a delicious state. She was half-way to sleep. The kitchen around her fell away, and she imagined herself in an old walled garden. The branches on the apple trees were covered with lichen and the fruit on the branches was red. There were daisies underfoot and white butterflies in the air. At the bottom of the garden was a stream, and sparkling amongst the brown stones in the water were sixpences and shillings.

She heard her three young uncles shuffling into old Pat's

231

bedroom. They were all complaining of exhaustion. There was laughter as her three uncles lay down on Pat's bed. Pat squeezed in with them. Then Mary Kennedy laid out a straw mattress on the floor beside them. As Mary Kennedy lay down, Katie heard the old woman complaining, 'It's a sad day indeed when my sons put themselves on the bed while I have to put myself on the floor.'

'Quiet now, Mother,' Katie heard someone say and everybody laughed.

Her aunt Bridget was sitting on the bench just in front of her. She had a sad face, Katie thought. Her mother was on a chair nearby. Her mother was yawning. Michael remained at the kitchen table. His back was towards her and she could not see his face. The only noises were the sighing of the fire and her uncles in the bed. Katie wished she would never have to marry a man like Michael, then she lifted her legs up to her chest, pulled herself into a tight ball and fell asleep.

Fire hissing, pleasant, restful, thought Bridget. Hip hurting, slightly. But surprisingly, not as much as it ought. Bad burn though, big white blister. Seen it when dressing. Skin down the leg sort of red and tight. Scorched. Otherwise not too damaged. Miracle really, escaped so lightly. Treacherous day though. The shilling business. What was all that about? Rubbing it on the thigh. As for Hogan and Smyth, totally useless. Smoked their pipes and ran away. Couldn't stand it. Too much tension. Michael pacing up and down like a caged animal. Madman more like it. Where does he get it? 'You are a fairy. You are . . .' Bridget is what! Lunacy. Although, has to be said, today not bad. Not like yesterday. Signs of improvement in Michael. And Old Boot Polish largely absent too. Another cause for joy. All in all, not a great day but it could have been worse. And actually, amazingly, head not so painful, throat not so sore, chest not so tight. Sickness in retreat and modest improvement noted. Tomorrow better and next day better again. Sunday – St Patrick's Day. Might be well enough to go to the parade in Clonmel. Go with Michael. Day out. Bring Father of course. Not a bad idea. Suggest that. Not yet though. Silence the better part of valour. Keep quiet for the time being. Remember Carmel. Keep very still. Don't talk. Don't confront. Don't argue. Don't even suggest. And all this will go away. Just disappear. In six weeks, six months, six years, 'Fairy – what fairy!' no more nonsense about fairy blasts and changelings. Jesus, Mary and Joseph, where did all that come from? Old Boot Polish, bloody interfering lunatic. Well, he was for the high road. Watch out! Once Bridget was better, a few home truths whispered in Michael's ear and his bacon would be cooked. He'd be old news. Dead meat. Out on his ear. Yes, sir. Hooray! Lovely feeling – anticipating revenge. But she had to pick her time. Oh yes. Gauge opportunity. The *Kidnapped* story could be taken up the wrong way, she shouldn't forget. Michael mad, yes. He might think Bridget ensnared Old Boot Polish by playing the harlot's part. He might, yes. Very good. Point taken. Absolutely. Now what? Bridget wanted something. What did Bridget want? Tea! Good idea. Tea. Mouth dry. Yes. Where was Michael? Over at the table. Doing what? Holding bread-knife, staring into space. Best left. Good for him . . .

Sitting at the kitchen table, holding the black-handled knife in one hand, his other hand resting on the loaf, Michael felt himself growing quiet, then tranced. His mind, it seemed to him, had been whirring and turning at a frantic pace for days if not weeks. And it wasn't until he had sat down a little while ago, and had allowed himself to stare vacantly at the back of the front door without thinking about anything, that he had come to realize just how tired he was.

But then of course, he thought, he had hardly slept. He was bound to feel exhausted.

He remained like this, awake and yet with his mind

unfocused on anything, for some minutes. The only noises were those of the fire hissing and, more occasionally, one or other of the Kennedys or their mother murmuring as they turned in their sleep.

'Can I have a cup of tea, Joanna,' he heard his wife saying at last.

After several minutes of blissful silence the sound of a human voice was almost hurtful. He felt himself suddenly feeling very deeply irritated, even angry. It was the same as the feeling he got when, having just fallen asleep, he was woken abruptly.

'Yes, of course,' he heard Joanna reply.

She stood up, scraping the legs of her chair on the stone flags on the floor.

The noise was unbearable, he thought. Then a moment later his anger vanished and he was filled with an inspiration. Now he knew exactly what to do next.

'You'll eat something first before you get a cup of tea,' he said, and he added, 'Nourishment. That's what you need, Bridget. No wonder you're ill.'

He began to saw at the loaf with the bread-knife and two thick slices fell on to the breadboard. They reminded him of the log sections which they sometimes had in the workshop.

He stretched across the table, swiped his knife across the soft butter, and spread the yellow stuff over the two slices.

The food was going to do Bridget good, she was going to enjoy it, and it was going to make her better. This certainty was a new and pleasurable feeling.

He fetched the blackberry jam from the dresser and spread it thickly. He even made sure the top edges of the crusts were covered.

Then, looking up, he saw Joanna was handing Bridget a cup of tea. He felt offended. His irritation shot back to the level of a few minutes earlier.

'Didn't I say food first?' he shouted.

In one step he was by the bench where Bridget was sitting. He snatched the cup from her.

'Didn't I say food first?' Michael shouting.

Oh no. What in heaven's name now. Michael suddenly wrenching cup and saucer out of hand.

'My mother always said you got sick putting food down on a stomach filled with liquid,' Michael shouting.

What was this? The wisdom of Agatha. Where was Joanna? What was she doing? Why wasn't she here? She could do something. Oh yes, there she was. Gliding away. Conspicuous by her absence. As usual.

'You must eat first,' Michael shouting.

All right, yes. Michael was tipping tea towards fire. Embers hissing. Joanna, why aren't you helping? Why aren't you saying something? Intervening?

'What are you looking at?' Michael shouting.

What was this? Bridget was not looking at anything. No, of course, Michael was not speaking to Bridget, no. It was Katie staring up at him. Never did like the child, did he? No, never. Now Joanna settling down with her daughter. Comforting . . . Lucky Joanna. Katie to snuggle up to. Must be good, time like this, warm body. Where was Michael now? Had to keep eyes skinned. No knowing what was coming next. Oh yes, there he was, getting plate. No food, hours seemingly, quite hungry actually, yes.

'Move along,' Michael saying.

Michael sitting. Michael's body against hers. Michael shoving her along the bench some more. Michael's arm was round her shoulder. Michael was trying to be friendly. Human touch. Better than human hurt. Certainly was.

He had lifted his right arm, draped it across her shoulder and squeezed. That felt nice. She had thinned down the previous weeks but Bridget was still a fine woman. He felt the side of her breast pressing against his chest. When was the last time they had slept together? He could not remember. It was several weeks, anyhow. That was the trouble with having so many callers to the house. They stopped a couple being a normal husband and wife. But he'd get Bridget better, he'd get rid of the pack of them, and he'd have her back to himself.

'You have one of these, now,' said Michael quietly, not shouting. Bread and jam. On a plate. Two slices. Took one. Lifted it to mouth. Sweet taste of blackberry first, butter next, bread lastly. It was soda bread, brown. Teeth moving. Tastes all mixing. Food quite welcome. Second bite. Third. Fourth. The slice was eaten.

'Here. Have the other.'

Her stomach was full. She shook her head. But plate stayed where it was with the slice in the middle. Three colours she saw. Brown crust, yellow butter, purple jam. Appetizing, yes, but she was full.

'Go on. Take it,' Michael saying, not quite shouting but nearly.

'I've had enough.'

Amazing, her powers of speech still there, intact. And sentence quitely spoken, nicely pitched too.

'You'll take it,' Michael shouting, a fully fledged roar from the back of the throat. But she couldn't. Not another mouthful. She was packed with bread and jam, from the stomach right up to the back of the throat. Felt like that, anyway. Tea now, yes, that was what was required. Hadn't it been promised?

'I want some tea, please.'

Hats off. Thoughts into words. But what was this? Michael staring. Strange, rapt expression. Michael blinking. Michael staring again. Angry now. Yes. No doubt. Oh hell! About to start again.

As she stared back at him, he saw what he had noticed sometimes before and then lost sight of. Her eyes weren't Bridget's lovely eyes, they were cold, grey and lifeless. Seeing this, he knew suddenly that all the work of the night before had been in vain. The fairy was still there, looking back at him, while the real Bridget was locked away in Kilnagranagh he didn't doubt, because that was where it had all started when she had been waiting for Mr Hagan. And she was waiting there for him still. Waiting for him to come and rescue her. He saw it all now, instantly, in another flash of inspiration.

'You'll do what I say,' he said. 'Come on, now, eat!'

He gripped the fairy's neck in the elbow of the arm over its shoulder. The bench was shaking beneath them.

'I'm warning you . . .'

He pushed the bread against its mouth. The fairy wrenched its head away.

'Eat it,' he shouted.

The creature wriggled and writhed. The bread crumbled and lumps of butter and jelly rolled on to the floor.

'Bridget, I'm warning you . . . You eat this now . . .'

The fairy was stubborn. Then it dug its nails into his arm. Nothing else for it. He flipped it backwards off the bench. It landed on its back, its head hitting the flagstones an instant after with a crack.

He shoved the bench aside, knelt down and shoved what bits of bread were left in his hand into its mouth.

'Swallow it,' he shouted, and then a moment later, 'Is it down?'

'Is it down?' he asked again.

He could see its pink tongue, and the edges of its teeth. He wanted to see it swallow. It was coughing and gagging.

'Bridget Cleary, come back,' Michael called.

Moving her tongue, touching teeth, she was spitting out the

bits of bread. How was the breathing? Still there? Yes. Was she alive? Yes. Hanging on.

'Leave her alone, don't you see it's Bridget and you're choking her,' Joanna shouting.

Joanna, yes, at last, after so long a silence. She would speak up. No! Had to speak up herself. Make a word. Yes. What word? Any.

'Joanna.'

Yes, again.

'Joanna.'

'You'll choke her,' Joanna shouting.

'Don't mind her. It's not Bridget I've had at home these past weeks,' Michael shouting.

Eyes closing. Wrong, wrong. This was Bridget. Now what was this? Michael was holding wrists, hand was flopping down. Move it. Move fingers. No, too tired. Too much effort. Couldn't be done. What about . . . Yes. She had to lift eyelids. Open them. That was right. That way Michael would know. She was alive.

'She's alive,' Joanna speaking.

Yes, Joanna, louder again. Speak for Bridget. Now Michael holding lamp and looking down at her.

'I got you by the law of God and I'll get you back by the law of God,' Michael shouting.

Oh no. Fairy lore. Speak. No one else would. No one else could. Pronounce name. Enunciate. Mouth opening . . .

Nothing though coming out, no words, no word, mouth speaking but what? Speaking silence. Mouth speaking silence. Now eyelids lowering, breathing fading, eyelids closing, sliding, darkening.

There was froth, he saw, on the side of its mouth. It opened its mouth to speak but he heard no words coming out. Then the eyelids closed. There was no sound of breathing.

'I believe it is dead,' he said calmly.

It was done. He had laid down the law and the fairy had departed. Simple as that.

And now another inspiration came to him.

The following night he would go to Kilnagranagh rath. Bridget would ride out from the trees on a white horse. She would be tied to the saddle with ropes. He would cut her free, and then he would have his smiling, handsome, original wife back.

He had never felt so tired. What a struggle.

Suddenly, he became aware that great clouds of smoke were billowing out of the chimney of the lamp he was holding.

He set it down on the table and turned the wheel which worked the mechanism inside. The wick shrank and the smoking stopped. Now he noticed that the glass chimney was black with soot. He made a mental note to clean it the next day.

He looked around the room. There were cups and saucers on the mantelpiece. The floor was filthy. Ash was piled up under the grate. In fact, he decided, he would get the whole place tidied up and ready for Bridget's return. She would want to come home to a clean house. Yes, it would be a nice thing to do.

He bent down and undid the buckle of the fairy's belt. After he had pulled the belt from around the waist, he pulled the skirt off.

He could hardly wait for Bridget to come home again. He had missed her terribly over the preceding weeks. Of course, they had had their difficulties down the years; that was inevitable – they were married; and he had said hard things and done hurtful things. However, he was truly sorry now, yes, he was.

He undid the buttons on the jacket. Then he lifted the body into a sitting position and pulled away the sleeve from one of the arms. It was a difficult task, he thought, stripping an inert body, and another pair of hands would make it easier.

He looked across at Joanna. She was crouched on the ground, huddled against Katie. He tried to catch her eye but failed. Obviously, he thought, unwilling to help.

In the weeks without her, he had come to see how important Bridget was to him. Yes, so when she came home, he was going to shower her with love. He was going to prove this to her.

Every morning, from now on, he was going to smile at her. He was going to bring her tea in bed, as he used to do at the beginning of their marriage. And every night he was going to hold her tight in his arms.

Bridget would never be sad any more because he would never make her sad any more.

Holding the body propped up with one hand he managed to pull the jacket off the other arm with some difficulty. Then he let the body fall back to the floor.

'Don't you realize there's a wake to be organized?' he called across.

There was going to be a Christian burial even if it was a fairy.

'Come on, Joanna, there's work to be done,' he continued. 'Turn down the bedclothes on Bridgie's bed.'

He watched as Joanna dragged herself to her feet and slowly traipsed across the kitchen, her daughter following. They filed into Bridget's old room, and before long he heard the sound of the bolster being plumped up.

Good, he thought, that was right.

Instead of sitting around and moping, Joanna was off her arse at last and doing something constructive. It was her slatternly laziness at a time like this that he found so particularly irritating. Didn't she have eyes? Didn't she realize what had to be done? Actually, now he came to think about it, it was staggering that he had even had to ask her to get the bed ready.

He picked up the left hand and began tugging at the wedding ring on the third finger.

He managed to work the ring down as far as the knuckle but he couldn't get it any further.

Obviously, this fairy had much bigger hands than Bridget.

Well, he thought, there was no alternative.

He put its finger into his mouth and sucked on the skin.

After a few seconds he took the finger out of his mouth and turned the gold band under to get it wet all over. Then he was able to slip the ring over the wrinkled flesh and off the end of the finger.

He stood up, opened his handkerchief and put the ring into the middle. That was a particularly cunning ploy on their part, to provide the interloper with the same ring. It showed what? – a great determination to pull off the swindle. But he'd seen through it.

For a start it was the body. The fairy was big and gawky, whereas Bridget was finely boned and slight. And he knew Bridget too well, after eight years of intimacy; he knew every hair on her head, every scrap of skin, every joint and sinew of her body.

Then there was the matter of health and well-being. The substitute was sick the whole time, while Bridget was hardly sick a day in her whole life.

Finally, there was temperament. Bridget was always warm and funny, whereas this one was unstintingly peevish and cranky.

It was absolutely extraordinary, he mused, that they thought they could smuggle this counterfeit into his house and that he would live with it for the rest of his life as if it were his wife. It was extraordinary, he agreed with himself, yes, and quite ridiculous.

He heard a sound like a low moan and looked down. What was this? The fairy was moving.

He lifted the lamp across and peered down. Was it moving? It was very, very hard to see indeed. He lowered the lamp. Well, there was only one way to solve the matter, finally, and for all time.

He got on a chair and reached up for the paraffin can which lived on top of the dresser. It was pale blue tin with studs down one side. They had lost the cap somehow, and as usual the neck was stuffed with a rag.

Yes, there was no alternative, he thought as he climbed down from the chair. He was just going to have to fight fire with fire.

He pulled the rag away and began tipping the paraffin on to the shape on the floor, soaking the chemise which was all that it was now wearing.

The paraffin fell in dribbles and splashes and its sharp smell drifted up.

When he judged the body was well and truly doused, he cleaned his hand with the rag. Then he took a long ash stick which was standing against the fireplace and carefully knotted the rag around one end. He put it into the fire. The rag caught and yellow flames jumped up.

He swivelled slowly, holding the burning stick well in front of himself, then he lowered it slowly. As the rag touched the pool of paraffin which had spread from the body across the floor, it caught with a whoosh. Suddenly the flames were everywhere, along the legs and up the back.

He heard a scream. For a moment, he thought it might be the fairy, but then he realized it was a childish cry. He looked behind and saw it was Katie. The child was standing in the doorway of Bridget's old room.

Now Joanna darted out, and before he could stop her, she took hold of the chemise. She gave a tug and the whole thing came away from the body. Suddenly, it seemed to him that if Joanna wasn't careful, there was a danger she too was going to catch fire.

He lifted his foot and kicked the flaming bundle out of her hands. It soared in an arc across the kitchen and landed on the hearthstone, where it flared and flamed noisily.

He turned back to the figure on the bare floor. He tipped

the gallon can several times, sploshing paraffin around the body. Every time the liquid caught it whooshed almost as if the paraffin itself were gasping for breath.

'Her eyes are open,' Joanna shouted. 'She's not dead.'

She tried to run forward but he blocked her path.

'I'll burn you too if you come any closer,' he shouted.

He pointed the brand at her.

'This is not Bridget my wife, on the floor here. I have not had Bridget at home with me for weeks now.'

Joanna stepped back. He tipped the can again. With each new splash the paraffin roared even more loudly. The flames were leaping as high as the mantelpiece.

'She's alive,' Joanna cried.

'Shut up, Joanna. You wait, you will soon see a witch going up that chimney.'

He heard a whimpering coming from the floor. It was pain, he realised. But that was none of his concern, he told himself. Rules were rules and as the creature must have always known there was always a right of recourse to fire. Flame had always been the test of a fairy, from the beginning of time probably.

The door of the other bedroom opened, and Pat Boland shouted out, 'What's going on?' Mary Kennedy and her three sons appeared an instant later behind him.

Joanna started shouting at her brothers, telling them to put the flames out. Bridget was burnt, Joanna screamed, but maybe she was not burnt too badly. They would get the doctor up from the dispensary. And she would go for the peelers, she said, as she ought to have done hours before.

The police, he thought. This was too much. Asking them in was only going to make a bad situation worse. What did they know? Nothing about this. Summonses and dog licences, that's all they were good for.

Pat was now advancing towards him.

'You're burning my daughter,' he shouted incredulously.

The three Kennedy brothers lined up behind him. So that was their game. Four to one. Well, he'd show them.

'You dirty pack,' said Michael, cutting the air with the brand as if it were a sword and making a whistling noise. 'Now I see you would all rather have her with the fairies than with me.'

'Oh my God,' muttered William.

'For the love of God, stop it, Michael,' cried James a moment later.

'She is not my wife,' Michael shouted back. 'She's an old deceiver sent in place of my wife, and she's been deceiving me not just these last twenty days, but these last eight or nine months. And she deceived the priest today, too. But she won't deceive anyone any more; and as I started with her, so I will finish her.'

Mary Kennedy now pushed towards him. 'What have you done to the creature? You're roasting her.'

Michael stabbed towards her with the brand and she jumped back.

'It's not Bridget.' He widened his eyes. He pointed the brand at them all. 'And I am not going to keep an old witch in place of my wife. I must have my own Bridget back.'

'Burn her, if you like,' James shouted at him, suddenly white-faced, and he guessed panic-stricken. 'But give us the key and let us out.'

The room was filling with smoke and Michael felt his eyes smarting. Everyone was coughing.

Michael sprinkled more paraffin over Bridget. As the flames leapt up, he felt their heat on his face, and fearing he might scorch himself he jumped back. Then he turned to face everybody again, and at the same time drew himself to his full height.

'Come on,' he appealed to them, 'let's put her on the fire and then we can all have Bridget back.'

Pat Boland was coughing and spluttering, as much from the smoke as emotion, Michael presumed.

'I'll do anything to keep my daughter,' Pat Boland shouted.

Michael watched now as Bridget's father turned to Patrick Kennedy who was standing behind him.

'Well then,' said Pat Boland, 'come on. Let's do it, and perhaps God will be good enough to send Bridget back.'

Pat took up the spade leaning by the wall near the front door and, together with Patrick and Michael, he helped to roll the flaming body round and round across the floor, until it was nearly up against the grate. Bridget was on her side, her back towards the fire. Now the men worked the spade under her hip. It was difficult work. The body was heavy and they could not get too close because of the flames. But at last they got the spade in place. Then they lifted, hoisting the body up by the middle but leaving Bridget's head and feet on the ground. Arms straining, and grunting loudly, they let Bridget slide off the spade and into the grate. Michael put in his booted foot then, to hold her there, while Pat and her cousin Patrick folded her legs over one end of the hob, and then her head and shoulders over the other.

Michael looked around. The others were standing stock still. He looked down. The flames from the grate were licking up around the middle of the body. The paraffin on the legs was still burning as well. He sniffed. The room smelt, it was like burnt pork. The smoke was growing thicker and blacker and he had to cough, a long hacking cough which left him feeling sore at the back of his throat.

'That should do it,' he said finally, for they couldn't go on standing there like this all night.

Using the spade like a rake, he dragged Bridget forwards. The fairy's corpse slid from the grate and on to the floor. There was no need to worry any more now, he thought. He had heard the cries of pain a little earlier and, he had to admit, they had almost sickened him for a moment. But now there was no more pain, because the fairy was dead.

'I think we've burnt the fairy out,' he said.

The others, seven of them, were now standing in front of the dresser. They were staring at him blankly and he wondered why none of them was saying anything.

Suddenly, William shouted at him, 'I'm going to break down that door and go.'

William ran to the door. You won't get out, he thought, and smiled as he watched William rattling the handle furiously and cursing. Then William ran back, took Michael's coat from where he had hung it earlier on the back of a kitchen chair, and frantically began to rummage through the pockets.

'You won't find it,' he called comically. The key was in his trouser pocket. A precaution he'd taken earlier.

'No damned key,' William shouted back.

He threw the jacket on to the floor, the inside-out pockets still sticking out. Like tongues, Michael thought, only they needed to be pink, not white.

'Let us out,' William shouted, running back to the others.

Then an anxiety came to Michael. Although the worst might be over the ordeal was not ended. There might be questions from neighbours. There might be tittle-tattle around Drangan. The fairies were clever, and who was to know what they might whisper in people's ears against him over the next day or so. So he would have to be ready for them. Those who had seen, they had to be sworn to silence.

He was about to demand this when, to his great surprise, William fainted to the floor with a sigh. Well, he thought, as he watched them dragging William into Pat's bedroom, they would all just have to swear later.

They closed the door but he crossed the kitchen, opened the door and went in after them. They had lifted William on to the bed, and Mary had found a bottle of holy water and was sprinkling it on his face.

246

Michael opened the chest in the corner, pulled out the tablecloths, blankets and sheets which were in it, until at last he found the flour sack he was looking for.

It was soft and white and still smelt of flour, and there was red writing on the front which gave the weight it had once held. He threw it over his shoulder, took an old sheet that he was also going to need, then turned and said, 'Joanna, it is not Bridget I have burnt. You will soon see the witch go up the chimney.'

In the kitchen he spread the sheet on the floor beside the naked fairy. The flames were out. Amazingly, her hair was unburnt, not even singed. He rolled the corpse into the middle with the spade. Next, he squatted down, sat the body up and rested it against his knees. The skin was oily with the paraffin and he wiped his fingers on his trousers. He dropped the flour bag over the head and pulled the drawstring tight around the neck. Finally he rolled the body up inside the sheet.

He felt breathless but there was no time to rest. He had to push on.

He took the spade and a lamp, unlocked the door and went out, locking it again after himself.

He went round to the back of the house and climbed over the wall into the field. There was a low hill. He walked to the top, carefully negotiated another wall, and descended several big long fields on the other side.

After about half a mile he reached a sunken area near a drain which he knew from walking this land was invisible from the road.

He marked a square in the turf which was roughly the creature's size, levered away the sods and began to dig.

The ground underneath was boggy and wet. It was with some difficulty that he managed to dig a shallow grave and pile the earth up on the side.

He returned to the house and found everybody in Pat's

bedroom, where he had left them. They were all reciting the rosary, everybody except for the child, Katie, who was asleep on the bed.

'God help us, he is going to murder us,' Mary exclaimed, and one of them inside closed the door in his face.

'Are you there, Patrick Kennedy?' he bellowed at the door. 'I'm going to count to three, and if you don't come out by then I'm going to come in and get you.'

On the far side of the wood he heard frantic whispers and finally Mary saying, 'Patrick, answer him.' Her voice quivered and Michael judged with pleasure that Bridget's old aunt was frightened. Maybe now he'd see a little more cooperation, which sadly, so far, had been lacking.

'I'm here,' he heard Patrick reply at last.

'Come out here,' he said. 'I have the hole nearly made; I can't drive the devil out the chimney, so I'm going to have to carry her out the door. And I can't do it by myself. You're going to have to help me.'

The door opened and Patrick walked slowly out.

'Come on,' Michael said, 'buck up.'

Patrick took the feet and Michael took the shoulders. They shuffled the body through the front door to the step outside. Then Michael closed the door and turned the key in the lock again. No one was going to go wandering, he thought grimly, not while they were away.

It took them over an hour to carry the body to the hole. They put the body in and he began to cover it with earth.

When all the earth was in place, it stuck up of course, forming a mound. He began to flatten it with his spade. Suddenly he felt very tired.

'Have you a cigarette?' he demanded.

Patrick did not appear to hear him.

'Patrick?' he said.

The boy was sobbing quietly.

Michael smacked down his spade again. What, he wondered,

248

might those tears lead to? Into sneaking down to the barracks, he thought grimly, that was what!

When they got back to the house and he opened the front door, Patrick bolted past him and ran into Pat's room.

Michael stepped in, closed the door, took the black-handled knife from the table, and walked over to Pat's door.

Inside the room, six faces stared blankly back at him. Frightened? he wondered. Not exactly. It was more that they were expectant, he would say. They were waiting for him to make a move.

'You will all now take an oath that you will not inform on me.'

'You've no need to use that knife against any of us,' said Mary from the end of the bed.

'I'm not in dread of any of you, except Joanna,' he heard himself shouting. His hand rose and he was pointing the blade towards her.

Steady, he told himself. He mustn't let them know that he was in any sense anxious. Weakness was fatal. If they saw the slightest sign of it, wouldn't they trample him in the mud?

'You need not be in dread of Joanna,' said Mary, 'neither she, nor I, nor any of us will inform on you. We don't need to. Wherever you put her, God will show where she is.'

God, he had completely forgotten God. He felt a sudden surge of panic rising inside. God saw. God would speak. God would inform.

So, he informs, Michael heard some inner voice agreeing. God saw a fairy and he saw you put her to the fire. So? So what?

Of course, he thought, and in an instant the panic was transformed into a sort of happiness. He hadn't done wrong but right and that was what God saw. And God would be happy he had done right. And if the people of Drangan turned against him, he would have God by his side, for He upholdeth the just and He smiteth the wicked, does He not? And then when Bridget rode from Kilnagranagh, he would show her to the disbelievers, and when any asked him for his source of strength he would tell them, which was the truth, that his strength came from God.

So there was no need to fear. Fear was a thing of the past. So Joanna carried tales. What did that matter? In a day or two she'd be proved wrong and he'd be proved right. They'd all laugh at her then in Drangan. She wouldn't be able to show her face, and he'd be a hero with beautiful Bridget at his side; Bridget, whom he'd sprung from her underground prison, and returned to her sweet life on earth.

He lowered the arm holding the knife to his side. The room was still. There was absolute quiet. Then the child Katie woke up. She knelt up on the bed and put her arms around her mother.

'Come on,' he heard Joanna saying quietly.

He watched as Joanna got off the bed, lifted Katie down, and walked out past him. Then a moment later, following her lead, Mary Kennedy and her sons walked out after her.

'Where are you going?' he called after them through the doorway.

Everybody froze.

'I'm going to my mother's,' Joanna said. She did not turn to face him as she spoke, but remained gazing steadfastly at the front door.

'No, you're not,' he said, stepping after them into the room.

'I'll go to my own home then,' he heard Joanna replying. 'I'll not go to my mother's if it worries you, but I must get my daughter to bed.'

'Yes,' he said. He could hear that Pat, who had remained behind in his bedroom, had begun to moan. They were loud cries and he guessed they came not from the throat, but the stomach.

Joanna pulled open the front door and led everyone out.

He went after them and stood on the step and watched as they walked down the path to the gate. Without a word being spoken, Mary and her sons turned left, towards Drangan, while Joanna and Katie went the other way towards Rathkenny. He listened to their footsteps for a few moments, then they died away and there was silence.

He re-entered his house, closed the door and locked it.

'Goodnight,' he called through the wooden door to Pat in his bedroom, but the old man was still sobbing and he did not hear.

He picked up Bridget's jacket and her other clothes, extinguished the lamps in the kitchen and went into the bedroom. The house seemed unnaturally still and empty and for an instant he felt a twinge of sadness, the kind he associated with childhood, with losing something precious, or being separated from your parents or someone you loved.

He pulled the box in which they kept old clothes from under the bed. The nightdress from Thursday night was lying in the bottom. There was a hole burnt in the side and it smelt of pee. He threw the good clothes he had in on top of it. They would all be washed together; another chore to do before Bridget came back.

He shoved the box back under the bed and sat on the chair and unlaced his boots. He felt sad again and told himself he was not to mope. He took his boots off. In a day, a couple of days, Bridget was going to be home again.

He got into the bed, dressed. He would have to get up in a few hours, so there was no point in taking anything off.

Sliding down now into the bed, he felt how tightly the sheet was stretched over the mattress underneath him. Yes, Joanna had made a good job of it earlier.

He blew out the candle and lay back in the darkness. He could smell Bridget's hair on the bolster, her skin, her body. He registered another twinge of sadness. He wanted Bridget. He was missing her, badly he sensed. He wanted to feel her hair against his cheek, to nuzzle the crinkly part of her ear, to stroke her belly.

Well, he couldn't have her now, he told himself. He just was going to have to wait. Why not pray instead, he thought. A good idea.

'Dear God,' he said out loud in the darkness, and as he lay there trying to think what to say next, the most enormous fatigue suddenly swept over him, and he fell into a deep, dreamless sleep.

As she walked home in the darkness along the lane, Joanna's thoughts moved backwards.

In her mind's eye, as if she were looking down on the scene from a great height, she saw herself and her brothers and her mother filing silently out of the door of the Ballyvadlea house, then going down the path and through the gate, where she turned right and they left, while Michael watched from the porch and waited until their footfalls had disappeared from earshot, before slipping inside, closing the door and locking it.

From here the viewpoint shifted to an even greater height, and now she was looking down on herself and Katie. They were two dark amorphous shapes stumbling along the coal-black ribbon of the lane. And the world through which they hurried was totally noiseless, except for her own shoes striking the stones in the dirt, Katie's lighter footfalls, and the child's breathing.

Then, without warning, this top-down view vanished. Watcher and the watched suddenly merged. She was her whole self again, and she was filled with painful desires. She began to imagine that her husband would be awake in bed, waiting for her, and that she would undress and creep into his arms. But no sooner had she admitted the idea than she knew it was hopeless. He was asleep. He did not know what had happened. But even if he had, and even if he were waiting for her, what good would it do? None at all. Because no matter how long they lay together, and no matter how passionate they were with one another, and no matter how much she abandoned herself to the heavy form of Thomas lying on top of her, it would never, in fact nothing could ever wipe away the image of the burning, bare creature, whimpering on the floor. Nothing could ever do that.

She stopped where she was, overcome not by tiredness but a feeling of being utterly alone, spent and hopeless. As she stood there, she noticed her eyes were watering, and the thought crossed her mind, but in a vague and distant way, that if she could possibly put off crying, that would be best. Yes, it would be, she found herself agreeing with herself, for she didn't want Katie to see her weeping.

But as this inner dialogue was occurring, she sensed an awful thought was hovering. If she walked on perhaps it would go, but before she could take a step, it dropped like a hawk from the air, and she was held fast by it and helpless. She was like a captured lamb or a young rabbit.

Why, she asked herself, why had she not gone for the police earlier or, at the very least, why had she not told someone other than her husband what was happening? She had had days in which to report what was going on, and yet she had done nothing.

There was a pain now in the back of the throat, and a tightness somewhere in the area of the stomach. She felt like a huge bag of water which at any moment was going to tear asunder and let its aqueous contents spill everywhere.

A first tear rolled out of her eye, and she felt the hot path as it moved down her cheek. Then a second and a third came, and she let out a great wrenching cry. Why had she stood by and let it happen? For a few moments this recrimination formed itself into a coherent thought, but then a great wave of grief swept over her and it was washed away.

Beside her, Katie squeezed her hand tightly and then blurted out, 'W–w–w–what is it?'

Katie was stammering, she observed, but in a curiously removed and objective way. This was new. Well, she thought, it would pass, and then she remembered that the child had asked her a question. She had to answer it.

'It's nothing,' Joanna said automatically, 'nothing.'

Joanna looked about herself but through her tears she could hardly see the dark lane below her feet, or the darker hedgerows looming on either side of them. Neither could she think clearly any more because the waves of pain and remorse were coming more and more quickly.

She could hear Katie wailing along with her now, and she knew she could not go a step further. She sank down on to the damp ground, put her face on Katie's shoulder, and let out a great cry as she began to weep.

CHAPTER EIGHT

Michael awoke. There was light bleeding around the edges of the shutter. He could smell Bridget's smells all around him. His mouth was dry and then he noticed the smell of paraffin. There was an imminent danger, he sensed suddenly, that a memory from the night before was going to flash before his inner eye. He knew what it was although he was not seeing it yet. It was the fairy stretched out on the floor; there were flames all over the body, and it was whimpering.

It was unbearable, the idea that he would now allow himself to recollect the picture, or worse, the noise which the creature had made when it was dying on the floor. No, no, no, he was not going to. Out, out, out, he thought. Then, as suddenly as a mist clears as the sun starts to shine, the memory went away and his mind cleared.

He stretched his legs into the bottom of the bed. It was cool between the sheets here. Now, his mind was moving back in time, slowly and steadfastly. What was it trying to get at? Oh yes. He hadn't thought about this, not for years and years, literally. He could almost say he had forgotten about it altogether until this moment . . .

He was seventeen. He was cleaning out the byre at his parents' home, when he noticed a loose stone over the door. He could tell that it was loose because there was a fringe of black shadow around it, instead of a vein of crumbling, yellow mortar. Strange, he thought, he had never noticed it before, and he decided to take a look.

He got the milking stool and climbed up. He pulled the stone free and dropped it on the ground. A musty smell wafted from the hole. He put his hand into the dark space.

There was something in there. He pulled the bundle out and opened it. Inside he was greatly surprised to find a spinning top and eight lead soldiers. The tin top was rusty and the soldiers had lost most of their paint, yet he recognized them at once. These were the offerings he had left on the stone in Kearney's rath. He felt around to see if there was anything else inside – perhaps his pennies – but there was nothing, just mortar dust. His money, he decided, had been spent on tobacco and beer.

He took the toys to his mother in the kitchen.

'I found these in the byre,' he said to her.

At first Agatha was puzzled, then her expression changed to one of alarm.

'Your toys,' she began uneasily. 'You left them above in Kearney's ring and your father found them and brought them home.'

'Why didn't he give them back to me?'

Agatha flushed. She blinked and wrung her hands.

'I don't know,' she said.

He nodded, solemn and blank-faced, but half an hour later, as he stalked across the Quarter field with the scythe resting on his shoulder, he began to feel furious. He had always believed his toys had been taken and that was why Agatha had been released. Now it turned out the toys were in the byre all along. How could his mother and father have deceived him in this way?

He sat down on a large stone covered with pale lichen. It was warm from the sun. He laid the scythe across his lap and began to stroke the grey whetstone along the curving blade.

But did he believe what his mother said? he asked himself. Frankly, as he thought about it, no, he did not.

He stood up and looped the leather harness across his shoulder.

Who was to say what had actually happened? And further-more, if his mother had not told him the truth when he was a boy of seven, was there any reason to believe she was telling him the truth now?

He gripped the pegs attached to the scythe handle.

No, he decided, what she was saying was just a complicated fairy trick.

He sliced at the nettles along the top of the bank, and the faintly metallic smell of their sap rose up from the ground.

Two months later, Michael remembered, lying still in his bed, he secured his apprenticeship at the cooper's in Clonmel. That was when he moved out of his parents' cottage; and once he was married to Bridget and settled into his house in Ballyvadlea, he never slept at home again.

Now, he started dreamily recalling the day he and Bridget had first seen the Ballyvadlea house, the two of them standing side by side in the then empty kitchen.

'Look,' she had said, and pointed to a moth with orange and black wings, fluttering against the window by the front door. He could see the sun shining outside.

The window was stuck; the house had been closed up for a few months. However, in the end he got it open, and the insect flew out. As he stood and watched it zig-zag erratically through the air, he felt Bridget's arms curling round his shoulders and then her lips kissing his cheek.

He wanted to linger with this memory, but his thoughts were trying to push it away. They had formed a question. It was an urgent question. And what was that question? he wondered.

What if your mother was right? What if the toys were never taken? What if they were found by your father?

Stop, stop, he ordered his thoughts. His knees, his legs, his whole body was shaking. No, no, no, he replied to himself. It was a fairy trick. The fairies hid the toys above the byre door and they did it deliberately to confuse him. It was a big trick and his mother was in on it and his father too. They intended him to find them – otherwise why else did they put them in such an obvious place over the door in the byre? Clearly, they wanted him to think there weren't any fairies.

And the trick might have worked too, he told himself. He might have fallen for it. And then what would have happened? He'd never have realized the stroke they were pulling with Bridget. Yes, that was it. He saw it all now, how everything fitted together. It was obvious; also ingenious, cunning and typical of fairy wiles.

But what if it wasn't a trick? came the question from his thoughts. What if the toys had *never* been taken?

But they were, they were, he replied in anguish.

But if they weren't, it meant, didn't it, that Agatha was never taken away?

No, he shouted back. That was never in question. He'd always known that was the case. Always, always, always . . .

And if Agatha wasn't taken, the inner voice continued relentlessly, then Bridget might not have been taken either?

No, wrong. Wrong . . .

But if Bridget wasn't taken – *if* – then who was it he had burnt the night before?

No, he refused to answer such a question. The very idea was unbearable . . .

Perspiration had broken out all over his face, yet his feet at the bottom of the bed were freezing. He wiped his face with his hands and curled his knees up to his chest.

But if Bridget was never taken, then who was it he had burnt the night before if it wasn't his wife?

Was this conversation going to go round and round in the same circle for ever?

But if it wasn't Bridget, then who, who was it?

Why, why the same question over and over again, hammering the same point . . . ?

'No, no, no,' he shouted at the top of his lungs, and as he did he sat up in bed.

Joanna ran through a meadow. She had no shoes on. Her eyes were fixed on the trembling wings of a cabbage white fluttering through the air in front of her. She was trying to catch it but she did not have a net. Instead, she had been given Cleary's gallon can – not the white one they used for milk but the blue one they used for paraffin. However, besides being far too heavy and unwieldy, the neck was far too narrow to catch the butterfly.

Then the dream changed to a place which was dark and warm. Someone helped her to undress; when she was naked she went and lay down. She was happy and smiling. Someone took her arms and lifted them above her head. This was Thomas, she assumed. It could only be Thomas.

Then someone came into her. It was Thomas of course. It had to be.

In her dream she opened her eyes and looked down. It was dark and at first she was not able to see much; only that the head and shoulders of her husband were covered with thick, chestnut-coloured hair.

She reached out and began to stroke the back of Thomas's neck. It took her a moment or two before she realized and as she did she froze. This wasn't Thomas. It was the head of a man and the torso of a horse . . .

Joanna opened her eyes. The sheets were wet. Her heart was pounding.

She washed and dressed and rushed back to Cleary's. As she approached the cottage, crouched behind the wall, it seemed like a terrified little creature caught in a trap.

She pushed open the gate purposefully and went down the path. The front door was open. Inside, she found Michael bent double in semi-darkness. He was scrubbing the bottoms of the trousers he had on. The room was still shuttered up from the night before. It stank of paraffin and herbs.

Michael looked up at her.

259

'You must give yourself up,' she said abruptly.

Michael scowled, dunked his brush into the bucket on the floor, and went on scrubbing. The room was filled with the rasping sound of the bristles rubbing on the material.

Michael continued cleaning his trouser ends for several minutes. Joanna wondered if he were waiting for her to leave. She was determined, however, to stand her ground and wait until she had an answer out of him. She cleared her throat; she was going to speak again, when suddenly Michael stopped without any prompting from her, sighed loudly and looked up at her.

'Oh God, Joanna.' His voice, she heard, was both hesitant and sad. 'There is the substance of poor Bridget's body.'

He held out the sodden trouser bottoms towards her. They were covered, she saw, with whitish spots and splashes. It was fat, she realized, the fat of Bridget's body.

As she looked down, first at Michael as he stared back at her with a crushed and hopeless expression on his face, and then at the trouser bottoms with their human stains where ordinarily there was only mud or muck, she suddenly understood the awful dream which had woken her up. The butterfly, beating its lovely white wings as it moved erratically through the meadow, was Bridget. Her soul had fled her body, and to get it back was as impossible as catching a cabbage white with a gallon can for a net. Bridget was dead. It was an indisputable fact.

'You must give yourself up,' she said suddenly.

'I'll go to America,' Michael's voice flowed back quietly. Then he added, matter-of-factly, 'But I'll make provision for you and Pat.'

He lifted the black-handled knife down from the mantelpiece. He scraped the blade over each of his trouser ends a couple of times, then suddenly got up and pointed the end at her.

'I'm not afraid of anyone but you and her father,' he said.

Joanna slid back towards the door, but he circled round and blocked this, her only route of escape.

'I'll cut my throat before I give the police the chance to catch me.'

He moved towards her, pointing the knife at her throat.

'Did you hear me?' Michael shouted.

Her knees trembled.

'Go to the peelers. It's the best thing you can do,' Joanna said faintly.

'Promise. Swear you won't inform,' he shouted.

He pushed her on to her knees on the flagstone floor.

'I promise, I will never, ever tell anyone what I know,' she heard herself agreeing.

'Do you swear?'

'I swear,' she said.

'Get up.'

Michael returned to the cold fireplace and she watched as he began to shovel the ashes into an ash-pail. As he worked quickly, clouds of ash rose around him. A pale beam of sunshine shone through the open door, lighting up the floating particles as they trembled in the air.

When the pan was full he carried it across the room. His bootprints in the ash reminded her of footprints in the snow. Why had she sworn to do wrong? she wondered. For the same reason, came the answer, the half-man, half-horse had given her such pleasure. There was bad in her, of course, that was why.

Through the back window she watched now as Michael crossed the yard to the manure heap. He made a hole in the brown mess then upended the pail over it. As he lifted the pail away, a cloud of ashes was caught by the wind and swirled across the yard.

She looked around the room hopelessly. The fire was out. She needed to do something. Automatically she took the broom from its place in the corner and began to sweep the floor.

Leaving Joanna at work in his house, Michael set off for Mary Kennedy's. He met Pat in the lane as he walked along. The old man said nothing to him when he called out, 'Good morning,' and then turned away as Michael passed him by.

When he came into the cottage, he found Mary sitting in her usual chair. There was a stub of a candle burning on the mantelpiece. There was a curious smell, as if dead flowers had been left standing in the room. He looked around quickly but there weren't any that he could see.

'How did you come? Across the fields?' she asked, looking at his trousers.

Michael pulled a chair over and sat down on the opposite side of the hearth from her. Patrick stood between them, supporting himself against the chimney breast with an out-stretched arm. His face was streaked. He had been crying, heavily.

'I came along the road,' said Michael.

He pulled his trouser bottoms, still wet from the washing and the scrubbing, towards the glowing embers.

'That isn't dew on your clothes.'

'No.'

'What is it then?' Mary asked curtly.

'I was cleaning them.' He glared at her.

'Mary,' he continued firmly, 'tonight we will go to Kilna-granagh fort and she will come out of there riding a white horse. I will cut her free and we will bring her home.' As he spoke, he monitored himself, and it pleased him that he sounded so certain.

Patrick turned towards him. He wiped the end of his sleeve over his eyes.

'Will Bridget come?' he asked. He sounded unconvinced.

Michael stared up at him and nodded. Patrick smiled back weakly.

'Maybe you're fools, both of you,' said Mary.

262

'No we're not,' her son said quickly.

'I'm telling you, tonight, we'll get her back,' said Michael confidently, 'So, Patrick, get all your brothers there.'

Michael headed back for home then. But instead of using the lane he went across the fields. He didn't want to run into Pat this time.

He felt cheerful, even to the extent that he smiled at Joanna when he got to the house. She was outside cleaning the front windows. They were speckled with grime from the night before. But then, just at the very instant he was stepping across the threshold, he realized that while emptying the fire earlier, he had probably made a mistake.

Bridget wore ear-rings; they were lovely gold hoops which he had bought for her in Clonmel, and there were tiny hallmarks stamped inside them which proved they were assayed in London.

When she returned from Kilnagranagh she would want them back, just as she would want her ring.

Knowing this, he had looked for the ear-rings. The night before, after he and Patrick had put the fairy into the grave, he had taken the flour sack off its head and checked the ears. However, he had only found one ear-ring. He had wrapped this in his handkerchief with the ring and replaced the flour sack.

So the other had obviously come out sometime during the evening before, and it had most probably come out in the fire, he reckoned. However, with Joanna distracting him with all her talk that morning while he had been cleaning the grate out, he had failed to notice if it was in the ashes.

Damn her, damn her distracting me, he thought, and he turned about, went round the house to the shed, found a rake and went straight to the manure heap, where he began combing through the ashes.

A few moments later he heard footsteps, and glancing up

from his work, he saw his friend John Dunne coming into the yard.

'I met your father-in-law on the road,' he heard John Dunne saying, 'and he says Bridget's gone.'

Michael stopped raking, for there was the golden ear-ring for which he was looking. It was in the middle of the ashes in the middle of the manure.

He picked it up quickly, so that John Dunne wouldn't see, and then turned to face his friend with a blank expression. Meanwhile, he wormed with his fingers through the handkerchief in his pocket, then deposited the ear-ring there with the other jewellery.

'Where has she gone?' John Dunne repeated.

'I do not know,' he heard himself saying, 'I cannot tell you what happened.' But he didn't need to think what to say next because somehow it was there in his grasp. 'Joanna was bringing in some stumps of wood last night,' he continued. 'She fetched them out of the shed here, and she was coming round the side of the house to the door.'

Michael pointed the way with a finger, sooty and filthy under the nail.

'As she goes in the door, Joanna meets Bridgie coming the other way. Joanna calls in to me – I'm stretched out on the bed – "Come quick, Bridgie's going." I get up, I come out to the front of the house, and I see Bridgie going away across the field right in front of the door with two strange men.'

Michael led John Dunne round to the front, where the two of them stood for some while looking over the wall. Joanna Burke had finished the outside, and they could hear her washing the windows inside now. Green fields and ragged hedgerows stretched towards the rounded shape of Slievenamon mountain.

'Why did you not follow her?'

Michael shook his head. 'It was no use for me,' he said enigmatically, 'they wouldn't let me have her.'

As he spoke Michael felt himself growing distressed. He knew that he was going to cry. Then a moment later it happened, and tears began to roll down both his cheeks.

'We'll have her back,' he heard John Dunne saying cheerfully.

'At the rath tonight, maybe, yes,' Michael agreed, and he repeated what he had said to Patrick about Bridget riding forth and cutting her free.

'She was always talking about Kilnagranagh,' John Dunne said suddenly. Then he continued, 'She used to meet Hagan, the eggman, down near my place. Perhaps she's gone down there. Let's go and have a look. There's no place around there I don't know, and if she is there, we'll find her.'

Michael could feel John Dunne's eyes burrowing into him as he spoke. He did not quite know why but he felt frightened. He looked across the landscape towards the mountain in the distance.

'Yes, why not,' said Michael eventually.

They set off along the lane towards Drangan. His father-in-law, Michael was happy to discover, who had been lurking out there for most of the morning, had vanished.

They passed Simpson's place. There was nobody about in the yard, only a few brown chickens scratching in the dirt. Michael felt nervous. He was going to have to be extremely careful about what he said. Yet he was also filled with a longing to tell John Dunne everything that had happened the night before and the doubts which had assailed him since he had woken up. His last secret had been safe with his friend, so why not these new ones? At the very thought of confessing his heart beat faster. The idea seemed not only necessary and vital, but he fancied it would almost bring him pleasure to tell his good friend. But then he decided no. His mind was turning like a weather-vane. He would keep quiet for a while.

They reached Dunne's cottage and went round to the back.

265

'We'll go along there,' said Dunne, indicating the direction.

Dunne leapt over the wall into the field on the other side, but Michael chose to sit on it and swing his legs over one at a time. The trouser bottoms flapped and he was thankful he had removed most of the stains.

The chosen path followed the course of a ditch. Now John Dunne jumped across this, his inverted reflection in the black shining water jumping with him.

They started to walk. The ground was firm; the water in the ditch was still. Michael saw a muddy patch ahead, with something sticking out of it.

Drawing closer, he found it was a green, half-buried bottle. Wherever one looked in the countryside, thought Michael, there were abandoned objects – bottles, jam jars, tins – as well as abandoned houses, castles and mills. They had all come out of the earth, and having served their usefulness, he thought, they were now returning to it.

Then in his imagination he was back at the burial site the night before. He was looking down at the hole he had dug, and the fairy in the sheet lying there bent double, while beside him Patrick Kennedy sobbed in the darkness.

To clear his mind he ran forward and kicked the bottle. The stem snapped, spun through the air, and landed in the water with a plop. John Dunne looked across at him.

'Just a bit of sport,' he explained.

Eventually the ditch led them to Kilnagranagh House. It had been abandoned by its owners years before. The rendering had fallen away and lay on the ground like gigantic pieces of icing. The exposed walls were brick, pitted by years of wind and rain. The windows were empty, the frames having long been carried away and burnt in fireplaces around the district. Inexplicably, however, the curtains had survived and hung in tatters behind the window holes.

In the hall an ash tree grew out of the bare earth with a

sycamore beside it, while overhead floor joists and roof timbers spanned the space between the walls. Above them was the grey sky.

In the old dining-room, the fireplace was filled with sooty lumps of burnt wood and pieces of bird nest, and some of the stucco, amazingly, was still in place around the ceiling edges. Where the french window had been there was a gap, and on the level walk beyond, where the old occupants had once strolled after dinner, a tangled mess of bushes had grown up.

In the offices at the rear they found a few mouldering remnants of human occupation – a rotten table missing a leg but still standing, a chipped enamel bowl, its entire bottom gone, the old pump wheel, rusted but still bearing traces of green paint.

They went through the back door into the yard. All the old flagstones were upturned by the roots of the trees and bushes growing everywhere. They passed the tumbled piggery walls, the stables where all the doors drooped from rotting hinges, and went into the kitchen garden. Here, using a stick, John Dunne cleared a path through the undergrowth to the old gardener's cottage. It was a bare brick shell with no roof, windows or door.

Michael had grown sadder and sadder since starting this ridiculous search with John Dunne. Bridget's absence hurt. He wanted her; he wished he could imagine her waiting at home. But she would not be waiting, not that day, not any day. The idea that she might never ever again wait for him at home pressed hard, painfully hard on his thoughts.

Now, as he stood there in the miserable shell of the gardener's cottage, he felt his energy draining away, his spirits sliding. At last his capacity to keep away the unthinkable vanished and his mind was filled with one single idea. He was never going to see Bridget again, never, ever. Then his eyes filled with tears and he felt the hot trail as one ran down his face. He was crying for the second time that day.

'She's not here,' said John Dunne, 'and we've been through the open fields. If she'd been anywhere we'd have seen her, wouldn't we?'

'Don't speak of it.'

Another hot tear rolled down Michael's cheek. He could not stop himself. He was going to have to tell his friend.

'She was burned last night,' Michael blurted, and he added, 'Bridget is dead.'

He wiped his hot eyes and stumbled back through the doorway.

'Are you a murderer?' John Dunne called after him, his tone curious more than condemning.

Nevertheless, he shouted back as if he were being accused, 'She was not my wife. She was too fine a woman to be my wife. She was two inches taller than my wife.'

The tears streamed on from Michael's eyes.

'I'll cut my throat,' he stammered, 'or do something to myself before the night; that way I will see her.'

'Go to the priest and the police.'

Dunne was standing in front of him. At the moment that he blurted out the truth, what Michael was expecting of his friend was some comfort. However, as he stood facing the older man, he saw that his expectation was misplaced. Of course, he realized, now the thought uppermost in John's mind would be saving his own skin.

But at the same time as he was thinking this, the distant looking-down-upon-the-scene part of himself was also working and thinking. Perhaps John's suggestion wasn't such a bad idea after all, he thought.

He could tell the authorities that there were others involved as well as himself. There were Bridget's cousins, the four Kennedy brothers; their sister Joanna; their mother, Mary; and there was John Dunne himself, of course. Every one of them had agreed that Bridget was not his wife. He had not acted alone; they were all in it together; it was not a lie.

'I'll go to the priest if you come along with me,' said Michael finally.

John Dunne took him by the arm and began to guide him back along the path through the undergrowth.

The confession box smelt to Father Ryan of old stone, leather and damp. Only a few had been and gone that morning. The curtain behind the latticework on the upper part of the door did not quite meet the edge and the light which showed through was like a silver line, floating beside him in the darkness.

He heard the door on the far side of the church banging shut and sat up in his seat. Boots rang out on the stone floor of the aisle. He anticipated the familiar set of sounds that would follow: the momentary hesitation for genuflection; further footfalls; another hesitation, this time just before the confession box, which to his mind was the parishioner debating whether to make a confession or not. Then the parishioner stepping on to the wooden floor and the whole confession box shifting; the creak of knees and the rustle of clothes as he or she knelt; the squeak of the grille as he slid it back. And finally, the overwhelming sense of a presence on the other side of the wooden wall, of a hot body with smells and breathing sounds . . .

However, instead he heard something like a heavy sack being dumped on the floor, and then a low wail of pain.

He opened the door of the confession box quietly. He saw Michael Cleary was lying on his side in front of the altar rail, his legs drawn up to his chest.

Father Ryan stepped down from the box and went forward. Cleary's forehead rested on the stone floor. He was weeping. His parishioner was prostrate with grief and distress, obviously, he reasoned; however, this was not grief as Father Ryan was familiar with it. Then he remembered a visit he had once made to an asylum for lunatics in Dublin. His contact with the inmates had been fleeting, but standing in his church and recalling their contorted bodies, gaping mouths and flailing limbs, he saw there was something of the same agitation about Cleary. But how could the man to whom he had spoken the day before in Ballyvadlea, who had seemed arrogant and almost bumptious then, how had he changed in so short a time? To Father Ryan the only answer was that he had gone mad.

'Are you all right?' he asked.

The wailing stopped. Cleary lifted himself on to his hands and turned to look up at him. His face was ashen, and under his eyes there were dark purple crescents, and his chin was covered with dark stubble. His hair, uncombed, stuck out from his head in tufts. The man clearly had not slept for days, or washed, and at three feet he could smell Cleary's clothes reeked of turf smoke, sweat and dirt.

'Hear my confession.' Cleary jumped to his feet and seized his arm as he shouted this.

Perhaps Michael Cleary was drunk, Father Ryan wondered. He sniffed but he could not smell alcohol. Cleary's eyes were shining and the man was now staring at him pleadingly. Obviously, it was some awful event – possibly his father's death – that had made him like this. Father Ryan, who at first had felt simply nervous, was now beginning to feel apprehensive and even alarmed. The mad were irrational and violent. He delicately disentangled his arm from Cleary's grip and stepped back a couple of paces.

'I don't think a confession today, under these circumstances, would be right, do you, Michael?' he said, with surprising calmness. 'Now come into the vestry, Cleary,' he continued, 'you're not doing yourself any good out here.'

Michael Cleary shuddered and waved his arms about as if he were shooing away a cloud of insects.

'I've done wrong. Hear my confession. Please, I beg you.'

'You're not in a fit state to give a confession. Now come with me like a good man.'

Cleary was staring around the church wildly. Father Ryan's heart was racing. Michael Cleary was either going to attack him or do himself some terrible harm. He needed to get him out of the church.

'I've done wrong. Will I ever be forgiven?' Cleary took hold of his hair and twisted his head from side to side.

'God forgives all who make proper amends,' said Father Ryan quickly.

He gently took Cleary's arm. He did not want to antagonize him but he needed to act firmly and quickly. Here was clearly one very desperate man.

Cleary staggered as Ryan manoeuvred him past the altar, through the door, and into the vestry.

It was a small room painted brown. A flypaper hung in a spiral from the ceiling, a portrait of an archbishop hung on the wall, and there were two bottles of Communion wine on the top shelf of the cupboard. The priest deftly closed the door with his foot and they vanished behind the brown wood.

'I think it would be best if you got some air. Come on, let's go outside.'

They stepped out of the door into the yard. Cleary was twitching and mumbling about forgiveness. The next task, thought Father Ryan, was to get Michael Cleary off the grounds. At that moment, he saw Mikey Kennedy and John Dunne standing at the chapel gate. He felt immediately relieved. They could look after him now. He beckoned them over. Mikey Kennedy came first and Father Ryan steered Cleary towards him.

'Take him home.'

Mikey began to lead Cleary away, coaxing him gently, 'Come on, Michael, let's go home.'

John Dunne, who had walked over from the gate at a slower pace than his companion, now sidled up to him.

'What's the matter with that man?' Father Ryan asked. He

watched and was puzzled as John Dunne rolled his eyes and made a sharp intake of breath.

'They burnt Bridgie to death last night and buried her somewhere. I've been asking him all morning to take her up and give her a Christian burial.'

Father Ryan got John Dunne to repeat himself.

'How did it happen?'

'I think there's three or four of them that did it.'

'Who?'

The older man shrugged.

'Did these four you spoke of go out of their minds simultaneously?' Father Ryan demanded.

He saw Mikey had brought Cleary as far as the silver gates, and that in a moment he would be off church property altogether. Then he heard Cleary beginning to shout, 'I must make my confession. I want to go back.'

'Go to your friend,' Father Ryan ordered Dunne. He said this because he wanted Cleary off the grounds. However, he had also reached the point, Father Ryan realized, that he had run into many times before. John Dunne had told him as much about the crime as he was prepared to say. If he told the priest any more, he became an informer.

At the gate, the two men took hold of Cleary. They pulled him out and dragged him away down the main street of Drangan.

A cart rumbled past heading in the opposite direction. Father Ryan could no longer hear Cleary's cries. The way was clear. He could go to the police station unobserved. He hitched up his soutane and set off.

As soon as Father Ryan finished his story, Acting-Sergeant Egan rushed from the day room and out into Drangan main street. He looked left and right. Michael Cleary was nowhere to be seen. He fetched his bicycle and set off for Ballyvadlea. Just as he was approaching the turning into the lane, he saw Cleary ahead of him with two other men.

'Stop,' he shouted after them.

By the time he reached them, Dunne and Kennedy were sitting on the wall of Mary Kennedy's cottage on the corner, while Michael Cleary had crossed the road to the ditch on the other side. He was staring intently at something in the hedgerow.

'What's this extraordinary rumour I hear, Cleary, about your wife?' said Acting-Sergeant Egan.

Cleary continued staring.

'Cleary, this rumour?'

Acting-Sergeant Egan turned to the other two men, and made a face as if to say, What's up with Cleary? Neither responded. He turned back. Cleary was still peering ahead.

'Cleary, did you hear me? Can you hear me?'

He shook him by the arm but Cleary did not react. Then, abruptly, Michael pointed and shouted, 'Look!'

Egan followed the line of his finger. It pointed to the shaft of a plough which had been thrown into the hedgerow. The metal parts were swollen with rust, the wooden handles rotten and splintered.

'Everything rots back to what it was,' murmured Cleary, and shivered.

Acting-Sergeant Egan looked from the old plough to Cleary's face. The man was distressed, clearly, but he was going to get nothing out of him. He walked over the lane to Cleary's friends.

'What's the matter with Cleary?' he asked.

Mikey shrugged. Dunne ignored him and stared into the distance.

'Dunne, do you know what's the matter with him?'

'No,' said Dunne, stonily.

As Dunne was the one who had been to the priest, Acting-Sergeant Egan imagined that he knew more. However, he also knew it was going to be pointless questioning the man; he was not going to talk. It was a pity; dislike of informing was

273

all very well, but when a woman had gone missing, he believed that scruples should be set aside. Be that as it may, he was not going to make any progress here.

'Good morning,' he said to Mikey and John Dunne. 'Good morning, Cleary,' he added.

Then Acting-Sergeant Egan mounted his bicycle and headed back to Drangan.

At three o'clock that afternoon, William Simpson gave a friendly rap on Cleary's front door. Michael came and opened up a moment later. Inside, Simpson glimpsed Joanna Burke kneeling at the hearth.

'May I have a word with you, in private?' Simpson asked in a hushed tone, and then he smiled in order to allay any suspicions on the part of his listener. Cleary looked awful, he thought. His skin was unnaturally pale and his eyes unnaturally bright.

'I suppose so.'

Cleary came out, closing the door after himself.

'Listen . . . ah . . . Michael,' Simpson began, 'I'm sorry to hear about your troubles.'

Cleary shook his head of filthy hair. 'Ah yes, my Bridgie . . . you've heard . . . she left me.'

'Yes . . . I heard that. Mikey Kennedy told me.'

Simpson stared away across the fields. Simpson had never liked drunks because of their unpredictability, and now he felt nervous of Michael for the same reason. His only comfort was the thought of Joanna Burke inside.

'You know,' continued Simpson, 'we've just had a visit from, ah . . . Colonel Evanson. And that half-sergeant, Egan.'

Michael Cleary glanced at him quickly and then looked away again.

'It was a very amiable visit and there's nothing to worry about,' Simpson swiftly assured him. 'And they stayed for tea, you know,' he added proudly.

Looking up, Simpson noticed a coil of dark blue smoke curling out of Cleary's chimney. He took a breath and continued: 'They wanted to know when I had last seen Bridget.'

Michael Cleary faced him again and blinked three or four times, his expression darkening.

'So, I just told them, Mrs Simpson and myself had seen her on Thursday, the day before yesterday, and that last night she disappeared.'

'Good . . . good . . . Well, of course, that's the truth. That's just it . . . She . . .' responded Michael Cleary in a staccato fashion.

Then in fits and starts and with considerable prompting from himself, Michael Cleary told Simpson the full story. Bridget had walked out of the door past Joanna Burke at midnight the night before, and had not been heard of or seen since.

'But Joanna inside,' concluded Cleary, 'she keeps telling me to go to the police. That what we did with the herbs was wrong. Yet we didn't do anything wrong, did we, Simpson?'

He felt Cleary taking his arm and squeezing it. He felt frightened.

'Why no, of course we did nothing wrong,' he promptly agreed. But why was he being connected to Cleary's maltreatment of his wife, he wondered, when it had nothing to do with him.

'Well, you go in,' he heard Cleary saying, 'and tell Joanna Burke that Bridgie's gone and that's all there is to it.'

'Sure, Michael, sure,' he agreed.

'You know what women are like,' he heard Cleary continue, 'they never like things simple.'

The two men went into the house and Cleary said, 'Go on, Simpson, tell Joanna,' and he nudged him hard with his elbow.

'There's been an investigation,' Simpson began. Joanna Burke was kneeling in front of the hearth. She was sweeping up the dirt and turf dust on the floor with a goose wing. 'Colonel Evanson and Acting-Sergeant Egan were up at my house just now,' Simpson continued. 'I told them what we all know. There was no foul play with Bridget.'

'What's an investigation?' asked Joanna Burke, naïvely he thought.

'It's an examination before the magistrate. They'll probably come to see you next, as you're Bridget's best friend. You'll be examined to see if we have the same story. So you tell them the same as me.'

He cleared his throat.

'We did nothing wrong on Thursday. On Friday night Bridget Cleary ran out past you, and she has been missing ever since. Nothing more has happened in the meantime, and there's no need for Michael to go to the police.'

'Do you understand what you have to say, Joanna, when we have this investigation?' Cleary continued. 'Bridget ran out past you and disappeared across the fields with two men.' His tone, Simpson thought, was menacing.

She looked very small and tired to Simpson, crouched on the floor in front of them. She snapped a twig and threw the pieces on to the back of the fire.

'I understand,' said Joanna without turning round to face them, 'I know what I must do.'

Around eight o'clock, Michael walked down the lane in the darkness with Pat beside him. He had the black-handled knife in his jacket pocket. There was a strip of hessian wrapped around the blade. He felt triumphant. He was on his way with his father-in-law to gather friends and relations, and together they were all going to Kilnagranagh rath to wait for Bridget to ride out.

The day was shortly about to end and it was going to end jubilantly. Earlier, he was assailed by doubts, but now he knew and he was certain. The smell of Bridget's hair, the shape of her breasts and the moist place between her legs were all he could think of. The feeling of desire which could not express itself was painful but also thrilling.

He knew the feeling well from those times in the past when he had been working away from home. In those last hours before returning, he had always been overwhelmed and intoxicated by an identical sense of her physical being. And when, finally, he had got home on these past occasions, it had always been to discover that Bridget was in the grip of the same excitement as he was.

Pat had always been tactful at these times. He would leave the house. Michael and Bridget would go straight to the bedroom. They would never bother to undress. He would just take off her skirt.

Afterwards, they would lie together, growing warm and drifting into the trance-like state that always came after intimacy. Then they would make love again, unhurriedly and more pleasurably. Then they would get up and Pat, who always seemed to know when to come home, would come in and put the kettle on . . .

The Simpson farm came in sight. Michael saw the pale white light of a lamp burning in one of the windows. He wondered if Simpson would like to come to the rath with himself and Pat, then decided against asking him. He might be a neighbour and even an acquaintance of sorts, but he was not the type you would choose to have at a celebration. And anyway, Bridget had never much cared for him. She always said she could never trust him or Mrs Simpson.

Then Michael remembered that Simpson had a gun. This could be very useful. It was far from clear what the forthcoming ordeal was going to involve. He knew that Bridget was meant to ride out on a horse and that she would be tied to the saddle with ropes. That was why he had brought the knife to cut her free. But what if they didn't send her out? What if he had to go into their ring of trees to reclaim Bridget? Or worse, and more unnerving, what if he had to go down the hole in the ground where they lived, and drag her out? Yes, he needed that gun.

They crossed the yard. The dog chained against the wall growled and barked. Michael knocked on Simpson's door.

A few moments later his neighbour stood before him. Michael glimpsed Minnie behind, disappearing into the kitchen.

'Can I have your gun?' Michael asked.

Simpson stared at him.

'I need to borrow it.'

'Why?'

'You see,' he began confidentially, 'I need to get Bridgie back and it may not be quite so easy.'

Simpson was still staring at him with stony impassivity.

'I can't,' said Simpson.

'I only need it to persuade the pishogues. It won't actually be used, I promise.'

'It's kept in Drangan barracks.'

A lie, thought Michael. What was the good of leaving a pistol with the police? At that moment, Minnie called from the kitchen.

'I have to go in now,' said Simpson abruptly.

Michael was about to turn and stamp away but Simpson held him by the arm.

'Listen to me,' began Simpson. 'I told the magistrate that Bridget ran away. Don't be making more trouble now, Michael.'

On the lane a minute later, Michael felt his heart beating; he was in a rage. How dare Simpson deny him the gun? He listened to Pat panting as he struggled along at his side, then squeezed the black handle of the knife in his pocket.

Two hours later, at ten o'clock that same night, Acting-Sergeant Egan cycled alone along the Ballyvadlea lane. He carried no lights, and neither moon nor stars showed through the cloud. The ground below and the hedgerows to each side appeared only as different shades of black. He had travelled like this before, yet tonight he felt strangely apprehensive. Perhaps, he thought, it was because he had never done anything quite so risky.

The place the Simpsons were caretaking appeared on his right. Acting-Sergeant Egan was grateful for the oil lamp glowing in the window.

He continued moving along the tunnel of dark. His bicycle ran over a rut and shrugged violently. He squeezed the handlebars to hold himself on. He did this instinctively, as he had done numerous times already. It was a very bumpy track and his forearms were aching.

Cleary's cottage came in sight at last. Acting-Sergeant Egan dismounted and stood very still. The house appeared to be dark and deserted with no lights burning inside. He held his breath and listened.

He could hear wind, water running somewhere and, most ominously, something rustling in the undergrowth. He screened out the other noises and concentrated on the last. Eventually he decided it was an animal. Its movements were too light to be that of a man.

He lifted the latch and swung the gate back. It was well oiled and quiet. Carefully and silently, he carried the bicycle round to the back, where he leant it against the wall of the empty piggery. Suddenly, the bell pinged, causing him to start. He had caught it with his cuff.

He returned to the front door and tried the handle. It was locked. He took this to be a good sign. In his experience, people round the country did not generally lock their houses, unless they had something to hide.

He went round to the sash window at the back. He put his face against the cold glass and peered through, simultaneously working his fingernails into the crack along the bottom. Inside he could just make out the shape of a bed. This was where Pat Boland slept.

The window rose slowly upwards. In a matter of seconds he was in. He fished out the piece of candle and the box of matches he had in his pocket. He lit the wick. The flame trembled momentarily, caught, and began to throw out its pale, yellow light about the room.

He looked around and saw the unmade bed, the bolster with a depression in it, the closed door with something hanging on the back.

It was a coat. He took hold of a sleeve and smelt it. The odour it gave out was a mixture of sour milk, animal and dirt. Perhaps it was Pat's working coat.

He went into the main room. There was a smell of scorch everywhere. There was also another smell which reminded him of burnt meat.

He passed the kitchen table and went into the other bedroom. He put his candle on the window ledge. There was a bottle here. According to the label it was a prescription for Mrs Cleary. He pulled out the cork and sniffed. It smelt like medicine all right. This was the bedroom of the missing woman.

He took the candle and got down on his knees. He lifted back the candlewick bedspread and looked under the bed. He saw the black springs of the bedstead, the battered bed legs, the dusty linoleum, and an oily box. He pulled it out. It was filled with clothes which gave off an overwhelming smell of scorch and paraffin. He burrowed into the bottom, found something and pulled it out. It felt like a cotton dress.

He stood up, letting the thing unfurl as he did. It was a nightdress. By the candlelight he could see the middle part was all burnt out, and the edges around the hole were black and thin like tissue paper.

With the evidence rolled into a bundle and stowed inside his jacket, Acting-Sergeant Egan pedalled away quickly.

He felt triumphant. If Bridget Cleary had been burnt, he had the means to prove it.

He approached Simpson's. There was a dog chained up in the yard. It barked as he went by.

He passed on. Why had Cleary kept the nightdress? Why had he not buried it? Or thrown it into some bog hole where it would never have been found?

It was obvious. Those who had no previous record, like Cleary, rarely took the necessary steps to avoid detection when they committed their first crime. In some way this was connected with their feeling that they were a special case, and would never be caught.

Mary Kennedy's cottage loomed ahead. It was a small, squat structure. There were no lights here either.

He approached the main Cloneen to Drangan road. He heard voices and stopped. There was a fire burning at the top of Kilnagranagh Hill, and it was from here the voices were coming.

He hid his bicycle in the ditch, crossed the road and made his way to the summit. At the top there was a grassy, level stretch but he stopped about twenty yards short of it and hid behind a tree. In the distance stood the fairy ring of Kilnagranagh. It was lit up by a vast fire which lay between him and it. The fire was spitting sparks out into the blackness. There were people standing around and he made out the stout form of Mary Kennedy with her four sons around her; the thin willowy frame of William Ahearn; John Dunne, very erect and with his chest puffed out; Tom Smyth and Francis Hogan with their wives; various other men, women and children whom he knew by sight from around Cloneen and Drangan; and in the middle of the group was Michael Cleary. He was shouting at the top of his voice, 'Come out now, Bridget Cleary, come out now, I'm telling you. I have the knife. Ride out and I'll cut you free and I'll keep you at my side, my darling, for ever. I have your ring, your ear-rings . . .'

Acting-Sergeant Egan could hear Cleary's voice quivering with emotion. He heard that he was crying. Acting-Sergeant Egan had never before heard a broken, weeping voice quite like this.

Now the others around the fire started to shout, 'Come out, Bridget Cleary, your husband's waiting,' and Cleary's voice was lost amongst the hubbub.

Acting-Sergeant Egan had seen enough. He slipped down the hill to the road and remounted his bicycle. He could still hear shouting in the distance. He reached down with his foot to pull the pedal around, and that was when he had his moment of inspiration.

He turned round and cycled back the way he had come, passing Cleary's, until he came at last to Mrs Burke's.

Acting-Sergeant Egan knocked at the back door and Thomas Burke admitted him. He found Mrs Burke in the kitchen sitting by the fire. He took the nightdress out from under his tunic and unfurled it in front of her.

'Mrs Burke,' he said. 'Is this Mrs Cleary's?'

She nodded.

'Would you like to tell me then what happened, Mrs Burke?'

He pulled his notebook out and sat down at the table, pulled the pencil out from under the fastener and licked the end.

'On the night of Thursday last, March 14th, around ten o' clock,' Joanna began, 'I arrived at Bridget Cleary's house in Ballyvadlea with my daughter Katie . . .'

CHAPTER NINE

At the side of the field ran an old stone wall with a ditch below. It was overgrown with nettles and long grass. Acting-Sergeant Egan made his way along the edge, stabbing through the greenery with the ash-plant he carried. All that he had found so far were two green bottles filled with mud and a rusting tin bath.

Acting-Sergeant Egan stopped and wiped his moustache with his handkerchief. Wooded hills and fields stretched away in every direction, and everywhere he looked he could see fellow policemen. They were all wearing the same dark green uniform of the Royal Irish Constabulary, and they were all probing with ash-plants into thickets, bog holes and waterways.

In the next field he saw Rogers, his sergeant. He was searching an old dyke. Acting-Sergeant Egan remembered catching frogs in the same muddy ditch when he was a boy; sometimes he had done this with O'Connor and Callaghan, who were now stationed with him in the barracks.

Suddenly, Rogers blew his whistle. O'Connor and Callaghan, both carrying spades, ran out from a copse at the top of the next field and hurried towards Sergeant Rogers. Acting-Sergeant Egan scrambled across the ditch and ran forward. He wasn't going to miss this.

The five policemen met up where the two arms of the water course formed a point. The whitethorn brambles here were broken, and underneath Sergeant Rogers had found a mound of freshly dug earth. It was just over four feet long and a couple of feet wide. An attempt had been made to flatten the top by beating it down. The black boggy earth was shiny.

Callaghan and O'Connor came forward with the spades. Callaghan forced his spade in, levered the handle and lifted away a heavy clump of soil. An earthworm, purple like a vein, came away with it.

'Must be after the same as us,' Constable O'Connor observed grimly.

'All right, thank you very much, Constable,' Sergeant Rogers reprimanded him.

Six inches under, something got in the way of the digging.

Sergeant Rogers nodded and Egan got down on his knees and started to sweep the earth away by hand. At any moment he was expecting the features of a face to appear out of the earth before him. He was therefore surprised that what he came upon instead was a saturated white sheet.

The body wrapped up by the sheet was on its side. He scraped off the earth all the way to the feet. Then the four policemen each took hold of the shroud and lifted. They carried the swaying load a few feet and tumbled the body out on to a patch of grass free from cowpats.

It was a woman in her twenties. She was naked except for a pair of black stockings on her feet, and a flour bag over the head that was tied around the neck. The middle of the body was burnt and charred, and at the hips the bones and internal organs showed through.

He cut the drawstring and pulled off the flour bag. It was the missing woman, Bridget Cleary. A fine coating of flour from the bag whitened her face. There was also flour on the grass. It lay in a whitish halo around her head.

He covered the body over. Sergeant Rogers told them all to have a smoke. Each man went off and stood alone. Acting-Sergeant Egan went to the edge of the ditch and stared at the brown water lying in the bottom. He lit his pipe and as he puffed he remembered coming here as a boy.

The frogs were fast and slithery and they often evaded a

284

child's grasp. So rather than trying to catch them, he would creep up from behind, and press them down with his feet a couple of inches into the soft mud. This gave him time to lift up the frog with a bit of slate and drop it into the jam jar of water which he always carried.

Now followed the best moment, for as the mud was washed away in the water, the colour of the catch was revealed, whether red, gorgeous vivid green, or a deep cobalt blue.

Acting-Sergeant Egan re-lit his pipe. In the open air the tobacco smelt good. On the other side of the ditch rose a long, low hill. The Clearys lived on the other side. It was nearly a mile, he thought, from their cottage to the spot where he was now standing. It cannot have been easy, he supposed, for Michael Cleary and Patrick Kennedy to have carried the body in the darkness.

Sergeant Rogers called the men back. The policemen took the sheet and dragged the body to the nearest farmhouse. The householder, John Anglim, lent them a table, and they laid Bridget Cleary out in one of his barns. Sergeant Rogers and the others returned to the barracks and Acting-Sergeant Egan was left on guard.

He found a stool and went to sit on it. There were birds swooping through the rafters overhead. Swifts, he thought. He lit his pipe again. Now they had found the body, and Joanna Burke had sworn her statement, the gossip would shortly start. The favoured explanation, he predicted, would be that either Bridget or Michael was in love with someone else. In Ireland, a rival was always believed to lie at the root of every domestic murder.

He exhaled and watched the blue smoke curl up. Judging by the injuries, it had taken hours for Bridget Cleary to die; and it was puzzling because, in his experience, killings by jealous spouses were always quickly done, with a sudden blow from a chair, or a knife picked up on impulse. Not by burning. But maybe she was killed some other way and only burnt afterwards, he thought.

His pipe had gone out. He tapped it on the wall.

The post-mortem was held in John Anglim's barn that afternoon and was finished by four o'clock. As the jurors filed out, the coffin maker, who had been waiting outside, crept in. He was not a local man, no local man would do the job, and Acting-Sergeant Egan, instructed by his superiors, had arranged by telegraph for him to come out from Fethard. His name was Clancy.

It took Mr Clancy an hour to knock up a plain pine box.

'That's the best I can do for her,' he said when he was finished, 'and now, if you don't mind, I want to be off.'

Colonel Evanson, the RM, and District-Inspector Wansborough had already given Acting-Sergeant Egan the cash; but then he and the other policemen felt they ought to contribute as well. Everybody felt sorry for the dead woman.

He counted out the money into Mr Clancy's palm, and when the coffin maker saw that his payment was twice the going rate, he smiled, said 'Thank you,' and slipped away.

The policemen put the coffin on the cart that Mr Anglim had lent them. Acting-Sergeant Egan climbed into the seat and took the reins, Sergeant Rogers climbed up beside him; the constables climbed into the back. The horse was an old piebald gelding, but frisky enough when he snapped the reins.

When they reached Cloneen they found Colonel Evanson and District-Inspector Wansborough waiting by the gate into the graveyard.

'The remains are not permitted on sanctified ground,' explained the magistrate, 'owing to the special nature of the case.'

So against a boundary wall, at the back of the graveyard and out of sight, a hole had been dug. There was no rope to lower the coffin into the ground. Callaghan and O'Connor dropped the foot of the coffin into the hole, then Sergeant Rogers counted, 'One, two, three . . .' and Acting-Sergeant Egan let go of the head. The coffin dropped with a dull thud.

The gravedigger had left two shovels leaning against the wall. They piled the earth back into the hole. The sticky soil stuck to their boots. A few onlookers watched across the graveyard wall. Callaghan had brought some flowers and a little cross made from two pieces of wood lashed together. Acting-Sergeant Egan stuck the cross into the ground and arranged the flowers on the mound. Then he led the policemen away.

Back at the cart, District-Inspector Wansborough offered round his cigarettes. Then he and Evanson went off in the Colonel's trap.

The policemen got back on to Mr Anglim's cart and moved off slowly down the road, a cloud of cigarette smoke hanging above them as they swayed along the lane.

CHAPTER TEN

The last notebooks are filled entirely with newspaper clippings relating to the Magisterial Inquiry, the trial, or other incidents relating to the case, which caught Mr Egan's eye.

Dr Crean

COLONEL EVANSON: Dr Crean, do you know Michael Cleary, one of the prisoners?

DR CREAN: Yes, I do.

COLONEL EVANSON: Did you, in the month of March, attend his wife Bridget Cleary?

CREAN: Yes, on the 13th, a Wednesday.

EVANSON: What was Bridget Cleary suffering from?

CREAN: Bronchitis, and nervous excitement.

EVANSON: Did you try to make any enquiries as to what caused the nervous excitement?

CREAN: I did but could not make any headway.

EVANSON: Did you prescribe for her?

CREAN: Yes.

EVANSON: Are you aware if she took the medicine?

CREAN: I don't know. I never saw her again.

Father Ryan

COLONEL EVANSON: How did you find Bridget Cleary?

FATHER RYAN: She was in a very nervous state, and I thought

possibly hysterical. I came to the conclusion that it might be the beginning of mental derangement.

EVANSON: Did you see her husband?

RYAN: No, he was not present.

EVANSON: Did she converse with you?

RYAN: Not except professionally, as a priest. Her conversation was coherent and intelligent.

EVANSON: Did anything more occur to attract special attention?

RYAN: No, nothing whatever.

Mary Kennedy

COLONEL EVANSON: Can you state your relation to the deceased?

MARY KENNEDY: I am her aunt.

EVANSON: Did you go up to see Bridget Cleary on Wednesday night?

KENNEDY: Yes.

EVANSON: What happened?

KENNEDY: I went into the room and asked her what way was she? She said very bad. I said it would be nothing with the help of God. 'I don't know,' she said, 'Michael is making a fairy of me.' 'Don't mind him,' I said. 'Oh,' says she, 'if I had my mother now I would not be this way.'

[*Later*]

EVANSON: Why did you bring the chamber pot to Cleary?

KENNEDY: I didn't.

EVANSON: You brought the chamber pot to Michael Cleary, did you not?

KENNEDY: No.

EVANSON: You didn't? Other witnesses have testified you did.

KENNEDY: Yes.

EVANSON: Yes, what? Yes, you did, or yes they have testified?

KENNEDY: I can't remember. I'm too old.

John Dunne

COLONEL EVANSON: What happened then?

JOHN DUNNE: Cleary told me Bridget should be brought to the fire. I thought it belonged in the cure, what we were doing. Cleary had told me it belonged in the cure.

EVANSON: Other witnesses say it was your idea to bring Bridget to the fire.

DUNNE: That's a lie.

EVANSON: Why would they lie?

DUNNE: I don't know. They mustn't like me. Mrs Burke certainly doesn't.

EVANSON: Why do you say that?

DUNNE: Because I can see her sitting over there, and I can see from her face and her movements what she's thinking.

Joanna Burke

COLONEL EVANSON: Why did you go into Bridget's bedroom when she was put into the fire the first time?

JOANNA BURKE: I couldn't bear to watch. I was a coward.

EVANSON: Why didn't you try speaking to your brothers?

BURKE: I didn't think they would listen.

EVANSON: Where was Katie?

BURKE: I took her into the bedroom with me.

EVANSON: What did you do in the bedroom?

BURKE: I closed my eyes and prayed for this to end, for everyone to go away, and for Bridget to get better. Then I saw my brother Mikey go down in a faint. I decided to help him and to put everything else out of my mind.

William Simpson

COLONEL EVANSON: After everyone came into the sickroom, did Mrs Cleary say anything?

WILLIAM SIMPSON: Other than answering the questions, no.

EVANSON: Did anyone refer to the ordeal she had been through?

SIMPSON: No.

EVANSON: Did anyone ask Mrs Cleary if she was in pain?

SIMPSON: No.

EVANSON: She was injured. Did anyone offer to fetch the doctor?

SIMPSON: No. All they kept saying was, 'Do you think it's she that's in it?', and when they all answered, 'Yes', everyone was satisfied that they had her and they were all delighted.

EVANSON: Why didn't you do something?

SIMPSON: I'm sorry.

EVANSON: In earlier testimony, you stated your reason for visiting was to enquire into Mrs Cleary's well-being. If so, why did you do nothing? Why did you stand around with the others in the room while she was being questioned after her ordeal?

SIMPSON: I didn't think it was my place. I wasn't a member of the family. I was just a neighbour, and I took the view that the exorcism was their affair.

Father Ryan

COLONEL EVANSON: Did anything else happen when you visited Mrs Cleary on Friday morning?

FATHER RYAN: As I was riding my horse from the yard, Cleary suddenly shouted in the house, 'Many people have some remedy of their own which would have more effect than a doctor's medicine', or something to that effect. I didn't know what he meant at the time.

EVANSON: Is it possible that during all this time, with your local knowledge, you had heard nothing about this witchcraft?

RYAN: No, nothing whatever. The priest is often the last to hear of these things. And I wish to state that if I'd had the remotest suspicion of foul play or witchcraft, I would have refused to say Mass, and should have given information to the police at once.

Joanna Burke

COLONEL EVANSON: When you went out for milk, you could have gone to the police barracks instead?

JOANNA BURKE: I could have, yes.

EVANSON: Did you think about doing so?

BURKE: I had thought about it before, yes, but by that time, which was dusk, my thinking, as far as I can recall, was that it wasn't necessary to go to the police. Everything was over, or so I believed. It was an error of judgement. I was exhausted. I was only just managing to stay awake although I had had a little sleep earlier. And I was confused besides – there had been so many changes that day.

EVANSON: How do you mean?

BURKE: Michael Cleary was in a great humour after breakfast in the morning; then later he became suspicious again; in the afternoon, Bridget seemed to pick up; but then when I got back from the dairy, Michael Cleary was in the sickroom with a bottle of holy water and it seemed as if we were starting the ordeal of the night before all over again. There was too much happening, in one day, for one person to take everything in, you know? First we went this way, than that way, then the other. By evening my mind was reeling. I didn't know where I was. Yes, I really don't believe I did. Yes, by Friday evening, the fact was, I couldn't think straight at all. And that was why I failed to do what I know now I ought to have done.

Michael Cleary

COLONEL EVANSON: Why did you throw paraffin oil on your wife?

MICHAEL CLEARY: I did not, and furthermore there was no paraffin oil in the house on that occasion which I could have thrown on her. There was only a little bit in a bottle which Mrs Burke herself used to fill the lamp that was then burning.

EVANSON: Why did you place your wife in the fire?

CLEARY: I would not have done that. I would sooner put myself in the fire, than put my wife in it.

Pat Boland

COLONEL EVANSON: Tell us what you want to say.

PAT BOLAND: To make a long story short, he burned her himself.

EVANSON: Who?

BOLAND: Michael Cleary.

EVANSON: Who did he burn?

BOLAND: Bridget, his wife. That's all I have to say. The priest here in the gaol told me to tell the truth and that's what I'm doing. I've nothing more to add.

EVANSON: Have you signed your deposition?

BOLAND: I cannot write my name.

EVANSON: Make an X then.

Michael Cleary

MICHAEL CLEARY: I want to make an objection to the statement of Pat Boland.

COLONEL EVANSON: Go on.

CLEARY: There is not a word of truth in it, and they are all the same – Pat Boland and Mary Kennedy and the four Kennedy brothers.

EVANSON: Do you mean that none of them is telling the truth?

CLEARY: I am asking for justice, and if I don't get it here, I will get it in heaven.

EVANSON: Could you answer the question?

CLEARY: Yes, none of them have spoken a word of the truth. Instead they are all doing their best to do me down, and the father, Pat Boland, he is the worst of them. They all say I burnt my wife but I did not. It is themselves that done it and buried her. They are the ones filled with badness and dirt. They're a rotten set, every one of them.

Joanna Burke

COLONEL EVANSON: On Saturday morning, you went to see Michael Cleary to persuade him to give himself up.

JOANNA BURKE: I did.

EVANSON: But instead he made you promise not to report what you knew.

BURKE: He did.

EVANSON: How was he able to do this?

BURKE: I must have been exhausted and he could be very persuasive. I couldn't resist him.

EVANSON: So you promised, even though you knew it was wrong?

BURKE: Yes.

Mary Kennedy

COLONEL EVANSON: You saw Cleary on Saturday morning?

MARY KENNEDY: I did.

EVANSON: How did he seem?

KENNEDY: The same.

EVANSON: Could you explain?

KENNEDY: He was tired and at the same time he was lively.

EVANSON: Did he talk about the deceased?

KENNEDY: Yes. He said she was coming back.

EVANSON: Do you believe he believed that?

KENNEDY: He believed when he was with us, but then he thought we might inform on him and we had told him to give himself up. But I don't know if he believed Bridget was coming back when he wasn't with us.

Joanna Burke

COLONEL EVANSON: Why didn't you go to the police?

JOANNA BURKE: Because I promised Michael.

EVANSON: Was that promise more important than what had happened?

BURKE: I didn't say that.

EVANSON: Did you tell your husband Bridget had been burnt and buried?

BURKE: No.

EVANSON: Why?

BURKE: He would have made me go to the barracks.

EVANSON: The idea of which frightened you?

BURKE: I was frightened of being arrested, yes. I was an accessary.

EVANSON: So it was not true that you did not go because you had promised Michael.

BURKE: No.

Dr Crean

COLONEL EVANSON: Dr Crean, did you make a post-mortem examination of the body?

DR CREAN: Yes, in cooperation with Dr Heffernan.

EVANSON: Were you able to identify the body as that of Bridget Cleary?

295

CREAN: Certainly.

EVANSON: What was the result of the examination?

CREAN: I found the spleen ruptured and I found a fusion of blood on the brain.

EVANSON: Was it the result of violence?

CREAN: I can't say.

EVANSON: What other injuries did you find?

CREAN: I found the stomach perfectly burned, and the intestines protruding; the bone of the right hip protruded through the flesh also.

EVANSON: Did you notice anything on the neck?

CREAN: Yes, there were black marks on the throat and a fusion of blood.

EVANSON: Was that the result of violence?

CREAN: I could not possibly say.

EVANSON: Might it have been?

CREAN: I can't say.

EVANSON: Was the stomach healthy?

CREAN: Yes, perfectly.

EVANSON: There were no traces of poison?

CREAN: No.

EVANSON: What in your opinion was the cause of death?

CREAN: The burns I have described.

EVANSON: Would the rupture of the spleen have caused death?

CREAN: No.

EVANSON: Was there any analysis of the stomach made?

CREAN: The coroner did not think it necessary; there would have been abrasions of the mucous membrane of the stomach if an irritant poison had been administered.

EVANSON: Were there any such abrasions?

CREAN: No.

EVANSON: Did you find any external mark corresponding with the fusion of the brain?

CREAN: No.

EVANSON: Was Bridget Cleary a healthy subject before?

CREAN: Yes, she was in perfect health.

EVANSON: Was she of good physique and well nourished?

CREAN: Yes. The only thing I noticed was that she was awfully nervous. I have been attending her for eight or nine years and always found her to have an irritable, nervous temperament.

EVANSON: Was that nervousness caused by dyspepsia?

CREAN: It may have been. I wish to add that I don't think Ganey ever did the woman any harm.

EVANSON: Oh, we can't enter into that now. [laughter].

The Sentences

Michael Cleary, twenty years of penal servitude; Patrick Kennedy, five years; John Dunne, three years; William and James Kennedy, one and a half years each; Mikey Kennedy and Pat Boland, six months each; Mary Kennedy, no sentence. Ahearn and Ganey were discharged.

After passing sentence the court then thanked Mrs Joanna Burke, the principal prosecution witness during the trial. It was noted that her contribution was of inestimable value.

A Fire

Feelings are running high in the Drangan/Cloneen district, our correspondent writes, for on the night of Wednesday last, a mob of young men from the area set fire to the cottage of Mary Kennedy, one of those convicted in the Ballyvadlea 'Witch-Burning Case'. The home of another of those convicted, John Dunne, also came under attack . . .

Cashel Guardians Act

We gather tourists are flocking daily to what has become popularly known as the 'Fairy House', the Ballyvadlea dwelling which was the scene of the recent 'Witch-Burning Case'. The enterprising Mr Simpson has somehow obtained the key to Cleary's cottage, we understand, and turned it into a 'peep show', wherein he displays items such as Cleary's fireside chair, which he describes as 'The Murderer's Chair'. (We have it, incidentally, on very good authority that the said chair is in fact the property of Pat Boland, the victim's father, who is currently serving a six-month prison sentence.)

However, only today we learn that the Cashel Guardians, who own the house, have given notice of intention to sue William Simpson for its return, a move we heartily applaud.

In Court Today

Having for some weeks anticipated this event we made certain we were at the courthouse in Clonmel early today in order to be certain of a seat from which to watch the proceedings in the interesting case of the Cashel Guardians versus Wilm Simpson.

First to speak in court was a representative of the Cashel Guardians. He produced the leasehold agreement under which the Clearys had rented the property. The magistrate read it and the following exchange ensued:

COLONEL EVANSON: I'm afraid Mr Simpson, you must hand back the key.

WILLIAM SIMPSON: This is unfair. I was the principal witness in the Cleary trial. He would never have been caught but for me.

EVANSON: I fail to see what that has to do with the business before us today.

SIMPSON: In the house where I live now I'm only the caretaker. I need somewhere else to go.

EVANSON: Then apply like anyone else. You must return the key.

SIMPSON: All right, but I keep the outhouses. I have my property
stored in them.

EVANSON: No. I order for the complete repossession of the property.

Fairy Redivivus – Apologia (by a Drangan Boy)

Oh, have they come the olden days,
    The days of *Crom* and *Maev*
When *Mab* in blooming beauty reigned,
    Beside Killarney's wave;
When mystic lights gleam'd thro' the groves,
    And pagan baelfires shone
O'er glen and wold and cromlec hoar,
    Around old Slievenamon.

And rev'lling in those legends of
    The dim, far distant years
When Druids sat 'neath oaken boughs
    In pride of no compeers,
Alas that in Tipperary's vales
    A group of peasants grew,
Who seem'd to think that *Crom* had come
    His empire to renew.

But oh! the tragic sequel that
    Has quench'd for all and aye,
Those dying rays of elfin lights,
    Which glimmer'd in our sky;
The Saxon bann'd the teacher and
    Let him not now recall
The crimson stain clung to his name
    In days of Erin's thrall.

He dimm'd the light in our fairy land
    Far as his torture could;

He draped its every window with
   A coat of Irish blood;
His fetters dangled overhead,
   Our every Irish school,
He conquered and he knows it
   And made each a fairy fool.

EPILOGUE

When he finished reading the poem, Mr Egan tapped the end of the cigar he was smoking on the rim of the 'Sweet Afton' ashtray at his elbow, and a piece of grey-black ash that was like pumice-stone to my childish eye fell away. Then he closed and fastened the last notebook.

'After I read this poem,' he said, puffing on the cigar again, 'which I thought was not only bad but quite preposterous – imagine believing it was the fault of the English; mind you, that was quite a common opinion round here – I set to work. These notebooks are the result and that's the end of the story.'

Looking past Mr Egan I saw through to the crab-apple trees in the garden. It was one of those rare Irish summer days with no wind and great white clouds like galleons sailing across a clear blue sky.

'Come on,' said Mr Egan. He was standing and, I realized, speaking to me.

I followed him out to the scullery and down the stone steps to the yard.

From there he led me across the garden to a greenhouse with green smeared glass.

Mr Egan opened the door and we stepped into the hot, damp air heavy with the smell of chrysanthemums.

'Look,' he said.

It was a mother cat and a kitten. The cat was black and white and its ribs were showing. The kitten was a tiny thing with closed-up eyes and a squished-up face. The kitten was nuzzling at the mother's upturned belly, searching for and then at last finding the little pink stud of a nipple.

'I found the mother under the hedge, crying,' Mr Egan explained.

I reached gingerly forward. The cat miaowed. I found her chin and began to stroke. I felt the sinews through the skin as the animal rolled her head with pleasure.

'You'll have to name her,' said Mr Egan, his slippered feet just beside me.

'Ruth,' I said, the word springing out without my thinking.

'Ruth it is.'

My mother's name. Of course I did not have to think.

Later, we sat with Mr Egan in his garden on striped deckchairs.

'Mr Christie,' said Mr Egan quietly, as I sucked lemonade through a straw, 'tell me, where is your wife? If you don't mind my asking.'

At the mention of Mother, every molecule in my body started to fizz, for here was the opportunity to augment my meagre stock of knowledge.

Lolling my head back against the canvas, I gave a good impression of being absent-minded, inattentive, lost in a world of lemonade and blue skies.

'I hope I am not intruding by asking,' continued Mr Egan.

'No,' said my father, and then he deftly lifted a hand and drew a finger savagely across his neck.

It was confirmation of what I already suspected but which I would not have been able to express. Mother was gone, but not gone somewhere; she was gone for ever. I was never going to see her again.

I remembered Michael Cleary and his supplication to the fairies as I sat there. Could they not do the reverse for me of what they had done for him? I was certainly of the age when I might have asked for their help, except that now, as I knew, they did not exist.

There was a big white cloud hanging in the sky above me, and as I looked at its swollen form I saw her face smiling back at me.

Later that afternoon, emboldened I think by the fact of having frankly hinted to Mr Egan what had happened to his wife, my father cleared his throat and said, 'Mr Egan, do you think I might borrow your notebooks?'

'I will want them back.'

'Of course,' my father promised.

My father took the notebooks away with him when we left that evening.

Two months later, Mr Egan wrote to us in London asking for their return.

My father did not answer the old man's letter.

Neither did he respond to the second or third request.

That was the last Father heard until, some months later, he gathered from Gerard, Mr Egan's grandson with whom he worked, that the old man was dead.

Why did my father not finish?

Because he thought Gerard would accuse him of theft? No. My father had the skin of an elephant.

Because he was not a finisher? No. He finished his articles. And he finished his wife.

Because – which is different from not being a finisher – he was not able.

Closer.

The reason he did not finish them was because the story was not what was properly regarded then as an Irish tale. It was not one which, in the late sixties, the early seventies or the eighties, anyone wanted to hear.

It was not a 'Big House' story.

It was not a 'green-eyed-colleen-making-buttermilk-at-the-end-of-the-glen-while-the-redcoats-search-for-her-sweetheart' story.

It was not a 'Troubles' story.

No, on the contrary . . .

This was a tale of violence by Irish people, for Irish people, against Irish people.

It was not what the *Zeitgeist* of those times demanded and, therefore, it could neither be told nor heard.

But today old pieties have lost their lustre.

So it's all a matter of timing, yes – but that's also a load of baloney.

It's because of what's happened to an author that a book gets written, not the social circumstances. All fiction is autobiography.

So why this now, told by me?

I would like to say my father was a thief. He stole and then, as if that were not bad enough, he kept his stolen treasure buried in a tin.

I would like to say, therefore, I am making restitution. I have dug up the chest and levered off the lid, and now I have spread them before you, the diamonds and doubloons of Bridget Cleary's story.

No. Let us be really clear about what this really is.

Father is dead. We had no relationship.

I have not one single memory of us doing anything together that made me happy, except for that one time when we listened to Mr Egan's story.

It was tragic, but it gave me something. I was moved.

Then came the bad part: that finger across the neck.

Every moment until that second, I was buoyed by hope.

After that, I had to swim for myself.

So, there you have it.

Happy times with Dad and my loss of innocence are tangled with this story, but for God's sake, let's keep a sense of proportion.

Another person's suffering and death – that is the principal thread. If Bridget had not died, none of this would have happened.

I have been as honest as I can. That is all I can say.

The weight of a human life is incalculable.

Enniskillen – Korakia – Newbliss